Survivor

Survivor

LESLEY PEARSE

MICHAEL JOSEPH
an imprint of
PENGUIN BOOKS

MICHAEL JOSEPH

Published by the Penguin Group
Penguin Books Ltd, 80 Strand, London WC2R ORL, England
Penguin Group (USA) Inc., 375 Hudson Street, New York, New York 10014, USA
Penguin Group (Canada), 90 Eglinton Avenue East, Suite 700, Toronto, Ontario, Canada M4P 2YR
(a division of Pearson Penguin Canada Inc.)
Penguin Ireland, 25 St Stephen's Green, Dublin 2, Ireland (a division of Penguin Books Ltd)
Penguin Group (Australia), 707 Collins Street, Melbourne, Victoria 3008, Australia
(a division of Pearson Australia Group Pty Ltd)
Penguin Books India Pvt Ltd, 11 Community Centre,
Panchsheel Park, New Delhi – 110 017, India
Penguin Group (NZ), 67 Apollo Drive, Rosedale, Auckland 0632, New Zealand
(a division of Pearson New Zealand Ltd)
Penguin Books (South Africa) (Pty) Ltd, Block D, Rosebank Office Park, 181 Jan Smuts Avenue,
Parktown North, Gauteng 2193, South Africa

Penguin Books Ltd, Registered Offices: 80 Strand, London WC2R ORL, England

www.penguin.com

First published 2014
001

Copyright © Lesley Pearse, 2014

Set in 13.5/16pt Garamond by Palimpsest Book Production Ltd, Falkirk, Stirlingshire
Printed in Great Britain by Clays Ltd, St Ives plc

A CIP catalogue record for this book is available from the British Library

HARDBACK ISBN: 978-0-718-15905-4
TRADE PAPERBACK ISBN: 978-0-718-15906-1

www.greenpenguin.co.uk

To my beautiful granddaughter Sienna Marie,
born 9 December 2012. Sister to Harley and bringing
extra joy to my daughter Jo, her partner Otis,
and to all the rest of our family.

I

Russell, New Zealand, 1931

'Mariette is so . . .' Miss Quigley paused, her thin lips pursed as she searched for a suitable adjective to describe her errant pupil. 'So defiant!'

Belle resisted the temptation to smile at the school-mistress's description of her eleven-year-old daughter. When Belle was a child, it was often said of her too.

It was around half past four, and Miss Quigley had called on Belle after dismissing her pupils for the day.

Belle had shown the teacher into the parlour as a mark of respect, but she had no intention of offering tea as she didn't want to encourage the woman to linger. 'I think what you are seeing is just a sign of a strong character. What exactly has she been up to that you find so distressing?'

'I have no particular incident to illustrate it, but she challenges everything I say. Just the other day I was telling the class how many New Zealand soldiers lost their lives in the Great War, and she claimed that France lost twenty-five per cent of her men.'

'But that's true,' Belle said. 'I wouldn't call it defiance to point that out – especially when her father is French and fought for his country.'

It was tempting to add that Etienne had been awarded the Croix de Guerre for his courage, but he wouldn't like her to boast about that.

Miss Quigley crossed her arms. 'But she has a view on

I

everything! I also get very irritated by her teaching the other children dubious French phrases.'

'I think you'll find there is nothing dubious about them, she just likes the sound of the language. I doubt very much that it is anything more than, "Please pass me a pencil," or, "It's very hot today." Both her father and I wish her to be bilingual, and we are delighted with her progress.'

Miss Quigley's disapproving sniff was evidence that she regarded teaching a child French as something subversive. 'She is overconfident.' She rapped this out like an insult. 'She's always the first child to speak out, takes the lead in everything.'

'I'm very sorry you find that troubling.' Belle thought this dried-up old stick of a schoolmistress should concentrate her energies on helping the less able children in the school and be glad she had at least one pupil who liked to learn. 'I would have thought a teacher would like to see such enthusiasm – it is, after all, a compliment to your teaching.'

'Pride cometh before a fall,' the schoolmistress retorted with another disapproving sniff. 'She may be a big fish in this little pool, but how will she manage when she comes up against even bigger fish?'

'A confident child will adjust.' Belle was growing cross. 'Now, shall we discuss her progress at school? I assumed that was what you came for?'

'She reads and writes very well,' Miss Quigley said begrudgingly. 'She is quick at arithmetic too. But she distracts the other children when she has finished her work and prevents them from finishing theirs.'

'By talking to them?' Belle felt they were at last getting somewhere.

'Yes.'

'Then I'll tell her that she mustn't do that. But maybe

you could give her more work or another job to keep her occupied?'

Belle had realized some time ago that Miss Quigley had taken against Mariette. She didn't think it was because the girl was quicker or smarter than other children of the same age, but purely because neither Mariette nor Belle sucked up to her the way that so many of the other children and mothers in Russell did.

A plain, thin and reserved woman in her late forties, Miss Quigley had arrived in Russell to teach around the same time that Belle had married Etienne. Rumour had it that she'd chosen to come to Russell to be nearer Silas Waldron, a widower who live in Kerikeri, whom she'd met in Auckland. Perhaps she'd hoped friendship would blossom into love and marriage, but it obviously hadn't.

It was never going to be easy for a single woman with no close friends or family in the area to adjust to living in such an isolated community after living in a big city. Miss Quigley had little in common with her pupils' mothers, whose lives revolved around their husbands and families, and she probably found them rather backward-thinking.

It didn't help that she was so starchy and prim – she had no small talk and rarely smiled, let alone laughed – and if she had hoped she might find a husband amongst the wealthy men who came here to fish for marlin in the summer, she was out of luck. Belle doubted any of them would want a plain middle-aged woman who looked like she'd spent her life sucking lemons.

'If you will forgive my plain speaking, Mrs Carrera, I do think you should curb Mariette's wild spirit by encouraging her to take up more ladylike pursuits than sailing. As I was coming here, I saw her pushing the boat out from the jetty with her dress tucked up in a most ungainly manner.'

Belle was suddenly all ears and looked at the school-mistress in alarm. 'You saw Mari taking the boat out? Wasn't her father with her?'

'No, she was alone, shouting back to someone on the shore like a fishwife.'

'Why didn't you tell me that straight away?' Belle ripped off her apron and made for the door. 'Do you really think we'd allow an eleven-year-old to sail alone?'

'That's my point, she's defiant,' Miss Quigley replied. But her point was lost because Belle was already out of the door, leaving her alone in the parlour.

Belle ran at full tilt along the shore towards the jetty, her heart thumping with fear. Etienne had promised to take Mariette out for a sailing lesson in the dinghy after school today, if he finished work early enough. But if Miss Quigley was to be believed, Mariette thought she had learned enough to sail the boat alone.

It was a beautiful, sunny October day, with just enough wind to make it ideal sailing weather, but Mariette wasn't strong or knowledgeable enough to control a sailing boat on her own. She had been told this by her father dozens of times. A sudden squall of wind could capsize the boat, and she could be struck on the head by the boom. Although she could swim well, the water out in the bay was still very cold at this time of year, and in some parts there were dangerous currents.

Seeing Charley Lomax up ahead, Belle called out to him. 'Mari's taken the boat out alone. Can you find Etienne for me?' she yelled. 'And if you see Mog, tell her too.'

Charley Lomax was one of Russell's characters, about fifty, hard-working when he was sober, but he went on benders that could last for days. He lived in a squalid shack at the back end of town, but Etienne liked him and they often worked on building jobs together.

The man waved his hand to signal he understood what she'd said and ran off so fast it was clear that he was sober today.

Belle stopped running for a moment as she had a stitch. Putting her hand up to shield her eyes, she scanned the bay. Their dinghy had a red sail, and when Etienne first bought it Belle had often stood here watching him put it through its paces. She had been worried when he started taking Mariette out with him to teach her, and she still wouldn't let him take Alexis or Noel as the boys were only eight and seven respectively and not strong swimmers yet. But she had relented with Mariette because the girl loved everything about the sea and boats and liked being alone with her father.

She spotted the dinghy, which was going at a fair lick, way out in the bay. Mariette was just a tiny dot leaning back from her perch on the side to keep the boat balanced. Belle's fear was that the girl hadn't the strength in her arms to bring the boat about, and she was heading straight towards the open sea where the waves would be heavy.

'*Belle!*'

Belle turned at the sound of Mog's shout and saw her racing towards her, clutching Alexis and Noel's hands. She collected the boys from school most days as they came out half an hour earlier than Mariette, and she usually took them for a walk so they could let off a bit of steam.

At any other time Belle would have marvelled that a woman of fifty-nine with a slight limp could run so fast. But Belle could only think of the danger her daughter was in.

'Mari's out there, alone,' she shouted back to Mog, pointing to the boat in the distance. 'Do you know where Etienne is?'

Mog reached her and doubled over with the exertion of running. 'Charley went to get him. He's only at the Baxters' place,' she wheezed out. 'He'll go straight to the jetty and take the other boat to get her. You'd better go with him to help.'

'If she capsizes out there, she'll drown,' Belle said in a quavering voice as they continued towards the jetty. 'I've told her a million times how dangerous the sea can be. Why does she always have to challenge everything?'

'Calm down, Belle,' Mog said. 'She's a naughty girl, disobeying you. But if you can still see the boat upright, then there's no need to panic yet. Etienne will be here before you can say Jack Robinson.'

Mog was right about that. As they reached the jetty, a cloud of dust heralded Etienne's arrival in the old truck.

Although fifty-one now, the years had been kind to him and he was still as lean and strong as he had been on their wedding day. He had more lines around his blue eyes, and his hair was more white than blond, but he still had the power to make women's hearts flutter a little, especially Belle's.

As she expected, he didn't stop for explanations, recriminations or suggestions, just told Alexis to run home and get a warm blanket, asked Mog to wait with Noel, then grabbed Belle's hand and charged down the jetty to where their small fishing boat was moored. He leapt in and started the engine while Belle hastily cast off and then jumped into the boat with him. Etienne pushed off from the jetty with a boathook and, within seconds, they were heading towards the dinghy.

Etienne looked at the little craft in the distance. 'She's handling it well,' he said with a certain amount of pride, but then glanced at Belle's terror-struck face. 'We couldn't have expected to have docile, obedient children, Belle! Mari has inherited the worst and the best of both of us.'

Belle was tempted to say he should never have bought the dinghy – and she'd never forgive him if Mariette was drowned, or even hurt – but she didn't, because she knew

Etienne would never forgive himself if anything happened. Besides, she had agreed that all children living by the sea should learn to swim and to sail, so she was every bit as responsible.

Neither of them spoke again, both silently willing the fishing boat to go faster. As they drew closer, they could clearly see that Mariette was struggling against the force of the wind in the sail.

'She's hanging on to the line for grim death and forgetting to use the rudder to put it about,' Etienne said. His teeth were gritted with fear for her because, if she continued as she was, the dinghy would be out on the open sea very soon.

As they chugged towards her, a sudden squall came up and, to their horror, the little dinghy flipped over in an instant and Mariette was thrown out into the sea like a little rag doll. They saw her fall, heard the splash, and yet she disappeared instantly.

'Where's she gone? I can't see her!' Belle gasped.

The water around Russell had been calm, but out here it was very choppy and the shock of sudden immersion in extremely cold water would make it hard for anyone to swim, especially a small girl.

'*Mari!*' Etienne yelled out at the top of his voice. 'Can you hear me?'

They had around fifty yards before they reached the capsized boat, and Belle was beside herself with fear as she scanned the water looking for her child. She glanced at Etienne and saw that his jaw was set grimly as he slowed down in readiness to jump into the water.

'Take the wheel and circle the dinghy, slow and wide,' he said. As she did so, he pulled off his boots. 'Shout and wave this if you spot her,' he added, handing her a piece of red cloth.

He dived into the sea, surfacing some ten yards ahead.

Belle did as she'd been instructed, slowly circling the capsized boat, calling out to Mariette as she searched the water with her eyes. Etienne kept diving under the water, then resurfaced moments later, only to plunge down again.

Terror threatened to overwhelm Belle, who was imagining that at any minute Etienne would come to the surface holding the body of their lifeless child. She tried to keep the lid on her panic by reminding herself that they knew Mariette hadn't been hit by the boom, so she wasn't unconscious, and that she could swim like a fish. But every second that passed without sight of her daughter meant she might have already drowned.

'Please God, keep her safe,' she whispered frantically as Etienne once again dived down.

Then, as if her prayer was answered, she saw her. A small and frightened white face emerged from a wave, and Belle saw that the girl was reaching out for the keel of the upturned dinghy.

'Stay there, Mari,' Belle yelled out, waving the red rag frantically. 'Papa's coming to get you. Hold on tight!'

Etienne emerged on the other side of the keel.

'This side! She's on this side of the boat,' Belle screamed and pointed.

Etienne raised one hand to let her know he'd heard. As he swam round the capsized boat, Belle steered the fishing boat in closer.

It took Etienne no more than a couple of minutes to reach Mariette and, holding her up, he swam with her towards Belle and passed her up into Belle's arms.

'I'll just go back to the dinghy and get it upright. We can tow it back to Russell,' he shouted out from the water, then turned and swam back.

'Oh, Mari, you are such a naughty girl,' Belle exclaimed as

she stripped off her child's soaked dress and wrapped an old coat of Etienne's around her. 'I was afraid you'd drowned.'

'Papa told me if I ever capsized, I was to stay with the boat,' she sobbed out, coughing and bringing up sea water. 'But I couldn't see it over the waves, and I was so scared. I was swimming the wrong way. I turned round and then I saw it.'

Belle hadn't the heart for lectures now, she was too relieved that Mariette was safe, so she hugged her tightly to her chest, watching Etienne righting the dinghy and fixing a tow line to it. There wasn't much he didn't know about boats – he'd learned to sail as a small boy in Marseille, and he was always in demand with the boat owners in Russell, both crewing for them and doing repairs – but he didn't know much about children, and she was angry with him for encouraging an eleven-year-old to think she knew enough to be out on the open sea alone.

If Miss Quigley hadn't noticed Mariette pushing the dinghy out, it might have been another hour or more before Belle went looking for her. Once out of the bay, the current would have swept the child away and perhaps her little body would never have been found.

But she said none of that to Mariette, who had had a big enough fright as it was. For now, all she wanted to do was warm the child up and hold her tightly.

Etienne was right in saying their daughter had inherited both the best and the worst of her parents. She was as fearless as her father, and as determined as her mother. She was also devious, opinionated and disobedient. Her looks too came from a blend of the pair of them, with her strawberry-blonde hair which was curly, like Belle's. She had Etienne's high cheekbones, but Belle's deep-blue eyes and wide mouth. She wasn't exactly pretty, but there was something arresting about her features, in the same way as there was with Etienne's.

9

'Are you very cross with me?' Mariette asked in a small, shaky voice once her father was back on board and stripping off his wet clothes.

'Yes, I am,' Etienne replied, looking very fierce. 'I've told you dozens of times that you are never to take the boat out alone. I can't believe that you would disobey me. You were very lucky that we found out where you were in time and were on our way to you. It isn't just about being a strong swimmer, the sea is very cold and even a grown man like me can become paralysed in the water in no time at all. Do you know what it would have done to your whole family, if you had drowned?'

'You'd all be very sad,' she said, hanging her head and trying to retreat further into the old coat Belle had wrapped her in.

'Not just sad, broken-hearted,' he said as he squatted down in front of her. 'You are just a little girl, you might have learned to sail quite well in calm water with a gentle wind, but you haven't got enough muscle yet to control a boat in a strong wind. You must learn to obey me and your mother, Mariette. We don't stop you from doing things just to be mean to you, but to keep you safe.'

'I'm s-s-s-sorry,' she stammered out, partly from being cold but also because she was in trouble. 'I wanted you to be proud of me, that I could sail so well.'

'You'd make us much more proud of you, if you were obedient,' Belle said, getting up to start the engine. 'If it wasn't for Miss Quigley spotting you, we wouldn't have known you were out here until it was too late. I hope you'll take this as a warning and never go off anywhere again – in a boat, a car or walking – without first asking either me or your father if it's alright.'

'I won't,' she sobbed out. 'Please don't be angry with me.'

Belle looked back at her daughter. She had snuggled into Etienne's side, the way she used to do when she was five or six. Her hair had been pure blonde then but, in the last few years, it had become more coppery and curly and Belle kept it plaited tightly or it became an unruly mop. She had mastered a wide-eyed, butter-wouldn't-melt look from an early age, which Belle and Etienne found endearing but sometimes worrying because she played both them and others with it. She was truly penitent, for now, but Belle was well aware that she was the kind of child who would never be meek and obedient. The very next time she took it into her head to do something that she shouldn't, today's lesson would be forgotten.

When they'd been choosing a name for her and Etienne had suggested Mariette, because it was his mother's name, he had laughingly told her it meant Little Rebel. Was it the name that made her behave that way?

No baby was ever wanted more. Belle had been told when she lost a baby while married to her first husband, Jimmy Reilly, back in England that she was unlikely to be able to have any more children. As things turned out, with Jimmy being severely wounded in the war, and all the problems that brought with it, Belle accepted that she was never going to be a mother, and she tried very hard to put babies out of her mind. But she had never quite succeeded. It was always a sore place inside her, a constant source of sorrow.

Then, right at the end of the war, Spanish flu flared up and, along with tens of thousands of others, Jimmy caught it and died, as did his Uncle Garth, Mog's husband.

Belle and Mog came to New Zealand to start a new life. And yet, young as Belle was, she had no expectations of finding another man to love. She once heard someone refer to her and Mog as the 'Two English Widows', and she guessed that was what everyone called them. She thought then that they would grow old together, making a living at dressmaking and millinery, and that the closest they would get to a child would be watching out for their neighbours' children.

Then Etienne, a man she had loved and thought had been killed in France, turned up looking for her. To this day she still considered it a miracle; she had accepted at that point in her life that she was never going to feel love and passion ever again.

She had shocked the people of Russell by failing to hide her desire for the gallant Frenchman, but she didn't care. She thought God – or just fate – had stepped in to make up for all the sorrow in the past. She was four months pregnant when they married, and no bride in history could ever have gone to the altar so proudly or joyfully.

So much had happened since then – hardships, disappointments, periods of great anxiety. And yet, having Etienne at her side, and the joy that came with each of their three healthy, beautiful children, made even the most troubled times seem insignificant.

But now, as Belle glanced over to Mariette again, she realized that children could bring even bigger heartaches than any of the bad things she'd experienced in the past. Mariette was far too brave and reckless for her own good, and as headstrong as both her parents. By the time she was fifteen or sixteen, her boldness and sense of adventure were likely to make her rebel against the quiet, sedate life here in Russell and search out excitement elsewhere. Belle knew only too well what dangers lay in wait for young girls, and just the thought that Mariette might be subjected to some of those made her blood run cold.

Mog had taken the boys home, and left two blankets on

the jetty. Etienne wrapped Mariette in one of them, put the other around his bare shoulders and, after securing the boat, he lifted Mariette into his arms to carry her home.

Back at the house in Robertson Street, Mog and the boys were waiting on the veranda. The binoculars on the table were evidence that they'd been watching the rescue anxiously from the shore and had only returned home when they knew Mariette was safe.

Mog was never one for dramatics; she just held out her arms for the shivering child and said she had a warm bath ready for her and that Etienne should get in it afterwards.

'Are you going to smack her bottom?' seven-year-old Noel asked, somewhat hopefully.

Both boys had Belle's dark hair, and their eyes were cobalt-blue, darker than hers, but they had their father's facial expressions – suspicious, watchful. Yet neither of them was as adventurous as their elder sister. Etienne always laughed when that was remarked upon, and said, 'Give them time!'

'Don't be silly, Noel,' Alexis said. 'She's had enough of a fright nearly getting drowned.'

Belle smiled at his superior tone. He used it often, as if to point out to Noel that he was a year older. He reminded Belle of her late mother, Annie, with his strong features and the same tendency to be frosty. But, fortunately, Alexis was sensible and could always be relied on to do as he was told.

Later that evening, after the children had eaten their supper and gone to bed, Mog fetched the bottle of brandy she kept in the pantry, and poured a measure into three glasses.

They were in the kitchen, the washing-up done and put away, darkness had fallen some time ago, but the golden glow of the oil lamp made it snug and conducive for a family talk.

'I know you're both worried about Mari,' Mog said as she

handed a glass each to Belle and Etienne. They had both been ominously quiet throughout the evening meal; all three children had picked up on it and had gone to bed without the usual delaying tactics. 'But perhaps it was a good thing she had a bad scare today. I doubt she'll be so quick to take such a risk again.'

Mog had bought the little clapboard house when she and Belle first came to Russell, but Etienne had extended it considerably since he married Belle. They were still waiting for electricity to come to Russell, but the kitchen was now much bigger and there was a separate wash house with a copper to heat up water for both baths and washing clothes. Etienne had built two rooms on to the side of the house for Mog, which she could access from either the hall or from the veranda along the front of the house. Above Mog's rooms were two new bedrooms, the boys sharing one and Mariette in the other.

They told people Mog was Belle's aunt, which was a far easier explanation than the truth. Mog had, in fact, worked as a maid for Annie Cooper, Belle's mother, and had virtually brought Belle up. Years later, Mog had married Garth Franklin and Belle had married Garth's nephew, Jimmy Reilly. Except for a couple of years when Belle was in America and Paris, and the time she spent as an ambulance driver in France during the war, she and Mog had always lived together. To Belle and Etienne's children she had the role of much-loved grandmother. As such, her opinion about the children – or, indeed, any other family matter – was always valued.

'I agree, Mog.' Etienne nodded. 'A bad scare is one of the best ways to teach a child about danger. Luckily, no real harm was done today, except to we adults. I think I would sooner be back in Ypres again than relive those heart-stopping moments while I was searching for Mari in the sea. I know it was the same for you on the shore, Mog, and poor Belle still looks shaken up.'

'We should get rid of the dinghy,' Belle burst out. 'Maybe Mari will be too scared to do it again, but one of the boys might try.'

Etienne took Belle's hands in his and smiled in understanding. 'We live in a place where the sea is an ever present danger, and we rely on boats to get about. It was the same for me as a boy in Marseille. I know it is far better to teach them to respect the dangers of the sea, and to handle a boat well, than to try to keep them away.'

'I agree. There is danger everywhere for children,' Mog said. 'Climbing trees, strangers who might wish to harm them, picking the wrong berries, infectious diseases, the list is endless. We can't protect them from everything. You know that better than anyone, Belle!'

Belle sighed. 'Yes, I do, but I thought that by bringing our children up here, in such a beautiful place, the chances of anything bad happening would be lessened. Do you know what Mari said to me as I tucked her in tonight? "I'd like to be a heroine like Grace Darling, or Joan of Arc. I don't want to work in the bakery or sew dresses." If that's the sort of thing she daydreams about, how on earth can we hope she'll marry a good, hard-working man and have a parcel of children?'

Etienne laughed. 'She's only eleven, Belle. I bet you had such daydreams too at that age.'

'Only about making beautiful hats,' Belle retorted. 'I didn't imagine rescuing people in a rowing boat, or leading a country to war.'

'I used to dream of meeting Queen Victoria,' Mog said. 'What about you, Etienne?'

'Having lots to eat,' he said. 'But then I was half starved most of the time.'

'So you two achieved your dreams,' Mog laughed. 'I didn't, I couldn't even face the crowds to watch Queen Victoria's funeral procession. You shouldn't worry about Mari day-dreaming of being a heroine, it won't hurt her to aspire to something brave and good. Besides, wait till the boys get bigger, they'll do things that will turn your hair white. You can't wrap any of them in cotton wool. You just have to teach them the right values, point them in the right direction and pray! One day, you'll sit out on the veranda with one of your many grandchildren in your arms and feel really smug because everything turned out well.'

Mog was always the voice of reason, and both Belle and Etienne loved her for it. It didn't matter what happened – Etienne losing money in an ill-fated attempt to start his own vineyard, a fire in the kitchen that meant they had to rebuild the house, or even the cow that wandered into the garden while they were out for the day and ate most of the plants and vegetables before they returned home and chased it out – Mog could always find the silver lining in the cloud. Belle remembered, after the fire, Mog saying that it was a good thing as they'd always planned to extend the house anyway. She even joked that if the vineyard had been a success, they might have all started to drink too much.

She was a happy soul with a simple philosophy that as long as she had her beloved family around her, enough food to eat and a roof over her head, nothing could hurt her. At fifty-nine she still had the energy of a woman ten years younger. She might wear glasses now, her hair might be snow white and her face wrinkled, but she was still a force to be reckoned with. Even now, when banks were foreclosing on mortgages and there was a worldwide depression, she remained optimistic, convinced nothing bad was going to happen to them.

'It's the years before the children settle down with children of their own that worry me,' Belle said. But she said it with a smile because, with Mog and Etienne beside her, she mostly felt invincible.

As the three of them sipped their brandy, Mog looked at Belle appraisingly. At thirty-six Belle was still a very beautiful woman, her curly hair as dark and luxuriant as it had been at twenty, and the few laughter lines around eyes, and the few pounds she'd gained in the last few years, added to rather than subtracted from her attractions. She was a woman men lusted after, and because of that some of the matrons of Russell watched her like hawks. But they didn't need to, Belle's heart was firmly in Etienne's keeping, she had eyes for no one else. Belle was safe with him too, he had no interest in other women, and only a complete fool would dare risk Etienne's wrath – one look at his cold blue eyes, the faint scar on his cheek, was enough to know he wasn't a man to upset.

Mog could remember only too well her reservations when he first turned up here to find Belle. He might have been a hero in the war, but the way he'd lived before that didn't bear close scrutiny. But she saw the light in Belle's eyes when she looked at him, sensed that he was her destiny, and so Mog had to accept him.

She loved him like he was her own son now. And he had proved himself again and again. He was strong, dependable, loving and faithful, with a wonderful sense of humour that never left him even in the most difficult times. Whether he was fishing to bring food to the table, doing building work, clearing land, or rocking one of the babies to sleep in his arms, he gave it his all. So maybe his plan of planting a vineyard had failed – something some of the more spiteful people in Russell liked to remember with delight – but, on balance, he'd been a good provider, and he was well liked in the community.

'What are you thinking about?' Etienne asked, looking at Mog with one fair eyebrow raised quizzically.

'Only how glad I am that it worked out for you two,' she said. 'We all did the right thing in coming to New Zealand, didn't we?'

'We certainly did,' Belle said with a smile. 'When I despair of us ever getting electricity here, modern plumbing and decent roads, I think of how cold and wet it would be back in England.'

'Times are going to get harder for us all, though,' Etienne warned. 'It's two years now since the Wall Street crash, seven million out of work in America, and things are getting as tough here. With farmers getting nothing for their produce, and factories in Auckland folding, the ripples will soon spread out to us.'

'It won't stop rich people coming here to fish and sail, though, will it?' Belle asked. Over the last ten years, they'd seen a big increase in the number of people arriving for the summer, mainly due to the American writer and sportsman Zane Grey coming to Russell in 1926 to catch marlin. The Duke and Duchess of York had spent a few nights in the harbour on HMS *Renown* the following year, and there had been scores of other rich and important people coming ever since. Mog and Belle had benefited from these visitors, mostly carrying out alteration work on clothes they'd brought with them, but Belle had sold quite a few hats and Mog had made shorts, skirts and blouses for wives who found their clothes were too formal for Russell.

As for Etienne, he'd taken out countless fishing parties on his boat, whole families wanting to picnic on a beach, and acted as a ferry boat for holidaymakers. Earlier in the year, the road from Russell to Whangarei had been completed, and this summer was the first when visitors would be able to arrive by road, even if it was as winding as a corkscrew.

'Maybe rich people will still come, but the little campsites all around here are already feeling the pinch now that people in the cities are losing their jobs,' Etienne pointed out. 'We may have to tighten our belts before long.'

'We'll be fine,' Mog said firmly. 'We might not have any money in the bank, but we have no debts and all three of us can turn our hands to anything. But what we should be doing now is deciding how we are going to handle Mari. By tomorrow she'll have forgotten what a close shave she had, so she ought to be punished in some way to remind her how serious it was. She is also a little too big for her boots. Miss Quigley was right in saying she's defiant, and that isn't good in an eleven-year-old.'

Belle bristled. 'She's just confident, that's all. I won't bring her up like you and Annie raised me, virtually a prisoner.'

'That's unfair, Belle,' Etienne spoke out. 'Mog had to keep you close as a child because there were dangers all around you in London. Mog doesn't want to do that with Mari.'

'Of course I don't,' Mog said. 'All she needs is some gentle curbing. She's been coming and going as she pleases for some time now. She should be helping around the house more, learning cooking and sewing, not climbing trees and playing ball with boys all the time. Another four years and she'll be a young woman, and I don't have to tell you, Belle, what dangers that can bring.'

Belle pursed her lips.

'Oh, don't give me that holier-than-thou look,' Mog said impatiently. 'Let's face it, between the three of us we know every last kind of trouble young people can get into. There's a lot less temptation here than there was back in London, or in Marseille. But it may be too dull for our youngsters. That will make them look for mischief.'

Etienne grinned. 'You are right, Mog, as you always are.

I'd be happier if Mari daydreamed of having a hat shop, or becoming a ballet dancer. But as that is unlikely, then we'll just have to steer her towards something safer than becoming another Joan of Arc.'

'Who told her about Joan of Arc anyway?' Belle looked accusingly at Etienne.

He did one of his Gallic shrugs. 'I tell the boys about King Arthur, so I tell Mari about a peasant girl who led her countrymen into battle. I thought you wanted equality for women?'

'I did. I do. But once you have a daughter, you just hope she'll marry a good, kind man and live happily ever after.'

'I hope for that too,' Etienne agreed. 'But I also want Mari to aspire to bigger things. She is clever, maybe her path is to be a doctor, a lawyer, or to succeed where I failed, with her own vineyard. We must do all we can to channel her strengths in the right direction.'

2

1938

Mog was in the workroom sewing pearls on to a wedding veil when Mariette came in, dressed to go out. She was wearing the green and white candy-striped dress Mog had only recently made for her, and she looked a picture.

Mog had always maintained Mariette would become pretty once she grew into a young woman, and she'd been proved right. At eighteen, five foot six, with an hourglass figure and stunning long, curly strawberry-blonde hair, she was the envy of her girlfriends and, no doubt, an object of desire to most men. Today she had her hair pinned up at the sides with two green ribbons.

'I don't think you should be gadding about on a Sunday afternoon,' Mog said. 'I was never allowed to, when I was a girl.'

Mariette laughed. 'Oh, Moggy! That's so quaint and Victorian. What's wrong with going for a walk on a lovely day? I bet Jesus didn't sit about on Sunday with his nose in a book.'

'They didn't have books then,' Mog retorted 'Besides, I thought you were going to help me. I've almost finished this veil, but there are hundreds more pearls to sew on the dress.'

'I'll help you with that when I come back. I just want a bit of exercise and some fresh air.'

'But you told your parents the reason you didn't want to go over to Paihia with them today was because you were going to help me.' Mog looked at Mariette suspiciously. 'Are you planning to meet a young man?'

'No! Why do you and Mum always think I'm meeting boys?'

Mog noted Mariette's flushed cheeks, and the false indignation in her voice, and knew her suspicions were correct. 'There isn't much your mother and I don't know about young girls,' she said tartly.

She adored Mariette but she wasn't blind to her faults. The girl was self-centred, devious and manipulative, with, seemingly, none of Belle's compassion – or her father's capacity for hard work.

They could all be proud that she was so bright, and her lovely face would melt a heart of stone, but Mog was very afraid that she would get herself into serious trouble one day.

She had helped Dr Crowley deliver Mariette, and from the moment she held her in her arms and looked down at that angry little red face, she'd felt an enormous surge of love for her. She had loved Belle just as much, as a baby, when she'd had sole charge of her. But Mog had been just the maid then, and because she knew that Belle's mother, Annie, could have thrown her out on her ear at any time, she'd learned to stifle her feelings and to keep her mouth shut until Annie asked for her opinion.

But both Belle and Etienne thought of Mog as their baby's grandmother and, as such, she had no need to hold anything back – not her help, her opinion or her devotion to their little girl. But loving a child so much was a double-edged sword. Mog might have the joy of knowing she was as important to Mariette as her parents, yet with that came the fear of something bad happening to her.

Belle had been abducted by evil men when she was only fifteen, and there had been times in the two years she was gone when Mog felt she would lose her mind with the agony of not knowing her precious girl's fate. While it was unlikely such a thing could happen to Mariette, there were many other dangers for a young girl to walk into. Mog felt it was her duty to keep her safe, and if she failed because she hadn't taken a firm enough line with her, then she'd never be able to forgive herself.

Once, that had meant merely making sure Mariette didn't play in dangerous places, ate the right food to keep healthy, and knew how to tell right from wrong. But then – and it seemed to have happened overnight – she turned into a young woman, and suddenly Mog saw new dangers. She couldn't keep an eighteen-year-old locked away, conceal those womanly curves or make her smile less dazzling.

Neither could she warn her what some men were capable of – not without telling her how she knew. Belle believed that Mariette was entirely safe in Russell, that no man would dare take liberties with her daughter out of fear of Etienne. Maybe she was right, but Mog knew Mariette was a little madam and she could very well be the one that did the leading on.

'Well, if you must go out, be back by four,' Mog said reluctantly. 'We need daylight to sew the pearls on the dress but, with just an hour at it together, we could finish it.'

Mariette agreed and hugged Mog. Then, before she got any further lectures, she snatched up a cardigan and raced out of the door.

Mariette *was* meeting someone. As she walked towards Flag Staff Hill to join him, she was afraid. Her fear was not because she'd lied to Mog – she'd told Mog and her parents so many lies in the past couple of months that she was beyond guilt – but because she had to end it today with Sam, and she expected him to turn nasty.

She'd first met him a year ago, when the cargo ship he worked on anchored out in the bay for some minor repairs. All the crew came into Russell and created quite a stir by getting very drunk and rowdy. Sam stood out because he was young, tall, blond and very handsome; the rest of the crew were short, tough-looking men with bad teeth and mainly well over thirty.

Mariette only spoke to him once. He asked her what there was to do in Paihia, and if it was worth getting the ferry over there. She told him it wasn't as pretty as Russell, and he laughed and said he was only interested in pretty girls, not scenery.

After the ship had left the bay, she heard her parents talking about the crew's bad behaviour. Not only had there been a fight in the Duke of Marlborough with chairs and windows smashed but several women and girls had been accosted, and the whole town was indignant.

Her father appeared to have some sympathy with the men. He said they'd probably heard that Russell was once known as the 'Hellhole of the Pacific', and they were disappointed to find it had turned into such a sober place, with no loose women and not even a dance hall.

The image of that handsome sailor, whose name she didn't even know then, stayed with her. She kept remembering the way he'd looked at her, like he was seeing right through her clothes, and how it had made her feel all fizzy inside.

For the remainder of last summer, she'd found herself thinking a great deal about boys. She had no shortage of admirers – she was, after all, said to be the prettiest girl in Russell – but they were just boys she'd grown up with, and not one of them made her feel the way the tall, blond stranger had. She practised on a few of them, led them on enough to kiss her, but it didn't set her on fire the way she'd read about kissing in books.

Mariette read every book she could get her hands on and, because of what she'd read about big cities and other countries, she considered Russell very dull. In her opinion it had nothing to offer other than its beauty. Apart from the odd dance now and then, the occasional film show or picnic, there was nothing to do. If she could go out fishing and sailing with her father every day, then she'd be happy. But he couldn't take her with him very often, and the owners of yachts that frequently needed a crew would never think a mere girl was capable.

As for old friends from school, she felt she'd outgrown them. They were content to help their mothers with the chores, to sit about giggling and gossiping; not one of them had dreams of travelling the world or doing something dangerous and thrilling, as she did.

She'd heard the sailor was an Australian, and so she never expected to see him again. Yet, to her surprise and delight, two months ago, he'd come back to Russell. He was no longer a sailor but was working as a truck driver for a timber company, collecting loads of timber from various forests in the North Island, which were then shipped further afield.

Mariette ran into him at the post office, and his broad smile told her he both remembered her and liked what he saw. They had a brief chat, and she flirted with him, but she knew her parents would never agree to her walking out with a grown man of twenty-five who was just passing through, so she didn't dare agree to meet up with him that evening.

She held out for three days, stopping to chat and flirt with him, but it was only when she heard he was moving on elsewhere the next day that she knew it was now or never.

Men always hung around the Duke of Marlborough, waiting for it to open at six, so she made sure she walked that way, wearing her prettiest dress. His eyes lit up when he saw her and the fizzy feeling she'd felt when she first met him all those months ago came back stronger than ever. In their brief chats she had been a little disappointed that he was somewhat coarse, using swear words and making crude remarks about her figure and legs. His worn checked shirt and moleskin trousers were a bit grubby too, but he had beautiful blue eyes and long dark lashes, and she couldn't resist the whiff of danger that seeped out of his sunburned skin.

That day she'd already taken the precaution of telling her parents she was going to a friend's house, and readily agreed to go for a walk with him. She was convinced he was already smitten with her because he didn't appear to care that he'd miss the six o'clock swill in the pub, and few men would pass that up.

Once they were away from the town and any prying eyes, he kissed her, and it was all Mariette had hoped for and more. She lost all track of time in his arms; he made her heart race, her knees go weak, and there was a strange yet wonderful tugging sensation in her belly that made her lose all sense of caution.

Yet he pulled back. 'I can't do this with you,' he said. 'You're too young, and I have to go away. It isn't fair on you.'

He left Russell early the next morning, and he hadn't even said if he would be back. But those last few words had convinced her he was a gentleman at heart, and his coarseness was just because he wasn't used to being in women's company.

A fortnight went by before he returned, and for all of those fourteen days she'd thought of nothing but him and his kisses. She'd had to hide it away, not even daring to tell one of her friends in case they passed it on.

When he did return, he told her that she'd been on his

mind the whole time he'd been away, and that he had fallen in love with her. What girl wouldn't believe that claim? And how could she not let him make love to her, when she believed she was in love with him too?

That first time was up on Flag Staff Hill, behind some bushes, and she knew as he pushed her down without any thought for her comfort that she'd made a mistake. She had wanted something romantic and beautiful, but all she got was prickles in her bottom, bruised thighs and disappointment. Then, when he said he had to get back to the pub to meet a friend, she'd felt cheated and humiliated.

But, like a fool, she thought it would get better. She'd read several books where the heroine felt like she did the first time, and it always came right in the end. Once, when he'd left Russell, not telling her when – or if – he'd be back, she even managed to convince herself he'd behaved that way with her because he was afraid of loving her.

Without having anyone to confide in, and also terrified her parents would find out, she was in a state of perpetual anxiety. Sometimes she even hoped Sam wouldn't come back to Russell, and then she could forget him. Yet, a week later, when she spotted him from her bedroom window, leaning against the tree at the shore end of Robertson Street and looking up at her house, she felt she had to rush out to meet him again.

Stupidly, she thought she could change him by trying to make him just talk to her, kiss and cuddle her, without anything else.

'I'm not too happy with the way you've been with me,' she said. 'I want to talk to you, get to know all about you. So can we just go for a walk and do that, without the . . .' She hesitated, not really knowing what to call it. 'You know, the thing?'

He stroked her cheek in what she thought was a really tender way. 'Look, sweetheart, you've been on my mind ever since the last time,' he said earnestly. 'I want you so badly. Don't do this to me?'

Looking back now, it was obvious that he didn't care about her at all, that all he wanted was sex. But she didn't see that then; all she saw were his pleading eyes, and so she went along with what he wanted.

By the fourth time, he was becoming even rougher with her, tossing her down on the ground and forcing himself upon her. After he was done, he degraded her still further by telling her to run along home as he had to see someone about some business.

Mog had an expression she used when she suddenly realized the truth about someone or something: 'The scales fell from her eyes.' Mariette had often laughed at it, saying only fish had scales. But she finally understood what the expression meant ten days ago, the last time Sam had been in Russell.

He had been really vile to her. He'd pushed her down on to her knees in some bushes and entered her from behind like a dog. There hadn't been even one kiss. As he buttoned up his trousers afterwards, he told her to meet him there again a week on Sunday – and she wasn't to be late.

It was like having a bucket of cold water thrown over her, but it did finally bring her to her senses.

Since then, she hadn't stopped smarting with shame for allowing him to treat her in such a callous manner. She fervently hoped that he wouldn't come back to Russell ever again, and that could be the end of it.

But that wasn't to be. Yesterday, as she was walking along the Strand, there he was, waiting for the Duke of Marlborough to open.

He was very dirty, he smelled of stale sweat, and it wasn't a smile he gave her but a leer, which said everything he felt about her.

'Don't forget our arrangement tomorrow,' he said, and rubbed his crotch in a suggestive manner. She had walked on quickly without stopping.

As she saw it, she had two choices. One was just to not turn up, but there was always the danger he might come to the house and alert her parents to what had been going on. The only other choice was to meet him and show him what she was made of. The latter appealed to her much more, and she knew it would make her feel better about herself.

But now, as she spotted him up ahead sitting on the grass smoking a cigarette, her stomach lurched with fear. He looked round as she got nearer, but he didn't even smile or stand up to greet her.

'I'm not stopping,' she said as she got within earshot. 'I just came to tell you I don't want to see you any more.'

'Is that so?' he replied with a lazy sneer. 'You could've said that yesterday and saved me the effort of walking up here, but I guess this is the usual Sheila's trick to get me to say something soppy. No chance of that, love, you've picked the wrong man.'

She went right up to him and looked down at him. 'I certainly did pick the wrong man,' she retorted. 'You've treated me shamefully, and I never want to see you again.'

He jumped up then. 'I gave you what you wanted, didn't I?'

'Do you really think any girl just wants that?' She was incredulous at his arrogance.

'You were desperate for it,' he said. 'All that fluttering your eyelashes at me and the come-on looks. Sheilas like you are ten a penny. They lure you into screwing them, and then they want you to marry them.'

'*Marry* you!' she said indignantly. 'You fancy yourself,

don't you? I wouldn't marry you if I was paid a million pounds to do it. You're uncouth, arrogant and plain nasty. I can't imagine what made me think there was anything to like about you. But I've said my piece, and I'm going home now.'

'Not so fast,' he said, grabbing her arm. 'No two-bit whore insults me and gets away with it.'

'You didn't mind insulting me with your animal behaviour,' she shot back, and tried to get out of his grip.

He dug his fingers harder into her arm so it hurt. 'You think you are so high and mighty,' he snarled at her, putting his face right up to hers. 'What've you got to be so snooty about? They say your old man is a war hero, but he's a bloody Frog, and they give the French medals just for wiping their own arse. As for your ma, well, from what I've heard, she jumped on the first single man who turned up here and was up the spout at her wedding.'

Suddenly Mariette realized she'd been very stupid to come up here where there was no one to run to for help if Sam turned really nasty.

'Let me go,' she pleaded.

'I'll let you go alright,' he said. 'But only after you've sucked me off.'

Mariette didn't know what he meant by that until he began to unbutton his fly, pulled out his penis and started pushing her down towards it.

'On your knees,' he commanded her. 'And do it good.'

Just the thought of such a thing made her gag, and she had no intention of doing anything so utterly disgusting. But she was aware that he was a great deal stronger than her, and she knew the only way she could get the better of him was through guile.

Taking a deep breath, she forced herself to grin up at him. 'I suppose I could . . . for old times' sake,' she said as she reached out to grasp his penis. It was still flaccid, and it felt sweaty and nasty, but the moment her hand went around it and she bent her knees as if to kneel down, thankfully, he let go of her arm.

Under her grasp his penis rose up as thick as a baby's arm. She looked up and saw he had his head back and his eyes closed. It was the moment.

In one swift movement she brought her knee up and thumped him right in his testicles, then turned and fled as fast as she could.

She glanced back to see him doubled up with pain. He sank to his knees on the grass, holding himself and making a bellowing sound.

It was shock that made her cry. Her mother and Mog had always warned her not to trust strangers or allow people to take liberties with her. But such warnings had never meant much before because, until she met Sam, everyone she met had been good and decent.

Yet she did remember a few years back, when times were really hard because of the Depression, how anxious her mother had been when gaunt-looking men with ragged clothes came to the door asking for food.

'Don't open the door to anyone when I'm not here,' her mother had warned her. 'Hard times make people desperate.'

Mariette had found it odd that, after warning her against such men, both her mother and Mog would give the men food and drink, and often bathed and treated the blisters on their feet.

'They can't help the way they look, they are hungry and exhausted,' Mog explained to her. 'There are men like them all over the world now, travelling about in the hope of finding work. You've been sheltered from the harsh reality of what the Depression means for most people. Luckily, we've managed with the vegetables we grow, the cow and chickens, and your father catching fish for us. Otherwise, we might be starving too.'

Mariette did start to notice things after that. No one could afford to have a new dress or a hat made, and so her mother and Mog weren't earning any money. She became aware that they both ate like birds so that she and her brothers could have more food. At night they would only light one lamp, old dresses were taken apart and made into something else, and both she and her brothers were expected to go down to the shore every day to pick up driftwood for the fire.

Her father spoke out in disgust about the relief camps that were supposed to help men feed their families. But in order to qualify for the pitifully small amount of relief money, they had to go to labour camps miles away from their homes. There they built roads with only a pick and shovel, cleared undergrowth, dug ditches or carried out hard, soul-destroying and often pointless work. They lived in tents with dirt floors, and the food they received was barely fit to give a dog.

She also learned that many children in the cities were dressed in rags, without shoes, and that babies were dying because there was no milk for them.

Tens of thousands had lost their jobs, shops and factories had closed down, and farmers were facing ruin. For many people the soup kitchen was the only thing that kept them from dying of starvation.

Her family clustered around the wireless at night to hear 'Uncle Scrim', just as people all over New Zealand did, but along with the shared laughter they heard reports of hunger marches in England and even riots in Wellington and other cities in New Zealand.

Thankfully, things had begun to improve in the last year. Men were leaving the relief camps and going home, factories were opening again, and the banks were becoming more lenient with the farmers. There was even free milk for all schoolchildren. Yet the only work Mariette could find was helping her mother and Mog with their dressmaking and millinery. She wanted something of her own choosing, but there just wasn't anything else in Russell.

She dried her eyes as she reached the small group of shacks at the bottom of the hill, because she knew all the Maoris who lived in them and certainly didn't want anyone seeing her in tears. As she passed the Komekes' house, Anahera, the younger sister of her friend Matui, waved to her. She was only fifteen, and heavily pregnant. Mog had commented recently how another mouth to feed in that family was the last thing they needed.

The sight of Anahera's swollen belly brought Mariette up sharply. What if she herself was pregnant?

She didn't know why she hadn't considered the possibility before – after all, she'd had the whole baby thing explained properly to her at the age of twelve. So she didn't have the excuse of ignorance as, perhaps, Anahera had.

Fear clutched at her heart and made her feel nauseous. It was bad enough that she'd allowed herself to be used by Sam, without the thought of carrying his baby too.

Her parents and Mog were generally lenient, understanding people. Mariette couldn't count the number of times they had stood by people who had shocked their more narrow-minded neighbours. They never sat in judgement on anyone, and they were the first to offer help to anyone in need.

But she couldn't hope for understanding about her becoming pregnant by a rough man she didn't even love.

Mog knew something was wrong the moment Mariette came in. Her eyes, so much like Belle's, had a fearful glint in them;

she looked edgy, as if she was expecting to be caught out about something. When Mog asked what was wrong, Mariette said she was afraid of being late getting home to finish the wedding dress.

Mog's active sixth sense told her there was a great deal more to it than that, but she didn't ask anything else. She'd learned years ago with Belle that to push for an explanation usually resulted in her clamming up permanently. Mariette was much the same.

They were now sitting either side of the workroom table, with Janet Appleby's satin wedding dress spread out between them. Sewing pearls to the hem was an intricate task which required patience and excellent eyesight, but it was the kind of job they both enjoyed and, usually, when they worked together they chatted and laughed.

But today Mariette looked haunted; she'd barely said a word since she sat down at the table, put on her thimble and began sewing. Normally she would have said where she'd walked to and who she'd seen, often making Mog laugh with sarcastic comments about the clothes that passed as 'Sunday best' on some of their neighbours. Women in Russell were not very fashion-conscious – many of them wore dresses that only fitted where they touched.

As Mariette had been such a tomboy when she was younger, Mog was both surprised and delighted when she took to sewing. She was now almost as adept as Mog, and far better than her mother. Mog often remarked that her tiny, neat stitches looked like the work of a fairy.

She looked over her glasses and watched Mariette as she rethreaded her needle. She had a true amalgamation of her parents' best features, with Belle's eyes and Etienne's sharp cheekbones. But the strawberry-blonde hair, which was a common result from one dark and one blonde parent, gave her a distinctive look that was all her own. She also had an enviable complexion, as clear and flawless as a porcelain doll.

'You're very quiet,' Mog said casually. 'Something on your mind?'

'No,' Mariette retorted, a bit too sharply. 'Sometimes it's nice to be quiet.'

After another twenty minutes of silence, Mog felt compelled to probe. 'If there's something bothering you, do tell me. I might be able to help,' she said.

Mariette looked up from her sewing, and Mog saw a flicker of something – maybe the need to confide? – in her face.

'Nothing's bothering me,' she said. 'Well, apart from wishing I had a job.'

Mog was fairly certain that wasn't the truth. 'What about your mum's idea, nursing?'

'Hmm,' Mariette responded. 'I don't think I'm really cut out for that. All those bedpans, vomit and blood. But it would be good to go to Auckland.'

'You want to run away from someone here?'

Mog knew she'd hit the nail right on the head by the way Mariette's eyes widened – even though she gave a humourless laugh, as if such a thing was impossible.

'Of course not. But there aren't any opportunities for me here, are there?'

'You never know what's round the corner,' Mog said evenly. 'Summer's coming, and the people who come here for sailing and fishing are from all walks of life.'

'Is that all everyone thinks I want? To find a husband?'

'It's what most girls want,' Mog said.

'Well, I don't want to spend my life cooking, cleaning and washing clothes,' Mariette snapped. 'And that's what marriage is about, isn't it? Janet Appleby might be stupid enough

35

to think that getting married is just about a lovely dress and a big party, but not me.'

Mog shook her head in disapproval. 'You are far too young to be so cynical,' she said. 'And very wrong too. Marriage is about sharing a life with a man you love, nurturing your children, supporting one another. I didn't get married until I was almost middle-aged, and we only had a few years together before Garth was taken by the Spanish flu, but they were the best years of my life. Look at your parents, Mari – they are still as much in love as they were when they got married. I think your mother would tell you marriage is about a great deal more than washing clothes, cooking and cleaning.'

'But they had to get married, didn't they?' Mariette asked. 'Mum was pregnant on her wedding day.'

Mog was shocked to hear such a thing coming from Mariette's lips, and wondered who had told her. But she wasn't going to deny it, not even if most people saw it as a disgrace.

'The reason they married was because they couldn't bear to live apart,' she said reprovingly. 'And, in my opinion, that is the only reason to get married.'

'But you'd all be furious if I got pregnant and I wasn't married.'

It was Mariette's tone, rather than her actual words, that made Mog suspicious. She had spent much of her early life listening to conversations between other women and had learned to detect hidden undercurrents, to hear the faint inflections in remarks that revealed what the speaker meant, but couldn't actually put into words. Belle claimed she was impossible to fool.

'Are you pregnant, Mari?' she asked gently. 'Is that what all this is about? Going out today to meet someone, the long silences since you got back? You're worried?'

'Of course I'm not pregnant,' Mariette said with some indignation. 'Whatever gave you that idea?'

'You did,' Mog said. 'Or you think you could be. But the most worrying thing for me is that you've obviously been seeing someone who you know we wouldn't approve of. I think you ought to tell me who he is, right now.'

As rebellious as Mariette could be, when faced with a direct question she usually answered truthfully. She had her jaw clenched, which suggested to Mog that she was steeling herself against admitting anything.

'You know I'll find out,' Mog reminded her. 'No one can do anything in Russell without someone passing it on. It's better to tell me now than to have someone spiteful telling your mother with the sole intention of upsetting her.'

'It's over, so it doesn't matter,' Mariette blurted out. 'I won't be seeing him again.'

'If he's someone unsuitable, then that's fine. But unless he's just someone passing through Russell, it would be hard to avoid him,' Mog said. 'But my guess it's someone you've known for a long time. Is it Carlo Belsito?'

Carlo Belsito was a ferryman. Although born in New Zealand he had all the hallmarks of his Italian ancestry, with dark curly hair, spaniel eyes and a physique that few women in Russell could fail to notice. He was something of a Lothario, and many distasteful stories circulated about his prowess with women.

'Carlo!' Mariette said in astonishment. 'What do you take me for, Mog? I despise him.'

'Well, that's a relief,' Mog chuckled. 'I'd hate to think you wasted even a minute of your life on him. So let me think, who else is there?'

'Let it go, Mog,' Mariette pleaded. 'I've told him it's over. I just want to forget about him.'

Mog knew that more could be gained by backing off and coming back to the subject at a later date than by trying to force the issue now.

'Fair enough,' she said. 'Now, we've only got about another fifty pearls left, so let's try to sew them on before the light fades.'

She noted that Mariette looked very relieved at being given a reprieve. Mog was amused that the girl assumed that would be the end of it.

3

The following morning Etienne left early in his truck to pick up some timber from Waitangi, taking Mariette with him. Mog suspected she'd asked to go in the hope that, during her absence, the conversation of the previous day would be forgotten.

After the boys had gone off to school, Belle decided to spring-clean their room. Mog went along to the Reids' bakery, as she always did on Mondays. Belle had become friends with Vera Reid, the daughter of the owners, when they were both ambulance drivers in France, and it was Vera who encouraged Belle and Mog to emigrate to New Zealand after the war ended.

Vera had moved away to Wellington back in 1924, and had since got married and had three children, but Mog had remained a close friend to Peggy, Vera's mother.

Don, Peggy's husband, was serving in the shop as Mog came in, and his face broke into a cheerful grin. He was over seventy now and looked as if he'd shrunk to half the size of the portly, energetic man she and Belle had met on their first day in Russell. His youngest son, Tony, was the baker now – Don was no longer strong enough to lift the heavy trays of loaves or to knead the dough.

'Peggy's out the back in the wash house. Go on through, if you want to see her. She'll be glad to have someone to moan to,' he said.

Mog thanked him and went through the doorway that led to both the bakery and their home. The wash house was just outside their kitchen; the heat from the boiler, the smell of carbolic soap and the steam hit Mog before she even got to the wash-house door.

If Don had shrunk, Peggy had expanded. Always plump, she was now very fat and her hair was snowy white. She was standing at the copper, prodding the washing with the copper stick, perspiration running down her fiery red cheeks. But her big face broke into a toothless smile at seeing her friend.

'Come to watch slave labour?' she said.

'I bet you can't wait for the day the electric comes to Russell,' Mog said. 'I know I'm never going to miss lighting the fire under our copper, or trimming and filling lamps.'

Peggy pulled up her pinafore and wiped her face. 'Too right. I'm too old for all this drudgery. Our Vera's got one of those new-fangled electric boilers, it's got a mangle that turns by itself. What I'd give for one of those! But let me get us a drink and we'll sit outside for a chat, shall we?' Peggy got two glasses of lemonade for them, and they sat down in the yard under the shade of a fig tree.

They chatted about this and that for a little while, Peggy saying she was planning a little holiday with Vera soon. 'Why don't you and Belle come too?' she asked. 'Vera's got plenty of room, and she'd be thrilled to see you both.'

'I could come, but Belle won't leave the boys,' Mog said. 'You know how they are – up to mischief if you don't stand over them.'

Peggy nodded. 'I remember what mine were like – little sods, they were – and Vera was no better than the boys. But when they were all away in the war, I'd have given anything to have them back playing me up. I reckon that's why I've got so fat. Nothing to worry about any more!' She cackled with laughter, making her many chins quiver.

'Just between ourselves, have you heard any tittle-tattle about Mariette?' Mog asked. 'She's been seeing a boy, but won't tell me who he is. That's always a bad sign.'

Peggy thought about it for a moment. 'There was a mention of that Australian. You know, the one who was part of the crew on the boat that came in for repairs last year?' she said. 'He's hauling timber now, but he comes here every now and again. Avril Avery claimed she saw them out for a walk, holding hands. But then she'd accuse the Pope of giving poisoned lollies to Shirley Temple!'

Mog laughed at Peggy's joke about Avril Avery, who was the eyes and ears of the little town. Yet although she was a gossip, Avril was not a liar, so she must have seen Mari and that man together. 'I dare say Mari will tell us when she's good and ready. But I'd better collect the bread and go on home. Thanks for the lemonade, and I'll let you know about going to see Vera with you.'

Mog was too disturbed by what Peggy had said to go straight home. Instead, she went down on the Strand and sat for a while looking out to sea to reflect on it. She had seen the man in question several times, hanging around near their house, but it had never occurred to her that he might be after Mari because he was far too old for her. There had been a lot of talk about him too – tales of drunkenness, fighting, playing around with a couple of Maori girls – and as he slept in a tent when he was in town, and not in the hotel, goodness knows what else he got up to.

What if Mari was pregnant by him, and that was why she looked so troubled?

Tears ran down Mog's cheeks at that possibility.

'What is it, Mog?' Belle asked during the afternoon. She had been busy upstairs all morning. Once she'd finished up there, she'd joined Mog in the workroom to finish trimming a hat. Mog had a length of gingham spread out on the cutting table in front of her, but so far she hadn't even touched it. 'You've been staring into space for ages.'

Mog started. 'What did you say?'

Belle repeated herself. 'If you've got a problem, tell me,' she added.

Mog looked up at Belle's concerned face. Not for the first time, she wondered how it was that, at forty-three, she had managed to remain so youthful looking and had kept her figure intact. There were some grey hairs amongst the dark, and a few lines around her eyes, but Belle was still a head turner.

'I was thinking about Noah's last letter, when he suggested it might be good for Mari to visit England.'

'And? When you read it, you said that he must be nuts suggesting such a thing when war is threatened.'

'I know, but everyone – and Noah too, for that matter – is saying that it will be averted, and I got to thinking it wasn't such a bad idea. He is Mari's godfather, after all, and he's got a beautiful home, with so many useful connections. His influence could only be for the good. Mari needs work, and there's none here. And you know what they say about Satan finding work for idle hands.'

Belle looked at Mog with narrowed eyes. 'What brought this on? Do you know something?'

'No, I just think that she's got a very aimless life. She told me she wanted to go to Auckland, but not into nursing. We don't know anyone in Auckland to keep an eye on her. I just thought maybe London and Noah would be good for her.'

'I agree that she needs something more than just a bit of sewing and helping with the boys,' Belle said, sitting down across the cutting table from Mog. 'But to send her to the other side of the world!'

'Yes, I know, it's a bit extreme. But we can count on Noah and Lisette to take good care of her, and their daughter will be company for her. Think of the opportunities there would be there for her.'

'And all the opportunities to get into trouble,' Belle pointed out. 'Now, tell me what brought this on. I know that you would never suggest sending Mari away unless you thought something bad was going to happen to her here. So what is it?'

Mog pursed her lips. She always forgot that Belle was as good at reading people as she herself was. Now she was stuck; having started this, she'd have to continue, even if that meant telling tales on Mari.

'Tell me!' Belle ordered her. 'If Mari is in some kind of trouble, I have a right to know.'

'Oh, Belle,' Mog implored her. 'It's one of those situations where I'll be damned if I tell you my fears, and damned if I don't. You and Etienne will fly off the handle if I'm right, and possibly make things worse. If I'm wrong, Mari will never talk to me again. Anyway, I'm not even sure there is a real situation.'

Belle said nothing for a few moments. She picked up a pincushion and began arranging the pins in neat rows.

'Right!' Belle said eventually. 'We both know you are very intuitive, so the chances are that you're right about whatever you fear. So why don't you tell me? We can mull it over together calmly, and then decide how we deal with it. Mari won't need to know you said anything.'

Mog took a deep breath and then blurted out that she was afraid Mari had been seeing the blond sailor in secret.

Belle turned pale. 'Heaven help us,' she exclaimed. 'I didn't see that one coming! I knew, of course, that the man had come back to Russell – you can hardly miss him – but Mari's never mentioned him.'

'The best way to put us off the scent,' Mog sniffed. 'But bear in mind that I haven't got any proof he's the man she has been seeing. She also said it's over. But the way she was behaving yesterday, I suspect she's worried about something.'

'Maybe she was just afraid of him coming here? We all know Etienne would tear a man like that limb from limb, if he thought he'd taken liberties with his daughter. Do you really think they have been . . . ?' She paused, unable to finish her question.

'Yes, I do think they've been doing it,' Mog said bluntly. 'A man of his age and type isn't likely to waste time on a girl who won't cooperate. Besides, she's had something on her mind for some little while now – easily distracted, and off with the fairies too.'

'Etienne will kill him!' Belle exclaimed, as all the implications sank in.

'You see why I thought it would be a good idea to send her to London?' Mog asked. 'If Avril told Peggy she'd seen them together, you can bet she's told others too. And that lout may have boasted he'd had his way with her too. You know what people are like around here. If this gets out – and it's sure to – she'll be seen as shop-soiled goods, and that might make her find someone even more disreputable.'

Belle leaned on the cutting table, her head in her hands. 'Well, I certainly know what it's like to be the one everyone is talking about. Remember all the nasty stuff that was said about me when Etienne arrived here? Even now, donkey's years later, some women still think their husbands aren't safe with me around. Some things you just can't live down.' She looked at Mog fearfully. 'What was she thinking of?'

'You, of all people, should know that girls don't think at such times,' Mog said tartly.

Belle blushed at the oblique reference to her affair with

Etienne in France, while she was still married to Jimmy Reilly. 'I thought I'd done the right thing by telling her the facts of life and how girls have to protect themselves by waiting till they get married,' she retorted. 'But perhaps I should have been like other mothers and told her sex was something to be endured.'

'I doubt whether that would have made any difference,' Mog said. 'Mari is as hot-headed as both you and Etienne; she's never listened to advice or abided by any rules. In my opinion, this has come about because she has too little to do. Boredom creates a fertile ground for wrongdoing.'

'What are we to do, Mog?' Belle pleaded.

'We can pray she isn't pregnant, for a start. But I can't see how we can keep this from Etienne. To do so would make Mari think we are condoning her behaviour. She has behaved like a little trollop, and she has to face up to the consequences of that.'

Belle winced at Mog's harsh words. 'Oh, Mog,' she sighed. 'Once I'd married Etienne and we were all living so happily here, I really thought there would never be any bad times again for any of us. Now this!'

Mog reached across the table and took Belle's hand to comfort her. 'It might not be as bad as I fear, but the fact remains that we must do something. If we try to keep her under lock and key here, she'll just rebel. Maybe she could get an office job or shop work in Auckland, but she's too young to be without some sort of supervision.'

'You're right,' Belle agreed. 'But England seems so drastic, and so far away. Noah and Lisette are ideal in so many ways, parents themselves, and worldly enough to be aware of the dangers young girls can get into. They would be a good influence too, and inspiration for Mari. But how could we let her go?'

'You coped in America, under hideous circumstances, and you were far younger than Mari. But before we give that any serious consideration, we need to get the truth out of her, and I think that must be in Etienne's hearing.'

'Perhaps we've got it all wrong?' Belle said hopefully.

'Pigs might fly!' Mog retorted. 'We've both got too much experience of girls going astray to hope for a more innocent explanation. We should do it tonight, after the boys have gone to bed.'

Belle and Mog put their anxieties about Mariette on hold when the rest of the family arrived home. They all had supper together, and Mog saw the two boys off to bed just after seven. When she came downstairs, Etienne was still sitting at the kitchen table reading the newspaper while Mog and Mariette finished off the washing-up.

Mariette hung up the tea towel to dry and then went to leave the room.

'You can come back in here, and close the door,' Belle said sharply.

'Why?' Mariette asked. 'I was only going to get a book to read.'

'We have things we need to talk about,' Belle said. 'Now, sit down there by your papa.'

'What is this?' Etienne put down his newspaper and looked at Belle in puzzlement.

'Mari has something to tell you,' Belle said. 'In fact, she has something to tell us all. Come on, Mari, we want the name of this boy you've been seeing!'

Etienne was fond of saying he was an old man now but, at fifty-eight, he still had all his hair, his body was lean and fit, his eyes had lost none of their sparkle, and he was still as strong as a horse.

'You've been unusually helpful today – has that got something to do with this?' he said, looking hard at his daughter.

Mariette blushed. 'It was just a boy, nothing special. And it's all over now,' she said quickly.

'Name?' Belle roared at her. 'I already know, I just want to hear you say it.'

Mariette quaked visibly. 'Sam,' she whimpered. 'I couldn't tell you, I knew you wouldn't approve.'

Etienne looked stunned, but more by Belle's anger than by the name because he couldn't think of anyone called Sam.

'How could you expect us to approve of you going off alley-catting with any boy?' Belle asked, her voice harsh and cold. 'But that man! He's at least twenty-five, uncouth, always getting into fights and full of himself. You have clearly been lying to us constantly in the past weeks in order to see him. Why is that, Mari?'

'Because I knew you'd be like this,' Mariette retorted.

'Is this the blond Australian sailor?' Etienne asked, looking aghast.

Belle nodded.

'In that case, I agree totally with your mother. He's an animal, drunk every night, and I've heard other men say their girls aren't safe around him.'

'I'm sorry, Papa,' Mari said pleadingly. 'You are right about him, but I didn't realize it at first.'

'Just the fact that you were meeting him in secret tells me you knew full well that he was a bad lot. How far has this gone?'

Mariette folded her arms, looked insolently at the kitchen wall and didn't answer.

'Answer me, Mari,' Etienne commanded. 'Have you been lovers?'

Her silence was his answer, and his face flushed with

47

anger. 'You are barely eighteen. You have your whole life ahead of you, and you'd throw it all away for a roll in the hay with someone as worthless as him. Are you pregnant?'

He looked at Belle and Mog, waiting for them to confirm or deny this.

Belle shrugged. 'I don't know. I wasn't sure till now that it had gone that far.'

'Mariette! You will tell us all now,' Etienne roared. 'Are you pregnant?'

She continued to avoid his eyes. 'I could be, I suppose,' she retorted, hearing his sharp intake of breath. 'And don't come all high and mighty with me. I know perfectly well Mum was having me when you got married.'

Belle was incredulous that her daughter had no sense of shame, or respect for her father, and her fingers itched to strike her. But she managed to control herself. 'You'd better hope to God you aren't pregnant. Because if you are, you'll soon find out what real life is all about,' Belle spat out. 'Now, get upstairs to your room. I can't bear to look at you.'

Mariette scuttled out of the kitchen as fast as she could. Her mother's furious reaction, and the very fact that they'd all jumped to the conclusion that she was pregnant, made it seem even more probable.

What would happen to her if she was? There was no question of marrying Sam. Even if he agreed to it – which he wouldn't – she'd have a miserable life with him, saddled with a baby she didn't even want.

People were mean to unmarried mothers and, judging by her parents and Mog's reaction, it would start here in her own home.

She flung herself down on the bed and cried. She could hear the hum of their voices down below, and every now and then her father's became louder. That was the worst thing. She could live with her mother and Mog's disapproval, but she couldn't bear the thought of her papa being disappointed in her.

Downstairs, in the kitchen, Etienne paced around angrily. Belle knew that he wanted to rush out of the door and beat Sam to a pulp. She had to prevent that.

'He's young and very strong,' she insisted, standing in front of the door so her husband couldn't get out. 'If you go round there now, with all guns blazing, he'll retaliate, and you are likely to come off worse. Furthermore, the whole town will get to hear of it – and once that cat is out of the bag, we won't be able to get it back in.'

Mog intervened too. 'Mari did this willingly, remember. She wanted a bit of excitement and she got it. Now she has to learn the meaning of the word "consequences". As do you! If you go and beat Sam up, that will suggest to her that he is the only one to blame.'

'Are you seriously suggesting that I do nothing?' Etienne asked, bewildered that they weren't crying for the man's blood too.

'Of course not,' Belle said soothingly. 'But Mog is right, Mari is as much to blame. I could have understood her more easily if she'd said she loved him. Sometimes she is so cold-hearted, I can't believe she's my child. Please sleep on it, Etienne, before you rush off at half-cock. All you will achieve is giving the gossips far more ammunition.'

Etienne had felt hurt that both his wife and Mog thought him too old to give his daughter's seducer a good hiding. But he could see some sense in at least waiting until the morning before he did or said anything further.

As it was, he had a sleepless night, tossing and turning,

49

with unwelcome pictures of Mari and that unkempt sailor together running through his mind.

At first light he got up, dressed and quietly slipped out, leaving Belle still sleeping. The fury he'd felt on the previous night had abated. All he wanted now was to confront the man and at least try to understand what Mari had seen in him.

He had heard the ex-sailor was camping on a piece of waste ground close to the start of Flag Staff Hill and, as he walked towards it, he remembered the only time he'd spoken to him. The man had come lurching drunkenly out of the Duke of Marlborough one evening, just as Etienne was passing, and had bumped his shoulder.

'Steady up and look where you're going,' Etienne had said.

The man had straightened up and looked askance at him. 'You must be the Frog war hero, with an accent like that,' he'd said with a sneer.

'And you must be the drunken lout from Australia with an accent like that,' Etienne had retorted and walked on, ignoring a ridiculous further remark about whether he was out collecting snails to eat.

That brief encounter was as much evidence as Etienne needed in order to know the man was an ignorant buffoon, and it made the possibility of Mari carrying his child even more alarming.

He found the tent, half hidden behind some scrubby bushes, and he remembered then that there had been complaints from various people in the town about the man being there.

The tent was a small shabby affair that sagged in the middle as the guy ropes were slack. Etienne looked at it for a few moments, then kicked the ropes loose so that the tent collapsed. From inside came the sound of swearing as the man awoke to find himself buried in canvas.

Etienne waited – he suspected the man was enough of a

slob to stay where he was, regardless of the damp canvas covering him – but after a minute or two he crawled out rubbing his eyes, wearing only a pair of filthy underpants.

During the moments of waiting, Etienne had noted all the debris around the tent – mainly beer bottles and food cans. He wondered if the man ever bathed and how Mari, who had been brought up in a clean home, could possibly tolerate such a lack of hygiene.

'Did you bugger up my tent?' the man asked, squinting up at him. He had thick stubble on his chin and his blond hair looked filthy. And yet, even so, his bronzed muscular torso was impressive and he was very handsome.

'Guilty as charged,' Etienne said. 'Just be grateful I didn't attack it with an axe and chop your head off. On your feet! I know you are lower than shit, but I like to look a man in the eye when I'm talking to him.'

'What's this about?' Sam asked as he got to his feet.

'As if you don't know!' Etienne scoffed. 'You know full well I'm Mariette's father. But then, if you'd had any sense of decency, you would have called on me to ask my permission before walking out with her.'

'No one does that any more,' Sam growled. 'Go home, old man, and pick a fight with someone your own age. Mari threw herself at me. You might not like to hear that, but that's the way it was. Now get out of here.'

'I had hoped to find you had some saving graces,' Etienne retorted. 'But you live like a pig and smell worse than one. I think Mari must have temporarily taken leave of her senses getting involved with someone as low as you. You will leave Russell this morning on the first ferry, and never come back. If not, you may live to regret it.'

Sam laughed scornfully. 'And you think you're going to make me, old man? How do you plan to do that?'

'Like this,' Etienne said, and punched the man on the chin so hard that he reeled back and nearly toppled over.

Sam was momentarily stunned. He rubbed his chin and looked at Etienne, as if weighing him up. 'I don't want to fight with you because you'll never get up again from it,' he said. 'So clear off now, before I do you an injury.'

'Like this?' Etienne gave him a second punch in the belly with his right fist, then followed it up immediately with a punch from his left fist, smack on the jaw. 'Come on, don't hold back. I'm an old man, remember.'

Sam staggered back, blood trickling out of his mouth from a dislodged tooth. He lifted his fists to hit back, but Etienne danced out of the way and landed two further punches on the younger man's face before he could even blink.

Blood came gushing from his nose, and Etienne laughed. 'I thought you were going to do me an injury? But you're a little slow on your feet. This is how you do it,' he said as he zoomed in with an uppercut to the chin, knocking Sam's head right back, then followed it with an almighty blow to the solar plexus, which toppled him back and on to the ground.

Etienne went over to him, stamped his boot on the middle of the younger man's chest and held him there with it. 'For your information I learned to fight in the backstreets of Marseille,' he said. 'I'm handy with a knife too – would you like to see?'

He pulled a six-inch, narrow-bladed knife from a sheath on his belt and, leaning over Sam, held it to one of his nostrils. 'One of my favourite punishments for people who displeased me then was to slice their nose open. It leaves a man looking very ugly, girls don't look at them any more, they have to rely on ageing whores when they are desperate for a fuck,' Etienne snarled at him.

Sam gave a squeal of terror, and Etienne smiled as he looked down and saw he was pissing himself. 'They usually shit themselves as I start to do it too. Not such a big man now, eh! I can hardly wait to tell Mari that you never even managed to land one punch on me. Now, are you leaving Russell this morning? Or do I need to give you any more prompts to do as you are told?'

'No, I'll go,' Sam whimpered. 'Just don't cut me.'

'Afraid you'll lose your looks? I think I should make sure of that so you don't hurt any more young girls,' Etienne said. 'To be a real man, you have to treat women with respect. Every time you get tempted to do otherwise, think of me and my knife slitting your nose open.' He taunted Sam further by running the blade around his nostrils, enjoying the terror in the man's eyes, the way every muscle in his body was tense, waiting for the agony he was sure would follow.

Etienne straightened up and put the knife back into its sheath, but he pressed down harder on Sam's chest with his boot.

'I'll be off now. But I'll be waiting at the jetty to see you on the nine o'clock ferry. If you aren't on it, I'll be back for you. But just to make certain you obey me, here's something to think about.'

Etienne clenched his fist and slammed it down on to Sam's mouth. He took his boot off the man's chest, and took a couple of steps back. 'Sit up, or you'll choke on your own blood,' he said.

Sam did as he was told and spat out blood; with it came his two front teeth. His whole face was a bloody mess now.

Etienne smirked. 'Knocking front teeth out is almost as good as split nostrils for putting girls off,' he said. 'Remember, be on the nine o'clock ferry. Or there's more of that to come. This old man is going home for his breakfast now.'

Etienne walked away but, some fifty yards further on, he glanced back to see Sam trying to get to his feet, one hand on his belly, the other on his mouth. The pain he'd inflicted on him wouldn't help Mari if she was carrying the man's child, but it had made him feel a whole lot better.

When Belle woke up to find herself alone in bed, she guessed that Etienne had gone to have it out with Sam. She leapt out of bed and went downstairs to stir up the hot embers in the stove, adding more wood to boil the kettle for when he returned. But she was afraid he might be lying somewhere too badly injured to get home, so she decided she must get dressed and go to look for him.

At that moment, the door opened and he came in. One look at his face was enough to know his mission had been successful; he didn't appear hurt, except for some blood on his knuckles.

'What happened?' she asked.

'Nothing you need worry about,' he said, and his eyes were twinkling.

'Let me bathe that,' she said, pointing to his hand.

'No need – it's his blood, not mine,' he said calmly, and went over to the sink to wash his hands.

She didn't ask anything more, but busied herself taking some scraps out for the chickens and laying the table for breakfast. When she came down from waking the boys, she found Etienne sitting at the table staring blankly into space.

'Do you really think Mari has a cold heart,' he asked suddenly as she put the teapot on the table.

'Sometimes,' she admitted. 'She doesn't appear to have much compassion. And I hate to say it, but there are times when I think she takes after Annie.'

Belle rarely spoke about her real mother, who had died

five years earlier. The only contact between them since Belle had come to New Zealand was an annual Christmas card, and she only heard of her mother's death via Annie's solicitor. She had left everything she had to her daughter – a sum of just over £1,000 – but, as grateful as Belle was to have that money at a time when things were so hard for them all financially, she would gladly have traded it for one proper letter telling her that her mother loved her and was sorry for the neglect and stony-heartedness over the years.

Etienne caught hold of Belle around her waist and pressed his face into her breasts. 'How could we have had a child incapable of compassion?' he whispered.

'She isn't incapable of it. She just hasn't been through anything bad enough yet to learn to feel for others,' Belle replied. 'Did Sam say something like that to you?'

He shook his head. 'No, the only thing he said was that she threw herself at him. But I was thinking about how Mari was last night – she showed no emotion, not about Sam, or what this would mean to us. That's frightening.'

Belle lifted his face up and bent to kiss him. 'She was on the defensive – I think that man scared her. And she's ashamed too. My guess is she was holding all that in so tightly, it stopped her showing any emotion. But that doesn't mean she doesn't feel.'

'That young blackguard called me an old man, and I feel like one now,' he said. 'What will we do if she is having a baby?'

'You aren't an old man to me,' she said. 'Let's leave Mog to see the boys off to school, come upstairs with me and we'll talk in the bedroom.'

'I've got to finish the roof at the Apsley house,' he said.

'That can wait,' she said. 'Go on up, and I'll bring some tea in a minute.'

Ten minutes later, after asking Mog to take charge, Belle joined Etienne in their bedroom. He was lying on the bed looking defeated. She put his tea down on the side table, then joined him on the bed, pulling him into her arms. 'Did he hit you?'

'No, he didn't,' Etienne sighed. 'He didn't get a chance, but I inflicted a great deal of damage to his handsome face and ordered him to be on the nine o'clock ferry and never return.'

'Sounds like you've retained all your old menace,' she said with a smile.

'I feel a bit ashamed now that I enjoyed it so much,' he admitted. 'I even got the knife out that I use for gutting fish and threatened to slit his nostrils. I can't really believe I did that. But if you'd seen him, Belle! Filthy dirty, living like an animal, and all I could think of was that he'd had his way with our baby.'

Belle held him tightly to her breast and said nothing. She understood how he felt.

'I made him piss himself with fright. But what made me act so self-righteous, Belle? I've done things far worse than he can ever imagine. And I never stopped to think I might have got a girl pregnant.'

'I very much doubt you treated any young girl badly,' she said soothingly. 'And I can understand that you feel a bit of a hypocrite, because I do too – after all, I wasn't so pure either. But it's because we both went so wrong that we want better for Mari. I really hoped that she'd fall in love with a kind, caring man and float down the aisle in a white dress and veil, and it never occurred to me that she would be wanton.'

Etienne chuckled. '"Wanton", that's a great word. You were wanton as I recall too.'

'I was with you,' she admitted. 'I still am, on occasions!'

'Not often enough,' he said, sliding his hand inside her dressing gown and caressing her breasts.

'We came up here to talk,' she said reprovingly, but she didn't move his hand. 'Mog and I think this all came about because Mari was bored. She wanted some excitement and she found it in him. Even if she isn't pregnant, this sort of thing could happen again as she hasn't got enough to occupy her.'

'I hope to God she isn't pregnant, because then all the things we wanted for her won't happen,' Etienne sighed. 'I've known folk who pass off their daughter's baby as their own, but we couldn't do that here, we're too close to people.'

'Unless we all went to England, and then came back with the baby,' Belle said with a giggle.

Etienne laughed too. 'England's a bit drastic! Just going down to the South Island would make more sense.'

Belle looked thoughtful. 'I was only joking, but it's not such a bad idea. No one but us would know it wasn't ours. Women of forty-three do still have babies.'

'What has Mog suggested?' Etienne asked. 'She's usually good at coming up with solutions.'

'Well, that's what made me mention England. Before we thought Mari could be pregnant, Mog had suggested we send her to Noah. He is her godfather, after all, and there would be more opportunities for her there.'

'There are even more opportunities to go wrong there too,' he said.

'That's exactly what I said. But with you suggesting we make out the baby is ours, maybe it would be a good idea for all of us to go back? We've got that money from Annie; we could even write to people back here and say: guess what? We've had another baby! When we got back, Mari could do whatever she wanted with her life, but her baby would be safely here with us.'

When Etienne didn't answer, Belle thought he disapproved of that idea.

'But I'm going to pray hard that she isn't having a baby,' she added. 'We are too old to be parents again.'

He sighed deeply. 'Remember how overjoyed we were when we realized you were having Mariette? All babies should start life being wanted that much.'

'I agree,' Belle admitted. 'But Annie didn't want me and handed over the childcare to Mog. I turned out OK, didn't I?'

'Whatever happens, baby or not, we've got to make Mari take responsibility for her actions,' Etienne said firmly. 'We both know we'll love her child — even if the father was a snake and we're really too old to be going down that road again. But we aren't going to tell her that, no ideas of going to England, nothing. She must sweat it out for a while. She needs a good fright to bring her to her senses.'

4

As the days ticked slowly by, still without Mariette's month-lies appearing, Belle grew ever more anxious. Mog's usually smiley face had been replaced by a permanent frown, Etienne looked grim, and even Alexis and Noel kept asking what was wrong.

Belle had torn into Mariette later in the day, after Etienne had banished Sam, delivering a bitter, angry tirade about how she'd let her family down and risked her whole future. When Mariette retorted that Belle was no better – for hadn't she been carrying on her wedding day? – Belle slapped her face.

It seemed as if Mariette couldn't grasp the seriousness of her situation. She claimed she had no idea when her last monthly was. She had made no apologies, not even an attempt at offering an excuse for why she'd behaved as she did, and wore a sullen expression all the time. She didn't volunteer to help out more around the house – as anyone else would do when they realized they were in deep trouble – and when she was asked to do something, she flounced around as if she thought she was above such jobs.

'I can't bear this,' Belle confided to Etienne one night when they were in bed. 'I'm at my wits' end. I can't even get her to tell me how she feels about having a baby.'

Etienne held Belle tightly to try to comfort her. 'I would suggest I took her out sailing for the day – I might be able to get through to her away from here – but that looks too much like a treat, as if I'm condoning her behaviour.'

'I just want my happy little girl back,' Belle cried. 'I don't even recognize this Mariette, she's like a stranger.'

'I expect she's as scared as we are,' Etienne said. 'She must feel as if the weight of the world is on her shoulders. We, of all people, know what it's like to get carried away.'

'You are always so bloody understanding,' Belle snapped at him.

'If I am, it's only because I've made all the mistakes in the book,' he said. 'Imagine what it must be like to feel everyone in your family is against you?'

'She deserves it.'

'Does she? I'm not sure about that. She probably imagines we'll send her off to one of those institutions for delinquents.'

'Surely she wouldn't think such a thing of us!' Belle was horrified.

Etienne kissed her nose affectionately. 'You've got to remember that she doesn't know about the more shameful aspects of our pasts and the jams we've got ourselves into. God knows, I hope she never will. But that's what has defined our characters, and I think it made us better, more compassionate people. This is Mari's first hard lesson, and I hope to God she will learn something from it.'

It was two whole weeks after Sam's banishment when Mariette burst into the workroom where Mog and Belle were sewing.

'I'm not pregnant, my monthlies have come,' she said jubilantly.

'Oh, my sainted aunt! What a relief!' Mog exclaimed.

For a second or two, Belle couldn't respond. She had been so sure that Mariette was pregnant, however much she hoped she wasn't, and it took a while to really sink in that her prayers had been answered.

Finally, she got up and embraced her daughter.

'I'm so glad you've been spared,' she said breathlessly. 'But you must promise me you've learned from this? You have been very lucky this time, but I never want us all to go through the misery we've had this last couple of weeks. Never again.'

'Nor do I,' Mariette said, her face alight and glowing with the relief. 'I promise you, I'll wait until I'm married. And that won't be for years.'

Once Mariette had left the room, Mog and Belle looked at each other and burst into relieved laughter.

'I don't know why we are laughing,' Belle said. 'There's nothing funny about it.'

'Her promise that she'll wait till she gets married is funny,' Mog said. 'I think you must find a way to teach her a few tricks of the trade, Belle. Because as sure as summer follows spring, if she finds another young man she's attracted to, she won't stop at kissing.'

It certainly seemed that Mariette had turned over a new leaf. In the week that followed finding out she wasn't pregnant, she became a changed girl: she was docile and helpful, playing with her brothers, and didn't make any attempt to go out on her own. Belle was fairly certain it wasn't a permanent change in behaviour, but it did stop her even considering Mog's idea of sending the girl to England.

Late on Sunday night, after the children and Mog had all gone to bed, Belle and Etienne were sitting on the swing seat on the veranda because it was so stuffy indoors. To Belle's surprise, Etienne brought up the subject of England again.

'I think we should send her,' he blurted out. 'There's talk about her all over Russell.'

'Who's been talking?' Belle asked, alarmed because Etienne was usually the last person to pick up on gossip.

'I don't know where the talk started, but Angus said, "If I was you, I'd send her off to a relative until the talk dies down." As you know, Belle, he's not the kind to gossip, and he's got a soft spot for Mari.'

Angus was an elderly Scotsman who often went out fishing with Etienne. His wife had died a couple of years ago and his two sons had moved away to Christchurch. Belle knew that his friendship with Etienne meant a great deal to him, and that was why he felt he had to warn him about what was being said.

'No one has said anything to me,' she said.

'They wouldn't, would they? People love to chew over other people's misfortunes, but they are rarely brave enough to face up to the person they are tittle-tattling about.'

'How much do you think has got out?' Belle asked, anxious now, as she was sure it was more than just about Sam and Mariette holding hands.

'I think Sam must have talked to someone on the ferry. Anyway, word got around that I'd beaten him up, and it doesn't take much to work out why. If Mari stays here, she will be ostracized by many and become a target for those young men who will see her as "easy".'

'Couldn't we just send her to stay with Vera and her family?' Belle asked.

'We could, if Vera was agreeable. But too many people here have relatives there, and the gossip will just follow her. With Noah and Lisette she can start out with a clean sheet. Noah will help her to get a suitable job and, as Rose is only a few years older than Mari, she'll be like a sister to her. We can use some of the money Annie left you to pay for her passage. I think it could be the making of her. Would you have wanted to be stuck in a quiet little place like this at eighteen?'

Belle recalled her eighteenth birthday, by which time she

was already officially a whore. The so-called gentleman she'd had to entertain had been very fat, with the most rancid breath she'd ever smelled. That night she would've given anything to be somewhere as beautiful and serene as Russell. But she supposed you had to experience the wickedness of the world before you could truly know when you were in paradise.

But Belle never spoke about those days – not even to Etienne or Mog, who knew all about it. That was a former life, they were all different people then, and she'd drawn a shutter down over it all.

'You are right – at eighteen you want more than the sea and cows wandering along a dusty street. You want to see shops lit up with electricity, to go dancing and to wear the kind of clothes that would be impractical here. But what if war does break out? How will Mari get home?'

'We heard on the news about Chamberlain coming back from meeting Hitler and waving the document he'd signed, saying it was "Peace in our Time". No one in England or France wants a war, and Noah said in his last letter that he thought it could be averted. He should know, Belle. He was a war correspondent in the last one. Besides, there's no one I'd trust more to keep our daughter safe.'

'I agree with that; he's a kind and caring man. But isn't it asking too much to expect him to take responsibility for Mari? We both know just how headstrong she can be.'

Knowing how strong the bond was between Etienne and Mariette, she was surprised he would even consider sending her away. The fact that he appeared to have decided on this course of action meant that he really feared for her future here.

'Children are different away from their parents,' he said, putting his arm around her and drawing her close. 'She is behaving for us now, but how long will that last? A few months down the line and she'll be playing us up again, and resenting the fact that there is so little future for her here. But if we send her to England, maybe she will learn to value all she has here, and then she'll come back to us willingly.'

'How did it come to this?' Belle asked with a break in her voice. 'When she was born, we thought she would have everything we never had: love, security, a happy home in a place where nothing bad could ever happen. And now we are talking about sending her away from us.'

'All parents tend to think they own their children,' Etienne said, 'but we don't, we get them on lease. And when they become adults, they have to make their own way. In England she can find interesting and fulfilling work. Through Noah and Lisette she'll meet decent young men, make friends with other girls, and the whole experience of seeing England will be an education in itself.'

Belle knew he was right. But she was afraid for her daughter, going so far away.

'What if she gets there and she hates it? Or she likes it so much that she never wants to come back?'

'The first worry is easily rectified,' Etienne said calmly. 'As for the second, we both know girls usually end up where their husbands take them. We'll never have a guarantee she'll be living close to us for ever. I'd rather lose her to a good and happy life in England than see her marry the first man to ask her here, and watch her grow bitter and old before her time because she never experienced the love we have.'

Belle snuggled into his shoulder. 'You always present a good case,' she sighed. 'I'll try to see it the way you do. So what do we do now?'

'I will put a call through to Noah tomorrow,' Etienne said.

'But until we know if he is still willing to have her there, we won't say anything to Mari.'

Belle turned her face into her husband's neck. There was nothing further to say. She knew Etienne felt as badly about losing his little girl as she did.

5

Mariette was very aware that people thought she was cold because she didn't show emotion. She felt indignant that just because she didn't weep and wail, or say soppy things, they thought that meant she didn't feel anything.

The whole business with Sam had been the most hideous and hurtful thing she'd ever known. He'd not only made her feel dirty, ashamed and stupid, but her actions had made her parents and Mog feel horrified and let down. She so much wanted to find the words to tell them how bad she was feeling, how sorry she was that she'd hurt them, but she couldn't. Keeping quiet and out of their way had been her only way of coping with the situation.

Then, when she found out she wasn't pregnant after all, she had thought that was the end of it, they could all forget it had ever happened. But just helping more at home, trying to show them all how much she valued them and how sorry she was, didn't really make it go away. It was still there, like a faint bad smell that refused to leave, whatever she did.

Outside the house, it was even worse. She sensed that everyone was talking about her; older people were snubbing her, younger ones looking at her with a sneer. One by one, all her friends dropped her; no one came round, and there were no invitations to go anywhere.

Perhaps other girls in her position would have cried and made a scene, but that wasn't her style. So she put her nose in the air and made out she didn't care.

When her father said that her godfather in England had

asked if she would like to visit him, her first reaction was utter joy. The thought of leaving behind the past humiliation and disapproval was enough on its own. And who wouldn't want the adventure of going to London, and seeing all those amazing sights she'd seen in books and magazines? She loved the idea of being on a big ship for more than six weeks, and she felt excited at the prospect of getting a real job, meeting new people who would have a much broader view of life than those she knew here in Russell.

But the delight and excitement soon vanished when she realized it was banishment, because she'd shamed her family.

They didn't say as much. They talked of there being more opportunities for her, and of giving her the chance to see the world. Yet even though that was what they truly wanted for her, Mariette also knew they felt her past mistakes were affecting her brothers.

She didn't know Uncle Noah and Auntie Lisette. They were just names on a Christmas card, the people who sent presents to her and her brothers on their birthdays. Granted, they were always lovely presents – for her eighteenth they'd sent her a beautiful silver bracelet. She knew they lived in a splendid house, that Uncle Noah was an acclaimed journalist and author, and a good friend to both her parents. And yet, to Mariette they were strangers on whom she was being fobbed off.

She had learned her lesson. Sam was a horrible and worthless man, and she regretted ever having clapped eyes on him. She certainly didn't intend to make a mistake like that again. But however badly she had behaved, she didn't understand why the neighbours felt they had a right to judge her. She hadn't hurt any of them, and she could bet every single one of them had done something shameful in their life too.

In the past, when she had daydreamed of leaving Russell,

Mariette had always imagined her friends and family shedding tears as they waved goodbye to her on the jetty. She'd also thought that if ever she came back, it would be a joyous and triumphal return. But now she felt everyone would be whispering 'good riddance' as she left, and hoping that was the last they'd see of her.

Miss Quigley had always said she was defiant, and that's what she decided she would be now. She would act like she couldn't wait to leave because Russell was too small for her. Maybe, if she could put on a good enough act, she'd start to believe it too and stop being scared.

Alone in her room at night, though, she found herself crying. She was going to miss Noel and Alexis; however much they got on her nerves sometimes, she loved them. As for Mum, Papa and Mog, she couldn't imagine what life would be like without seeing them every day. Who would she turn to, if she was frightened or lonely? Her confidence had always been remarked on, but what if it left her when she got to England?

'I think you're being very brave,' her father said one morning, almost as if he'd read her thoughts. 'I'm sure you are a bit worried about going to the other side of the world without us, but you are going to love it, Mari. Along with seeing London, I'm sure Noah will take you over to France. He has a place near Marseille which used to be mine. Imagine seeing all the places your mother and I have told you about?'

Mariette had always wanted her father to be proud of her, and if the only way she could make that happen was to appear brave, then that was what she must do. So she didn't throw herself into his arms and tell him she couldn't bear the thought of not going sailing and fishing with him, which was the truth. Instead, she just forced a grin and said how much she wanted to see Buckingham Palace, the Tower of London, the River

Seine and the Eiffel Tower, and that she was grateful for the opportunity she'd been given.

Mog dug out a thick, brown wool coat with a red fox collar, which she'd brought here from England, and began taking it apart with the plan of remodelling it for Mariette. Her mother found some brown felt to make a hat to go with it, and she showed Mariette some beautiful feathers with which she intended to trim it.

They booked a passage for her on a ship leaving for England from Auckland on 18th December, at the height of summer, but she'd arrive in England in the dead of winter.

She had always been a bit confused as to why English immigrants moaned that New Zealand was upside down, how they missed big fires and the snow and ice that came at Christmas at home. Her parents didn't do this – in fact, they had always laughed at people who struggled desperately to keep up European traditions, including a roast dinner and plum pudding, when the temperature was up in the eighties.

Their family always celebrated with a special Christmas picnic on the beach, where they'd swim and play cricket. And although Mog often told them tales about the mining village in Wales where she grew up, she didn't make it sound like the views on the Christmas cards that came from England. They had pure white snow, horse-drawn sleighs and tables laden with food. Mog's were grim tales of eating a meagre rabbit stew, of a town coated in coal dust, of men and women who were old at thirty-five because of poverty and overwork.

Mog always said it made more sense to celebrate Jesus's birthday in a warm place, because that's how Bethlehem was. She loved to collect native wild flowers and greenery to decorate the house, and she would hang up dozens of gaily coloured Chinese paper lanterns on the veranda. When it grew dark, Dad lit candles in them and it was magical to sit out there with the various neighbours who dropped by. Mum said every year that it beat Christmas in England hands down.

Mariette didn't mind missing Christmas in Russell – it would probably be just as much fun on the ship – but she was a bit worried that an English winter would be very much colder than it was here in the North Island. Mog and her mother had often, in the past, talked of thick pea-souper fogs back home, of ice on the inside of windows, and although they both went out of their way to tell her now how warm and beautiful Uncle Noah's house would be, she was still apprehensive.

To take her mind off all the niggling worries, Mariette buckled down to help with the sewing of the new clothes she would need.

It was exciting to be making the kind of clothes she would never have the opportunity to wear in Russell. Earlier in the year, Noah had sent Mog some English fashion magazines and now she was in her element, deciding which dresses and costumes she could copy. She found some lovely cream lace in the trunk in which she hoarded fabric. That was going to make an evening dress, and there was some lilac crêpe which draped beautifully. But Mariette was doubtful about the checked wool which Mog planned to use to make a costume: it looked more suitable for Miss Quigley, the schoolteacher.

'I do know about fashion,' Mog said reprovingly when she saw Mariette's disdainful expression. 'Mrs Simpson wore a costume exactly like the one I'm going to make for you, just before the King abdicated. No one was more elegant than she was, even if none of us approved of her. You will find women in England take a greater pride in their appearance than they do here, and they have rules about dress. It's not done to go out without a hat, or to go bare-legged, not even in summer. When we go to Auckland to see you off, we'll have to buy you stockings and gloves. But once you are in England, Lisette will help you get it right; she's very chic, as you'd expect from a Frenchwoman.'

On 12th December, two days before Mariette was due to leave Russell, Belle woke in the morning full of misgivings about sending Mariette away.

They had decided that Mog and Etienne would accompany her on the steamer to Auckland while Belle would stay home with the boys. Once in Auckland, Mog would supervise buying the items Mariette still needed for England. Etienne was far better equipped than Belle to make sure his daughter and her luggage got on the right ship at the right time. Besides, it would be less painful for her to say goodbye here, rather than waving Mariette off in Auckland.

'I feel just the way I did in France, when they packed me into that coach to take me to the ship bound for New York,' she admitted to Etienne. 'If I feel like that, how must Mari be feeling?'

Etienne had got out of bed to dress, but on hearing the anxiety and dejection in Belle's voice he sat back down on the bed and enveloped his wife in his arms. 'It isn't anything like that for Mari. Firstly, you'd been through every kind of hell before that day,' he said. 'You also had no idea where you were being taken. And you were much younger than Mari. But Mog and I are seeing her off, and she's going to people who will love her as we do. She knows a great deal about England too. She's ready to leave us, Belle. She's outgrown Russell, and she wants a new start. You must let her go. We can telephone her from the bakery sometimes. She isn't being sold, as you were; she's free to make an exciting, fulfilling life for herself.'

'But what if war does break out? She might get trapped there,' Belle said fearfully.

A shadow passed over Etienne's features that told her he was as apprehensive and sad about Mariette leaving as she was. But he was made of sterner stuff than Belle was, and he would never admit it.

'Noah wouldn't make jokes about the government getting trenches dug in Hyde Park and stockpiling sandbags if he really thought they'd be needed,' Etienne said firmly. 'He said Hitler doesn't want to fight England. Besides, even if he's wrong, or if things change, he'll get Mari on the first ship back to us.'

'Are you sure?' Belle asked.

'How can you even ask that, Belle?' Etienne demanded. 'Have you forgotten all he did for us in the past? But for him we would never have got together again. Doesn't that tell you that we are putting our daughter in the safest of hands?'

'Yes, of course,' she sighed. 'But I can't help worrying.'

'Don't let Mari see it,' he warned her. 'She is all keyed up to go now, and we must send her off joyfully or she will get anxious too. Now let's make the most of her last two days with us. We'll prepare a picnic and go out in the boat to give her something good to remember.'

A few hours later, as Etienne was at the helm in his fishing boat, he glanced sideways at Mariette. As always when she was aboard, she was right at his side, eagerly awaiting the moment when he would let her take the wheel. Alexis and Noel were sitting astern with Belle and Mog. They hadn't yet developed their elder sister's passion for the sea. They were sitting quietly, far more enthusiastic about the prospect of reaching the beach for the picnic than about the joy of being out on the water.

It was days like this he was going to miss the most while Mariette was away. She was the only one in the family who loved to fish, swim and sail as much as he did. Some of the best times they'd had together had been out here in the bay, racing along in the dinghy with the wind in their hair, soaked by sea spray.

He had an ache in his heart at her leaving. She was so like him as a young man, determined, fierce and often ruthless, all character traits that had served him well but didn't sit well with femininity. He fervently hoped that Noah and Lisette would be able to encourage her to utilize her keen mind and would influence her to rein in her natural exuberance and wilfulness.

Belle had been beautiful at Mari's age, with black curly hair, a soft full mouth and eyes the colour of a summer sky, framed by thick sweeping lashes. She had the kind of devastating beauty that made people turn to look at her.

Mari was merely pretty in comparison, with hair the colour of new pennies, well-defined cheekbones and a sharp little chin. Her eyes were the same shape and colour as Belle's, but she had a habit of giving people icy stares, just like Etienne did. Yet he felt that in another couple of years she would become a real stunner. He hoped, by then, she would have learned poise and a sense of her own worth. The thought of another man bending her to his will made Etienne's blood run cold.

'It's been the most perfect day,' Belle said as Etienne helped her climb aboard later that afternoon. Mog came next, her skirt hitched up to save getting it wet.

They had lit a fire on the beach and fried sausages and bacon. The boys and Mariette had gambolled around in the sea while Mog dozed on a blanket. Belle and Etienne had built an impressive sandcastle which the children then decorated with shells.

Fourteen- and fifteen-year-old boys are, by their very nature, lacking in sentimentality. They had both tactlessly asked if they could have Mariette's room once she was gone. Alexis had said a few days ago that he wouldn't miss his sister sniping at him, or the rows she caused. Noel was more interested in rugby and cricket than considering whether he would miss her.

But they had both been less boisterous and argumentative all day today, so perhaps they weren't quite as keen to see her go as their past cutting remarks would suggest.

'This is what I'm going to miss – next to all of you, of course,' Mariette said, waving her hand at the turquoise sea and the vivid green of the trees which grew right down to the water's edge. The small sandy beach was a secluded spot which she had always liked to think no one but they knew about or came to.

'There's sea all around England too,' Mog said. 'But, I have to say, it isn't often blue, mostly it's grey and perishing cold. That's why I never learned to swim.'

'But there are lovely things in England that we don't have here,' Belle said. 'There're castles, palaces and little villages that are far prettier than anything in New Zealand. You are going to see shops in London that are so grand, you'll think you have to be someone important to go in them. There are trains that run underground too. When Mog and I left London, there were far more horses than cars and lorries, and few people had electricity in their homes, but all that's changed now. You won't know yourself, switching on a light as easy as anything, or turning on a tap and hot water coming out. When we stayed at the flat Noah had at the end of the war, every room was warm because there was a big boiler in the basement that heated radiators all over the building. I expect the house he lives in now is just the same. And no more going outside to the lavatory.'

Etienne started the engine and, as the boat began to move out into deeper water, Mariette asked if everyone in England had homes like Uncle Noah.

'Sadly not,' Belle said. 'There are still a great many people living in what they call slums, with a shared tap and privy out in the yard, but you won't be going anywhere like that. Uncle Noah lives in a lovely part of London.'

'I want to see all of London, not just the bits where the rich people live,' Mariette said. 'I want to go to the part where you used to live when you were a girl.'

'I expect Noah will take you to see the Ram's Head that my Garth used to own,' Mog said. 'The house where we lived when your mum was a little girl burned down, but there's a big market for fruit, vegetables and flowers called Covent Garden nearby. I don't suppose that will have changed much since our day; the smell of the flowers almost takes your breath away. It was your mum's favourite place.'

Just the thought of Mariette going to Seven Dials made Belle feel anxious. She didn't want her daughter to stumble upon the darker truths about what life had once been like for her and Mog. Noah knew it all, of course, and she knew he would never reveal it willingly. But what if Mariette kept probing and he let something slip?

Mog caught her eye. As always, she was quick to pick up on tension, and she was an expert on defusing it. 'You won't think much of that part of London, it's all a bit ramshackle and dirty,' she said. 'But you'll want to see Trafalgar Square and St James's Park, that's all nearby. Then there's the River Thames, that's a feast for the eye, so wide, so many boats. And the Tower of London, where they used to lock up lords and ladies for treason, that's just further along.'

75

Belle breathed a sigh of relief as Mariette got up and joined Etienne at the wheel. She just hoped Noah was good at diverting conversations away from dangerous ground too.

Late that night, when Belle and Etienne were in bed, she asked him if he was worried that Mariette would pester Noah for more information about both of their pasts.

'Why should she?' Etienne seemed surprised at the question. 'At eighteen you think anyone over forty is ancient and very dull. And even if she did ask him, he wouldn't say anything more than that he met me in Paris, where you were learning to make hats. Noah's smart, he'll be very good at being vague.'

'I do hope so,' Belle retorted.

Etienne gave her a sympathetic smile. 'Maybe one day, when Mari is older and more worldly, we can tell her the whole story, if she wants to hear it.'

Belle was satisfied that he knew best and nestled into his arms. 'It was a lovely day today. It was good to see Mari larking about with Alexis and Noel. She seemed very carefree.'

'And why shouldn't she be?' he asked. 'She's about to embark on an adventure. We have to trust her now to look after herself.'

'I just wish I was certain she will come back to us,' Belle whispered. 'Look at all the people we know here whose sons and daughters have gone off to Australia, America or Europe and never come back?'

'If she finds happiness in England and wants to stay there, then so be it,' he said. 'I'd sooner she was away from us and happy than with us and unhappy. I'm sure you feel the same?'

'I suppose so,' she sighed. 'But I'm not going to think about that, it makes me feel too sad.'

6

Mariette was glad when an announcement was made asking all visitors not sailing on the SS *Rimutaka* to leave the ship immediately. It hurt to see Mog and her papa so sad and emotional at her leaving. She felt like breaking down and sobbing herself, but she knew that would just make them feel even worse.

This morning at the guest house, when she'd dressed in the yellow dress and its matching bolero jacket that Mog had made for her, and secured the cheeky little yellow and white striped sateen and tulle hat at a rakish angle on the side of her head, she'd felt like a Hollywood film star. She even had new shoes with the latest Louis heel, and a trunk full of new, exciting clothes. But a new wardrobe didn't make up for leaving her family; it would never give her the comfort and security her loved ones did.

'You mind you behave yourself,' Mog said warningly, for about the twentieth time that day, as she dabbed her eyes with a lace-trimmed hanky that was already sodden. 'Or I'll come on over and give you what for.'

Mog enveloped her in a tight hug. As always, she smelled of her lavender cologne – a smell Mariette would always associate with home. Today had been the first time she had become aware that Mog was getting old; it was a hot day, and she'd been breathless and hesitant in her walking. As Mariette hugged her back, she thought how terrible it would be if Mog died before she came home, and her eyes filled up with tears.

'Don't work so hard, Moggy,' she managed to say. 'It's time you sat back and had a rest.'

Mog held Mariette by the shoulders, tears running down her cheeks as she looked at her. 'Let me get one last good look at you, my precious one,' she said, her voice faltering with emotion. 'You'll be in my heart and in my prayers. Write to us all the time, promise me?'

Mariette could only nod and turn to her papa. To her shock, she saw that he too had tears in his eyes. He was so much taller than her that she buried her face in his chest, and his hug almost crushed her.

'I can't find the right words to tell you what you mean to me, Mari,' he whispered. 'All I can say is it's like the wind out on the bay when we race the dinghy, or landing a huge marlin, or the first strawberries of the year. Now you must take full advantage of this trip to England, and enjoy it. But think before you act, and listen to your conscience. And come home safe to us, when you are ready.'

She felt rather than saw his kisses on her cheeks, and the final squeeze of her hands, because her eyes were blinded with tears.

Mog looked so small and vulnerable supported by Papa as they went down the gangway to the wharf. Even Papa, whom she had thought indestructible, seemed less sprightly and strong. Her whole being wanted to run after them and say she couldn't leave them, because she loved them too much, but it was too late. The ship's engine had started, the sailors were removing the gangway, and they were about to cast off.

So she clung tightly to the rail and waved, just one of 600 other passengers on a ship that was only three-quarters full. Many of them were crying at leaving loved ones, others were very excited because they were relishing a trip to England,

and there were a few families who looked both poor and glum with no one to wave to. She guessed these were people who had failed in New Zealand and decided to cut their losses and go home. Strangely, it was these families she identified with most; she guessed that, even now, in Russell there were those who would be gossiping about her and reminding each other that her father had lost money on his vineyard enterprise and his wife had been pregnant on their wedding day.

Saying goodbye to her mother and the boys had been awful. Only Peggy and Don from the bakery came to see her off at the jetty in Russell. Usually the whole town turned out for such occasions, and their absence brought it home to her just how much she had disgraced herself and her family. She could see her mother's anxiety and sorrow etched into her face, and although she tried very hard to appear jolly and happy for her daughter, Mariette knew she would go home and cry. She wouldn't even have her husband and Mog there with her to comfort her. Even the boys looked sad, hugging and kissing her without any prompting, and reminding her she was to send them postcards of every place she went to.

Until now, as the ship moved slowly away from the wharf, she hadn't had the sense that she was really leaving New Zealand – she'd half expected something would happen to prevent it – but this was it now, the gap between her and land widening with every second. She waved even more fiercely, even though she could no longer make out Mog or her father's features. All she could really see were their hats; Mog's was navy blue, trimmed with white ribbon, and her father was waving his panama with one hand and a handkerchief with the other. In a few days it would be Christmas, and new tears spilled over at the thought of her brothers opening their stockings without her being there to share their excitement.

'I'll be back,' she vowed to herself. 'Not with my tail between my legs but successful and triumphant. You'll see.'

The ship was picking up speed now and the people on the wharf were barely visible. It was time to go and stow her things away in the cabin she would be sharing with another single girl.

As she walked to the companionway that led down to the cabin, Mariette struggled to compose herself. She was not going to be a baby and cry, because the daydream she'd had for years of seeing the world was a reality now. She was going to cross the equator, go from one hemisphere to another, to the place her parents and Mog had talked about so often.

Of course, in her daydreams about such an adventure, she'd always imagined having someone with her, not doing it alone. She might have new clothes to wear, money to spend and people meeting her at Southampton, but it was so very scary.

She managed to find her cabin easily as her father had brought her down here when they first arrived at the ship. When she saw how tiny it was – two bunks with just a couple of feet of space next to them – she'd understood why she needed to pack clothes for the voyage in a small suitcase and let her trunk go in the hold.

But, as she opened the cabin door, she saw her cabin mate didn't appear to know this, because the entire floor space was strewn with clothes. Picking her way gingerly through the clothing, she saw a dark-haired girl lying on the bottom bunk with her face buried in the pillow, and crying.

'Hello,' she ventured. 'I'm sharing with you.'

'There isn't room in here to share, it's no bigger than a coffin,' the girl said, her face still buried in the pillow and her voice muffled. 'And I wish I was dead.'

Seeing another girl prostrate with grief had a galvanizing effect on Mariette. As much as she could easily have taken to her own bunk to cry at leaving home and family behind, she thought the girl looked and sounded drippy, and she wasn't going to copy her.

'That's a daft thing to say when we are less than a mile from land,' Mariette said. 'I'm sad at leaving my family too, but there's no point in wallowing.'

With that, the girl turned her head and stared at Mariette with eyes that were red and swollen. She looked as if she was in her mid twenties.

'Who the hell are you to say I'm wallowing?' she asked aggressively.

'Because your stuff is all over the cabin, and it seems to me more sensible to put it away before you lie down and feel sorry for yourself. I've got to share this cabin too.'

'There isn't enough room in here for one person, let alone two. It's not what I'm used to at all.'

'Well, it wouldn't be – not unless you'd spent your whole life on a ship.' Mariette was beginning to be irritated. 'You'll have to pack some of this stuff away and let the steward put it in the hold, like I did.'

'I need everything,' the girl said in alarm. 'I'm not taking it anywhere.'

Mariette paused for a second. She didn't like the girl's superior tone or even how she looked. She was big, and her face was as mottled as corned beef. But she didn't want to start the voyage with a row.

'What's your name?' she asked.

'Stella Murgatroyd,' she said.

'Well, I'm Mariette Carrera, usually known as Mari. So, Stella, we're in this cabin together for several weeks. And, as you point out, there isn't much room. That means we have to be tidy. There's a drawer under each bunk, a very narrow cupboard to hang stuff in and two shelves. So you'd better start stowing your stuff away, because otherwise I'll be trampling on it all as I unpack.'

'Who the hell do you think you are?' Stella got up from the bunk and stood several inches taller than Mariette, so close to her that her big breasts were almost touching her. 'I don't expect a child to tell me what to do.'

'Excuse me, you are the one that's behaving like a child,' Mariette said with indignation. 'And a very rude one at that. Put your case on your bunk, fold some of this stuff up and put it back in.' She bent down, picked up an armful of clothes and dumped them on the bunk. 'We're getting off on the wrong foot here. Just sort it all out, then perhaps we can go and get a cup of tea and make friends.'

With that, the girl's face crumpled and she began to cry again. 'You don't understand,' she said through her tears. 'I don't want to go to England. But they made me.'

Mariette was beginning to feel claustrophobic in the small space; it was tempting to run out of the cabin and leave this great blubbering lump to sort herself out. But her mother had always impressed on her that she should help those smaller and less able than herself. The girl certainly wasn't smaller, but she looked incapable of doing anything for herself.

'Right, we'll leave it all for now,' she said. 'Wash your face and we'll go and get some tea, and you can tell me all about it. How's that?'

Stella didn't even know how to pull down the folding washbasin; she just stared blankly until Mariette showed her how it worked. She showed no signs of being able to find a face flannel, so Mariette dampened the corner of a towel and wiped the girl's face as she would have done to her brothers.

'That's better,' she said. 'There might be some handsome sailors around. You wouldn't want them to see you with a blotchy face, would you?'

In the saloon, an hour and two cups of tea later, Mari had discovered the reason for Stella's distress. She was twenty-four, both her parents had died of Spanish flu in 1919, when she was five, and she and her elder brother and sister had gone to live with their grandparents in Wellington. When her grandfather died, he had left all three children some money. Her brother and sister had gone off to England, leaving fifteen-year-old Stella with her grandmother.

'I was intending to go to England and join them when I was twenty-one and got my money,' Stella said. 'But Grandma got sick just before that, and I couldn't very well leave her. I've had nearly three years of doing everything for her, and it's been awful, I can't even talk about how bad it was. But then she died a few months ago, and instead of me being able to carry on living in her house and having a nice life again, I found out she'd left the house and her money to my uncle, and he wanted me out. He never did a thing for Grandma, hardly ever visited her, and he didn't give a damn about what would happen to me.'

Mariette viewed this story with a dose of scepticism. From what Stella had said, her grandmother's house was large, with several servants, and so it was very unlikely she'd had sole care of her sick grandmother. In the short while she'd known Stella she'd learned enough to guess that the girl had led quite a privileged life. Perhaps her grandmother felt that as Stella had already been left money by her grandfather, she should build her own life, just as the other two siblings had done.

'So you are going to join your brother and sister in England then?' she asked.

'That was my plan,' Stella said. 'But my brother wrote just a few days ago and said that, although I can stay with him for a couple of weeks, I'll have to find a job and accommodation of my own. I don't know how I'm going to do that, I've never worked.'

Mariette tried hard not to smirk. 'You could get a job as a housekeeper as you've experience of looking after your grandma,' she suggested.

'Oh no, I couldn't be anyone's servant,' Stella said in horror. 'I wasn't brought up for that.'

As Mariette made some small talk about the ship and some of the other passengers she'd seen, she studied Stella. She was no beauty, she had all the grace of a carthorse, and her duck-egg-blue dress, though clearly good quality, was dowdy – more suited to someone of Mog's age than a girl of twenty-four. Her dark hair was fixed up in an untidy bun, but it was very shiny, and she had pretty hazel eyes. Now that the red blotches on her face were fading, Mariette could see she had a good, clear complexion too.

There was a brooch on Stella's dress that looked to Mariette like real sapphires and diamonds, not paste, and the opal and diamond ring on her finger looked as if it had been passed down from her grandmother. So her other clothes might be far nicer.

Mog had often said how much she liked bringing out women's real potential when she made clothes for them, and it occurred to Mariette that on this long voyage she could do worse than pass the time by turning this ugly duckling into, if not a swan, at least a more attractive woman.

'Well, Stella,' she said, 'we're stuck with one another for six weeks. I think we should spend the time improving ourselves, maybe learning new things or getting to know people who are very different from us, but first we have to sort out the cabin and your clothes. And as I'm good at clothes, let me decide for you what needs to be packed away.'

If Mariette had hoped to share a cabin with a like-minded, fun-loving girl, she would have been disappointed in Stella. Fortunately, she'd expected to be sharing it with a grumpy, elderly spinster who moaned about everything, so Stella didn't seem that bad.

She was lazy, slow and very unworldly, but Mariette soon found she was the easiest person in the world to lead by the nose.

It began with her clothes. Mariette went through them, dug out the ones suitable for hot weather and packed the rest away. Within two days, she'd persuaded Stella her hair was more attractive worn loose, and, having discovered there was a hairdresser amongst the passengers, she persuaded her to have it cut to shoulder length. It was a triumph: all at once she looked her real age, not as if she was fast approaching middle-age.

'Grandma said the only time a woman could wear her hair loose was in the bedroom with her husband,' Stella said, looking at herself in the mirror doubtfully.

'That went out with the sinking of the *Titanic*,' Mariette informed her. 'And all your dresses are far too long, they should be no longer than mid-calf, so we're going to shorten them.'

While it was quite satisfying sorting out Stella, it didn't actually prevent Mariette from getting homesick. It came over her in waves when she saw another passenger hugging her child, or when they had a meal which reminded her of home. There was an officer who looked just like her papa from the back; each time she saw him walking along the deck, it gave her a jolt. And at night-time, in her bunk, she missed her mother or Mog coming to tuck her in.

As they went into dinner on Christmas Day, Mariette felt quite smug at seeing one of the waiters smile flirtatiously at Stella and linger a little longer than necessary as he served her dinner. He wasn't much to look at, in his mid thirties with thinning hair, but it was evidence that the shortened skirt of Stella's red velvet dress and her new hairstyle were working.

When she'd woken that morning, Mariette had felt really sad imagining Alexis and Noel's excitement as they looked in their stockings – so much so, she cried for a little while. But although Stella was a poor substitute for her family, to see her new friend smiling and her eyes sparkling because she'd finally got some male attention did make Mariette feel a little less cast off and alone.

The first ten days of the voyage were pleasant and leisurely. She liked that there was no one giving her chores to do, or telling her off because she didn't help around the house enough. She had Stella for company, and although the girl was nervy and snobbish and they had little in common, Mariette could persuade her to do whatever she wanted. They lazed around in the sun, played quoits on deck, or card games in the saloon, talked to other passengers. And when Mariette tired of people, she spent her time either reading or gazing out at the vastness of the ocean.

But even for someone who liked the sea as much as she did, it soon wore thin when day after day she was looking at the same blue vista of sea and sky. There was the occasional school of porpoises or dolphins to excite her, and now and then another ship in the distance, but with each day these sightings grew less remarkable. She was bored, time passed so slowly, and she wanted some exercise – swimming, sailing or just walking. She could, of course, walk round and round the deck, but she thought that would drive her mad.

She also found herself becoming irritated by many of the

passengers because all they could do was gripe about New Zealand. Only a few of the English people aboard were going back to visit relatives; in the main, they were returning because they hadn't been happy in New Zealand. Some had lost their jobs and their money during the Depression, others found farming too hard a life, and there were those who had emigrated thinking they'd love the wide open spaces, only to discover they missed the crowds in English cities. It was disappointing for Mariette to find out that so many of the passengers were dull and timid, whereas she had fully expected them all to be bold and adventurous.

The equator was crossed with the ceremony she'd been told about by her mother and Mog. A sailor dressed as Neptune was doused with water and then other members of the crew acted out shaving him with a giant shaving brush and razor. Those on board who had never crossed the equator before, including Mariette and Stella, were dunked into a bath of water and given a certificate of crossing the line.

It was soon after crossing the equator that Stella and quite a few of the other passengers became seasick. Mariette wasn't affected by it at all, and she didn't have much patience with those who were. She kept telling Stella that she'd feel better on the upper decks in the fresh air, but the girl didn't listen and lay in her bunk getting worse. The smell of vomit never seemed to leave the cabin – sometimes Mariette could hardly bear it – but because Mog had said she must be kind and helpful to those who were sick, she did begrudgingly look after Stella, washing her face and hands, brushing her hair and emptying the sick bowl when necessary.

Stella recovered when they got to the Panama Canal, and the novelty of passing through locks and seeing land close by meant that Mariette was on the deck watching all day. She couldn't wait for the ship to reach Venezuela, where they would be stopping at Curaçao for two days and could go ashore.

7

The day before they were due to arrive in Curaçao, Mariette became ill. She was in perfect health until about an hour after lunch, when she suddenly felt as if she was on fire, her tongue seemed to have swollen up and a rash sprang up all over her. She felt so bad that she was glad when Stella fetched Dr Haslem, who took her to the sickbay. She heard him telling Stella that he thought it could be measles and she would have to stay in isolation without any visitors.

She was glad to be in that cool room and to be allowed to sleep. She barely noticed the next morning that the ship's engines had stopped, nor did she care when she heard clattering feet and excited voices from the deck above as the passengers disembarked. She must have slept all day because, the next thing she knew, it was dark again outside and she could hear faint sounds of music which, she assumed, were coming from the port. During all that time she was vaguely aware of a man with an English accent coming in and out, getting her to drink water, giving her some medicine and putting something cool on her forehead. But she was aware of little else.

When she opened her eyes again, there was a shaft of sunshine coming through the porthole. It took her a moment or two to remember why she was in the tiny white room and where it was. Gingerly, she sat up and poured herself a glass of water from the jug beside the bed. Her tongue felt its normal size again, she was no longer on fire, and, looking at her arms, she saw that the rash had vanished.

She had no idea how long she'd been in the sickbay, but as the ship wasn't moving it couldn't be more than two days. She got out of bed to use the chamber pot, and looked out of the porthole. Unfortunately, it was facing out to sea and all she could see were some small boats, most of them like canoes, with bare-chested brown- or black-skinned men paddling them.

She had been looking forward so much to going ashore, and she was incensed that she'd missed the chance. She looked down at the cotton gown she was wearing and realized her clothes had been taken away, but when she tried to open the door to find them, she found it was locked.

While she knew this was purely to prevent any passengers coming in and exposing themselves to infection, it still made her feel neglected and imprisoned.

Getting back into bed to wait for someone to come, her stomach began to rumble with hunger. After about half an hour of listening to it, and craving at least a cup of tea, she got out of bed and began hammering on the door and calling out.

'Hold on, I'll get the key,' a male voice called back.

'I'm starving,' she shouted. 'There's nothing wrong with me now. I want to come out.'

'Alright, don't get yourself in a tizz,' he retorted. 'Get back into bed, and I'll go and see if I can find the doctor.'

As his accent was English, and all the crew members she'd met until then were either New Zealanders or Italians and other Europeans, she thought he must be the man who had been looking after her since she was brought here.

After another interminable wait, the door was unlocked by Dr Haslem, a scrawny little man with a big nose and horn-rimmed spectacles. 'Now, what's all this fuss about?' he asked, looking very annoyed at being called.

'I'm better,' she said, sitting up on the bed. 'And I'm really hungry. I want to go back to my cabin.'

The doctor closed the door and peered first at her face, then picked up one of her arms to look at it, then the other. 'The rash has gone,' he said, and put a thermometer in her mouth. As he waited for the result, he looked at both her legs and her back. Then, taking the thermometer out of her mouth, he pronounced her temperature normal.

'Well, you obviously don't have measles,' he said. 'It must have been a reaction to something you ate. But I can't let you go until you've eaten something, and I'll see how you are then.'

'But if you know I'm not infectious, surely I can go back to my cabin, or at least up on deck?' she asked. 'And can I have my clothes back?'

Somewhat reluctantly, he agreed he would get the steward to bring her clothes and also a meal for her. But he said she was to stick to a light diet for the next few days, and she was not to go ashore. 'If you begin to feel ill again, you must come straight back here,' he said.

Some while after the doctor had left, the sickbay door opened and the steward came in with a tray of food. All Mariette had been able to think of while she was waiting was food, but the sight of the English steward made her forget how hungry she was.

His likeness to Errol Flynn, the Hollywood actor, was incredible, with dark hair swept back from a devastatingly handsome face, perfect white teeth and dark eyes that sparkled. As he smiled at her, she saw there was a deep cleft in his chin.

'Not exactly a feast,' he said, handing the tray to her. 'But I was ordered to get something light. It's good to see you looking better; you've been in a bad way. I was really worried about you.'

It wasn't just his looks that affected her. His voice made her think of home because his accent was something like Mog and her mother's, and the tone was as deep as her father's. Mariette glanced down at the pallid-looking omelette and the bowl of rice pudding. If anyone else had brought it to her, she might have been sarcastic, but coming from him it looked like the nectar of the gods.

'It's lovely, thank you,' she said, blushing because she knew he'd seen her looking her absolute worst, and she just had to hope she hadn't said anything stupid. 'Aren't you going ashore today?'

'No, I've got to stay here in case anyone else becomes sick.'

'That's a shame. I really wanted to see Curaçao, I'm sure you did too.'

'I've seen it before. It's not much to write home about. I'd only get drunk, and it can be tough dealing with sick people after a night on the tiles.'

'Are there any other people here for you to look after?'

'No, only you. Everyone else miraculously recovered as we came into port. We were all concerned about you, though, you were really poorly. Are you really feeling OK now?'

'Fighting fit,' she said. 'Will you get my clothes, so I can go back to my cabin?'

'I will, and you eat that food. I'll be back in a minute.'

Mariette noted how quiet and peaceful the ship was as she left the sickbay. No throbbing of the engines, or passengers milling around. Most of the crew appeared to have gone ashore too. She showered, did her hair and changed into a blue and white striped sundress that she felt really flattered her slender waist. It was also short enough to show off her legs, which people had said were one of her best assets. Then she went back to the sickbay.

While she was eating her lunch, the handsome steward had stayed with her. He told her his name was Morgan Griffiths, he was twenty-five and had been in the Merchant Navy for six years. He also told her he'd drawn the short straw when he was made a sickbay steward. But he laughed as he said it, so she felt he quite liked it really.

He had also dropped into the conversation the comment that his day would drag as there was nothing to do until the passengers began to come back later in the afternoon. She was certain that was a hint for her to come back.

It obviously was, because his face lit up as she came through the door. 'Not sick again already, I hope?' he said.

'No, I thought you might like some company.'

'I was just going up there to sit in the sun and have a smoke,' he said, pointing out the narrow stairs that led to the upper deck. 'If anyone needs me, I can hear them from there.'

Morgan was one of the easiest people to talk to that she'd ever met. Conversation just flowed between them about anything and everything. He told her he wanted to leave the Merchant Navy because he was tired of being at everyone's beck and call. 'You just wait till we leave port and it turns rough across the Atlantic,' he said with a deep sigh. 'Seasickness will strike nearly everyone. Going back to England isn't usually quite as bad as coming out, because most passengers have experienced it before, but there're quite a few first-timers on this voyage. They all think they're dying, and it can be hell.'

He was vague about his background, only mentioning that he'd spent some of his childhood in London. 'I ought to have become a mechanic, I'm good at that, but for some reason I got the idea that going to sea was for me. I'd be happier in the engine room, but they made me a steward. If I stay at it much longer, I'll go mad. I want a real man's job.'

'If war does break out, you'll get one,' she said. 'You could join the Royal Navy.'

'Spare me that,' he laughed. 'It's bad enough being at sea for weeks waiting on people, but to be under fire with very little chance of escape would be even worse. I wouldn't mind the army so much, if I could be driving trucks or tanks.'

Mariette couldn't imagine him in a job where he'd get mucky. He looked so right in his clean white jacket, his hair as immaculate as if he'd just come from the barber's. She thought he was the perfect man – he had both charm and looks – and she loved the way he asked her questions about her family and their life back in New Zealand with real interest. All he'd seen of New Zealand was Auckland, but he said he'd heard the Bay of Islands was beautiful and hoped to get there one day. He also wanted to know what she was going to do in England, and he talked about places there which he thought she ought to see.

'Your father and your uncle in England would probably want to knock my block off for suggesting this, but along with seeing all the sights, Buckingham Palace and the Tower of London, you should also go to the East End of London,' he said, with that wide, lovely smile he had. 'It will give you a more balanced view of what England and English people are really about. It might be squalid and grim, but it's also vibrant and real. We lived there for a time when I was growing up, and I learned more there than I ever did in school. You won't learn anything much in St John's Wood. It's all about money and position there.'

There were some things about Morgan that reminded her of her father. He had always been staunchly on the side of the underdog, he didn't kowtow to people just because they were rich or influential, and he also had that keen interest in people that Morgan appeared to share.

But she felt that, like Papa, Morgan wasn't a man to cross. All her life, Mariette had heard people in Russell remarking on this fact about Etienne. They implied he could be dangerous – in fact, Peggy often joked that in olden days he would have been a pirate. Mariette had always been baffled by such remarks because she thought Papa to be absolutely perfect. He was strong, protective, kind and understanding. But when she'd heard how ferociously he'd beaten Sam and forced him to leave Russell, she realized that this was the side of him others had always sensed.

She had grown up with boys boasting about how tough they were, but when put to the test they usually failed. Morgan had said nothing to imply he was tough – if anything, when he was talking about caring for sick people, some might have thought him very soft – but she sensed he had a harder centre. And from what little he'd said about his childhood, she guessed it had been harsh, as her father's had been.

Mariette knew she shouldn't even be thinking about any man so soon after getting her fingers burned by Sam. And yet, sitting out on a secluded bit of deck in the hot sunshine, just talking, it seemed like the most natural and harmless thing in the world. It wasn't as if he was trying to seduce her.

Their conversation ended abruptly when a booming voice from below called out, '*Griffiths!*'

Morgan jumped to his feet and threw his cigarette overboard. 'That's Lieutenant Hoyle. I've got to go,' he whispered. 'Don't come down the stairs to the sickbay. Walk round the deck, or I'll be in trouble for mixing with the passengers. See you again soon.'

He kissed his index finger, and then touched her cheek with it before disappearing down the stairs.

8

When Stella came back late that same afternoon on the ship's tender, her face was scarlet with sunburn. While she changed for dinner, she talked constantly and animatedly about the day. She had spent it in the company of three couples who Mariette thought were the dullest people on board. From what Stella said, they had been affronted by the squalor in the port, the number of drunken sailors and the young native girls who appeared to be selling themselves.

'I've never seen anything like it,' Stella kept repeating. 'Men kept pressing us to buy things, they said such cheeky things to me, and I'd have been really scared if I'd been there alone.'

Mariette felt a pang of jealousy that she hadn't seen it. The ship had been moored so far out of the port that she'd been unable to see any detail, only getting a tantalizing sense that it was a colourful and boisterous place. But then, if she'd been able to go, she would never have met Morgan.

Stella didn't shut up for about an hour, and it was only when she ran out of steam that she remembered to ask how her friend was.

'Oh, my goodness,' she squealed. 'Whatever must you think of me going on about the port, when you were so ill.'

'I'm better now,' Mariette snapped. She thought Stella could be such a drip sometimes. 'The doctor says I probably had a reaction to something I ate.'

'Mrs Jago said that yesterday,' Stella agreed. 'Her sister gets ill if she eats anything with almonds in it.'

Mariette bit back a sharp retort. Stella couldn't help but be influenced by people like Mrs Jago, who thought they knew everything. But Stella would be hurt if she said as much.

'I expect it was that spicy dish I had for lunch,' Mariette said. 'Heaven only knows what was in it! It tasted a bit strange and, within an hour, I was feeling bad.'

'I bought you something today,' Stella said, pulling a colourful scarf out of her bag. 'I expected you to still be in the sickbay, and I thought it might cheer you up.'

The scarf was all different shades of blue, and very lovely. As annoying as Stella could be, she was a generous soul. Mariette gave the older girl a hug and said it would always remind her of this voyage, of how she missed seeing Curaçao, and of her dear friend.

'I didn't think we'd get on at the start,' Stella said, glowing not only from her sunburn but also from the compliment. 'I thought you were a bit hard, but you aren't really. You're just as soft as me.'

Later that evening, after dinner, Mariette went out on to the deck and made her way round to where she'd sat with Morgan earlier in the day, hoping to see him again. The ship was due to leave the port early the next morning. One of the stewards in the saloon had told her many of the crew were still ashore, but she didn't think Morgan had gone.

It was a beautiful, very warm night, and an almost full moon was casting a silvery path on the dark sea. She could hear someone playing 'Puttin' on the Ritz' on the piano in the saloon, but from the port wafted the sound of less genteel music, brass instruments playing something wild that made her want to dance.

She knew that in a few days they'd be sailing into much colder, stormy weather. But here, where the warmth was like a gentle caress on her bare arms, it was hard to imagine that she'd soon need to open up her trunk to find woollens, the coat Mog had made for her and thick stockings.

'Looking for me?' Morgan's voice made her turn from the ship's rail she'd been leaning against.

'I ought to say no, that I was just passing by,' she laughed. 'But you'd know that wasn't true.'

'To tell the truth, I've been up and down these steps a dozen times this evening, hoping you'd show,' he said with a wide smile. 'In a few days' time, it will be far too cold to linger out here. It will be hard to see you then.'

They chatted for a little while. Morgan said the sickbay was still empty, but he and the two nurses who worked there had been preparing for what they knew would be a busy time in a day or two. Mariette told him about Stella coming back with a sunburned face, and how she'd been shocked by the dirty, noisy port.

'She wouldn't like Cairo then,' he chuckled. 'I was on a ship that called there a couple of years ago. That would make Curaçao look and smell like paradise. Not a place for the squeamish, but I loved it.'

'What kind of music are they playing in the port?' Mariette asked. 'I like it, it's very wild and makes you want to dance.'

'Jazz. Haven't you heard it before?'

'No. In Russell we get a piano and a fiddle player at a dance, and occasionally someone visiting has a guitar or an accordion. People do have gramophones, of course, but mostly the records they have are classical or opera. On the wireless we hear popular music, but I've never heard anything like that.'

'Jazz is basically Negro music,' he explained. 'I love it, and I'm told there are great nightclubs in Harlem, in New York, where the best musicians play. There are some places in London too where you can hear it, but swing music is much more popular – big bands with lots of brass, and singers too. It's got its roots in jazz, and it's easier to dance to. But you must have heard that.'

Mariette nodded. 'Yes, I think I have, on the wireless. But this is very different.'

'The musicians improvise, they kind of make it up as they go along. It's different here from what you'd hear in America or England because it's got South American and West Indian influences.'

'It sounds as if you really like music. Can you play anything?'

'The piano,' he said. 'But I'm not very good. When we were living in the East End of London, the lady downstairs to us had a piano and she taught me. Maybe one day, when I've settled down somewhere permanent, I'll get a piano and take it up again.'

'Where would you settle down?' she asked.

He laughed. 'How can I answer that, Mariette? Anything can happen. I go in and out of ports all the time; some I love, others I can't leave quickly enough. Where you come from sounds perfect, but I probably couldn't make a living there. Anyway, if we do go to war, I'll have to join up. And who knows where that might take me? I might not even survive it.'

'Don't say that!' she said reproachfully. 'Do you think there really will be a war?'

'I don't think there's any doubt about it. The officers are all convinced of it; some of them served in the last war, and they can read all the signs.'

'But my Uncle Noah was a war correspondent in the last war, and he said it will all blow over.'

Morgan looked at her with a grave expression. 'Then I

think he must be burying his head in the sand. Because those that know say it isn't a case of if war might come, but when.'

'Oh dear,' Mariette exclaimed. 'No one back home really thought it was going to come to that.'

'Don't look so glum,' he said, and lifted her chin up with one finger so he could look right into her eyes. 'Do what I do. Think of the adventure. War can create opportunities and, like I said, anything can happen.'

She felt that familiar dizzy, bubbly feeling as she looked into his dark eyes.

'You are pretty enough to make any man lose his head, Mariette,' he said with a smile. 'Do you think one kiss would seal my fate for ever?'

She licked her lips nervously, not knowing whether to move closer, or if he was just teasing her. 'I don't know,' she whispered.

'Let's find out then,' he said. Moving his finger from her chin, he cupped her face in both his hands and his lips came down on hers.

His words, 'Anything can happen,' ran through her head as his tongue flicked into her mouth, and she felt shivers run down her spine. She put her arms around him and lost herself in the sensual delight of his kiss.

It went on and on, as their breathing became heavy and Morgan's hands slid down on to her bottom, drawing her even closer to him. She could feel his erection through his clothes. Although a small voice at the back of her head reminded her that she knew where this could lead, she couldn't draw back.

'I'd like to take you down to the sickbay, but someone might catch us,' he murmured in her ear between passionate kisses.

'I daren't go that far. I might have a baby,' she whispered back.

He drew back from her slightly, looking affronted. 'I wouldn't let that happen, I've got some johnnies,' he said, with a touch of indignation.

Mariette had to assume a johnny was the same as a sheath, something her mother had mentioned just before she left for Auckland. 'It's too soon,' she said, trying to sound like she really meant it. 'I mean, I hardly know you.'

Morgan sat down on a seat and pulled her on to his lap. 'Then we'll have to find moments on the way back to England to get to know each other better,' he said, kissing her neck and making all the hairs on her body leap up. 'I really like you, Mariette. I could be tempted to jump ship in England to be near you.'

'You can't do that,' she said. 'Besides, I doubt my uncle will let me out of his sight. I wouldn't mind betting my parents told him to keep a close eye on me.'

'There are always ways and means.' Morgan smiled at her. 'You toe the line for a while to win his trust, and then later . . .' He broke off, leaving her to imagine how she could escape. 'But I can't really jump ship at the end of this trip. In any case, you need to find out if you like me enough to take the risk with me.'

Mariette was already convinced she'd risk anything to be with him, but she was glad he wasn't holding a gun to her head just so he could have his way with her.

They had just begun kissing again, when a voice yelled for him from down in the sickbay.

'I have to go,' he said, looking very disappointed. 'Try to meet me here at midday tomorrow.'

Mariette went back to the cabin floating on air. Stella was already in her bunk, with thick white cream smeared all over her face.

'Mrs Jago gave it to me,' she said. 'She reckons it's so good the sunburn will have gone by the morning. Where have you been? I looked everywhere for you.'

'Just up on deck looking at the sea.' Mariette wanted to confide in her friend about Morgan, but she was afraid Stella would tell someone else and it would get around the ship. 'I was thinking we ought to sort out our warmer clothes tomorrow, after we leave Curaçao,' she said, intending to put her off the scent. 'We shouldn't wait until it's really cold because, by then, you may be seasick again.'

Within two days, the sea became choppy and the clouds gathered. At first all that was needed was a cardigan when on deck, but soon people began wearing coats, and deck games were forgotten.

Mariette wanted to be excited about reaching England. But all she could think of was that when the voyage ended, she wouldn't see Morgan any more. They had just two hours sitting in the sunshine by the stairs leading to the sickbay, the day after they left Curaçao, but he warned her it would probably be the last time he'd get more than a few minutes to see her.

As he had predicted, the minute the weather turned bad the sickbay suddenly became very busy. Not just seasickness but falls on wet decks, on companionways, and even passengers falling out of bunks. While it meant they could meet up on deck without much fear of being spotted by anyone, it was too cold and wet to stay up there for long.

The moments they did share, though, were very sweet. Morgan was everything Sam had never been; he would slide his hands inside her coat and hug and kiss her, but he was never crude and always thought of her comfort and reputation rather than trying to get her into some dark corner for his own ends. He liked to talk and laugh with her too, and he often said he wished they could go into the saloon to have a drink and just be comfortable together. But though the ship's officers were allowed, and even encouraged, to mix with the passengers, the crew were not.

Each time they met up, passion flared between them. Mariette found it hard to eat or sleep for thinking about him. At night, she lay in her bunk imagining how it would be if he did jump ship in England. But she knew it was only a fantasy as he said he had to do at least one more return trip to New Zealand, and that would mean over three months before she had any chance of seeing him again.

Besides, he wasn't saying the kind of things she wanted to hear – that he'd write, that he wouldn't be able to wait to see her again. With Sam still looming in her mind, she was afraid she was merely a diversion for him on a long voyage, and he'd find another girl on the next trip.

As Mariette had expected, Stella became seasick again as the weather worsened. But this time it was far more serious: her face was as green as pea soup, and she vomited constantly. It fell to Mariette to take care of her as the stewards were all rushed off their feet. The dining room at mealtimes was almost empty because so many passengers were sick.

'You must have salt water in your veins,' Morgan joked because she wasn't affected at all, however rough the sea was. 'Even some of the crew are sick now.'

'I think it's because I've been out in boats since I could barely walk,' she said. 'But I'm getting so tired looking after Stella, I'm up and down most of the night, changing her bed, sponging her down. And the smell in the cabin is horrible.'

'The sickbay stinks too,' Morgan said. 'If you weren't ill when you went in there, you soon would be.'

The following day, Stella was barely conscious and Mariette became so frightened for her that she asked the steward to get Dr Haslem. When he came into the cabin, he was alarmed at how dehydrated Stella had become and decided she must be moved to the sickbay immediately so that she could be put on a drip.

'And you should get some sleep, my girl, while she's gone. Or you'll become ill too,' he said to Mariette before Stella was taken away on a stretcher.

As soon as Mariette had stripped off Stella's soiled sheets, remade her bed and tidied up, she climbed into her own bunk gratefully.

Moments later, the sound of someone coming into the cabin woke her. But it was dark, so she must have slept for a good few hours.

'Who is it?' she asked.

'It's me, Morgan.'

Mariette snapped on the light. 'Is Stella worse?' she asked.

'No, she's a lot better now they've got some fluids into her. But I'm off duty now, and I hoped you'd be pleased to see me.'

'I am. But I don't want you getting into trouble,' she said. She was a bit shocked that he would take such a risk – the two stewards who looked after the passengers on this level were older men, and not the kind to turn a blind eye to another member of the crew flouting the rules.

'You're worth the risk,' he said, leaning on to her bunk to kiss her. 'Anyway, as long as I leave at first light no one will be any the wiser. So can I stay?'

She hesitated for just a moment. But as there had been so many nights when she'd lain in her bunk imagining him with her, how could she turn him away now?

'We don't have to do anything, if you don't want to,' he said, and he stripped off his white jacket, shirt and trousers. 'I only want to hold you.'

But the moment he slid into the bunk, gathered her into his arms and she felt his bare chest against her, she knew she was going to break the vow she'd made back in New Zealand to never have sex again until she was married.

He kissed her so tenderly, and when he stripped off her nightdress and began sucking at her nipples, she wanted him far too much to stop him.

She realized as Morgan caressed, stroked and kissed her that this was what lovemaking was supposed to be like, and it bore no similarity to the animal-like rutting she'd had with Sam. She was entirely lost in the delicacy of his touch, loving the way his fingers explored her secret places, rubbing her in a way that sent spasms of delicious sensation throughout her body.

The bunk was so narrow there was no room to move around, yet somehow he managed to put her in positions that made it easier for him to lick and suck at her. She could hardly believe that a man would put his tongue into her sex, or that it could be so thrilling. An orgasm erupted within her under his tongue, and she must have cried out because he put one hand over her mouth.

'You taste wonderful,' he whispered. 'And I'm going to do it to you again and again because I love hearing you moan.'

'I must go now,' Morgan whispered, much later. 'Look, it's getting light!'

Mariette glanced at the porthole and saw that he was right. Instead of a circle of pitch darkness, it was now grey. They hadn't slept at all; in between bouts of long lovemaking they had cuddled and talked in whispers. It had been wonderful, and Mariette sensed that he was as reluctant to leave her as she was to see him go.

'I doubt we'll get another chance like this,' he said as he

slid out of her arms and on to the floor to dress. 'And we must be careful no one finds out about us. I'm not so worried for me and my job. But if it gets to one of the officers' ears, they might contact your uncle.'

A tremor of fear ran through her. 'They wouldn't do that, surely?'

Morgan pulled a face. 'It has been known, when young girls are travelling alone. They feel they have a moral duty.'

'But will I see you again in England?' she asked nervously, leaning over the side of the bunk and ruffling his hair. She had a feeling he was trying to say this was the end.

'I've got to be honest, Mari,' he said, taking her hand and kissing her fingers. 'I can't promise anything right now because of the job. But promise you'll wait for me? Don't start thinking I'm gone for good, if you don't hear from me in a while. I'll write when I can. And next time I'm back in England, we will meet up.'

He finished dressing, kissed her once again and then he was gone, slipping out so silently she didn't even hear the door click.

9

Mariette was too exhausted to try analysing what Morgan had said to her, too sleepy to even get up and straighten the tangled sheets. She was woken later by Alfred, the steward, banging on the cabin door.

'Are you alright, Miss Carrera?' he called out.

She got up, pulled on her long nightdress and a wrapper, and opened the cabin door.

'I was worried that you were sick as you didn't go up for breakfast,' Alfred said. He was portly, middle-aged and a bit of an old woman, but he'd been very kind and helpful to her and Stella.

'I'm fine. I was just tired,' she said. 'Don't worry about the cabin today.'

'I won't have time to do it anyway,' he said with a slight edge to his voice, which suggested he was annoyed at having his routine disturbed. 'It's after one. If you want some lunch, you'd better go now.'

Mariette thanked him and said she wasn't hungry. She was, but she knew she must go and have a shower before dressing, and she hadn't got the energy to rush. 'Have you heard how Miss Murgatroyd is today?' she asked.

He shook his head. 'With nearly all the passengers sick, I've got too much to do to go down to the sickbay.'

Mariette closed the door and leaned back against it while she gathered herself. She was sore from so much lovemaking, and still very tired. But when she closed her eyes and thought of the things she and Morgan had done to each other, a delicious quiver of excitement ran through her.

Once she had showered and dressed, Mariette made her way down to the sickbay to inquire about her friend. One of the nurses said Stella was a lot better and that Mariette could go in to see her. If Morgan was there, Mariette didn't see him.

Stella's face lit up to see her. Although she looked gaunt, her colour was normal again and she was well enough to sit up and talk.

'I thought I was going to die,' she said dramatically. 'To be honest, I welcomed death because I felt so bad.'

'Does that mean you can come back to the cabin?' Mariette asked, hoping that wouldn't be the case.

'I've got to wait for the doctor's permission,' Stella replied. She sighed, as if she hoped he would refuse it. 'Have you seen that steward who works down here? He's a real heart-throb, and so kind too. It's worth being ill just to be near him.'

'The dark-haired one that looks a bit like Errol Flynn?' Mariette asked, knowing it must be Morgan.

Stella went all dreamy-eyed. 'Yes, that's him. I thought I must be delirious, seeing someone so handsome bathing my forehead. But he came in again this morning, and I hadn't imagined it. He really is that gorgeous.'

Mariette didn't trust herself to continue this line of conversation. 'If you're well enough to get ideas about a steward, you must be on the mend,' she said. 'Do you want me to come back later and collect you?'

She wondered where Morgan was – he'd been awake all night, and must be exhausted – but she couldn't very well ask. Coming back for Stella would be the ideal excuse for returning later.

'No, don't bother,' Stella said. 'I'm quite happy to stay here. I like it now I feel a bit better.'

Mariette left the sickbay and went up to the saloon. As the sea was calmer now, there were many more people in the saloon than she'd seen in the past few days. She got herself a cup of tea and was soon drawn into conversation with several different people who all began by asking how Stella was, but it soon transpired that this was just an opening gambit to tell her how sick they'd been, and what an awful time they'd had in New Zealand.

Mariette felt like reminding them she was a New Zealander and perhaps suggesting their lack of success and happiness in her country was because they'd been stupid enough to imagine New Zealand was just like England. Back home, she'd often heard people laughing about immigrants who didn't attempt to adjust but instead spent all their time comparing New Zealand unfavourably with their homeland. But she bit back her sarcasm, smiled in sympathy and secretly hoped they'd find winter in England far worse than they remembered.

But after an hour or so, she'd had enough of being polite and went out on deck, hoping to find Morgan.

It was extremely cold, the sky was leaden and sullen, and although she watched the waves curling back from the bow of the ship for a few minutes, she was soon chilled to the bone and had to retreat down to the warmth of the cabin.

She lay on Stella's bunk and tried to read, but her thoughts kept turning to Morgan. Was this the end for them? Perhaps it was true what people said, that once a man had his way with a girl he lost interest. But why would he ask her to wait for him, if he didn't mean it?

Lying in his arms, she had allowed herself to believe that he wanted her for ever, that he only had to do one more return trip, and then they could be together. But even if Morgan had meant what he said, now that she was here on her own she could see problems. The chances were that her father had told Uncle Noah about Sam, and warned him to keep her on a tight rein in England. But even if he hadn't, it wasn't likely that her uncle was going to welcome a man she'd met on the voyage, coming to call at his house. If Morgan was an officer, it might be different – Mog had told her that English people were very snobbish about class.

A knock on the door startled her out of her reverie, and she jumped off the bunk to open it. To her amazement, it was Morgan. He came in quickly and shut the door behind him.

'You're taking a risk during the daytime,' she gasped.

'You're worth it,' he said, and pulled her into his arms to kiss her. 'I doubt we'll get the chance to be alone again before we get to England, and I didn't want to leave you not knowing how I feel about you.'

'How you feel about me?' she repeated.

'Isn't it obvious? I'm nuts about you. I wouldn't have risked coming to your cabin in the day otherwise.'

His words made the anxiety she'd felt minutes earlier disappear, and she kissed him passionately.

Morgan pulled away first. 'I need to know you trust me,' he said. 'I can't give you a date, or even the month, when I'll be back in England again. I'm not much of a letter writer, and the post can take for ever to reach home anyway. But promise me you won't lose heart and forget me? As soon as I get back, I will send word to you. I'm sure people will tell you sailors have a girl in every port, but you'll be the only girl in my heart.'

'And you'll be the only boy in mine,' she said, thrilled at his words. 'I'll give you my uncle's address now, just in case we don't get another chance after today.'

She wrote the address down, and he tucked it into the pocket of his white jacket before lowering her down on to Stella's bunk.

He pulled off her jumper, undid her blouse, then kissed her as he slid his hand down and under the top of her petticoat to caress her breasts.

Mariette arched her back, and he responded by bending to kiss and suck at her nipples. She held his head in her hands, transported into another world where nothing mattered but the thrilling sensations his lips were creating.

They were so wrapped up in each other, neither of them heard the cabin door open. They only knew they weren't alone when they heard a gasp.

'How could you?' Stella's irate voice boomed out.

Morgan jumped, banging his head on the upper bunk and exposing Mariette, who was naked to the waist, beneath him.

They were so aghast, they could only stare at Stella.

'How could you?' the girl repeated, loudly enough for any-one outside the cabin to hear. 'On my bunk! That's disgusting! I can't believe that of you, Mariette.'

'Now calm down, Stella,' Morgan said, standing up and putting his hands on her shoulders. Mariette quickly pulled her petticoat back over her breasts and slipped her jumper on. 'We care a great deal for one another, we just wanted some time alone together.'

'It's shameful, that's what it is,' Stella exclaimed, breaking away from Morgan and wagging a finger at Mariette. 'How can you behave like that with a steward!'

'It would be alright if it was the Captain, I suppose?' Mariette retorted. 'Oh, don't make such a fuss, Stella. It's not a crime to kiss a man, even if he is a steward. Only this morning you said how kind and lovely he was. Are you jealous that he likes me?'

'Jealous of you behaving so improperly? I should think not!'

'Now, Stella,' Morgan said soothingly. 'I'm sorry that you had to walk in on this, we are very embarrassed, as I'm sure you are too. We're both pleased that you are well enough to leave the sickbay. But don't forget that it was Mari who has been looking after you for most of this voyage. She doesn't deserve you to turn on her just because we fell in love with each other.'

At those words Mariette didn't care what Stella thought of her any more, or even if the whole ship got to hear of it.

'I wanted to tell you,' Mariette said. 'But you know Morgan would be in trouble, if one of the officers got to hear about it. And you've been so ill, it wouldn't have been right to upset you, would it?'

Stella glowered at them both. 'Don't think you can charm your way out of this,' she said. 'I'm going to see one of the officers.'

'Please don't do that, Stella,' Mariette pleaded with her and caught hold of her hand to prevent her rushing out. 'Morgan would lose his job, and he has a widowed mother to support. Take it out on me, if you must, but not on him.'

Stella shook her off and pushed Morgan back towards the door. 'Just get out of here, and don't you dare try to come in here again.' She wrenched the door open. 'To think I believed you were a gentleman!'

As she slammed the door shut behind him, Mariette continued pleading with her. 'I love him, Stella. He looked after me when I was ill in Curaçao, and we spent the afternoon while you were in the port getting to know each other. He only came here this afternoon because it was too cold to meet on deck. We just wanted to talk and be together, is that so bad?'

'You weren't talking,' she retorted, her face flushed red with outrage. 'If I hadn't come in, he'd have been having his way with you. I'm disgusted that you could do such a thing.'

Mariette kept apologizing, almost grovelling to the older girl, but nothing she said made any difference. Stella kept a wooden expression on her face, repeating over and over how disgusted she was.

Such a strong reaction had to be jealousy, but Mariette didn't dare charge her with that again for fear she'd make good her threat to speak to an officer. It wasn't in Mariette's nature to grovel to anyone, but she knew she must this time. Not just so that Morgan could keep his job, but because she was a minor and it was quite likely the Captain would consider it his duty to contact her uncle and tell him what he knew. She couldn't let that happen.

'I wouldn't have upset you for the world,' she pleaded. 'We've been such good friends, don't take against me for this. I know it looked bad, but we just got a bit carried away.'

'I really don't wish to have anything more to do with you,' Stella said, giving Mariette a look that would freeze a brass monkey. 'I won't report you, not this time, but just keep away from me for the rest of the voyage.'

At first, Mariette was so happy Morgan had said he loved her that she didn't care if Stella wanted nothing more to do with her. But after just one day of being totally ignored by her friend, she found she did care. Stella only spoke if there was no alternative, and at mealtimes she made sure she was seated with other people, excluding Mariette.

It became terribly cold, and Mariette hoped the sea would become rough again so she could take care of Stella and win her forgiveness. But the sea remained quite calm, Stella stayed well, and her demeanour was as frosty as the weather.

The extreme cold made it impossible for Mariette to hang around on deck in the hope of seeing Morgan. She considered faking illness to go down to the sickbay, but that might turn out to be asking for more trouble.

But two nights before they were due to dock in Southampton, Mariette bundled herself up in warm clothes and decided to brave it. To her delight, Morgan was there at the doorway which led down to the sickbay.

His face lit up on seeing her. 'I've been coming up here all the time,' he said. 'I was beginning to think Stella had put you off me.'

'She couldn't do that, but she has been horrible,' Mariette said. 'I feel entirely friendless now. She won't speak, gives me dirty looks all the time. I'm convinced it's jealousy.'

'Well, there is a lot to be jealous about. You're pretty, you're great company and you've got me. By the way, what made you say I had to support my widowed mother?'

Mariette giggled. 'Desperation. I didn't think she was cruel enough to see a widow go hungry.'

Morgan smiled. 'I like it that your brain works that fast in an emergency.'

'Well, it was self-preservation too. I didn't want her blabbing.'

'When I come back to England next time, we'd better do it all properly. You tell your uncle I looked after you when you were sick, and that I want to call on you. Would he refuse?'

Mariette shrugged. 'I can't see why, it's perfectly reasonable. I shall just have to be careful I don't look too excited about seeing you.'

'But would you be?' he asked.

She looked at his lovely face – those dark twinkly eyes, golden suntan and brilliant white teeth – and felt weak with wanting.

'You know I would be,' she admitted. 'No one would stand here on a freezing deck unless they were seriously smitten.'

That was the last time Mariette saw Morgan. She went out on deck the following night, but he wasn't there. And the next morning, as the ship sailed into Southampton, all the crew were so busy that she knew there was no point in trying to find him.

As she stood on deck, wrapped up in her brown coat, holding on to her hat for dear life, her initial impression of England was that it looked grim. Everything was grey – the sky, the sea, the buildings – and so very cold. Mog had said that, as soon as March came in, she would see green shoots on the trees, daffodils in the parks, and the sun would shine. But February was clearly not a good month to see England for the first time.

Her suitcase was stacked with everyone else's on a lower deck, ready to be taken ashore. When she'd left the cabin, Stella was panicking because she couldn't get everything into her suitcase. Mariette could have packed it for her but, after being ignored for so long, she didn't feel inclined to help in any way.

She had a recent photograph of Uncle Noah and Aunt Lisette. He was portly, with receding hair, and Aunt Lisette looked like Mrs Simpson, the lady the King had abdicated for. Her mother said Lisette had been very beautiful as a young woman, with dark hair and eyes. She was in her fifties now, her marcel-waved hair turning grey, but she was still lovely. She would be wearing a brown fur coat and hat, with a red flower pinned to her coat to make it easier for Mariette to recognize her. She just hoped she would.

The people on the dock were just becoming visible now, but it would be a while before she could see the details on faces. Morgan's face was stamped on her mind, and his features stopped any other images registering. She remembered the cleft in his chin when he smiled, the way one corner of his mouth went up higher when he asked a question, and the perfect arc of his dark eyebrows. She could recall their first kiss so clearly, but not the last one. Why was that?

Mariette looked around, hoping he was standing somewhere near, watching her. But she couldn't see him. Did he love her? She wished she could be absolutely certain of that.

With only a hundred yards of water now until they docked, the crew were standing ready, and there were more sailors on the quay too. She scanned the line of people waiting behind a barrier. They could only wave for now; all passengers had to have their passports checked before they could be greeted by friends and family.

She couldn't see anyone who looked like Uncle Noah and Aunt Lisette, and she had a moment of panic in which she felt certain that they'd forgotten about her.

Finally, the ship's engines stopped, she was secured, and the gangway put in place.

Mariette looked around again, but there was still no sign of Morgan, even though many of the stewards were out on the upper deck waving goodbye.

All Mariette was aware of, as she joined the throng of jostling people to have her passport examined, was the biting cold. Her feet and legs were like ice, the lisle stockings Mog had bought for her in Auckland no protection at all from the cruel blast of the wind.

There were so many people, all pushing and shoving, so much noise and confusion. She let herself be drawn along by passengers whose faces had become familiar in the past weeks. She didn't know where her luggage would be taken and, if Uncle Noah wasn't here waiting for her, she had no idea of what she would do. Then, just as her eyes began to fill with tears of fear and panic, she heard her name being called.

'*Here, Mari! We're here!*'

The voice came again, and through the crowd she saw a man in a dark overcoat, waving a trilby hat. Dodging through the crowd, Mariette reached him, and he flung his arms around her and hugged her tightly.

'You poor thing, you must be so cold and confused,' he said as he held her to his chest. 'Welcome to England. It may be freezing, but we are thrilled to see you.'

Mariette hadn't really been aware of Lisette until she heard a gentle voice with a French accent say, 'Don't cry, little one. We've been dying to meet you and can't wait to get you home.'

10

It wasn't until after ten that same night, when Mariette was tucked up in the prettiest bedroom she'd ever seen, that she was able to reflect on all she'd experienced during the day and put it into some kind of order.

Although she knew Uncle Noah had become a celebrated journalist and author since the days when he was her father's friend, she hadn't for one moment imagined him living like a millionaire, or being so warm and lovable. From the first moment, when he hugged her, she felt really comfortable with him.

His car was a black Daimler, driven by a uniformed chauffeur called Andrews, and as she had only ever been in old ramshackle cars and trucks before, she couldn't quite get over the grandeur of the leather seats, so much legroom and the sublime comfort. Uncle Noah sat up front, by Andrews, but he spent almost the whole journey turning round towards the back seat to speak to her and Lisette. He asked so many questions about her parents and her brothers. Interspersed with this, he told her about all the places in England he wanted her to see.

His looks belied his true nature. While his plumpness, thinning hair, hand-tailored suit and beautiful overcoat were all that she had expected of a wealthy middle-aged man, his personality was irrepressibly youthful and excitable. Within minutes of being in his company, she began to think of him as far younger than he actually was.

Lisette had the classical look of a ballerina, partly due to the way her hair was pulled back into a tight bun, but she was also slender, graceful, elegantly dressed and very serene. Her fur coat, which Mariette suspected was mink, was a light biscuit colour with a very fluffy collar that emphasized her high cheekbones and beautiful skin. Yet she gave the impression that she didn't fuss about her appearance. While being very interested and attentive, she let her husband do most of the talking. When she did speak, her voice was soft and soothing, her French accent reminding Mariette so much of her father's.

It seemed a very long drive through farmland, woods and small villages that were so old and quaint they could have been illustrations in a child's picture book. As stark and bare as the countryside was in its winter mantle, there was still so much beauty in the leafless trees, the small humpback stone bridges over streams and the hills covered in grass so much greener than anything she'd seen in New Zealand.

They stopped for lunch in what Noah said was an old coaching inn in Godalming, a very pretty village. The inn had wooden beams across the low ceiling and a huge fire, and she was rather surprised to see women in there.

'Women aren't allowed in public houses in New Zealand?' Lisette exclaimed. 'How very odd! English women don't tend to go into pubs alone, of course, but it's becoming very common these days for women friends to come in together for lunch, or for a drink in the evening. Pubs are at the centre of village life in England.'

When they drove into London, Mariette's eyes nearly popped out of her head. Noah had asked Andrews to drive over Westminster Bridge so she could see the Houses of Parliament and Big Ben. They drove round Trafalgar Square, then up the Mall towards Buckingham Palace. Although she'd seen many pictures of these places, everything was so much larger and more splendid than she had expected.

'There's an awful lot more to London than we've shown you today,' Noah said, smiling because she was so overawed. 'But we'll wait until you've got used to the cold before we take you to see the rest.'

Finally, they reached Noah's house and Mariette's jaw dropped at the size of it. Noah said it was built in 1795, which made it much older than any house she'd ever seen in New Zealand. Old it might be, but it was so graceful and beautifully proportioned, with a portico over the central front door and three long windows, arched at the top, on either side of it.

Mog and Belle had both used words like 'cosy' and 'homely' to describe the home Uncle Noah and Aunt Lisette had when they left for New Zealand. But this house had been bought since then. Cosy and homely would certainly not describe it. Grand, palatial – even spectacular – would be more apt.

Mariette tried very hard not to show her astonishment as Mrs Andrews, the housekeeper and wife of the chauffeur, opened the front door and welcomed her into a huge hall with a floor polished to a mirror finish and a grand staircase sweeping up and round, the like of which she'd only seen in films.

'We're rattling around in all this space since Jean-Philippe got married two years ago,' Noah said, while Mrs Andrews took her coat and hat. Mr Andrews was already carrying Mariette's suitcase up to her room. 'We never realized how much space he took up until he moved out. Now it's only us and Rose. She's away at the moment, with friends, but she'll be back tomorrow.'

The drawing room to the right of the hall was huge, decorated in soft pastel shades, with floor-length curtains and elaborate braid-trimmed pelmets above. In front of a roaring fire there were large sofas which begged to be curled up on, and in front of the window there was a polished wooden table covered in silver-framed photographs.

Mariette was thrilled to see herself amongst them. There was one of her as a baby in Noah's arms, when he'd come out to New Zealand to be her godfather, another of her at fifteen, taken while sailing the dinghy, a lovely one of her mother and father on their wedding day and one of Mog and Belle, presumably taken at the end of the war, when they were leaving for New Zealand, because they were both very dressed up.

'This is Jean-Philippe,' Lisette said, pointing out a young man with very dark hair and a very serious expression. 'He's thirty-one now, but that was taken when he was around twenty-six.' She then touched his wedding picture. 'And this is him with his bride, Alice.'

Mariette knew that Jean-Philippe was Noah's stepson, and she wondered if he would come round soon to meet her.

'Rose?' Mariette asked, picking up a photograph of a girl in her twenties. She reminded Mariette of the way Mog had described Noah when he was young, with a round face, very curly hair and a brilliant smile.

'Yes, that's my Rose — and aptly named, for she is much more English than French,' Lisette said. 'She's twenty-four now but still young enough to be good company for you.'

'It's lovely to see Mum, Papa and Mog here too,' Mariette said. 'I didn't expect that.'

Lisette put her hands on Mariette's shoulders and looked her full in the face. 'Your mother and father mean a great deal to Noah and me. There is a bond between us stronger than just family ties. So, of course, your pictures are all here in our home. I'm just waiting for them to send me a photograph of Alexis and Noel, and then they will be here too.'

'I have one in my case, Mum said I was to give it to you,' Mariette said.

'You will miss your parents, being so far away,' Lisette said, and put her arms around Mariette to hug her. 'But you must think of Noah and myself as stand-in parents. Don't be afraid to tell us things. We are not – how do you say it in English? – ogres.'

Mariette wasn't normally one for hugging, but she was glad to be enveloped in Lisette's arms. She liked her, and she wasn't surprised now that the Frenchwoman and Belle had been such good friends. There was a similarity about them, not looks, but something indefinable which she felt, but couldn't quite put her finger on.

As Mariette reached out to switch off the bedside lamp in her new room, she remembered how Mog had said she wouldn't know herself once she discovered the joys of living with electricity. She'd already got used to it on the ship, but here in this pretty cream and pink room, which Lisette said had been inspired by Belle's hat shop, she hoped she would never have to light an oil lamp again.

It was touching that Lisette had been thinking of Belle when she planned the room, yet it seemed very French to Mariette. The gilding on the ornate dressing table and matching stool reminded her of pictures she'd seen of furniture in Versailles. There were two pictures on the wall above the bed, both of outrageous frothy hats. Lisette said she'd found them in a flea market in Paris, and both she and Noah knew immediately that they would be perfect for this room.

The house back in Russell was very simply decorated and furnished, which made this house seem even more grandiose and decadent, but it wasn't just the sumptuous carpets, polished furniture and the like that impressed Mariette so much, rather the way she was taken care of and the sheer comfort of it all. While they had been eating their supper, Mrs Andrews had come up and unpacked her suitcase for her, taking away everything that needed washing. There was a cream chaise longue by the window, and there were radiators all over the house so that every room was warm. Even the bed she was in was a double one, with sheets that felt as smooth and soft as silk.

She'd had a bath in a bathroom which was just for her, adjoining her room. There were fluffy towels warming on a heated rail, and going outside to a lavatory was now a thing of the past. It was all beyond her wildest dreams.

But there were two things missing. One was the sound of the sea. Ever since she'd been a little girl, she'd lain awake listening to the waves breaking on the shore, and on the voyage from New Zealand the sound had surrounded her. Here there was just traffic, a faint hum now it was getting late, comforting enough, but not in the way the sea was.

Then there was Morgan. She'd managed to avoid thinking about him for most of the day, but now she was alone she ached for him. Was he thinking of her right now? Or had he forgotten her already and gone off into Southampton to dance, get drunk and find another girl?

The first two weeks of being in London were such a whirl-wind of new experiences that Mariette didn't miss Morgan quite as much as she'd thought she would. It was really only late at night that he crept into her thoughts, and although her stomach would churn with wanting him, it wasn't as bad as she'd expected it to be.

She adored London. It wasn't just seeing the famous sights – the Tower of London, St Paul's Cathedral and London Zoo – but simple things, like a ride on a bus, eating fish and chips, or taking a toboggan out on Primrose Hill when it snowed. She'd never seen snow before – they had it in the South Island, but never in Russell – and she couldn't quite believe that a man like Noah would gleefully hurtle down slopes on a toboggan with her.

When she wrote home, the words flooded out in her excitement to make her family share her experiences and the sights she'd seen. She felt obliged to tell them she missed them all, but the truth was that she was far too happy with her new life to give them more than the occasional sentimental thought.

She loved living in such a busy street. In the mornings, when she looked out of the window, there were gentlemen in bowler hats with furled umbrellas, going off to the City. There were so many smartly dressed office girls too, mothers taking small children to school and older children larking around as they found their own way there.

Later in the day, there were the tradesmen: a baker delivering bread from his horse-drawn cart, a coal merchant, even a man who sharpened knives. Nursemaids pushing prams came out when it was sunny, while housemaids scrubbed doorsteps and polished door brass.

She thought of the streets in Russell. Cows meandered along them at will, and when it rained they were like swamps. Now that she was here, in London, she couldn't imagine going back to such a primitive way of life.

The thought that Noah and Lisette might get fed up with her – and might send her home – worried her, and to make this far less likely she made sure she was always on her best behaviour. She spoke French to Lisette, because she knew she liked it, and she offered to help around the house. Mrs Andrews did all the housework and so, invariably, Lisette would say there was nothing to do. But Mariette made her own bed, kept her bedroom really tidy and remained alert for anything else she could do to please Lisette.

She loved running errands. The little shops nearby were like Aladdin's caves stuffed with goods, and the big shops, further away in Oxford Street and Regent Street, were so amazing that she could wander around them all day without getting bored.

Rose had returned home on Mariette's second day in London. Although Mariette's first impression of her was that she was like one of those aristocratic, earnest young women she'd seen in British-made films, she liked her.

'I expect Mama and Papa will overdo the sightseeing,' Rose said with an infectious grin. 'So I'll take you to the jollier places. Have you ever tried roller skating? I love it. There's a rink in Finchley Road, not far from here. Shall we go tomorrow night?'

Mariette had only ever seen roller skating on a film, but it looked a fun thing to do, and she agreed with enthusiasm.

It was all Rose had said, and more. Mariette hung on to the side of the rink at first, too scared to let go, but then Rose and one of her friends held her hands and took her round with them.

She got the hang of it very quickly after that, and by the end of the session she could even skate backwards. She was complimented for learning so quickly.

Rose and her circle of friends were very different from women of the same age back in Russell. Although few of them did any paid work, they all appeared to have had very good educations. They spent their days visiting friends, having lunch and helping out in various charities. Rose told her it wasn't done for middle-class girls to work and that she was an exception, having been trained as a bookkeeper. But even Rose didn't go to work every day; it seemed the bookkeeping work she did was for people known to her father, and she slotted this in between her social engagements and charity work.

Yet, despite not working, none of Rose's friends seemed the least bit concerned about getting married and raising families. They travelled, took a great deal of interest in world affairs, went to concerts, visited nightclubs and took part in sport. Next to them Mariette felt like a real country bumpkin who hadn't the least idea about anything.

'My parents expected me to work while I was here,' Mariette confided in Rose. 'But I don't know anything, so what work could I do?'

'What do you enjoy doing?' Rose asked.

'Sailing and fishing,' Mariette joked. 'But I don't suppose there's much call for those talents in London. I like sewing too.'

Rose smiled. 'There's sailing on the Serpentine in summer, but sewing's a real asset. I bet my mother could pull some strings for you there. She knows most of the couture places in London.'

Rose must have spoken to her parents about this because the following evening, when Rose had gone out to a concert with a friend, Noah brought up the subject over dinner.

'I know Belle and Etienne felt you should work while you are here, but Lisette and I just wanted you to enjoy being in London for a while before thinking about that. However, Rose mentioned you wanted to do dressmaking.'

'It's one of the few things I'm good at,' she said. 'But then, I had good teachers in Mum and Mog.'

Noah frowned. 'While you may love dressmaking, Mari, I think you may get very disillusioned about working in a couture house. The pay is abysmal, the hours very long, and you are likely to be put to work on just one tiny part of the garment, never doing the whole thing. How about doing a secretarial course? Once you can type, you can get work anywhere in the world, and when you go back to New Zealand too. I wish I'd learned to type properly when I was a lad. As it is, I've had to struggle and get by with two or three fingers for all these years.'

Mariette had heard him tapping away at a typewriter in his study. She'd grown up seeing his hugely successful book on the 1914 war on the bookshelf at home. Her parents always showed it to people and proudly told them he was their friend. Mariette felt a bit ashamed now that she hadn't tried to read it, especially as her father's input had been huge, telling Noah the inside stories about how it really was for the enlisted men, and exposing the mistakes of the generals. Since that bestseller Noah had turned to writing fiction, penning a series of very popular gritty detective stories. She had read two of those on the ship, and really loved them.

'I think I'd like to do that, Uncle Noah,' she agreed. Even though she did like sewing, she wasn't sure she wanted to be cloistered in a totally female world. 'And I think Mum and Dad would approve too.'

Noah beamed. 'First thing tomorrow, I'll make some phone calls,' he said. 'I think Lisette would agree that dressmaking is a rewarding hobby, but hardly a career.'

Later that evening, Noah went off to his study and Lisette and Mariette sat by the fire together speaking in French. They made a point of speaking French every day now – often just for a few minutes, while they were doing something together – but on a night like this, when they were alone, they would keep it up for an hour or more.

Papa had also done this since Mariette was old enough to speak, and she really enjoyed it. But speaking to another woman brought new words into her vocabulary, and

Lisette worked hard on giving her a more Parisian accent, rather than the Marseille pronunciation she had heard from her father.

They chatted in French about fashion for some little while, then Lisette suddenly changed back to English.

'I hope you didn't agree to train as a secretary just to please Noah?' she said. 'He can have some odd ideas about women's jobs. Since he became so successful, he has also become a bit of a snob.'

'Do you mean he thinks dressmaking is a bit like working in a factory?' Mariette asked.

Mog had often made jokes about the class system in England, but her comments had been wasted on Mariette as class didn't really exist in New Zealand. But Morgan had made sharp remarks about the differences between officers and ordinary seamen. And once she'd been in England for a few days, she'd begun to notice certain things for herself, accents in particular.

All Rose's friends had very posh accents, like people on the wireless. One of them had made a cutting remark about someone who was a 'shop girl', giving Mariette the idea they saw people who did the more lowly jobs, or spoke with a different accent, as another species.

It was this attitude which made Mariette realize that Rose's friends would not approve of Morgan. She had already identified his accent as cockney, much like the very jolly milkman who called her 'ducks' and Lisette 'missis'. Mr and Mrs Andrews spoke much the same way too, though not quite so obviously.

Lisette made a funny little sucking noise with her mouth, as if considering whether her husband thought dressmaking was as lowly as factory work. 'It is very hard for me to explain how people in England think about such things, my dear.

Noah has many friends in high places now, and that has changed his outlook a little.'

'And he wouldn't like to tell them his goddaughter was working as a seamstress?' Mariette prompted her.

Lisette blushed. 'You are so like your mother, Mari. Belle always said everything as it was, not what people wanted to hear.'

To Mariette making beautiful dresses was as skilful as being a surgeon, and it made no sense to her that anyone could classify one as being lower class, and the other as upper. 'But a secretary is fine?' she asked.

'It is a job girls from good homes do,' Lisette replied, and made a gesture with her hands as if that made no sense to her either.

'You mean, if they aren't clever enough to be an accountant or a doctor?'

'Now you sound like Etienne,' Lisette said with a wry smile. 'He was always a champion of the working class. Belle and Mog too struggled with class distinctions. I remember, when they first moved to Blackheath, they made a real effort to appear more genteel, just so they would fit in. They had a book they read, called *Correct English*, and when I visited them all three of us would try phrases. We used to laugh so much doing what Mog called "posh voices".'

Mariette laughed too. She remembered how, just before she left New Zealand, her mother and Mog had done this to illustrate how some people in England spoke. Their London accents had mellowed after nearly twenty years in New Zealand – they mostly sounded like people who had been born there – but when they talked to each other, especially about England, they tended to lapse back into their old ways.

'I have an advantage, in being French, for some reason anyone hearing my accent assumes I'm a "lady",' Lisette said with a chuckle. 'But it took me some years to understand what is meant by that. Even now, when I see Mrs Andrews who is ten years older than me lifting a heavy coal scuttle, I want to help her. But she would be horrified, if I did. She thinks it is her place to do such jobs.'

'I'm not sure I know what place I should be in,' Mariette said. 'My father fishes and does building work, and my mother makes hats. So that makes me working class, doesn't it?'

'The whole class system is ridiculous.' Lisette patted Mariette's knee to stress she too found it baffling. 'Both Noah and I came from humble beginnings, but because Noah made a name for himself as a very good journalist and author, we found ourselves shunted upwards. This is exactly why your parents felt we were the right people to guide your future.'

'But Dad doesn't have any time for the class system,' Mariette said with a touch of indignation. 'I don't think he'd want me to get airs and graces.'

'It isn't about that, it's about acquiring polish, knowing how to behave in company, so you can mix easily with all kinds of people, Mari. Noah and I had to learn that, just as Belle had to when she had her hat shop. It is that polish that your parents want for you. They would never want you to become a snob, but they do want doors to open for you.

'Maybe, in six months' time, you will go home and marry a carpenter, or a fisherman, and be as happy as your parents are. But it is always good to have choices, to know about the possibilities there are in life. And that's what Noah and I want to help you with. Do you understand what I mean?'

'Yes, I do,' Mariette agreed. Lisette had put it very well. 'But I don't think Noah would like it much if I wanted to walk out with a bus conductor, a train driver or a ship's steward, would he?'

'Did you meet a nice steward on the ship?'

The inquiring tone in Lisette's voice brought Mariette up sharply. The word 'steward' had slipped out, and it was clear Lisette had picked up on its importance.

There was no sense in trying to lie her way out of it. 'Yes, I did,' she admitted. 'His name is Morgan Griffiths, and he took care of me when I was in the sickbay. I really liked him.'

'I see,' Lisette said thoughtfully. 'Is there a reason you haven't mentioned him before?'

'Well, as you probably know, I was a bit foolish over a man back home,' Mariette said cautiously. 'I expect Mum and Papa warned you to watch me like a hawk.'

'Strange as it may seem to you, your parents told us nothing like that. Of course, we did suspect something,' Lisette smiled. 'But you are not alone in being foolish. It is something we all expect from young people. Rose has had her moments, and Jean-Philippe too when he was your age. Both Noah and I did things that we aren't so proud of now. The biggest danger for young girls is that they often get carried away by a handsome face, and fail to look at the man's character. Do you think Morgan is a good man?'

'Yes, I do. But it is hard to be sure when you only have a short time with someone.'

'And on the ship you only saw him for moments here and there?'

Mariette nodded.

Lisette took Mariette's hand in both of hers and squeezed it. 'When you meet a man in secret, you only see what you want to see. You are often so caught up by the excitement and by the way he makes you feel, you don't question anything, or look too closely. I have discovered the best way to find out how a man really is, is to watch him in the company of other people you know well. Both good and bad points become apparent then.'

'But other people said how charming he was.' Mariette felt that Lisette was dismissing Morgan out of hand. 'You would too, if you met him.'

'I hope so, *ma chérie*,' Lisette smiled. 'So when he is back in England, we invite him here. Yes?'

The first week of March was cold, with rain and strong winds, but the weather turned warmer in time for Mariette's birthday, on the 8th. Suddenly there were swathes of daffodils in the parks and gardens, green buds on the trees, and Mariette understood why Mog had said England was beautiful in the spring.

Lisette and Noah gave her a beautiful silver locket for her birthday, with an inscription from them inside it. Rose gave her a fluffy stole, and a parcel came from home with a turquoise crêpe de Chine dress made by Mog, a white hat with a turquoise ribbon from her mother and, from her papa, a replica of his little fishing boat which he'd carved and painted himself. The name of the boat was *Little Rebel*, which made her eyes prickle with tears.

Lisette made a special birthday tea, including a cake with nineteen candles. After Mariette had blown out the candles, Rose announced they were going to be picked up later by Peter Hayes and taken dancing in Soho.

'So you'd better put your glad rags on, Mari,' she said. 'I know you've been dying to wear that divine cream lace dress ever since you got here. Now's your chance.'

Peter Hayes took Rose out quite often. She had confided in Mariette that he was the man she wanted to marry, but she played hard to get, often accepting dates with other male friends.

Mariette liked Peter, as did Lisette and Noah. He was twenty-eight, tall, with soft brown eyes. Although not exactly handsome, he was, as Rose described him, 'presentable' and a solicitor. Rose made much of him coming from a very good family, and she often spoke about their huge house out in Berkshire, but however much Rose made out that she was selecting him for his family and position, Mariette knew that wasn't his only attraction. He was not only lively, intelligent, kind and generous, but sexy too.

Rose was a virgin and intended to stay that way until she married. But Mariette could see by the way her friend lit up in Peter's company that she was itching to go to bed with him.

'You'll have a lovely time with Peter and Rose,' Lisette assured her. 'I know we can trust Peter to look after you. Now, run along and get ready.'

As the two girls went upstairs, Rose whispered, 'Peter's bringing a friend. I know you'll like him. His name is Gerald Allsop; he's younger than Peter but they went to the same school.'

'Is he a solicitor too?' Mariette asked.

'No, not yet, he's still doing his articles. I didn't tell Mother and Father he would be with us because they would want to meet him and quiz him first. That's a bit of an ordeal for anyone, they are so old-fashioned sometimes. So he'll meet us there. But if you do like him and want to see him again, I'll just tell them tomorrow that Peter introduced you to him, which is more or less the truth.'

'Are you sure you want me coming along with you and Peter?' Mariette asked. She was a little afraid Gerald would prove to be stuffy and earnest, and that Rose had only asked her to come with them tonight to stop Gerald being a gooseberry when she wanted to be alone with Peter.

'Of course I do,' said Rose, slipping her arm around Mariette's waist. 'You are nineteen now, quite old enough to be shown off, and I want to see if you remember all the dances I've taught you.'

'You look an absolute picture!' Noah exclaimed, when Mariette came into the sitting room with Rose an hour later.

Mariette blushed. She adored the cream lace dress; it had a silky underdress with shoestring straps and a low neckline, but the overdress had elbow-length sleeves and a higher neck, which resulted in a peek-a-boo effect with enough flesh showing through for glamour, but not enough to look common. The skirt was cut on the cross, so it clung to her hips and then flared out in handkerchief points that reached to mid-calf.

'Perfect!' Lisette clapped her hands in approval. 'I always envied Belle having Mog to make her clothes; she is such a marvellous dressmaker.' She took the new fluffy stole from Mariette's hands and arranged it around her shoulders. 'So chic and beautiful.'

'You don't think I ought to have put my hair up?' Mariette asked. She had wanted to put it into a roll – a popular style amongst Rose's friends – but her hair was too curly to stay in place, so she'd clipped it up on either side of her face with two little slides.

'It would be criminal to hide that pretty hair,' Noah said stoutly. 'In my opinion, all women should have flowing locks until they are at least thirty.'

Lisette laughed. 'He would still have me wearing mine loose and grey, if he had his way. But he is right about you, Mari, your hair is too pretty to put up.'

'And you look beautiful too,' Noah said to Rose. 'I always like you in that dress.'

Rose was wearing a dropped-waist pale pink crêpe de Chine dress with panels of slightly darker pink embroidery.

Mariette thought it a little old-fashioned, but it suited Rose as she was rather flat-chested. Her satin shoes had been dyed to match her dress, and she had a pink flower in her hair.

The doorbell rang.

'That will be Peter,' Rose said. 'Come on, Mari, it's time for dancing.'

'Have a lovely evening,' Lisette said. 'But remember, not too late coming home.'

Mariette had heard Rose talk about Soho a great deal; her eyes lit up when she mentioned it. She said it was where all the fun people went for a daring night out, and the Bag O'Nails, where they were to celebrate Mariette's birthday, was right at the centre of it.

The club was dark and smoky, and full to capacity. A five-piece band of black musicians were playing jazz, that wild music she'd heard before in Curaçao. As they squeezed through to a table reserved for them, Mariette could see by all the shining, rapt faces around her that she wasn't alone in liking the music.

The dance floor was packed with energetic dancers, and it was a startlingly different scene to anything she'd imagined. Up until now, all the English people she'd met seemed very sedate, and so she expected people to be waltzing, or doing the quickstep, not throwing each other around as they were doing here. But the music made her want to lose all her inhibitions and dance like that too.

Gerald was waiting for them at the table. As he got up to be introduced to her by Peter, she knew immediately that he would never be able to make her heart race, however 'suitable' he might be as a boyfriend.

He was tall, slender and wore his dinner jacket with the confidence of a man born to it. He was, in his own way, attractive, with light brown well-cut hair, puppy-dog brown eyes and a bright smile. But the hand that shook hers was too smooth and soft, and his teeth were yellow and crooked.

Yet Gerald looked at her as if he'd just been offered a wonderful and unexpected gift, and Mariette assumed by this that he'd got the idea that all girls from New Zealand were bound to be as plain as a pikestaff.

A bottle of champagne was already chilling in an ice bucket on their table. Gerald filled their glasses and offered up a birthday toast to Mariette. 'I'm told New Zealand is a very beautiful country,' he said, smiling at her. 'But I wasn't told the girls there were beautiful too.'

Mariette had never had much opportunity to drink alcohol. On special occasions, since the age of around fourteen, her father would pour her a glass of wine, but he always topped it up with water. She'd had a few sneaky sips of brandy or whisky at friends' houses, when their parents were out, but although she liked the idea of drinking, she'd never liked the taste. But now she found she did like the taste of champagne, and the loosening-up effect it had on her.

'Mother will never forgive me, if I take you home drunk,' Rose said in warning. 'So drink it slowly, and not too much.'

Mariette had to admit that Gerald was a perfect gentleman. And he was fun too, laughing readily, and all too willing to dance with her.

The music was too loud to have a conversation, and she didn't want to talk anyway – not when she could dance and get swept away by the music. By the time the tempo slowed, she was feeling distinctly woozy from the drink, and it was lovely to be held in Gerald's arms during the slower dances.

'May I take you out again?' he asked. 'We could go to the theatre, or have dinner.'

'That would be lovely,' she said, leaning into his shoulder. 'I'd like that very much.'

Then suddenly Rose said it was time to go. The last thing Mariette remembered thinking, as they left the club, was that if this was a taste of nightlife in London, she was never going back home.

11

As March turned into April, Mariette noticed that there was a great deal about the Spanish Civil War in the newspapers, but far less about a war with Germany. When people talked about the possibility, it was spoken of in such a light-hearted manner that it was hard to take the threat seriously. Even so, gas masks had been handed out to schoolchildren back in January, and each day there were more sandbags appearing in front of public buildings. People were told to stick tape to their windows in a criss-cross pattern, to avoid flying glass in the event of an air raid, and trenches were being dug in many parks to provide air-raid shelters.

But there was still no letter from Morgan.

Mariette veered from thinking it just took a long time for a letter written at sea to get to England, to being convinced he'd forgotten her the moment she left the ship. But letters from home reached her within eight weeks, and she asked herself why he would say he loved her and ask her to wait for him, if he hadn't meant it.

She had begun her secretarial course at Marshalls Secretarial College for Young Ladies, at Swiss Cottage, at the end of March, which was a distraction from thinking about Morgan. On her first day at college, there had been a lot of talk about Hitler invading Austria. And almost every evening, when Mariette arrived home, Noah was either talking to people on the phone or on his way out to meet people to discuss what this might lead to.

At the end of April, Noah said that he wanted to go to

Germany, to try to gauge the mood of the people there for himself. He said he'd been blinkered when he thought that war could be averted, and he now believed it was inevitable.

He left for Germany a week later, but when Belle and Etienne telephoned one evening during that time, she didn't tell them where Noah had gone, or his opinion about the likelihood of war. As her parents could only ever talk for three minutes, because of the cost, Mariette filled the time with tales of what she'd seen or done, and asked about her brothers and Mog, anything rather than give her father an opportunity to ask leading questions. She knew if he found out Noah's opinion had changed, he'd insist she book a passage on the next boat home, and that wasn't what she wanted.

She missed her family more than she had expected to, but she loved being in England far more. She felt free here, people weren't watching her every mood or judging her. Rose had become like an elder sister and friend rolled into one. Some evenings, she would put her latest record on the gramophone up in her bedroom, and she'd teach Mariette to dance. Other times, they went to the pictures or out roller skating. Rose was a bit bossy, and an awful snob sometimes, but that amused Mariette more than it offended her.

There were lots of evenings too when Rose went out without Mariette, to meet her friends alone. But that was fine with Mariette; there was the wireless to listen to, Lisette to talk to in French, and books to read.

She fitted in well at Marshalls Secretarial College too. None of the other girls had ever met someone from New Zealand before, and everyone wanted to be her friend. Shorthand seemed terribly difficult, but she really liked typing and was already one of the quickest in the class. She loved talking to the other girls in the lunch break; none of them were as narrow-minded and naive as the girls back home. She listened to them talking about the places they'd been, about their families and the young men they walked out with, and she felt she was learning more in a week than she would learn in a year in Russell.

But it was London that she had lost her heart to, and she didn't want to leave. The city was beautiful and exciting, maybe a little dangerous, and she felt she belonged here.

Morgan was another reason why she didn't want to leave. Just the thought of his lovemaking made her shiver and bubble, and she had to trust that he would write, and eventually come back to her. If she had to go home now, she would always wonder if he was truly 'the One'.

Getting a typing and shorthand diploma would help her case to stay in England. Her parents would be proud of her. And if she found a job she loved, she didn't think they'd insist on her returning home.

The night Noah returned from his ten-day trip to Germany was one Mariette felt she would never forget, because it brought home to her the reason why war was inevitable.

His expression had been grave enough to give them some inkling of his concerns. But the way he hugged each of them was evidence that he was afraid.

'I didn't like the look of things over there at all,' he said over dinner. 'Everyone seems to be in thrall to Hitler. While it's true that he has brought Germany out of the Depression and created full employment again, he's won his power by destroying or imprisoning anyone who opposes his ideals and methods.'

'So you think there really will be a war?' Lisette asked, her face stricken.

'I have no doubt any longer.' Noah shook his head sadly. 'Chamberlain may be intent on appeasement, but Hitler's

Nazi party is all powerful, they will sweep away any opposition. They have Austria now, and Czechoslovakia – and who knows where else? They are victimizing Jews too. I spoke to a group on their way to Hamburg, hoping to get a passage to America. They were born in Germany, fought for their country in 1914, and yet they told me they would fear for their lives if they stayed.'

'But why would Hitler do that?' Mariette asked.

Noah sighed. 'Hitler and his Nazi party appear to see the Jews as the worm in the apple. They blame them for the terrible inflation that began in 1929, and for just about everything else. In Berlin, I saw some old Jewish men being forced to get down on their knees and scrub the street. I couldn't believe what I saw.'

'That's horrible, Daddy,' Rose gasped. 'Couldn't you stop it?'

Noah looked at her and sighed. 'How could I, when people all around me were laughing and jeering at those poor old men? I would have been lynched. I saw a rally where Hitler spoke to a vast crowd, thousands of people. I couldn't understand much of what he said, but I saw a terrible fervour in the eyes of all his followers. They see him almost as a god, a leader who is going to give them back everything that was taken away from them in 1918.'

'Don't let's speak of this any more tonight,' Lisette begged him. 'I find it frightening.'

A few days after Noah's return from Germany, Mariette got her first letter from Morgan, posted in New Zealand. She was so excited, she thought her heart would burst. But as she read it, her heart sank because she could hardly believe it was Morgan who had written it. It was so badly scribbled – childish printing, terrible spelling, no punctuation – and there were no references to anything they'd talked about or shared when they were together.

He did say he loved her and couldn't wait to see her again. He said too that his ship was undergoing some repairs, but he didn't say how long this was going to take, not even when he expected to return. As he hadn't dated the letter, and the postmark was too blurred to read the date, for all she knew he could already be back in England by now.

She spent the next two or three days brooding on it and realized Morgan had obviously received little or no education. He had been vague about his upbringing and, apart from mentioning living in the East End for a time, he'd told her little else. But he was bright and articulate, so how could he write so badly?

Maybe being able to write a good letter wasn't the be all and end all, but Mariette had been brought up to value the written word, and she felt very uncomfortable knowing that Morgan didn't have such basic skills.

By the beginning of May, Mariette was doing so well at secretarial college that she was now the fastest typist in her class. Although she still had a way to go to be up to the eighty words a minute required to get her certificate, and she was still slow at shorthand, her teacher said she was nearly there.

Just a few days later, while Mariette was still in a rosy glow about her teacher's encouraging comments, and imagining a bright future for herself, a letter came from Morgan. She hadn't expected to hear from him again so soon, and it threw her into a tailspin.

He was in London, staying in Whitechapel, and he asked if she would meet him on Saturday afternoon in Trafalgar Square.

While her heart leapt involuntarily at the thought of seeing him again, she wasn't sure it was such a good idea to meet him. It would be easy enough getting out on a Saturday afternoon – she could say she was going shopping with a friend from college and then going on to the cinema – but she didn't want to deceive Noah and Lisette.

She'd discovered life was far easier with approval, and she was happy going to college and making friends with girls who were as well behaved as Rose. Her night out in Soho had shown her that she could have a wonderful time without being sneaky, or being expected to have sex.

Meeting Morgan would involve both things.

Just the previous day, Rose had been talking about one of her friends who had fallen for a man who was, as she put it, 'from the wrong side of the tracks'.

'I can see a certain romance in it,' she'd said thoughtfully. 'But she isn't going to like living in a couple of rooms in a rough area. I like my comfort too much to be happy in squalor, even if I did adore the man.'

Rose might be a bit of a snob, but she had a point. Mariette had grown used to the luxury of her godfather's home, and she knew this was how she wanted to live for ever. She was fairly certain Morgan would never be able to offer her that.

Was it enough to have a man who made her pulse race? Wouldn't it be better to write back to Morgan and offer up some excuse, then try to forget him?

And yet, on Saturday afternoon, Mariette was in Trafalgar Square in her prettiest floral dress and a white hat. It was a beautiful day, and the small inner voice that urged her to be sensible and to think of her future had been overcome by her desire to be in Morgan's arms again.

She was watching a woman feeding the pigeons, with the birds perched on her shoulders, arms and even her head, when Morgan came up behind her and put one hand on her shoulder, making her jump.

'Hello, beautiful,' he said. 'Sorry to startle you.'

One look at him and her knees felt they would buckle. She thought she might have imagined how handsome he was. But here he was, in bright sunshine, and he looked even better than she remembered. He wore a white open-necked shirt, grey flannels and a tweed jacket; his dark eyes were just as twinkly, the cleft in his chin was adorable, and his bronzed face was almost startling after being surrounded by pale Londoners.

'It's good to see you again,' she said, suddenly feeling shy. 'How long before you go back to the ship?'

'I'm not going back, I'm joining the army. I've got my medical on Monday.'

He didn't give her a chance to ask any further questions because he swept her into his arms to kiss her. She found then that her feelings for him hadn't changed; her heart pounded, tingles ran down her spine and she wanted him.

'Let's go to St James's Park?' he suggested, when he finally let her go. 'A band plays on Saturdays.'

The warm sun had brought out hundreds of people, courting couples walking hand in hand, whole families, many of them picnicking on the grass, and elderly people taking a stroll.

The deckchairs were out in rows in front of the band-stand, most of them already occupied by people waiting for the band to arrive. People with children were feeding the ducks on the lake.

Morgan put his jacket down on the grass for them to sit on. He explained why he thought it was better to enlist now, rather than waiting to be called up.

'This way, I get to choose what I do. I've asked for a transport division or ambulances. If I stayed on the ship till war was declared, I'd have just been pushed down into the engine room or something. They certainly won't be taking passengers anywhere. And you, Mari, if you want to get back to New Zealand, you should go now while you still can.'

'I don't want to go home,' she admitted. 'I'm just hoping my father won't order me back.' She went on to tell him about the secretarial course she was doing, and about her life with her aunt and uncle. 'I miss my family, but there's nothing in Russell for me and I'd like to do something to help out here. My mum drove an ambulance in France in the last war; I couldn't do that, but there must be something I could do.'

'As you speak French you could apply for a job with the government, they might need bilingual secretaries,' he said, and then went on to tell her about some of the passengers on the ship and their reasons for wanting to come back despite the threat of war. 'People never know how patriotic they are till they feel their country is threatened. One man, well into his sixties, told me he didn't feel he could stay in New Zealand while younger members of his family here would be facing hardships and danger. I thought that was a bit mad, like putting your head in the lion's mouth, but then I want to do my bit too.'

The clarity and passion in that little speech reminded her of her concerns about his badly written letter. She worked the conversation around to asking him where he went to school.

'Is this about the bad letters?' he looked at her, shame-faced. 'I wanted to get someone else to write to you. But I couldn't keep that up, and I'd have had to own up sometime. I bet you think I'm a right numbskull?'

'No, because I know you aren't. But I was a bit shocked,' she admitted. 'I knew there had to be a good reason for it:

perhaps you didn't get much schooling. So tell me now, and then we can forget about it.'

He hesitated, eyes cast down. 'My folks were gypsies,' he eventually blurted out. 'They were always on the move. I told you I spent some time in the East End, and that's where I started school. I got as far as learning to read and then we were off somewhere else. I never got more than six months in any one place. All gypsies live that way, and my folks didn't think it was necessary for me or my brothers to have a proper schooling.'

Mariette had never even seen a gypsy. All she knew about their lifestyle was from books, which made it look very romantic. 'Did you live in a caravan?'

'Yes. Well, at least when Dad worked the fairgrounds or circus. Mum would be running a sideshow too. But in the winter we'd get a couple of rooms somewhere. The only time we stayed put for more than a few months was in the East End because Dad could get casual work in the docks. But they didn't like that way of life, so it was back on the road.'

'Are they still alive?'

'No, they died in a road accident a few years back. Dad was driving in a convoy of circus trucks, up on the coast road in the north-east of England, and there was a terrible storm; the lead truck hit someone coming the other way and they all piled into one another. Dad's truck and the one behind him teetered over the edge and were smashed to pieces on the rocks below. Altogether, seven people died that night and a few more were injured.'

'How awful,' Mariette gasped.

'Yup, it was terrible. But I didn't even know about it until after their funeral because I was at sea. The last time I'd seen my folks was over a year before, and I'd had a row with Dad about Mum. I tried to tell him that she wanted a permanent home but, as always, he flew into a rage. He was a vicious bully who didn't care about anyone else's feelings, so he smashed me in the face and told me to bugger off. I told him then he would never see me again.'

She could tell by the way he almost spat this information out that he was still hurting about it. 'I'm so sorry,' she said.

He gave her a glum smirk. 'Don't be – well, not for my dad, he had it coming to him, and worse – it's Mum I feel bad about, she had a miserable life with him. If she hadn't been with him that night, if she'd been left a widow instead, I could've found her a little place and looked after her. She deserved better.'

'What about your brothers?'

'The two elder ones are just like Dad,' he sighed. 'I haven't kept in touch with them. My younger brother, Caleb, is more like me, and I would see him if I knew where he was. But I don't, so that's it really.'

'Did you join the Merchant Navy so you could have a different life?'

He reached out and ruffled her hair. 'Yes, that was the plan, but I found it was the same life, only on water instead of land. So I guess I haven't lost the gypsy in me, or got an education either.'

'But you must've learned a lot?'

He shrugged. 'About people perhaps, and geography. But I still can't spell, or write a good letter.'

'You can learn those things, if you read,' she said. 'Do you read?'

'I can read a kids' book OK, but that's about it.'

They stayed in the park until about five, when it became chilly, then went to the Lyons' Corner House in the Strand for some tea.

It was packed with people, and very noisy, but they managed to get a table in a corner where they could at least hear one another speak. At first, Morgan continued to talk about the ship and the places he'd seen, but then he suddenly changed tack.

'Will you come back to where I'm staying?' he asked.

There was something in his eyes – it was almost as if he was challenging her – and it made her feel wary.

'I'm not so sure that's a good idea,' she said.

'Why not?'

She hesitated. How could she admit she didn't want to be taken to some seedy room in the East End?

'I thought you loved me,' he said. 'You've changed your mind, now you know I'm an ignorant gypo, have you?'

'Don't be like that.' She whispered it, because he'd raised his voice and the people on the next table were looking round. 'It isn't that at all.'

'Well, prove it then, and come with me.' He got up, put some money down on the table for the bill and held out his hand for hers.

As they swept down the stairs and out into the street, Mariette felt very nervous. 'Don't be fierce like this, it's scary,' she said.

He caught hold of her two forearms and put his face up close to hers. 'I'll tell you what's really scary. It's finding a girl who says she loves me, and I start to think I can have a better life with her, but the minute I tell the truth about where I'm from and why I don't read and write so well, she gets chilly on me.'

'That isn't why,' she protested. 'I'm just not sure about going back to where you're staying.'

'Why not?'

'It's too soon. You might think it's all fine because of how we were on the ship, but as lovely as that was, it was very risky, and I daren't take that risk again now.'

He shook his head in disbelief. 'I didn't think you had all the prejudices other people carry around with them. I've met them all in my travels – Jews, coloured people, Chinese, Indians, even Irish are all looked down on – but gypsies are almost always top of the list of undesirables. Now I find you are the same.'

'I'm not prejudiced about you being a gypsy,' she retorted indignantly. 'That's a ridiculous thing to say. What I don't like is feeling that I'm being pushed into a corner. I don't want to find myself pregnant when I'm not married, especially with a war about to start.'

'I'd be careful,' he said.

Mariette shook her head in despair. 'If you keep on like this, I just might work up a prejudice against you. But if you must know, it isn't only about being afraid of having a baby. I just don't want to go to a nasty, squalid place in Whitechapel and feel bad about it afterwards.'

He let go of her forearms and took a step back from her, looking a little confused. 'Well, where do you want to go then?'

She felt he might be hoping she'd say a hotel, but she wasn't going to.

'My mother used to live somewhere near here. In a place called Seven Dials. Could we go there? I'd really like to see it. She lived in a pub called the Ram's Head.'

He shrugged his shoulders and looked none too enthusiastic. 'If that's what you really want. It's almost as squalid around there as in Whitechapel, but it's close by.'

As they walked along the Strand, a wide, grand road lined with lovely shops, it seemed as if Morgan had snapped back into how he was before his outburst. He pointed out the Savoy Hotel, telling her it was the first hotel in London to have electric light, and said he'd worked in their kitchens for a few weeks before he joined the Merchant Navy.

Mariette was still a bit wary of him, anxious to get things back to the way they'd been earlier in the afternoon, so she asked him questions about joining up and how soon it would be before he was in uniform.

'I think once you've passed the medical, it's off to a training camp immediately,' he grinned. 'They won't want to give me any time for second thoughts. My guess is that by Tuesday or Wednesday, I'll be doing square bashing.'

Once they'd turned off the Strand towards Covent Garden Market, the streets were markedly narrower and dingier, and there were very few people around.

'Saturday evening and Sunday are the only times when it's quiet around here,' Morgan said. 'During the week, it's bustling almost around the clock as the fruit, vegetable and flower traders in the market open up their stalls for business in the early hours of the morning. By nine in the morning, when the office workers arrive, the market folk have done almost a whole day's work.'

Mariette was rather shocked to see a group of shabbily dressed women sifting through the rubbish left behind by the stall holders, salvaging fruit and vegetables which weren't entirely rotten.

'Our ma used to send us up to do that on a Saturday evening,' Morgan said. 'Down in Whitechapel, the pickings weren't as good as here. She used to make a stew with the vegetables and a bit of scrag end of lamb. She'd make it last for about three days.'

Mariette shuddered at the thought of that, then swiftly turned her attention to the many very well-dressed people getting out of cabs amongst all the debris of the market. 'What are those people here for?' she asked.

'The theatres,' Morgan said. 'It might look rough around here now, before it's all been swept clean, but along with some of the best theatres there are some very good restaurants. It's the only place you can get a drink in the early hours of the morning too, as they open up for the market men. You often see toffs in there, having a couple more drinks before staggering home.'

Once they were beyond the market, the surroundings became very squalid. There were narrow, dirty little lanes that looked like the places Charles Dickens described in his books. Mog had often talked about her time around here, but Mariette had always imagined it to be more colourful and quaint; she hadn't expected the soot-blackened buildings, filthy windows and the stink of mould and refuse.

'There you are, the Ram's Head,' Morgan said, pointing out a public house on the other side of what appeared to be one of the slightly better streets in the neighbourhood. 'Shall we go in and have a drink?'

Mariette didn't reply immediately because she was suddenly remembering Mog's story about how she came to be living there. The house where she had been housekeeper to Annie, Belle's mother, had been burned to the ground. They were rescued by Garth Franklin and Jimmy Reilly and taken to live with them at this pub. A few years later, when Belle returned from Paris, she married Jimmy and Mog married Garth before moving away to the other side of London.

The Ram's Head was what she'd come to recognize as a traditional old English pub. It had bow windows, with panes of bottle glass, and a low door that meant tall people had to stoop to get in, but it was desperately in need of some paint and general care.

Mog had described the upstairs of the pub as being like a 'midden' when she first moved in. If the ragged curtains at the upstairs windows were anything to go by, it was still a slum.

'Well, shall we go in? Or not?' Morgan said.

She really didn't want to, but was afraid that admitting her feelings might make Morgan think she was a snob. 'Of course we'll go in,' she replied, trying very hard to look eager. 'I can't wait to write home and tell them I've been to see it.'

It was still too early in the evening for the pub to be very busy – there were only about twenty or so people in, mostly men still in their working clothes – and to Mariette's relief it was surprisingly well kept. The stone floor was scrubbed, the tables were polished and the mirrors behind the bar gleamed. She assumed the portly man behind the bar, wearing a striped waistcoat and sporting a handlebar moustache, was the land-lord, and the older of the two barmaids must be his wife. The younger one was a bottle blonde, wearing a low-cut red dress with lipstick to match. She was very flirtatious, flutter-ing her eyelashes and tossing her hair as she poured pints.

Morgan ordered a pint for himself and a port and lemon for Mariette, and they sat down near the fireplace.

She had told Morgan a little about her mother and Mog whilst on the ship. Now she reminded him that they had been married to uncle and nephew, and that both men died of Spanish flu right at the end of the last war.

'Mog said people were a bit scared of Garth when he owned this place,' she added. 'It's very strange to know this was the pub she cleaned, and where she fell in love with her husband.'

'A lot of villains used to hang around here back then,' Morgan said. 'And there were dozens of brothels in the area too. Your Garth would've needed to be tough to keep the punters in line. Didn't you say he sold the pub and moved away to Blackheath?'

Mariette nodded.

'We used to go with the fair to Blackheath for the August bank holiday every year,' he said with a smile. 'Mum used to love it there: she'd take us to Greenwich Park to see the deer and we'd watch the rich people's kids sailing toy boats on the pond. I only ever remember it being warm and sunny there.'

'Mum and Mog had to learn to be "ladies" there; Mum's customers in her hat shop were all snooty. They don't say too much about it because Jimmy lost an arm and a leg in the war, and I think everything must have turned sour for them.'

'They were brave to emigrate to New Zealand after their husbands died,' Morgan said admiringly. 'So where did your mother meet your father?'

'It was in Paris, before the war. Noah was there too, and they all became good friends, but Mum came back here and married Jimmy. Years later, through Noah, Dad found out what had happened and where she was, and he came out to New Zealand to find her. And they lived happily ever after.'

Morgan smiled. 'Sounds very romantic. My poor mum had no choice of who she married, her family arranged it. I never knew the half of what she'd had to put up with until I was about fourteen.'

They stayed in the Ram's Head for a couple of hours talking, but Morgan seemed different from the man he'd been on the ship. Every time she mentioned something she'd done with Rose, or somewhere she'd visited with the family, he came up with something about the poverty and deprivation in his childhood.

It was as if he was jealous of her, but that seemed ridiculous. Surely any man who claimed to love her would be glad she was being so well looked after in London?

When the bar became crowded later, they left and walked around the West End. Morgan showed her the Windmill

Theatre, with its daring showgirl dancers, Tin Pan Alley, where musicians went to buy sheet music, and so many theatres in which famous actors and actresses were starring. He was his old self again, interesting and fun to be with.

He stopped to kiss her so many times in dark little alleys, pressing himself up hard against her in a way she found thrilling, but also a bit frightening, because she was afraid he might try to drag her off somewhere.

And yet, at ten o'clock, when she said she ought to go home, he seemed absolutely fine about it.

'We'll walk down to Green Park station,' he said. 'You can catch the tube home to St John's Wood from there, and I can go to Bethnal Green. Unless you want me to come the whole way with you?'

She was touched that he was prepared to do that, but said she was fine to go home alone. The last thing she wanted was Noah or Lisette spotting her with him before she'd had a chance to admit where she'd really been today.

'Just a few more kisses,' Morgan said as they got to Green Park, and he drew her into the park instead of the tube station.

Holding her hand, he led her over to the bushes at the side of the Ritz Hotel. The dining room in the hotel was lit by huge chandeliers. There were big mirrors on the walls, crystal glasses and silver on the tables, and the whole place seemed to shine and twinkle.

'Look at all those toffs,' Morgan said, indicating the diners in evening dress. 'One of these days, Mari, we'll stay there. I bet the bedrooms are out of this world.'

They stood with their arms around each other's waists, looking at the people in the dining room for a few moments. The women wore elegant evening dresses and beautiful jewellery, and the men looked distinguished in their dinner jackets and bow ties.

'You'll look very handsome in a dinner jacket,' she said. 'But I think to eat and sleep in there would take more money than we're ever likely to have.'

Morgan turned to kiss her, gathering her into his arms. As he kissed her, he moved her closer to a huge tree by the hotel's dining-room windows. His kisses were thrilling, but all at once Mariette had a creepy feeling. He had manoeuvred her out of sight of anyone walking in the park, but they were in full view of anyone looking out of the hotel windows.

No one was looking out – they were too intent on conversation and enjoying their dinner – but, all the same, Mariette felt it was Morgan's way of making a statement. He might not be able to afford to eat or stay in the Ritz, but he could have his way with a girl right outside the window.

She tried to disengage herself from his lips so she could say she wanted to move away, but he held her all the tighter. His hand was under her dress, groping into her knickers, and all at once she realized that he really did intend to have his way with her, whether she was willing or not.

Shocked, she managed to get her hands on his shoulders and push him away enough to stop the kiss. 'I must go now, Morgan,' she said, hoping he would say something which would prove she'd been wrong about his intentions.

'Not yet, I'm going to fuck you first.'

Appalled that he would use that ugly word, she tried to push him away more forcefully. 'I don't want this, it's not right,' she said.

'You thought it was just fine on the ship, and it's the very same cock,' he said, putting his hand down to his fly and unbuttoning it.

An image of the humiliation she'd suffered with Sam came

155

into her mind. 'I said no,' she yelled out, pushing him away with as much force as she could muster. 'Stop it.'

'You don't mean that. You love it,' he said, pushing her back hard against the tree and using the weight of his body to hold her there.

She saw red. He was not going to treat her like this. She moved her head, as if to kiss him, and as his lips came close to hers she opened her mouth and bit down hard on his lip. At the same time, she brought her knee up swiftly to his groin.

He reeled back, staggering. She'd drawn blood on his lips.

'How can you be like this!' she snarled at him. 'You call that love?'

She ran for it then. She heard him call out that he was sorry, but she didn't stop. The tube entrance was just outside the gates, and she ran down the steps into the station, rushing to buy a ticket. She was just going through the barrier to the escalator, biting back tears, when she heard him call out.

'Wait, Mariette!'

She glanced round to see him coming down the steps, two at a time, into the station. 'I didn't mean it, let me explain!' he yelled out.

Tossing her head in defiance, she walked on swiftly to the escalator.

Yet when he didn't come running down after her, contrite and loving, prepared to take her home without any further funny business, tears welled up in her eyes. What a fool she'd been to think he loved her. All he wanted was some furtive sex before joining up, and that was so very humiliating.

Lisette and Noah were in the kitchen when Mariette opened the front door. Lisette called out to say she was just making some cocoa. All Mariette wanted to do was go up to her room and sob out her disappointment at Morgan's behaviour. But she knew Lisette and Noah would find it odd, if she didn't join them.

As she'd expected, Lisette asked what she'd done and if she'd had a good time.

'I told you a fib,' Mariette admitted. 'I didn't go out with a girlfriend. I met Morgan from the ship.' She looked at Noah and explained that Morgan had been the steward who looked after her in the sickbay when she had an allergic reaction.

'Why did you lie about it?' Noah asked. He didn't sound angry, just puzzled.

'I thought you wouldn't approve,' she said, hanging her head. 'But he's left the ship now and is enlisting in the army.'

'Did you like him as much today as you did on the ship?' Lisette asked. She was looking hard at Mariette, as if she suspected something.

'No, not really.' Mariette shook her head. 'He's handsome, good company, but he's not for me.'

'A pretty girl of your age should have lots of admirers, and not take any of them too seriously,' Noah said with a broad smile. 'Speaking of admirers, Gerald telephoned this evening. He wants to take you to the theatre next week, and he's going to ring again tomorrow.'

'Lovely,' she said weakly. 'That will be nice.'

The way she felt now, she didn't think she would ever trust another man. But she wasn't going to say anything that would make Lisette question her further about Morgan.

Later that night, while Mariette was sitting at her dressing table and giving her hair the hundred brush strokes she'd been brought up to believe were necessary for shiny hair, Morgan was slumped on the front doorstep of the rooming house in Whitechapel.

He hadn't been able to go after Mariette because he had to queue for a ticket, and by the time he'd gone through the barrier she was already on the train going home. He'd done it all wrong; he might have known that a few months in London with relatives that were toffs would change her. What on earth possessed him to paw at her like a bloody savage?

The truth was that he knew, just from the way she spoke about her life in London, she was never going to settle for someone like him. He saw the way she looked at those people dining at the Ritz, her eyes shining like she'd just seen God. It hurt because, on the ship, she'd looked at him the same way. It wasn't much of an excuse to come up with for the way he'd tried to force himself on her, but it was the only one he could offer. Maybe he'd thought that, if he could arouse her again, that look would come back into her eyes for him.

He rested his elbows on his knees and held his head in his hands. The street was still as noisy now, at nearly midnight, as it was during the day. Drunks were staggering along, shouting to anyone they passed, and further along the pavement a whole family were sitting out drinking; a piano jangled from somewhere near, some youths were play-fighting down under the street light on the corner, and every now and then someone would stick their head out of a window and shout for someone.

Morgan had always loved this part of London – he understood the people – but how could he ever have thought Mariette would like it too?

All she'd see was the squalor, ignorance, overcrowding and deprivation. She would never see the spirit of the residents, laugh at their rich sense of humour, or want to make friends with anyone here.

It was bad enough to know that Mariette had her heart set on a way of life he could never give her. But it was far worse to think that her last memory of him would be of how he had tried to force himself upon her.

He was so ashamed.

I 2

As Mariette walked back from her final day at college in early July, carrying her diploma, she felt very dejected. She had passed her final exams with distinction, but the elation of her achievement was deflated by knowing she would have to go home to New Zealand now.

War was imminent. Noah had worn a permanently worried expression for weeks. She'd recently seen him and Lisette having whispered conversations, which stopped when she came into the room, and she knew they were talking about getting her a passage home. It was futile to beg them to let her stay as her parents were insisting she must return home; they had already met her halfway by allowing her to finish the secretarial course and get her diploma. But now she had it, she would have to go.

She really didn't want to leave. She loved everything about England, and although all the accelerated preparations for war were scary – barrage balloons appearing up in the sky, more trenches being dug in the parks, sandbags being stockpiled outside buildings, windows being taped up and more bomb shelters being built – she still wanted to stay.

It didn't help that the weather was hot and sunny, and Rose and her friends were all talking about summer balls, picnics and open-air concerts. There was an atmosphere of 'do it now, for tomorrow may be too late' in the air; men of twenty and twenty-one had already been called up, and London was full of men in uniform.

She tried to think about the positive aspects of going home. But apart from seeing her family, and swimming and sailing, nothing else sprang to mind. To be stuck on the other side of the world, twiddling her thumbs while every able-bodied man went off to fight, was not a pleasing prospect.

She had felt so low immediately after the incident with Morgan that she might have welcomed going home then, but she'd put that behind her. He did write to apologize, but the letter was brief and inarticulate, giving her no real idea of his reasons, that all it did was confirm how unsuitable he was for her.

That didn't stop her thinking about him, though, and wondering why he had suddenly behaved as he did. She wished she could sit and talk to him face to face, and try to find out.

But, meanwhile, she had Gerald to take her out. She might not feel anything but friendship towards him, but he was fun, kind and he was too much of a gentleman to pressure her into more than a goodnight kiss.

Mariette walked round the side of the house to go in through the kitchen, then stopped short in astonishment at the sight in front of her. A long table had been set up for a dinner party on the lawn. It was laid beautifully, with flowers and dozens of candles. All at once it dawned on her that it was for her, a surprise leaving party, and this was what Noah and Lisette had been whispering about recently.

She might not want to go home, but it was very kind of Noah and Lisette to send her off in style.

Lisette came out of the kitchen, stopped short and then laughed at Mariette's stunned expression. 'Yes, it is for you, we wanted to celebrate you passing your exams. I have been praying for warm weather for weeks so we could have it in the garden, and my prayers have all been answered.'

'It looks so lovely.' Mariette's eyes began to well up; she was so touched that Lisette would pretend the party was for her exam results, rather than her leaving. 'Fancy you doing all this and keeping it secret!'

'It's been a pleasure.' Lisette came closer to Mariette and wiped her tears away with a corner of her apron. 'Let me see your diploma, we must put that up somewhere so everyone can see it.'

Mariette took it out of the envelope and handed it to Lisette.

'Passed with distinction!' Lisette exclaimed. 'Noah is going to be so proud of you. But off you go, and get ready now. You must look your best to greet all the guests. Rose is up there already.'

At six thirty, Mariette was ready, wearing her cream lace dress. Rose had pinned her hair up for her and fastened a couple of pink rosebuds amongst the curls.

'Papa wanted us down before the guests arrive so we can have some family moments on our own,' she said, giving Mariette's hair a few little tweaks. 'I do hope he isn't going to say this is a farewell party too, and that he's going to put you on a ship any minute. I really don't want you to go, Mari. I know that's selfish of me, when you want to see your family, but it's been so lovely having you here.'

'I don't want to go either,' Mariette admitted, touched that Rose felt that way. 'But it's what my parents want. So let's make the most of tonight as we may never get the chance again. '

Down in the drawing room Noah handed them both a glass of champagne, and they had a little toast to Mariette.

Then Lisette asked Rose to come and help her in the kitchen. Mariette sensed this was because Noah had something to say to her, and her heart sank.

'Lisette thinks I ought to wait till tomorrow to tell you this,' he said, looking very serious. 'But as I know all your friends will think this party is also a farewell dinner, I felt I had to tell you now.'

He paused, as if he didn't know how to say it. 'I have been a little blinkered,' he went on. 'I didn't think there would be any problem getting you home, but it seems almost all the ships going to New Zealand are now concentrating on carrying cargo, and the few remaining ones taking passengers are already fully booked. I am so sorry, my dear, but unless something turns up at the last minute, I think you will have to stay here.'

Mariette was unable to speak for the shock.

'I've tried pulling strings,' he said, clearly thinking her silence was due to distress. 'But it's been to no avail. I feel I have failed you and your parents. I am so very sorry.'

A bubble of glee burst inside her. She wanted to hug him, dance around the room with him, tell him it was her dream come true. But she resisted the temptation. It was more seemly to appear anxious and disappointed that she wouldn't see her family in the near future.

She put her hand on his arm. 'It's alright, Uncle Noah,' she assured him. 'No one could've known what was going to happen. You did your best. And anyway, as I have an English mother and a French father, maybe it is right that I should stay and make some contribution to the war effort.'

His frown vanished. 'That is both brave and noble, Mari. I must say that none of us wanted to lose you, we've all become so fond of you. But I'm looking into finding a house somewhere outside London, where you girls will all be safer in an air raid.'

'Don't let's talk about it any more tonight,' Mariette said. 'Auntie Lisette has gone to so much trouble, and we must show her how much we appreciate it.'

It was a wonderful party. Most of the two dozen or so guests were people Mariette had become friends with through Rose. They had all been very welcoming when she first arrived in England, including her in so many outings and parties, and they all said they were delighted she wasn't going home so they could have even more fun together. The food was superb, the wine flowed, and when darkness fell the dozens of candles and the strings of coloured lights in the bushes made the garden look enchanted.

Mariette found it a little odd that Jean-Philippe and his wife, Alice, weren't here. Surely they must have been invited to a family party? She sensed a bit of a mystery there; she had met them twice, and only fleetingly, but even in those brief moments she'd felt a strained atmosphere. Lisette did go on her own sometimes to see her son – just for lunch, mainly – but she never said anything about the meeting when she came home. Mariette had asked Rose about it, but she shrugged it off. 'Jean-Philippe is an odd fish,' was all she would say on the subject.

But Mariette's thoughts about Jean-Philippe were only passing ones. There were so many people here who she wanted to chat to, and she was soon busy making arrangements for future outings.

Rose brought out her gramophone and played some records later. But Mariette held herself back from much of the dancing and revelry because she wanted to convey to Noah and Lisette that she was a little shaken by what she'd been told earlier.

Mog had often claimed that Mariette was devious, but

she'd never quite grasped what Mog meant. But she knew now. Back home, she had never cared if her family were cross with her, but as soon as she'd realized England was where she wanted to stay, she'd gone out of her way to make her hosts love her so they wouldn't want to send her home.

She knew it was a bit devious to be helpful, appreciative, sunny natured and affectionate to suit her own ends. But then, it wasn't hard to be that way here because Noah, Lisette and Rose were such lovely, reasonable people who were intent on giving her a good time.

Maybe she did pile on a little extra admiration for Rose, to keep her happy, and she certainly never opposed any plans she made for them both. She went out of her way to spend time with Lisette too, something Rose didn't do, and she asked Noah endless questions about his writing, about English history, or anything else that he cared about.

What had begun as a plan to butter them up became unnecessary as she really did like them a great deal. She had found Noah to be a fascinating man, and Lisette had hidden depths that she wished she could delve into and discover her secrets. She would admit that, had she met Rose back home, she would have cut the girl down to size immediately – because she was opinionated, a snob and sometimes mean-spirited – but she had other qualities that more than made up for the irritating things, such as her patience in teaching Mariette to dance, her sense of fun, and the fact that she was so loyal. She never told tales, she didn't belittle Mariette in front of friends, and she was always supportive.

She was more ashamed of her deviousness with Gerald. She acted all breathless and happy to see him, pretending his kisses excited her to maintain his interest, because she liked being wined and dined and treated like a lady.

She could see him now, enjoying the party. He was chatting with Rose, Peter and a couple of other people, but he kept looking around longingly for her with his puppy-dog eyes. He was a considerate man, so he probably sensed she wanted a bit of time to herself and would wait for her to go over to him. She liked that about him – in fact, she liked a great deal about him – but as a friend, nothing more.

She'd become so good at playing the ideal guest that she found herself becoming the ideal daughter too. When she spoke to her parents on the telephone, she was always careful to say how much she missed them, her brothers and Mog. She took an interest in everything they were doing, knowing all this would convince them she had grown up and become a responsible person. She only told them news that smacked of culture or education, such as the plays she'd seen at the theatre, the ballets at Sadler's Wells, or her friendships with fellow students at college. She left out the parties and wilder entertainment.

A few weeks ago, while in Noah's study, she'd seen and sneakily read a partly written letter to her parents. He wrote with warmth and affection about how mature she'd become, how charming she was to their friends, and how helpful to Lisette. He had broken off at the point where he said how much they would all miss her when she went home, and she had wondered if he was considering pleading for her to stay.

If she could just rid herself of nostalgic thoughts about Morgan, she would claim to be the happiest girl in the world tonight. She didn't understand why he kept creeping back into her mind after the shocking way he'd behaved towards her.

But perhaps it was just as well he'd shown his true colours because living here in St John's Wood had given her a taste for the finer things in life, and he could never have matched it. Maybe that did make her mercenary, but she couldn't think of anything worse than living in a couple of shabby rooms and wearing the same dress day in and day out, not even if Morgan treated her like a queen.

'That's what I want,' she thought as she watched Noah and Lisette dancing cheek to cheek. It was obvious to everyone that theirs was a marriage made in heaven. Even when they had a little tiff about something, one of them would start to laugh, and suddenly it was all over and they would be hugging each other. Mariette couldn't imagine anything or anybody ever coming between them. Her parents were the same, although her mother was a lot less docile than Lisette.

She wondered if you knew when you'd met the right man, from the very first meeting. And if not, how long did you have to give it to be absolutely certain?

In the weeks that followed her graduation party, Mariette observed that people had become much more focused on what was important and what wasn't. Everyone kept talking about making the most of everything because they didn't know what was around the corner, the implication being that death could snatch them away at any time. It helped that the weather in July and August was beautiful, with long periods of hot sunshine. Noah said he'd never before seen so many people picnicking on Hampstead Heath and swimming in the ponds there.

People were remarkably calm about the prospect of war, but that could be because they weren't very well informed and still imagined it would be averted at the last moment.

Mariette was informed, thanks to Noah. He had been incensed, back in March, when Hitler sent his troops into Czechoslovakia. And when Germany and Italy agreed the Pact of Steel, in May, he'd said no one could possibly claim they hadn't got aggressive intentions.

It was his sense of duty, and the need to keep his finger on the pulse, as he put it, that prompted Noah to pack Lisette, Rose and Mariette off for a holiday in a cottage near Arundel at the start of August, while he stayed at home in London.

'You don't want me around, harping on about war,' he said to Lisette as he saw them into the car. 'You have a good time together, it might be the last chance you get for some years to enjoy a relaxed holiday.'

As Andrews drove the car out of the driveway, Mariette looked back at her godfather standing on the doorstep. She thought he looked suddenly older, and a little fearful.

'He is haunted by things he saw in the last war,' Lisette said, picking up on the same thought. 'He was so sure all those millions of brave young men, on both sides, had died to ensure lasting peace. Now he finds he was wrong, and that is hard for an idealist to come to terms with. He told me this morning he is going to find some kind of war work, and I'm hoping that will pull him round.'

Lisette's words jolted Mariette and made her think of her father. She hadn't ever really considered before what he went through in the last war. She had always known he had been a war hero and was awarded the Croix de Guerre, France's highest military honour. But was he feeling the same as Noah now, thinking that perhaps the sacrifices made by so many of his countrymen had all been for nothing? He was getting old and it must be hard for him to watch young men full of fire and patriotism enlisting, knowing that many of them would die.

Was he worrying about her too? Afraid that she might be hurt or killed? She had spoken to him on the telephone, just after Noah had explained why she couldn't go home, and he sounded calm, not even slightly emotional. But he had said something which she thought sounded very odd.

'War can bring out the best or the worst in us, Mari. True courage is when you can hold on to what is right, whatever the cost to yourself, even when it seems all hope has gone. I hope you will never find yourself in that situation. But if you do, remember what I told you.'

All gloomy thoughts of what war might bring to them and their families vanished when Lisette and the girls arrived at the quaint thatched cottage in Arundel. It was tiny, with just a living-room-cum-kitchen and two bedrooms. There was no bathroom, and the lavatory was out in the garden, but it was so pretty and had a view over fields to the river, so they didn't mind. Rose said it was like a doll's house, and she suggested they all take turns to cook and tidy up so that Lisette could have a real rest.

She grinned at Mariette. 'Of course, that means we'll only get a decent meal every three days, when it's Mama's turn. And expect salad from me, I can't do much else.'

It was good to see Lisette relaxing; at home, she was always busy with voluntary work, gardening and jobs around the house. Mariette had often wondered why she didn't get Mrs Andrews to do a little more – she was, after all, supposed to be the housekeeper.

'Isn't it odd that when you go away you enjoy the ordinary things so much more?' Rose said on the second morning, while they were eating breakfast at a little table just outside the kitchen door. 'I mean, we eat toast every day at home. But this toast, with this superb marmalade, tastes so much better in the open air. At home, I think it's a terrible chore going to the shop to buy some eggs or something. But the thought of wandering up the lane later to buy a few groceries fills me with delight.'

'You'd soon get bored, if you lived here all the time,' Lisette laughed. 'And speaking of going to the shop in the village, we ought to start buying up some sugar, tea, flour and such like. It will all be rationed as soon as the war starts.'

'Isn't hoarding food frightfully bad form?' Rose asked.

'Maybe. But I remember going without, and how awful it was, in the last war. I used to go over to Blackheath sometimes, when Belle was in France. Mog always seemed able to lay her hands on meat and cheese, I think Garth must have got it on the black market. I envied that so much. She always stuffed some little parcels in my bag before I went home. We had a day bottling fruit together too, and that's something we should do when we get back – in fact, we can probably buy a lot of plums to take home with us.'

'Mog still bottles fruit, makes jam and chutneys,' Mariette said, suddenly seeing an image of Mog stirring a huge saucepan on the stove with rows and rows of sparkling jam jars lined up on the kitchen table. 'We ought to grow vegetables in the garden, Auntie Lisette, and maybe get some chickens. That was what kept us going, when times were hard a few years back – that, and Dad going fishing. I know all about chickens, I could look after them.'

Lisette laughed at Mariette's earnest expression. 'I never expected to hear you suggest growing vegetables or keeping chickens,' she said. 'But you are right, that's exactly what we should do. We kept chickens, pigs and grew vegetables when I was a girl in France. Back then, I used to wish for a pretty garden with lots of flowers. When Noah bought the house we live in now, I was so excited that I could finally have my flower garden. Now you want me to dig it all up to grow things to eat?'

It was the first time Lisette had ever said anything about her childhood, and Mariette wanted to know more.

'You could keep some flower beds,' she said. 'But were your family poor?'

'Very poor,' Lisette said with a grimace. 'I was one of five children, and I can remember being hungry many times and having holes in the soles of my shoes. I used to dream of food – roast beef, pork and big fruit cakes. I wanted pretty dresses and dainty underwear, a warm coat and shoes that fitted properly. I ran off to Paris when I was only fourteen, believing all these things were waiting for me there. I soon found out that there is only one way to get them, and that is to work very hard.'

'Or marry a rich man,' Mariette said.

'Rich men don't marry poor little country girls with ragged clothes,' Lisette said sharply.

Mariette blushed, sensing she'd touched a raw nerve with her remark.

'You never say anything about your brothers and sister. Are they still alive?' Rose asked her mother.

'My sister died of pneumonia in 1911. My brothers may have died in the war. But if they survived, they would be in their late sixties and seventies now as I was the youngest. We fell out a very long time ago. They were mean-spirited people, I do not want to know them.'

Mariette was sure there was a great story behind the little that Lisette had revealed, and resolved to tackle her about it another time.

Meanwhile, it was the best kind of holiday. The weather was beautiful, and they went for many long walks exploring the countryside, caught the train to Littlehampton, or sat around in the garden reading. They bought Kilner jars, bottled gooseberries and plums, and made a large quantity of raspberry jam to take back to London. In the evenings, they played card games or just chatted.

As the end of August approached, it seemed that everyone in England was holding their breath, waiting for an announcement about the war on the wireless. As there was no wireless in the cottage, their elderly neighbours invited them in on Sunday, 3rd September, at eleven o'clock to hear Prime Minister Neville Chamberlain make his speech.

The day was hot and still. As they clustered around the wireless, somehow as soon as they heard the grave tone of Chamberlain's voice, they knew he had only bad news.

'This morning the British Ambassador in Berlin handed the German government a final note stating that, unless we heard from them by eleven o'clock that they were prepared at once to withdraw their troops from Poland, a state of war would exist between us.

'I have to tell you now that no such undertaking has been received, and that consequently this country is at war with Germany.'

Everything seemed to go into slow motion for Mariette as Chamberlain continued his speech. She watched a tear trickle down Lisette's cheek, saw the alarm on the faces of the old couple who, she already knew, had lost both their sons in the previous war. Rose just stared into space, as if she'd been turned to stone.

Mariette noticed there was a bee stuck on the lace curtains at the window. She wanted to go and help it get free, but it seemed wrong to do something so trivial at such a moment.

'Now may God bless you all,' Chamberlain finished up. 'May He defend the right. It is the evil things that we shall be fighting against – brute force, bad faith, injustice, oppression and persecution – and against them I am certain that the right will prevail.'

The old man was the first to speak. 'Well, war or not, I need to water my runner beans,' he said.

That broke the silence. Lisette got up and thanked the couple for allowing them to hear the broadcast. Then they went back to their cottage.

Without anyone saying a word, they all sensed that the holiday was now over. Lisette put the kettle on, and Mariette and Rose sat at the table waiting to be told what they must do.

'I should go to the telephone box and ring Noah,' Lisette said. 'I expect he's already told Andrews to come and get us. So, while I'm ringing him, you had better start packing.'

'How long will it be before bombs start dropping?' Rose asked anxiously.

Lisette moved closer to her daughter and caressed her cheek comfortingly. 'I don't know, darling, but I would assume Germany will attack France first. But, as you know, they began evacuating all the London children on Friday. And they've been urging us to take our gas masks everywhere for weeks now, so maybe the government are expecting bombs immediately.'

'Is it wise to go back to London then?' Rose said fearfully. 'Why can't Papa come and stay with us here?'

'I don't want to stay here. I want to do something useful for the war, and that means being in London,' Mariette said eagerly. She liked Arundel for a holiday, but she'd be bored stiff if their stay ran into months. 'I'm sure you want to do something too, Rose. And won't all your clients need you back?'

'I think a great many of them will leave London too,' Rose said.

'Noah will decide where we go for the duration of the

173

war,' Lisette said firmly. 'I know I would prefer to take my chances in my own home. We have, after all, got a fine cellar beneath it. Besides, my place is with my husband.'

Just the day after they returned from Arundel, Peter and Gerald called round to say they'd enlisted in the RAF. As both of them had been in the RAF cadet corps at school, and they had some flying experience too, they were going straight to pilot training school the following morning to learn how to fly Spitfires and Hurricanes.

Mariette applauded them both, but Rose burst into tears, throwing herself into Peter's arms and saying she was afraid he'd be shot down.

'Come on, old girl,' he said, looking a little embarrassed. 'I've got to do my bit for King and country and all that. We will get leave, you know. We'll only be in Kent, easy enough to get back and see you.'

Gerald suddenly looked far more attractive to Mariette. Later that same evening, when the four of them went up to Hampstead Heath for a drink, she kissed him passionately in the pub car park and promised to write to him.

'It will mean so much to me, knowing you are my girl and are waiting for me,' he said, showering her face with kisses. 'You mean the world to me.'

'I'm very fond of you too,' she said, suddenly aware that she really was. 'Just keep safe, Gerry.'

As it turned out, for the general public there was no need for panic or hasty decisions, because nothing happened at all. There were no bombs, no threat of imminent invasion, nothing. The newspapers reported that Poland had been taken by the Germans, but in England it became known as the 'Phoney War'. People complained about the ration books that were issued, and about the blackout regulations, as if they didn't believe the real war would ever affect England. In fact, by Christmas, many of the children who had been evacuated were back in London with their parents.

When they first returned from Arundel, Lisette's pleas to stay put and the stringent petrol rationing that was about to be enforced persuaded Noah to change his mind about moving away from London. He decided to put the car into the garage for the duration of the war, and got Andrews to clean and whitewash the cellar in readiness for using it as an air-raid shelter.

Mariette really enjoyed the challenge of making the cellar cosy. When Noah bought not only beds but also paraffin heaters and oil lamps too, in case the electric went, Mariette took charge of the lamps. She found a sense of irony in that, just a short while ago, it had been her job at home to fill lamps and trim the wicks. And now she was doing it again. Lisette let her go up into the attic, where she found some old pictures, a bookcase and various other small pieces of furniture. She arranged these in the cellar, filling the bookcase with books and collecting up a few games and jigsaw puzzles too.

'I don't know how you can be so enthusiastic about spending time in here,' Rose said when she came down to have a look. She wrinkled her nose in distaste. 'It smells nasty and it's so cold. I think Mama is wrong to want to stay here; we'd be far happier in the country, nearly all my friends have gone already.'

A great many of their neighbours in St John's Wood had boarded up the windows of their homes and moved away from London. Mr and Mrs Andrews decided they would leave too, to go to stay with relatives who had a farm in Dorset. 'They'll need us more than you will,' Mrs Andrews said to Lisette. 'With all the young farm workers being called up, they'll be in a pickle.'

The morning after Mr and Mrs Andrews left, much to Mariette's shock, a letter arrived from Morgan, as badly written and inarticulate as the previous ones. He wrote:

I know I behaved bad. But I do, I love you. And didn't mean to harm you. Please say you've forgiven me and write back. Because I'm off to France now with my regiment. And please send me a photo.

She felt she should be outraged, but instead she could only shake her head in wonder at his cheek. He'd only written now because he was scared of what lay ahead of him and wanted to think he had a girl back home. She didn't want to be that girl any more, but she couldn't help feeling a bit anxious for him.

The next morning, she went out early for an interview for a job in Baker Street. As she walked there, her mind was on how different Morgan and Gerald were, yet both were desperate for her to write to them. If only Gerald set her on fire the way Morgan had, then she would agree to marry him right now, if he asked. He had all the right credentials – family, education, prospects – he was excellent company, the kind of man everyone wanted for her.

While she had no intention of writing back to Morgan – only a complete fool would do that after the way he'd treated her – she couldn't help but feel a little wistful when she remembered how handsome he was, and what a great lover he'd been before he disgraced himself.

But then, with the war just beginning and all the new experiences in store for her, perhaps it was a good time to be fancy free?

13

London, May 1940

Mr Greville came through from his office and loudly cleared his throat to get everyone's attention. Mariette, who was typing up a letter to a supplier, looked up at her boss expectantly, while the other girls in the office stopped what they were doing.

'Mr Chamberlain has resigned as Prime Minister,' he announced with his customary pomposity.

'Who will take his place, sir?' Doris asked. Doris was in charge of accounts and considered herself a cut above everyone else in the office.

'It's sure to be Winston Churchill, he's the only man with the right credentials, even if he is something of a bounder,' Mr Greville replied. 'I would imagine that will be verified shortly. One thing is certain, though, which is that even more uniforms will be needed now. It's an ill wind, as they say.'

He disappeared back into his own office, leaving Mariette thinking that his obvious delight at profiting through war was a little distasteful.

At the time of her interview to be his secretary, back in September – eight months ago – the only good thing she could see about the job was that it took a mere ten-minute walk to get there. A company which made uniforms sounded deadly dull, the Baker Street office was gloomy, and she thought Mr Greville was slimy. But she was very aware that she was young and inexperienced, and that she was unlikely to get a better offer, so she felt she had to accept it.

Rose had called here once and proclaimed Greville – who was around forty, with oiled dark hair and a droopy moustache – to be 'an East End spiv, only one step up from a barrow boy'. Yet, in Mariette's opinion, there was no doubt he was a sharp businessman, whatever his background. Eighteen months ago, he had been manufacturing ladies coats in his Shoreditch factory, but he'd been quick to tender for government contracts for uniforms, and then turned over the entire production line to supply them.

Despite all Mariette's reservations about the position, it had turned out to be much better than she expected. She liked both Polly, Doris's assistant, and Susan, who did the filing, and her expectations that Mr Greville would be making passes at her within a week, as he certainly looked that kind of man, were wrong. He had never said or done anything to her that was improper.

Nor was she bored. She'd imagined her job would merely be taking dictation and typing up letters to woollen mills in the north of England. But it soon transpired that there was far more to the job. Along with having to chase up orders of buckles and buttons, get samples of fabrics, and many other related tasks, she often had to go to the factory in Shoreditch to find out how production was going. She took shorthand notes of Greville's meetings with senior military personnel, and now and again he would ask her to accompany him to lunch or dinner with men who would put more business his way.

'A pretty face and a touch of class will sway most men,' Greville said the first time he asked her to accompany him to the Savoy for dinner. He was to be even more impressed with her when one of his guests was French and she translated for him.

Mariette knew she owed the 'touch of class' to Noah and Lisette. She could attribute every improvement in her character since leaving New Zealand seventeen months ago to their influence. It wasn't just sending her to college, taking her to the theatre, or Lisette's encouragement to be chic and ladylike, it was more that they'd opened her eyes to her own potential.

Back in Russell, her only talents had been sailing, fishing and sewing. And they hadn't made her a good conversationalist because these were her only interests. But Noah's enthusiasm for history and world events had rubbed off on her, and Lisette had taught her by example to be interested in other people. She could now hold her own at a dinner party; she'd learned to ask the right questions to allow other guests to shine, which made them think she was intelligent and caring. Once she'd thought that being reckless was the best way to get attention, but now she found she got that without even trying.

She could remember waking up in the mornings, back in Russell, already bored before breakfast because each day was so predictable. The same old routine, the same faces, the same conversations about the weather, peppered with a little gossip.

But now she could have a real conversation with a total stranger on the bus. People wanted to air their horror at the atrocities in Poland, and praise the courage of the Poles, who had tried so hard to defend Warsaw. Often these strangers told her that the company they worked for was moving out to a 'safe' place in the country, or young women confided they were going to join the Land Army or the WAAFs. But whether or not people were talking about the war in general, or only their small part in it, there was no doubting the excitement and expectancy in the air.

While there was still no real evidence of war in London – apart from almost every able-bodied man being in uniform – it was coming closer every day. In April, Denmark and Norway had been invaded by the Germans and Noah had said, the previous night, that it was only a matter of days before they swept through Holland, Belgium and Luxembourg. He was seriously concerned for France as their troops were sitting on the Maginot Line of forts and anti-tank defences, on the German frontier between Switzerland and Luxembourg, and he couldn't understand why they were too blinkered to see that the attack would come through Belgium.

But here in England daily life was still much the same as it had been before war broke out. Rationing, the blackout and having to carry gas masks everywhere were all irksome. But so far, the worst danger Mariette had encountered was tripping up or banging into something in the dark.

She and Rose were anxious about David and Gerald as they were fully trained pilots now, and they could be called upon any day to fly against the enemy. Yet whenever they came home on leave, they were always in high spirits, ready for a night on the town with the girls, and from the stories they told about their fellow airmen they were having a lot of fun back at the base too.

Mariette had become very fond of Gerald, and although she had never once felt a surge of passion for him, she could say she loved him as the dearest of friends. She liked his company, he was fun, kind and so easy to talk to, and it made her sad that his kisses left her unmoved. She wished with all her heart that he could make her feel the way Morgan used to do.

Morgan was somewhere in northern France now. She had relented and written back to him, purely because she needed to tell him just how appallingly he'd behaved that night and to explain that it had killed off any affection she'd once felt for him.

However, he'd written back to her, saying he understood her feelings and was ashamed of himself. But he begged her to write now and then because there was no one else he could expect to get a letter from.

So she had continued writing because she felt sorry for him. But his inability to write a good letter was as frustrating as Gerald's inability to make her feel lust. Morgan couldn't convey what he was feeling – not about her, what he was doing, or even how he was getting on in the army.

He still claimed he loved her. But she couldn't tell if he really meant it, or if he was merely holding on to an image of her for comfort while he was away.

As for her own feelings about him, they were confused. She did still think about his lovemaking, and his looks, but she felt she didn't really know him.

She did know Gerald. Along with coming home often and taking her out for dinners and dancing, he also wrote wonderful letters. He took a real interest in what she was doing; he often slipped in a bit of poetry that he liked, told her about books he'd read, and there were always amusing anecdotes about the other flyers. While it was clear he couldn't wait to go out on his first mission, he also told her that sometimes he was scared. It was his letters that had made her see what a good man he was – brave, honest and very open.

Rose had once said she thought a woman had a better chance of a long and happy marriage with a man who was 'suitable' and her best friend, and she believed people talked a lot of baloney about falling in love. Perhaps she was right, but Mariette didn't think Rose had been 'awakened' by a man. Maybe if she had, she might think differently.

*

Just after lunch, and a few hours after Mr Greville had made his announcement about Chamberlain's resignation, he called Mariette into his office.

'I want you to go to Shoreditch now with some instructions for them,' he said, putting some papers into a large Manila envelope. 'I've just received a huge order for more uniforms, which means the girls there will have to work harder, and longer hours, to fill it. I'd go to the factory myself to talk to them, but I've got to catch the train up to the mills in Yorkshire and step up my order with them. So I want you to stand in for me.'

Mariette wasn't sure what he meant by this, and her blank expression must have told him as much.

'For goodness' sake, Miss Carrera, surely that isn't difficult to understand? I want you to give them a pep talk to make sure they understand that their work is vital for the war effort. Now can you do that?'

Mariette gulped. The factory girls were a hard lot, and they were unlikely to appreciate anyone telling them they'd got to work harder, and for longer hours, especially if that person was an office worker who was younger than most of them and who knew nothing about sewing uniforms. But she was touched that Greville thought her capable of doing it, and she was delighted to have an afternoon in the East End.

Rose couldn't understand why Mariette liked going there – she shuddered at the very thought of the overcrowding, disease and poverty – but Mariette understood now why Morgan had said she needed to see it. Living in St John's Wood, and mixing only with the wealthy and privileged, would have given her a very narrow view of London.

However, her first reaction had been one of sheer horror. She had known in advance that whole families sometimes lived in one room, that a single outside lavatory and one tap might serve twenty or more people, and that most of them had appalling diets.

But what she saw during that first visit was hopelessness. There were dirty, grey tenements with even greyer washing hanging across the fetid yards, where little sunshine ever shone. She saw ragged children with pale faces and hollow eyes sitting listlessly on doorsteps. A careworn mother struggled home with an ancient pram loaded not only with a baby but a toddler, a sack of coal and a bag of washing too.

That day her stomach had been turned by the smells, and she'd had to avert her eyes from a severely crippled man who was being dragged along in a soapbox on wheels by a girl no more than seven or eight years old. She had wanted to run back to St John's Wood, where she felt safe and secure, and she couldn't understand why Morgan thought she ought to visit such a place.

Yet months later, after many more visits and having got to know many of the staff at the factory, some of whom lived in those same tenements that she'd found so repulsive, she had a different view.

They might have very little, and many lived in conditions which were terrible, but they weren't downtrodden. Against all the odds, most managed to keep themselves, their children and their homes surprisingly clean. She'd heard talk of rats and bedbugs, and how living in such close proximity to others meant that they knew their neighbours' bodily functions as well as they did their own. But these were things they laughed about. And laughter, it seemed, was as important as food and drink in the East End.

Mariette saw the people she'd got to know as brave little terriers, prepared to take on another dog twice their size. She admired the factory girls, who sang as they worked, made jokes about everything and shared what they had. She saw how neighbours looked out for the elderly, the sick and other people's children. There was a camaraderie there that Mariette had never experienced before. Sometimes, she almost wished she could be one of them because they struck her as far more genuine and warm-hearted than some of the people she'd met through Rose and considered to be friends.

'You can do this, Miss Carrera,' Mr Greville said. 'You are good with people, and I have been told that many of the women at the factory like and admire you. So don't let me down!'

'I'll try not to, Mr Greville,' she said, and went back to the general office to get her jacket and handbag.

Mariette wished she'd had the nerve to speak out and say that the women might be more inclined to help him out if Mr Greville was kinder to his machinists, if he took into consideration the fact that many of them had small children and ageing parents to take care of along with their job. But Mr Greville was a hard man — only a week ago, he'd sacked a woman for taking home scraps of wool to make a patchwork blanket. The scraps would only have been thrown away, they were no good for anything else, but he'd felt he had to make an example of her.

Mariette caught the underground to Bethnal Green station and then made her way to Greville's factory. For once, she wasn't noticing the mean little houses or the dank, musty smell that wafted out of open doors. She was too intent on thinking about what she could say to inspire the machinists to want to work longer hours.

Greville's factory blocked off the end of a short street lined with small terraced houses. It stood behind tall iron gates, giving the ugly stone-built factory the look of a prison or a Dickensian workhouse. In fact, it had been built in the

1800s as a slaughterhouse. The front, which must once have been where the animals were herded, ready to be slaughtered, was now a loading bay. With its soot-blackened stonework, and the rusting hooks and pulleys that had been left behind, it still retained a sinister appearance.

Mariette went through the side entrance and up the stairs to the first-floor workroom. The noise of thirty or so sewing machines all going at once was deafening. Blasts of steam were coming from the pressing area, and the smell of machine oil, damp wool, sweat and cheap scent was over-powering.

The first time she'd come here, she thought a person could easily go mad in such an environment, especially as the women shouted to each other over the noise of the machines. But they seemed unfazed by it.

She found Solly Freilich, the manager, in his office. She liked Solly. He was perhaps fifty-five, small and thin with a hangdog expression, but his dark eyes were full of merriment, and she knew from the staff that he was a fair man. She handed him the notes from Mr Greville, and explained that he'd said she was to talk to the workforce.

'I wish you luck,' he said, his dark eyes twinkling. 'They will heckle you! But take no notice.'

Coming out of his office with her, Solly blew a whistle to get everyone's attention and asked them to turn off their sewing machines.

Mariette's legs turned to jelly as the big room went quiet and everyone looked up expectantly. There were around thirty female machinists, their ages ranging from eighteen to fifty. The male cutters had all been called up and their places taken by some of the older women, who had worked for Greville for years and quickly adapted to being cutters. There were only four men other than Solly. Two were in their fifties, too old for call-up, the third was a young lad of fifteen or so, and the fourth man appeared to be in his early twenties, with dark curly hair. She hadn't seen him before, but he was looking at her appraisingly.

'Mr Greville has sent Miss Carrera over to have a few words with you,' Solly announced. 'Please pay attention and don't interrupt.'

All the women wore the same dark green overalls and had a scarf tied turban-style around their heads. Mariette had spoken to many of them in the past and found them to be welcoming and interested in her because she came from the other side of the world. But now, guessing that she had been sent here with bad news, they folded their arms across their chests and glowered at her in an intimidating manner.

Mariette had a strong desire to just run from the building. But she knew, if she did, she'd lose her job.

'Today we received a very large order for more uniforms —' she began.

'And you want us to work harder to get them out?' a woman shouted from the back. This created a wave of indignation and intimidated Mariette still further. But she was determined to give as good as she got.

'Is your name Gypsy Rose Lee?' Mariette called back to the woman, a bleached blonde who she knew often stirred up trouble. 'I think it must be, as you've obviously been looking in your crystal ball.'

A ripple of gentle laughter went through the workforce, and she knew then they were prepared to listen.

'Well, Gypsy Rose Lee's prediction is correct,' she went on. 'The message from Mr Greville is that he wants you all to work longer and harder to get this new, big order completed.'

As she expected, there was dissent. Someone shouted out that Greville could stick working longer hours unless he was offering to pay them extra. Several women got to their feet as if to walk out, while another woman yelled out that Greville was lily-livered to send a mere girl to do his dirty work.

'Please sit down and hear me out,' Mariette shouted over the raised voices. 'I haven't been told anything about extra pay. And I know that asking you to work longer hours when so many of you have children who need you at home is going to cause difficulties. But there is a very good reason why you should all push yourselves a bit harder. Hands up all of you who have a husband, sweetheart or brothers who have enlisted!'

Almost everyone put their hand up.

'And I bet you were all really proud to see them in their uniform?'

There was a general nod of agreement.

'Well, every one of those uniforms was sewn by women like you,' she said, letting her eyes travel along the rows of workers. 'Here in Shoreditch it's very hard to imagine what our men are facing, and I'm sure most of you are afraid that those you love won't come back to you. But those who have already enlisted and are now in France are just a small part of the army that England needs so we can win the war. Each day, thousands more join up. And that means thousands more uniforms.

'I'm asking you to work faster and longer so that every one of those men can look smart and feel confident in his new uniform. A confident man will make a better soldier. And the better our soldiers feel, the more likely we are to win this war.'

She paused for just a second, letting that sink in.

'But that's not all I ask,' she went on, and raised her voice a little. 'I'm asking you to sew love into each seam, and to send your good wishes for the safety of the man who will wear the uniform. You will never know the name of the man who will be wearing it, but it could be one of your husbands, brothers or sweethearts. Here in this factory none of you will ever face bullets and tanks. But the men wearing the uniforms will. So is it too much to ask that each of you gives a few extra hours a week so those brave men of ours look their best? You may not get rewarded in money, but when the war is over and your men come back, you too can be proud that you did your bit to help.'

There was silence for a moment, then suddenly they all applauded very loudly. She even saw a couple of women wiping tears from their eyes. Not one of them stood up to demand more money.

Solly came forward then to address the women. 'Back to work now,' he said. 'I'll talk to you about the rota for extra hours tomorrow.'

As the machines were switched on again, Solly took Mariette's elbow to show her the way out.

'I didn't really know what to say,' Mariette admitted once they had reached a quieter area where Solly could hear her. 'I mean, looking smart in a uniform won't protect our boys from bullets or mines.'

Solly clapped her on the shoulder. 'No, it won't. But you made the women think about the men who will be wearing the uniforms, and that is enough motivation for them. You know, you were born for public speaking, Miss Carrera! When you told me what Mr Greville wanted you to achieve, I half expected a riot. But instead they took your words to heart. Let's just hope they don't get the idea of sewing love letters into the seams.'

Mariette laughed; she was so relieved it was over. 'I think people need reminding of the importance of a job they are doing, and then it seems more worthwhile.'

'My father and my grandfather before him were tailors,' Solly said. 'I was taught to take pride in how good the gentlemen looked in the suits I made for them. In hard times, all I had was that pride. I think you have given the machinists that same idea. But I think you must also try to influence Mr Greville, persuade him to offer the workers some kind of bonus too. Pride in your work alone does not put food on the table.'

Mariette nodded in agreement. She didn't know how Greville had the cheek to expect the women to work longer hours without extra pay, while he was making a fortune.

'I'll suggest it as soon as he gets back from Yorkshire,' she said.

As she left the building and was walking to the gate, the dark-haired man she'd seen inside the factory came up to her.

'You've got the gift of the gab,' he said with a wide grin. 'I was fully expecting them to throw things at you, but you charmed them.'

He had a fascinating face, with very green eyes and sharp cheekbones. His were not matinee idol looks, by any means, but the kind anyone would look at a second time.

'To tell the truth, I was expecting trouble,' she admitted. 'It wasn't as if I had anything to sweeten the bitter pill.'

'Well, you did good. They all know what a mean cove Greville is and what a packet he'll be making from the war.'

Mariette couldn't openly agree with him, it might get back to Greville. 'The war is getting closer and closer, everyone will need to do their bit and make a few sacrifices,' she said. 'But what's your job here?'

'Jack of all trades, that's me,' he grinned. 'Mechanic when the machines break down, driver, packer, floor sweeper and tea maker.'

'How come you haven't joined up?' she asked.

'Reserved occupation,' he said. Seeing her look of surprise, he laughed. 'Not jack of all trades! I mean the Fire Brigade. I just help out here in my time off. I'm Greville's nephew, John Abbott, his sister's son.'

'Good to meet you, Mr Abbott,' she said.

'Johnny to everyone,' he said. 'Come and have a cup of tea with me, there's a café round the corner.'

'I have to get back to the office,' she said, but she found herself looking into his green eyes and feeling tempted.

'Solly is bound to ring my uncle and tell him what a marvel you are, so if you're a bit late back he's not going to fire you.'

'He's gone to Yorkshire, so he won't know anyway,' she said. 'And I could do with a drink.'

The café was grubby, with broken lino on the floor, and a pall of cigarette smoke hung in the air from a dozen or so people who all appeared to have taken root. The oilcloth-covered tables needed a good wipe down, and the red-haired woman behind the counter looked half asleep. But Johnny grabbed the table by the window, then told her to sit down while he got the tea.

'It's a bit of a dive,' he whispered when he got back with two mugs of tea. 'But, believe it or not, they do the best bacon sandwiches you've ever tasted. Funny, really, because the owner is Jewish and they don't eat pork.'

Johnny, it seemed, knew quite a bit about Mariette already – that she had just turned twenty, was from New Zealand and living with her uncle and aunt in St John's Wood. He said his uncle was impressed at her secretarial skills and claimed she was the best he'd ever had. 'Mind you, he's had some old trouts in the past,' he laughed. 'And he's bowled over that you can speak French. What made you work for him, Miss Carrera? Surely, with your looks and brains, you could have found a better job?'

'I had to get some secretarial experience somewhere, and the office is only a short walk from home,' she said. 'But I've grown to like it there. And do call me Mari – that's short for Mariette.'

'Mar-i-ette,' he said, sounding each of the syllables. 'A very pretty name, and very *ooh la la*!'

She smiled. 'It means "Little Rebel". But I haven't done any rebelling since I arrived in England.'

'Does that mean you were a rebel back home?'

'I suppose I was,' she agreed. 'But it was a sleepy little town with nothing much to do. There weren't many opportunities, and my folks thought coming here would be good for me.'

'Are you walking out with anyone?'

She was a little surprised by such a point-blank question. 'That's a really silly expression.' She giggled. 'It's so very English, implying that the relationship is one that only involves walks.'

'Well, how about I ask you if you have a sweetheart? That implies kissing and cuddling.'

'No one serious,' she said. 'I have a couple of men friends I'm writing to while they are away. One is in the army, the other in the RAF. What about you?'

'There are girls I see now and then, but no one special. The way I see it, this war is going to offer opportunities. I'm not sure exactly what shape they'll take, but I want to be unattached when the moment comes.'

That remark made her feel a little uncomfortable, but she didn't know why.

'When the bombing starts, you'll be kept very busy with fires,' she said reproachfully. She could see he was what Rose called a 'Jack the Lad', a bit too cocksure, someone who wouldn't hesitate to bend the rules or break the law, if the price was right.

'That's true,' he sighed. 'I almost wish it would start, and then we could get it over with. All this hanging around waiting for something to happen wears me down.'

'That's a terrible thing to say,' she exclaimed, but she couldn't help but smile. It did seem like the whole of London was holding its breath.

She had to go then, but as they stood outside the café he took hold of her hand.

'Can we meet up again?' he asked, looking right into her eyes. 'I could take you to a club, dancing, whatever you like. Just have some fun, nothing serious. And very little walking.'

'I'll have to give that some thought,' she said, and began to walk away.

But she couldn't resist looking back over her shoulder. He was leaning against the wall, his hands in his pockets, watching her. There was something about his stance, and the way he was looking at her, that made her think he could be fun.

'Ring me at the office,' she called back.

Just three days later, it was announced that Winston Churchill had been signed in as head of the wartime coalition government. Not a minute too soon as the Germans were thundering their way through Holland, Belgium and Luxembourg. That frightening news drove Johnny from Mariette's mind.

The Dutch Army surrendered a few days later, and it was said that the British and French troops were retreating to the French coast.

She hadn't heard from Morgan, but when she and Rose went to the cinema to see *Gone with the Wind*, the Pathé newsreel of what had happened in the Low Countries was very alarming. Columns of massed German tanks backed by motorized infantry and preceded by accurate aerial bombing smashed through outmoded defences in Antwerp and Brussels. They saw on the screen the smoking ruins of what had once been homes, churches and schools. Thousands of people, many with babies and young children, were taking to the roads to try to reach some place of safety.

A couple of women in the cinema became completely hysterical, yelling out that the Germans would soon be here in England. Mariette had seen the huge coils of barbed wire all along the coast while in Littlehampton, and there had been warning signs that the beaches were mined too, but the German Army looked invincible. She didn't think mines and barbed wire were going to deter them from making their way across the English Channel.

The day after that film, the sky seemed to be full of Spitfires and Hurricanes. Compared with the German planes she'd seen on the news, they seemed pitifully small.

Rose got herself into a terrible state at the thought of Peter being shot down.

'They won't stand a chance in those little planes once they're hit,' she sobbed. 'I can't bear the thought of losing him.'

Mariette could hardly reassure her that he would never be shot down in his plane – it was all too obvious that many airmen would be lost – and yet, when Peter came to the house with Gerald a few nights later on a twenty-four-hour pass, they seemed untroubled and couldn't wait to be sent out on a mission.

'Aren't you scared?' Mariette asked Gerald later, as they sat in the garden alone together.

'Not of flying, I love it,' he grinned. 'But I expect I will be scared when I'm faced with a Messerschmitt on my tail. Doesn't do to show it, though, got to keep a stiff upper lip and all that.'

He asked for a photograph of her, and she gave him one taken on the night of her surprise party when she'd left college. 'I shall kiss you for luck each time I go out,' he said as he tucked it into his wallet. Then he kissed her with all the abandonment of a man who thought it might be his last embrace.

'I love you, Mari,' he whispered when he finally broke away. 'You are on my mind all the time, I go to sleep imagining us getting married one day and never having to say goodbye ever again.'

She couldn't bring herself to say she would happily marry him. But his passionate kiss had stirred up feelings inside her, so she held him close and kissed him back. If he took that as meaning she felt the same as he did, well, she couldn't help that. And besides, if he kept kissing her that way, she might find it was true love.

It was through anxiety for Gerald that she turned Johnny down when he rang her to ask her out. She really wanted a fun night out dancing, especially with a man who wasn't in real danger of being killed in the near future, but it seemed wrong when Gerald thought of her as his special girl.

The evacuation of thousands of British and French soldiers from the beaches of Dunkirk began on 27th May. Noah went down to Dover the following day to write an article about the evacuation. He stayed on there until 4th June, when the evacuation of the troops was completed. During that time, Mariette, Lisette and Rose all remained glued to the wireless each evening as reports came in that, aside from the troopships that had been sent for the evacuation, hundreds of ordinary people all along the coast had taken out their little boats to rescue as many soldiers as they could. It was reported that some people did the forty-four-mile round trip in heavy seas twice, crossing the English Channel with German aircraft firing down at them. It was so stirring and heroic that all three of them listened with tears running down their faces.

They saw it all on the Pathé news at the cinema, watching the film showing thousands of French and English soldiers patiently waiting on the beaches of Dunkirk, even though they were under heavy fire. Even more telling were the images of the wounded being carried off ships at Dover and Folkestone on stretchers.

Each day, Mariette waited anxiously for the postman to call, but there was no letter from Morgan telling her that he was safely back in England. She wondered whether anyone would even know to contact her, if the worst had happened. His brothers were his next of kin, after all.

On 18th June, they listened to a stirring speech by Winston Churchill in which he said that the Battle of France was now over, and the Battle of Britain was about to begin. 'Let us therefore brace ourselves to our duties,' he said, amongst other lines that both chilled and thrilled, ending with, 'Men will still say, "This was their finest hour."'

The very next day, an exceptionally brief letter arrived from Morgan, sent from a hospital in Folkestone. It said:

> *I copped some shrapnel. But I'm OK. Don't come here, I don't want to see you while I'm like this.*
> *Yours*
> *Morgan*

She didn't know if that was just bravado, or if he really wanted her to visit him.

But Lisette said she should take him at his word. 'He might be in a lot of pain, and perhaps he can't walk at the moment. Some men like being babied, but some hate anyone to see them looking vulnerable. Besides, all the trains coming back from there will be packed with wounded men. That's no place for you.'

Winston Churchill had been right in saying that the Battle of Britain was about to begin. On 14th June, the Germans entered Paris. With the enemy now just across the Channel, and the Luftwaffe firing on British shipping, suddenly invasion looked imminent.

The newspapers reported that wolf packs of German U-boats were inflicting enormous damage on shipping in the Atlantic, and the Italians had joined with the Germans to attack British troops in Egypt. For Gerald, Peter and their fellow airmen there was no leave now as they bravely set off in their little Spitfires and Hurricanes again and again to defend England. Airfields in the south of England were being targeted by the Luftwaffe. Noah reported, on returning from some business near Brighton, that he'd witnessed fierce dogfights overhead.

It was clear to everyone that, despite the indomitable courage of the British fighter pilots, Germany had a huge advantage in deploying so many more aircraft.

The arrival of thousands of Commonwealth troops in England was heartening. And yet, at the same time, everyone suspected they were here because the invasion of England was about to start.

On 2nd July, Mariette arrived home from work to find Rose and Lisette sitting in the kitchen, both in tears.

'Whatever's happened?' Mariette asked, her stomach beginning to churn with fear. 'Where's Noah? Is it him?'

'No, Noah's fine,' Lisette croaked out. 'It's Gerald . . . he was shot down today.'

Mariette sank down on to a chair in shock. She didn't need

to ask if he was dead, she could see it on their faces. 'How do you know?' she asked.

'Peter rang. They went out this morning with three other pilots,' Lisette said quietly. 'Gerald had shot down a Heinkel, and they were all returning to the airfield in formation when another Heinkel came out of the clouds firing at them. Peter said Gerald's plane was hit on its tail, it went into a spiral and then burst into flames. He didn't stand a chance.'

Mariette covered her face with her hands. She remembered Gerald's passionate last kiss, and how he'd said he loved her. If only she'd told him she loved him too, let him go off with the belief one day they'd get married. She doubted if she would ever meet another man with such wonderful qualities, and it hurt so much to know she'd never see him again.

Suddenly the war became very real to her. Thousands of men might have been killed all over Europe – two women in the factory at Shoreditch had lost their husbands at Dunkirk, and another pilot, who was a friend of Gerald and Peter's, had been shot down on his first mission – but she hadn't known any of them. She hadn't heard them laugh, hadn't danced with them, and certainly hadn't been kissed by them. Gerald's death brought the war into sharp focus, right in front of her, and all those sandbags, air-raid shelters and gas masks had real meaning for her at last. People were going to die, here in London – not just strangers, but people she knew well – and life as she'd known it was never going to be the same again.

That night, she stayed up late writing a long letter home. She was no longer devious Mariette; the words she was writing came straight from her heart. Alexis was seventeen now, Noel sixteen, and the thought that her brothers were close to the age when they would be called up made her blood run cold. Suddenly her family seemed so much more precious to her, and she felt she had to tell them. She wrote:

Getting the news today that Gerald was shot down has made me realize what war really means. It's being afraid for those you love, realizing that nothing will ever be quite the same again. I hope I can be as brave as you two were in the last war. And I wish I'd asked you about your experiences then. I've been awfully self-centred, haven't I?

She closed her eyes for a moment, imagining them all sitting around the kitchen table. She could almost smell one of Mog's wonderful meat pies cooking in the oven, and hear the faint hiss of the oil lamps and her brothers' chatter. For the first time since she had left home, she really wished she was back there, with nothing more troubling on her mind than what she would wear to the next dance.

14

From early August enemy raiders had begun targeting convoys in the Channel and Dover harbour, then moving on to bomb aerodromes and dockyards. Britain was fighting back with all the force it could muster; from every airfield in the south of England Spitfires and Hurricanes flew out to intercept enemy planes and shoot them down. Doris from the office, who lived in Kent, reported that the sky was full of RAF fighters at first light, bravely setting out in tight formations. But the casualty figures were high, and each time the pilots returned there were fewer of them.

Then, on 19th August, there was a heavy attack on the docks in the East End of London. Mariette heard about the attack at first hand, from Johnny, because he'd been there fighting the fires.

Two days after the bombs dropped, he met her from work to take her for a drink. His eyes were still red-rimmed from the smoke.

'I can't even describe how bad it is, just that it's bloody terrifying,' he admitted. 'I've got to get back there tonight an' all, cos it's still raging. You think you've put out one fire, then up it pops somewhere else. The old hands reckon it'll take us a fortnight to put it out completely.'

Mariette had met up with Johnny twice since Gerald's death. The first time had been the day after his funeral at the church in Finchley that his family had always attended. Rose, Lisette and Noah were with her. Peter and his parents were there too. Gerald's CO and two of his closest RAF pals had a few hours off to attend the service, and the rest of the congregation were family, neighbours and Gerald's childhood friends. To see his parents, grandparents, two sisters and a younger brother all bowed down with grief was heart-breaking. It was clear to her that Gerald must have told his family that she was the girl he was going to marry; when they bravely put aside their own grief to offer her their deepest sympathy, it made her feel such a fraud. But her tears were real that day. She couldn't believe he'd been snatched away so young, before he'd had a chance to fulfil any of the ambitions he'd confided in her. They were such simple ones too. He wanted to learn to ride, because he loved horses, to go sailing with Mariette and to ski in Switzerland. She wished so much there had been time to do all those things with him, and that she could have truly loved him.

Johnny had telephoned her at work the following morning, catching her at her lowest ebb, when she was dreading going home that evening. She knew Rose would want to talk about Gerald and her fears for Peter. So she agreed to meet Johnny when she finished work.

She was glad she went because he took her out of herself. He didn't take life seriously and he saw no reason why she should either. First he took her to a little restaurant on the Marylebone Road, and during the meal he told her funny stories about the firemen he worked with, then they went to a nearby pub where he plied her with drink.

She told him about both Gerald and Morgan. 'One is dead and the other doesn't want me to visit him,' she said glumly. 'I feel bad because Gerald cared far more about me than I did about him. What does that make me?'

'Honest,' he said, and grinned at her. 'There's some who would've made out he was the love of their life just to milk the sympathy. You liked him, cared about him, but you can't make yourself fall in love with someone just because that's what they hope for. As for this other geezer that don't want to see you because he's injured, I reckon he either thinks he's being a hero, or he's got some other girl he don't want you to run into.'

'I really don't think he's got another girl,' she said indignantly.

Johnny raised one dark eyebrow quizzically. 'Well, thinking he's a hero is just as bad. He ain't got his leg blown off, has he?'

She didn't know whether to be offended by his bluntness or glad of it.

'If he has, he hasn't told me so,' she said. 'He said it was just some shrapnel.'

Johnny shrugged. 'I ain't got much time for people that can't be straight. If you want my opinion, you're wasting your time worrying about him. A man don't tell his girl not to visit him for nothing, it don't make sense.'

Although Johnny's lack of sympathy for Morgan seemed heartless, he did have a knack of putting things into perspective for her. She didn't love Morgan – he'd killed that off by his behaviour towards her – and if Morgan cared for her, as he claimed to do, he should be totally honest with her. Whether that meant admitting his injuries were worse than he'd said, or that he had another girl.

But she'd begun to realize that few people were totally honest. They might not lie exactly but they dressed things up to be more palatable. Noah wouldn't have approved of Morgan, if he'd met him. But on hearing he'd been wounded at Dunkirk, he put on a show of concern which she knew he didn't feel. She'd heard people at Gerald's funeral say that he would have preferred to die a hero, rather than live a long and ordinary life. That was rubbish: Gerald had wanted an ordinary life, the war just got in the way of it.

Noah and Lisette wouldn't approve of Johnny either. 'A cockney spiv' would be Rose's opinion, and it was true that he was a bit rough around the edges and not even devilishly handsome like Morgan. But he was bright, funny and it took as much courage to face huge fires and deal with them as it did to fly a plane. So maybe he wasn't going to be Mr Right, but she liked his green eyes and the mischief in them, she liked the way her hand felt very small in his big one, and she knew she wanted to see him again.

His red-rimmed eyes and his obvious bone-weariness at their second meeting had made her like him even more. There was something very gallant about a man who had been fighting a fire for two days and could have opted for dropping into the camp bed at the school which had been pressed into service as a fire station. But he'd found the energy to rush off to meet her. He even insisted on escorting her home after their supper together, and when he kissed her at the corner of the street she'd wanted it to go on for ever.

'I don't know when I can see you again,' he said, running the tip of his finger around her lips and looking right into her eyes. 'These bombers aren't going to give up, I've got a feeling it's going to get a whole lot worse too. But I'll ring you when I can, and next time I'll take you dancing.'

Soon after it was the congested commercial areas of the City, and then on 5th September the enemy bombers turned their attentions to the huge oil installations at Thames Haven and Shell Haven, at the mouth of the river, setting one tank alight with an incendiary bomb.

Johnny rang her the day after and described how he'd been standing on the roof of an oil tank, aiming his hose to cool the other threatened tanks, when a Messerschmitt roared in low with its machine guns blazing.

'Most of the blokes ran for cover,' he said quite cheerfully. 'But I was up higher and didn't have anywhere to go. And besides, if I'd dropped the bleedin' hose and tried to scarper, the tanks might have caught fire, and then my mates would all have been trapped, surrounded by fire, so I had to stay put. Luckily, I didn't cop it.'

Just that morning, at breakfast, Noah had been speaking about the attack on the oil installations. He said that, because of the good safety record enjoyed by the oil companies in the past, there were few firemen in England with experience of fighting oil fires. He had gone on to say that the men who'd been dealing with this fire were true heroes because, if it had spread to the other tanks, it could have led to complete disaster.

Maybe she should have admitted then that she knew and liked one of those heroes. But coming so soon after Gerald's death, it didn't seem right.

The next morning the air-raid siren went off. Mariette leapt out of bed and went out on to the landing to see Noah in his pyjamas, looking out of the window.

He looked round at her. 'It must be a false alarm,' he said. 'It's going to be a beautiful morning, the sky is completely clear and cloudless.'

Mariette looked out of the window with him. As Noah had said, there was nothing in the clear sky to warrant any concern. 'Maybe bombers are heading towards the area south of the river again,' she said. 'Or even the coastal towns. It must just be a general warning.'

They all went downstairs for a cup of tea, and it seemed that Noah was right. Everything was calm outside, there were no people rushing around, and there was the promise of a warm day ahead.

'Shame you've got to work this morning, we could have gone for a picnic on Hampstead Heath,' Rose said.

'I'm only working until one. And Mr Greville always gets in by seven on Saturdays, so if I get there early maybe he'll let me off by eleven,' Mariette said.

'It's funny they haven't sounded the all-clear, if it was a mistake,' Noah said pensively a little later.

'I don't suppose they are allowed to, as long as something is going on somewhere,' Rose said.

The plan for a picnic was very appealing. Leaving Rose to organize it, Mariette got dressed and hurried off to work. The streets were very quiet still; she didn't see more than five people on the way to Baker Street, and they all looked totally untroubled, just going to work as she was.

Mr Greville was already in the office and, judging by the crumpled state of his clothes, she thought he'd probably been there all night. Perhaps he'd been out with friends and couldn't make it home. He never said anything about his private life. She knew he lived near Epping Forest, and that he had a wife and two sons, both of whom were in the army. But Mrs Greville never came to the office, and Mariette had a feeling they weren't very happy together.

She explained why she'd come in early, and he merely grunted his agreement that she could leave at eleven. So she sat down at her desk and began typing the letters he'd dictated to her the previous day.

She hadn't been there more than fifteen minutes, when the telephone rang. Greville answered it, and she saw his face blanch at whatever he was being told.

He thanked whoever he was speaking to, then put the receiver down. 'They've struck Thames Haven again,' he said. 'There are squadrons of bombers supported by hundreds of fighter planes. Ford Motor Works has been hit, and Beckton Gasworks. They are making for the docks now and dropping incendiaries.'

'Oh no! Then that siren this morning wasn't a false alarm!'

'If the factory takes a hit, then I'll be finished,' he said, wringing his hands.

Mariette thought this was a very selfish worry. She had walked around that area many times now and had seen huge warehouses full of foodstuffs and other goods vital to the war effort. There were large cargo vessels, moored like sitting ducks in the bright sunshine, grain silos, flour mills, tar distilleries, chemical works, paint and varnish works, and acres of timber stacks which, if once set alight, were likely to explode and spread the fire for miles. But worse than that – and what Greville ought to have been thinking of – was the number of houses in that area with so many, many people about to be killed or injured.

It was then she heard the thudding of bombs in the distance.

'Our Johnny!' Greville said, dabbing at his forehead with a handkerchief. 'It will break my sister's heart, if he loses his life.'

Mariette thought perhaps her boss had a heart after all. She hadn't let on to him that she and Johnny were more than passing acquaintances. But as her fear for him began to mount, she wished she could admit that she cared for Greville's nephew, if only so they could share their anxiety.

But this wasn't the time to tell Greville such things.

'The warehouse is quite a way from the docks,' she said, getting up and laying a hand on his arm. 'It may be safe. As for Johnny, he's been trained to fight fires, so I'm sure he'll be fine. It's the machinists we should be afraid for; an awful lot of them live down by the docks.'

Mariette made tea for them both. But as they drank it, the sound of the bombs grew louder and louder. They heard the drone of British planes flying overhead too, clearly hoping to fight the enemy planes and make them turn back.

'You'd better go home,' Greville said. 'And I must go and see what I can do at the factory.'

'I'll come with you,' she said, without stopping to think what that might entail. 'It's the sturdiest building around there, people might go to it for shelter. There is a cellar beneath it, isn't there?'

He looked at her, almost as if seeing her for the first time. 'Yes, there is. We might be able to get some of the goods down there for safety.'

She hadn't been thinking of the bales of cloth or sewing machines at all, only the people, but she could work out a plan on the way there.

The taxi driver turned them out at the start of Whitechapel High Street. They could hardly expect him to go further as acrid black smoke was billowing over from the docks. The drone of planes above and the thud of bombs dropping below, mingled with the sound of ambulance sirens, was enough to make anyone turn tail and run.

Greville hesitated as they turned into a narrow side street. 'Perhaps we should go home while we can,' he said.

'No, we go to the factory,' she insisted, taking his arm firmly. 'There have been no bombs here yet. We're safe enough.'

It looked to Mariette as if all the people had fled to shelters, or were cowering indoors, as the streets were totally deserted. She was afraid now. The black smoke, the fumes of chemicals, the thumping sound of bombs, the noise of ack-ack guns and the wail of fire and ambulance sirens made her think they were making their way into Hell.

They quickened their steps to reach the factory but didn't speak. Mariette knew she ought to have phoned home before leaving the office. Once Noah heard the bombs, he would ring one of his many contacts to find out what was happening and where. When he rang her at the office and found no one there, he would be worried about her.

As they reached the factory gates, Mariette resolved to ring home as soon as they got inside. But the moment Greville had pushed the gates open, a handful of people appeared in the road.

'Can we come in, mister?' asked a woman with a baby in her arms and two small children clinging to her skirt.

When Greville didn't answer, Mariette spoke for him. 'Yes, come on, we'll all be safer in the cellar.'

An hour later, there were over fifty people, mostly women and children, in the large cellar. They all came from homes in the neighbouring streets, and some of the women worked at the factory. The cellar had never been used for storing material or machinery as it became damp in the winter. But now, at the end of the summer, it was dry. Greville had got the few men, all of whom were either over or under conscription age, to carry some of the sewing machines and bales of cloth down there. Mariette and some of the women had brought chairs and a large trestle table, used for cutting out the uniforms, in an effort to make everyone a little more comfortable.

The cellar was lit by only two light bulbs, but as they kept flickering Mariette had found a box of candles for backup if they went out completely. Down here the bombing was muted, but she'd heard a little girl ask her mother if they were safe now. She hoped they were.

When she risked a trip to the workshop, two floors above, the sound of the mayhem by the river seemed to be coming closer. Because of the thick black smoke she couldn't see more than twenty yards from the windows, but she could hear the sound of falling masonry and hissing hoses, and that sounded ominously close by.

Noah answered the phone when she rang home. 'Whatever were you thinking of, going there?' was his immediate response.

'I have to try to help,' she said. 'I think we're safe enough for the time being. But should the air raid get worse, will you ring someone to tell them there are people in the cellar here?'

He agreed he would ring the Civil Defence people, and advised her to make sure there was adequate ventilation in the cellar and to take water down there for everyone. 'If your Mr Greville had had any sense or foresight he would've made preparations for an eventuality like this,' he said. 'You can't just fill a cellar with people without making some provision.'

'Is it better for them to die in crushed houses with a sandwich in their hands? Or to be hungry and alive?' she said sharply, and put the phone down.

There was what passed for a kitchen at the back of the loading bay. It was very dirty – the factory workers had always used a kitchen just off the main workroom to make their tea – but, whatever its shortcomings, it was safer to use the dirty one than risk people going up another flight of stairs. Mariette collected up all the cups and mugs and tea-making equipment and took it down there. There was also a lavatory beside it; she hoped against hope that the bombing wouldn't become so bad that they had to resort to using buckets in the cellar.

Everyone apart from the children, who were too young to know what was going on above them, looked terrified. They sat huddled in small groups, alert to the slightest sound. Iris and Janet, two of the machinists, dished out cups of tea and tried to act as if it was all just a bit of a lark, but the smiles they got back were forced ones.

Greville kept himself busy by collecting up files and documents and bringing them down to the cellar. 'Thank goodness that big shipment of uniforms was collected on Thursday,' he said to Mariette at one point. 'I suppose the girls could work down here on Monday, if the bombing continues – that is, if I could get some power down here.'

Mariette was astounded that he could only think of his business. 'If you don't mind me saying, sir, we ought to be thinking of how we can get some blankets, milk for the babies and some food for everyone. Not thinking about making uniforms.'

Some of the children were already saying they were hungry. But just as she was about to suggest that it might be a good idea to get a few volunteers together to go to the nearest houses and get some food and milk, there was an explosion. It was loud and forceful enough to shower dust and mortar down on everyone. Many people screamed involuntarily, some covered their heads with their hands as if that would protect them, and a few ran towards the door.

'Have we been hit?' Mariette asked Greville. But she might as well have saved her breath because he was trembling with fear. 'Get a grip,' she hissed at him, shaking his arm. 'I'm going out to see what damage has been done.'

She opened the cellar door tentatively, half expecting the way out would be blocked. But it wasn't, so she ran up the concrete stairs to the loading bay. That was still intact, as were the open factory gates, but the houses on the right-hand side of the road outside the gates had received a direct hit. The whole row, about ten small houses, had come down like a pack of cards. The air was thick with swirling brick dust and mortar; as she stood there, too shocked to move, the wall right at the end of the terrace came crashing down too.

Hearing another plane, she turned to look towards the docks, in time to see a German bomber drop its load less than half a mile away. At the sound of the deafening explosion that followed she ducked back into the factory, and ran down the stairs to the cellar.

Iris came over to her. 'What's been hit?' she asked.

Mariette hesitated. One of the destroyed houses was Iris's home. She had four children, all of whom were in the cellar with her, and her husband was in the army.

'Come on, put a girl out of 'er misery,' Iris laughed.

Mariette liked Iris. She was always laughing. She claimed to have nothing to be miserable about. She was thirty-one and had given birth to her first child at seventeen; the other three had come one after the other in close succession. Because of her bleached-blonde hair, and a voluptuous figure which she poured into tight low-cut dresses, some of the more shrewish machinists called her a tart, but she didn't care. One of her favourite put-downs for those who gossiped about her was, 'Men like an angel in the kitchen and a tart in the bedroom. I'm no great shakes in the kitchen, but I can be a tart in any room they like.'

'I'm sorry, Iris,' Mariette said. 'But your house, and the whole terrace, has been hit.'

Iris blanched and put her hands over her mouth in horror. But to Mariette's astonishment, she forced a laugh. 'Bloody good job I was behind with the rent then,' she said. 'I'd 'ave been 'opping mad if I'd just paid it.'

Most of the other residents of the terrace were in the cellar, but none took the news as bravely as Iris. One, a very fat middle-aged woman, began a terrible keening noise, rocking backwards and forwards in her chair, and couldn't be comforted.

The all-clear sounded then, and almost everyone got up to leave. Mariette went out into the yard with them. When they saw the devastation before them and the black, greasy smoke almost blotting out the sun, they looked shaken, helpless and undecided about what to do.

'If your home has been hit, or if the siren goes off again, you can come back,' Mariette told them. 'It might be a good idea to bring some food with you.'

She watched them clambering over the rubble in the road; even the young women looked suddenly old and careworn. The ones whose homes had been hit began picking through the rubble for things to salvage. Only the children seemed undeterred by the carnage. She saw one little girl picking up a rag doll from the wreckage of her home and shouting to her mother gleefully that it only needed a wash.

'What will we do?' Iris said at her elbow.

Mariette knew she meant about getting another home. 'I think the Civil Defence people help with that,' she said. 'I told my uncle to ring them and tell them about all the people here, so they are bound to send someone round very soon. But tonight you and the children had better stay in the cellar. Shall we go and see if we can find some clothing and bedding?'

There was far too much to do for Mariette to even think about going home. Some of the women were too stunned by the destruction of their homes to think for themselves. And although Mariette assumed there would be no further bombing today, that couldn't be relied upon.

She had made a list earlier of everyone who had been in the cellar, including their addresses. She'd also got each of them to tell her the names of other people who lived at the same address but weren't with them, just in case their house should be bombed. As far as she could tell, all the people from the flattened terrace next to the factory had either come to the cellar, or weren't at home, so it didn't appear that there was anyone who might be trapped under the rubble. But someone had to inform the Civil Defence of this, so when she saw Greville locking up the upper floor in preparation for going home she was shocked.

'But what about all these homeless people?' Mariette said.

'I'm leaving the cellar open. That's enough, isn't it?' he said, looking surprised that she expected more of him.

'Don't you think you should stay till someone from the Civil Defence comes?'

'To do what?' he said impatiently. 'None of the people here earlier were hurt. They're not sick, they can speak for themselves, can't they? You should go home too.'

'I will, once I'm sure someone in authority knows about the cellar,' she said.

'Well, leave as soon as someone comes,' he said. His tone was terse, as if he was irritated by her. 'If I see a policeman as I walk up to the main road, I'll direct him here.'

Mariette began to help the bombed-out women salvage blankets, quilts and clothing from the ruins of their houses. Whilst there, some of the people who had left earlier came back. Most of them were in tears, or looking dazed.

'It's like the end of the world,' one woman sobbed out to Mariette. 'Whole streets gone, just piles of bricks and broken furniture. My grandfather clock was smashed to pieces, lying in the road. There're people who've been killed, we saw the rescue teams laying the bodies on the road.'

Mariette put her arms around the woman to comfort her. 'Did they tell you where to go?'

'We told them we'd been in the factory while the bombing was going on, so they said to come back here.'

A red-headed boy of about twelve gave Mariette more information. 'I talked to one of the rescue men, he told me the fires down on the docks are real bad and just about every fire engine in London is there. There's people trapped under rubble too, just a couple of streets away from here. They're trying to get buses in to take people away to somewhere safer, but it will take a while as most roads are blocked with rubble. The rescue man told us to come back here for the night. He said he would send someone with blankets and sandwiches for us.'

A man with a handcart arrived around half past five with a pile of blankets, a box of cheese sandwiches and a few bottles of milk. The people living in the houses on the left-hand side of the street, which hadn't been knocked down, brought over whatever they could spare. One of them made up bottles for the babies and shared out some old nappies.

Mariette was about to make her way home, when the wail of the siren began again. Everything had looked organized and even a little homely in the cellar up until that moment. People had claimed their space with their family and friends, put their blankets down, many had lit a candle in a jam jar, and the atmosphere was calm and quite jovial, especially considering what they had all experienced such a short while ago.

But it all changed when other people hammered on the door to be let in. It wasn't only those from the undamaged side of the road, who had been here earlier, but also new people from neighbouring streets. Suddenly there was mayhem as they walked across carefully laid-out blankets, and the owners protested. Babies cried, small children rushed about, and arguments broke out.

Mariette was forced to take charge. She blew the whistle she'd found earlier in the day to make everyone pay attention.

'They may start bombing us again at any minute. So before they do, please listen to me. This cellar is big enough for all of you, but please remember your manners and don't walk across blankets or frighten small children by arguing. We're all in this together. It's not very comfortable, there is only one lavatory up in the loading bay, so I'm relying on everyone to be kind to one another and share what little we have. Can you do that?'

'Sure, love, you can share my blanket any time,' a wild-haired man of about thirty called out.

She didn't get the chance to respond as they heard the drone of approaching aircraft, growing louder and louder until it became a roar. Then there was the bark of anti-aircraft guns, followed by the scream of falling bombs and the earth-shaking thump as they exploded.

It seemed to be far worse than the bombing of the morning. People held hands or clutched children to their chests; in the dim light their faces showed their terror. No one knew how far down a bomb could penetrate, and there was real fear of being buried alive.

Mariette made her way round to everyone, making sure she had all their full names, addresses and dates of birth on her list. It crossed her mind that, if the factory did receive a direct hit and they were buried in here, the list would never be found. But busying herself, getting to know these people, and perhaps giving them some comfort by taking charge, helped take her mind off the danger.

The bombing went on all night. There were lulls, now and then, during which people rushed to use the lavatory and empty the bucket the small children had been using. Some of the children fell asleep, but for the adults there was no respite.

Iris took it upon herself to be the tea maker. Alfie, the red-headed boy who had spoken to rescue workers earlier, played snap with some of the children. One elderly woman propped herself up against bales of cloth and knitted. Mariette asked her how she could do it when the light was so bad.

'I've been knitting all me life,' she said. 'I don't need to look any more. Me old man used to say he'd put needles and a ball of wool in me coffin with me. But he died two years ago, so I knits fer all me neighbours' kids now.'

At 6 o'clock in the morning, the all-clear finally sounded. But no one rushed to leave the cellar.

Iris offered to make another round of teas before they braved the outside world. 'If you come back tonight,' she yelled out, 'all bring a cup. And if anyone's got a big tray or teapot, bring that too.'

Mariette went out into the yard. She wanted fresh air, but there wasn't any with the dust swirling about and the fumes from all the fires. Her dress was filthy, she suspected she might have got a few nits in her hair from the children, and she was sure she must stink. But, above and beyond that, she'd had enough of being kindly, brave and helpful. It wasn't in her nature to be like that for long.

She wanted to get home, to wallow in a hot bath and then sleep for eight hours. But she didn't know how she could leave here without it looking like she was running out on everyone.

As she stood there in the swirling dust, to her surprise Johnny came walking through the gate.

He looked bone-weary and was still in his uniform, which even at a distance stank of wet wool and fire. 'So my spies got it right,' he said, his soot-blackened face breaking into a wide smile. 'I was told that people were sheltering in my uncle's factory. They said a girl was in charge who spoke funny! Thought it might be you.'

Mariette laughed. 'I speak funny, do I? Am I glad to see you! It must have been terrible out there.'

'The worst,' he said. 'I've been on duty for thirty-six hours, and it never let up once. But I had to check you were all in one piece.'

'As you can see, I am. But let me get you a cup of tea and something to sit on.'

'If I sat down now, I'd never get up,' he said. 'Is my uncle about?'

She had to admit he'd gone home before the air raid.

Johnny whistled through his teeth. 'What a bleedin' hero he is,' he said.

Iris came out then with a mug of tea for him. 'I saw you, Johnny, from the kitchen. I 'spect you've seen my 'ouse is gone?'

'Yeah, my sympathy,' he said. 'But after the sights I've seen just walking up here, you are one of the luckier ones.'

'Me and the kids would be dead, if it wasn't for Miss Carrera,' Iris said. 'If it 'ad been up to your uncle, the factory would've stayed locked up. None of us along the street knew where we was supposed to go to when the siren went off. That bully boy of an air-raid warden is always quick enough to report anyone showing a chink of light at the window, but 'e never came near yesterday when we needed 'im.'

'You must report him then,' Johnny said. 'And you can go to the nearest air-raid shelter anyway. But maybe my uncle will let the cellar be used all the time now. Actually, he'll probably have no choice, it's a lot safer down there than in some of the shelters the government threw up. One down the road got a direct hit, and everyone in there was killed. But I don't want to talk about sad stuff, I came to see Mari.'

Iris put her hand on her hip and made a comic face. 'She's Mari to you then? Something going on here I ought to know about?'

Mariette giggled. 'No, we're just friends.'

'Well, the poor bloke looks done in, so I don't think you'll need a chaperone,' Iris retorted, then turned on her heel and walked back towards the kitchen.

'How she can be so cheerful when she's homeless with four children, I don't know,' Mariette said. 'I'd be in pieces.'

'There's a lot like her around here,' Johnny said. 'Born with steel in their spine. There's women down the road digging in the rubble with their bare hands to find their loved ones. But give us a kiss, if you can bear to touch someone so dirty?'

'Of course I can bear it,' she laughed, and moved closer to put her arms around him. He did smell terrible, his uniform was soaked and his lips were blistered from working so close to the flames. But all she could think of was how glad she was to see him, and what a brave man he was.

'That's breathed new life into me,' he said when she broke away. 'Sorry I messed up your dress.'

She looked down at herself and saw that along with the dirt she'd noticed earlier, it was now black with soot from hugging him. 'It will wash, and you must go and get some sleep. But thank you for coming, I was worried about you.'

'This wasn't how I intended it to be,' he said sheepishly, hanging his head. 'I wanted to take you out and show you a good time, both of us dressed up to the nines. I wanted a sweet romance with you.'

Mariette's eyes prickled with emotional tears. She hadn't given much thought to what she wanted with him, but a sweet romance sounded perfect.

'Our time will come, Johnny,' she said. 'I'd rather have a dirty but brave man than a slick weasel just out for himself.'

15

Early March 1941

Mariette paused in the letter she was writing home, torn between telling them the exact truth and a watered-down version to save them any anxiety.

She couldn't say she went dancing with Johnny every time he got a night off, not without explaining who he was, and admitting that Noah and Lisette hadn't met him. If she made light of the bombing, they'd think she was hiding the true facts. But, by the same token, if she said how it really was, they would worry about her safety.

They already knew that since the beginning of the Blitz she had dropped to working two days a week for Mr Greville, and spent the rest of the week in the East End doling out clothes to bombed-out families and helping them fill in forms to be rehoused. She suspected it must have been quite a shock to her parents as the Mariette who had left New Zealand wouldn't have volunteered for anything unless there was something in it for her. But they didn't express surprise, only pride in her putting others before herself. Mariette was the one to be surprised that her parents' approval meant so much to her.

In previous letters she had told them little stories about some of the people she'd got to know, but writing about people being bombed out, with sons or husbands missing or prisoners of war, was getting a bit too depressing.

She certainly wouldn't tell them she wasn't frightened by

air raids any more, because that implied she was still reckless, so it was easier to write bland, everyday things, about shortages of food, the irritation of the blackout, and funny stories about some of the girls she'd met through Rose who had become land girls. Most of them were frightened by all the farm animals, even the chickens. To find they were expected to muck out stables and pigsties, learn to plough, and live in a place where having a bath meant heating up kettles, was a rich seam of comedy – although she wasn't sure it would sound as funny in Russell. And perhaps Mog and her mother had never met posh, privileged girls to understand how drippy they could be.

Rose hadn't become a land girl, but she had taken her accounting skills to the Ministry of Defence to do her bit for the war effort. The department had moved out to somewhere in Hertfordshire and she lived there too. It was some kind of hush-hush work she was doing, but Mariette liked to tease her by claiming she believed her friend requisitioned lavatory paper and bars of soap for the troops. Rose laughed at this, which made Mariette suspect she was actually using her fine brain for something really worthwhile. On the few occasions she'd seen Rose lately, she seemed very happy – despite hardly ever seeing Peter – and it made Mariette wonder if there was another man in her life.

The house seemed very big and empty now with Rose gone. Noah was either writing articles about how the war was for ordinary people, or out doing his bit with the Home Guard. Lisette had gone back to nursing at the local hospital. But then, Mariette wasn't home much either; on the days when she helped out in the East End, more often than not the sirens went off, and she ended up staying the night in a shelter.

She couldn't remember how many dead bodies or body

parts she'd seen now after air raids. Or how many people she'd comforted when they'd lost loved ones. She'd taken children whose parents had been killed to stay with relatives; she'd written letters to husbands in the forces to tell them their wife and children were seriously injured in hospital. Just last month, when it was bitterly cold, she'd found an old man dead outside the office in Baker Street. People must have seen him in the doorway as they went by but thought he was a tramp, sleeping off the effects of too much to drink. The ambulance men said he died of cold.

Mr Greville had a new factory now, out in Berkshire, and much of the office work was done from there too. He'd made a fuss when Mariette told him she wanted to help out in the East End, but in fact it had all turned out for the best because Doris could run the Baker Street office almost single-handedly. Greville only came in on Mondays, when he dictated all his letters to Mariette, and she typed them the following day.

He'd found the new premises shortly after that first terrible air raid, and took on new machinists in the same area. All the employees in the East End had been astounded when he gave them all an extra five pounds in their last pay packet. Clearly, he felt bad about laying off people who had worked for him for years. But, as it was, most were happy enough to go into jobs at munitions factories, or become clippies on the buses, as it paid better. That extra five pounds meant a great deal to all of them, though, and they talked about it for a long while afterwards.

The cellar of the old factory was now a real air-raid shelter, complete with wooden bunks and a proper washroom. The workroom above was used as a rest centre during the day, and it was here that Mariette worked. People donated clothes, bedding and household equipment to the rest centre, and those who'd lost everything could find whatever they needed. It was also open to everyone in the area; they could get a cup of tea and a sandwich and talk to people who could help them with any problems they had. Homelessness was the worst problem, and no one seemed to know how to tackle it. There just wasn't enough housing stock available to shelter these people. Some went down into the underground stations each night, others camped out in schools and church halls. Then there were other people who just stayed in a badly damaged house, hoping they could get it repaired.

The factory cellar was Mariette's first choice as a shelter in an air raid as so many of the old staff used it too. Some nights, it was almost like going to a party with everyone mucking in, sharing food and drink and inventing games to pass the time. They laughed about how scared they'd been during the first few air raids, and the other girls would tell her little stories about the adventures and romances they'd had since then.

It was astonishing how blasé everyone had become about the danger. After fifty-seven consecutive nights of bombing they spoke knowledgeably about the difference between high-explosive bombs, incendiary devices and parachute bombs, as if they had always been part of their life. Young lads of eleven and twelve had been roped in to put out small fires caused by incendiaries, using a bucket and a stirrup pump, to save calling the Fire Brigade. And they did it with speed and thoroughness, taking pride in being useful. People would spend the night in a shelter, often going home in the morning to wash and change, only to find their house had been bombed. Yet they didn't sit down and wail, they went off to their work as if nothing had happened. Shops too carried on, even without windows. Mariette had seen one such place with a big sign reading 'More open than usual'.

Again and again Mariette was reminded of what Morgan

had told her about East Enders. They were the most resilient of people. They took anything that was thrown at them on the chin, laughed in the face of calamity, stuck together like glue, cared for each other's children, shared everything they had, and when one of their number was bombed out, they all rallied round.

People took risks, running home in the middle of an air raid to get their knitting, or call on a neighbour who hadn't come to the shelter, or check they'd turned the gas off. They all seemed to have the same fatalistic idea that, if a bomb had their name on it, there was nothing they could do to avoid it. Nearly everyone she knew had had very close shaves. Mariette had flung herself down on the ground one night when she heard a bomb coming, covered her head and said a last frantic prayer. But it landed thirty or so yards away from her, and the only damage had been to her coat, which was covered in brick dust.

Johnny was a fatalist too. He would tell her hair-raising stories about being trapped by a ring of fire, truly believing these were his last few moments of life, then suddenly and miraculously something would happen. A wall would fall down and create an exit. Or someone on the outside of the ring of fire would turn their hose on the flames hard enough to create a gap for the trapped men to jump through to safety. Once, when he was trapped with four other men, they pulled up a manhole cover and climbed down into the sewers to emerge stinking to high heaven several streets further on. He said that each time he got lucky, he wondered when his luck would run out.

Mariette talked about him sometimes to Noah and Lisette, but only ever as her friend the fireman, Mr Greville's nephew, not as a sweetheart. But that was what he was – her sweetheart – and their relationship was just as Johnny said, a sweet romance. She hadn't had sex with him, just kissing and holding hands, cuddling and laughing together. It was almost like being eighteen again, innocent and trusting, yet burning to see him, without the guilt that she was doing anything wrong. In a world that was, at times, both cruel and nightmarish, he made her feel safe. But she still felt unable to tell Lisette and Noah that Johnny was more than just a friend, because she knew they wouldn't approve. And there was no point in making them anxious when even she had no idea where this little romance was going.

Back in New Zealand, when she had first fallen for Sam, she thought she knew what love was. She soon discovered how wrong she was, and still smarted at what Sam had put her through. Then along came Morgan, who showed her how wonderful lovemaking could be and made her think this was true love. But then he'd turned brutal and made no attempt afterwards to explain why. Gentlemanly Gerald had put her on a pedestal, but all she felt for him was friendship.

Johnny was completely different from the other men. He could communicate in every possible way, from the tender way he smoothed back her hair, to the expression in his eyes, his laughter, and even his silences. He had a knack of turning up just when she most needed him, yet he would never be a doormat in the way Gerald had been. He didn't make sweeping promises, he didn't even talk about the future, but perhaps that was because he flirted with death every night fighting fires. They always had so much to talk about, but so little time together.

Did she love him?

It certainly felt like love when her heart leapt to see him lounging against the factory wall in the morning after another night of bombing. Sometimes he was still in a wet uniform, face all grimy, but on other mornings he'd washed, shaved and was in civilian clothes. Almost always he was exhausted, though. But he'd said more than once, 'If I only saw you after a good night's sleep, I'd never get to see you.'

Their romance was all snatched moments. An early morning cup of tea together in a steamy café while, out on the streets, people were sweeping up broken glass and rubble from the night before. Or an hour in the afternoon, when they'd walk together, trying to pretend the cold wind wasn't cutting them in two, knowing that as darkness fell he'd have to go back to the fire station.

Yet there was something very unreal about their relationship, almost as if they were characters in a film. She had confided in her cockney friend Joan about this.

Joan just laughed. 'Well, I'd call the film a bleedin' melodrama. You dole out old togs, Johnny puts out fires. You come from the posh end of town and 'e comes from the rough end. You never get long enough together to find out if you're suited. On top of that, you'll be going 'ome to the bottom of the world when and if this sodding war ends. Not sure I can see a 'appy ending, ducks.'

There had been a lull in the bombing in the New Year because thick fog, or snow, deterred the bombers. There had been a few nights when she and Johnny had put on their best clothes and gone dancing in the West End. For a few hours, while he held her in his arms, the horror of war was put aside and they could be the way sweethearts used to be before the war.

But as soon as the skies cleared, and the moon shone down on the Thames, the bombers were back, following that shining silver ribbon to guide them into central London to destroy more of the capital.

Tonight, there had been no air raid. St John's Wood hadn't seen the massive destruction that had taken place in the east and south-east. People around here made a big deal of the few sticks of bombs that had dropped, but in fact it was next to nothing. The cellar under the house was very comfortable as a shelter but Mariette had been in it only four times, and on those occasions the closest any bomb came to the house was 300 yards away.

Mariette turned off the bedroom light and pulled back the blackout curtain to look out. As always, searchlights scanned the sky for bombers approaching. She smiled, knowing that Noah was manning one of those lights on Primrose Hill. He was out most nights now, and he seemed to enjoy it. That was another odd thing about the war: people did seem to be happier having a part to play. And, despite all the hardships they had to endure, it was said there had been no suicides during the Blitz.

But in two days' time, on 8th March, Noah wouldn't be manning searchlights, Lisette wouldn't be dressing wounds, and Rose would be back here all dressed up ready to go to the Café de Paris to celebrate Mariette's twenty-first birthday. It was Rose's suggestion because it was not only the place to go in the West End, but it was also considered the safest as the dance hall was four floors below Leicester Square.

Hanging on the wardrobe door was Mariette's new evening gown, a slinky body-clinging dress made of silvery-grey silky velvet that flared out behind into a fishtail. Noah had bought it for Lisette in Paris during the early twenties. But Lisette insisted she was far too old at fifty-six, and too thick around the waist, to ever wear it again. She had been delighted that it fitted Mariette perfectly without any alteration.

'Belle and Etienne would be so proud to see you in it,' Lisette had said the day she tried it on. 'Their little girl all grown up, and so beautiful. We must have some photographs taken to send to them. It will be hard for them on your birthday, not being with you to share your special day.'

Mariette went over to the dress and stroked the soft, sensuous material. When Lisette had first got the dress out to show her, she'd thought silver-grey would drain her of all colour, but she'd been wrong. It reflected light back on to her face and made her glow. She couldn't wait to wear it. Lisette was also right about her parents being sad: birthdays had always been a big thing in their family, with bunting put up around the kitchen and in the garden. Belle always made an elaborate crown for the birthday boy or girl, which had to be worn throughout the party. All their friends and neighbours came, Mog would make a fantastic cake, and everyone had to wear their best clothes and play party games. Often, the adults carried on drinking and dancing until the early hours, and Mariette could remember wishing she was grown up so that she could stay up with them.

Mariette could imagine both Belle and Mog crying a little on the 8th. Maybe Mog would make a cake anyway, and they'd all raise a glass of wine to toast Mariette. But it would be a very quiet affair as Alexis had been called up as soon as he'd turned eighteen, in January. He was off at a training camp now, waiting to hear whether his regiment would be sent to Europe or North Africa. In less than a year it would be Noel's turn. Mariette could hardly believe her skinny little brothers had turned into young men capable of firing guns. She wondered too how her parents and Mog would cope without any children in the house.

She wished she could go home and see them; all those scathing thoughts she'd once had about Russell being a primitive backwater where nothing ever happened seemed so stupid now. She'd give anything to be sailing out on the bay, or climbing up Flag Staff Hill to look at the spectacular view.

Just to sit in the quiet of the evening on the veranda, with a warm breeze fluttering her hair, seemed like paradise.

Returning to her letter, she wrote down those thoughts about home and how much she wished she could be there with them. She added:

As I'm writing this, it will be early morning for you. I can almost hear Mog raking out the stove and calling up the stairs for Noel to get up. I expect Mum is outside feeding the chickens and collecting the eggs, maybe Papa has already left the house to take someone out fishing. I didn't appreciate how lovely it was when I was there, but I do now.

Tears filled her eyes as she remembered how she'd played her parents up. She recalled the deceit, all the fibs, and thinking she was somehow deprived because Russell was so small and quiet. She knew now, after seeing children who really were deprived, that she'd had the best childhood anyone could have. She'd always had enough food, and so much love and attention. No one had ever taken a stick to her. Her father never came home drunk and nasty, turning on anyone in his way. Her mother made things fun, and Mog was the comforter. Her lap was one of the best places on earth to be when Mariette was small.

She knew now she wanted a marriage like her parents had – sharing everything, good and bad, their love for each other shining out like a beacon – and how foolish she had once been to daydream that this was how it would be with Morgan. And yet, she found it very annoying that she couldn't forget him either. The last message she'd had from him arrived just after the Blitz began. She couldn't call it a letter as it was so brief. He wrote that he was leaving the hospital any day now, and he hoped she would keep safe.

There was not a word about his injuries, whether he was

going back to his regiment or to another hospital, and she'd heard nothing from him since.

Johnny maintained that Morgan had someone else and wasn't man enough to admit it. But that made no real sense, because why would he have bothered to write from the hospital?

She just didn't understand him at all. But from what she'd seen and heard about people's behaviour in the last six months, nothing would surprise her. She'd seen married women with children have a torrid fling with someone else while the husband they professed to love was serving overseas. Two women she knew were pregnant with the child of a man they'd met at a dance, and would never see again. Iris's husband had gone AWOL and was caught in Portsmouth with a girl of just sixteen. He'd written to Iris while waiting for his court martial and said he didn't love her and never had. He'd only married her because he had to. An elderly man living near the factory had reported his wife missing after an air raid. A couple of days later, her body was found under some rubble, but her injuries were consistent with being struck several times on the head with lead piping, not being hit by falling masonry. When the police began investigating the crime, the husband broke down and confessed it was him. He said he was convinced he was going to die in an air raid, and he couldn't bear the thought of her being left alone.

It seemed to Mariette that war altered everyone's character to some extent. The meek could become brave, the mean become generous, and mild-mannered men could turn into little Hitlers once they put on an air-raid warden's uniform. She knew she had changed too. She could hardly believe how self-centred she used to be, and yet now she chose to spend her days sorting out old clothes for people, when she could be earning good money as a secretary, and going out nightly to dance and flirt with off-duty officers.

Peter was bringing a fellow pilot with him to her birthday celebration. His name was Edwin Atkins, he was twenty-six and, according to Rose, very handsome and good fun.

Mariette wished Rose and Peter would give up on playing Cupid; this was the third man they'd tried to push on to her since Gerald was shot down. She expected he'd be much like the other two – well bred, hearty, a bit full of himself. Fighter pilots might be national heroes and most girls' dream, but they weren't hers.

Noah perched on the padded top of the fireguard in the drawing room, smiling as the photographer he'd booked to call at the house before leaving for the Café de Paris took some pictures of Mariette on her own.

She looked sensational in the silver dress, her strawberry-blonde hair cascading in loose curls over her bare creamy shoulders and the elaborate necklace Lisette had lent her sparkling like real diamonds, even if it was only paste. But the bracelet on her wrist was the real thing, his present to her for her twenty-first.

It was just on two years she'd been with them, and he'd grown very fond of her. She had Belle's easy manner, a ready smile, and a genuine interest in other people. When she'd first got here, he thought she was a little calculating, as if she was weighing up everyone to find their weak points. But that must have been just his old journalistic mind seeing shadows where there were none, or perhaps it was because Annie, her grandmother, had been like that. Annie had felt no loyalty to anyone, particularly not to Mog who had been devoted to her. Etienne, Mariette's father, had some worrying traits too. He was the best possible man to have on your side, but cross him at your peril.

Yet, whatever he thought two years ago, he was wrong,

and Mariette was now very much her own person. She might have her mother's dogged persistence in doing what she wanted to do, with her father's courage and a sprinkling of Annie's arrogance thrown in, but she also had a big heart. He was hoping she was going to fall for Edwin tonight. He was made of the right stuff – intelligent, charming and from a good family.

Lisette kept telling him that he must stop trying to marry the girl off to a 'toff'; she thought Mariette needed a man similar to Etienne to make her happy. But Mariette was his god-daughter, and he couldn't help but want the best for her.

'Come on now, a group picture,' the photographer said, arranging Mariette in the centre with Rose and Lisette either side of her, and beckoning to Noah.

'Take one of the three most beautiful girls in London first,' Noah said as he got up.

Rose was wearing a fabulous pink evening dress, and Lisette was as elegant as only a Frenchwoman could look in black lace.

'Aren't I the lucky one taking you three beauties to the Café de Paris!'

16

The air-raid siren sounded just as Noah was paying off the taxi at the Café de Paris by Piccadilly Circus. It was chilly, and both Mariette and Rose wrapped their fur stoles more tightly around their shoulders before hurrying to the door of the club. When dance halls and nightclubs were closed down at the start of the war, the Café de Paris had remained open because it was underground and considered safer than any shelter. It had a long and illustrious history, attracting the rich and glamorous ever since the Prince of Wales had announced that it was his favourite nightclub. Rose, Noah and Lisette had all been here before the war, but tonight they were just as excited as Mariette because they wanted to see the resident band, Ken 'Snakehips' Johnson and his West Indian Orchestra.

A long staircase led down to the first of several galleries, each table lit with a small lamp. Mariette was bowled over by the decor of the club as it was reminiscent of the ballroom of the White Star liner *Titanic*, with lots of gold leaf and beautiful chandeliers.

Peter and his friend Edwin were at the table waiting for them, looking very dashing in their uniforms. Mariette was pleasantly surprised that Edwin was every bit as handsome as Rose claimed. He had a rugged face with a square chin, brown hair and soft brown eyes. She liked his smile; it was slightly bashful, reflecting the fact that he wasn't sure he wanted to be fixed up with Rose's relative. But even if he was reluctant, he didn't show it. He jumped up to shake her hand and then led her to the chair next to him.

Their table was on the lowest gallery, looking down on to the stage and the dance floor. At present there was a quartet playing, and the leader was singing 'Stormy Weather'. Mariette was so busy looking at all the beautifully dressed women, their partners either in evening dress or uniform, that she didn't even notice the waiter pouring them all champagne and Noah proposing a toast, until Edwin nudged her arm.

'To our beautiful Mariette on her twenty-first,' Noah said as he raised his glass. 'I wish Belle and Etienne could have been with us tonight, they would be so proud of you. But let's drink to a happy birthday and to absent friends!'

'Happy birthday and to absent friends,' everyone chorused.

'You must feel a little sad to be so far from home on your birthday,' Edwin said to her after the toast.

She was touched that he should be so sensitive. 'Yes, I was rather homesick this morning when I got up, my mother always made such a fuss on our birthdays. My elder brother has just been called up, which leaves only the younger one, Noel, for Mum to run around after.'

'Do they hear in New Zealand just how bad the Blitz is? Or do the newspapers there focus more on the North African campaign and the Japanese?'

'They never comment, but I'm quite sure that my dad is very well informed about all the action, all over the world. But then, they'd know better than most New Zealanders what war is really like as my father was in the French Army in the last war. And my mother drove ambulances in France.'

'From what Peter tells me, you've got the same spirit. You help out in the East End, I believe?'

'I got into it by accident really. I was caught up in one of the first bombing raids there. Once I'd got to know people and had seen the problems they face, I sort of had to help.

They have had such a hammering there. But I don't need to lecture you about that!'

He smiled at her, his blue eyes as warm as a summer sky. 'We tend to concentrate only on shooting the enemy down and getting ourselves home unscathed. We don't see the suffering that bombs cause to civilians, at least not in the way you do.'

She was touched by his lack of ego, loved his deep voice, and she felt a little shiver down her spine. Maybe she would want to see this man again after tonight.

The meal was disappointing – the steak was small and tough, and the vegetables were overcooked – but this was how it was now in almost every restaurant, and no one commented on it. But the champagne and the wine that followed were good, and it was lovely to be surrounded by people having a good time.

Mariette was taken with Edwin; he was funny, chatty, but didn't try too hard. He wanted to know about New Zealand, and said he'd even given some thought to emigrating there when the war ended. 'If it ever ends,' he said ruefully. 'I love sea fishing and sailing, I want to live in a country with space.'

'There's plenty of that,' she laughed. 'And more sheep than people!'

'What do you think of him?' Rose whispered later, when Edwin and Peter had gone to the men's room.

'He's very nice,' Mariette admitted.

'Does that mean you'll want to see him again?'

Mariette laughed. 'Let's see what tonight brings first.'

The meal was finished by nine, and the waiter cleared the table except for their drinks. 'Snakehips' Johnson was due on now, and Mariette and Rose could hardly wait to see the handsome young singer from Guyana who had got his nickname because of his smooth moves and undulating hips.

They were not disappointed. Ken Johnson was even better looking in the flesh than in the pictures they'd seen, and his West Indian Orchestra played swing music that made them all leave their table to go down on to the dance floor.

'We won't be able to move on this tiny dance floor after ten,' Edwin told her as they danced. 'That's when most people arrive. But one good thing will be that I can hold you tighter.'

Mariette smiled. She would be glad to be held close by him. But she was aware that more people arriving would mean long queues in the powder room, so she excused herself to go there now.

She paused to look back just before she went through the powder-room door. 'Snakehips' was singing the hit song 'Oh Johnny, Oh Johnny, How You Can Love'. The words made her feel a little guilty that she was having such a good time with another man, but she quashed that thought and reminded herself that this was a family party, not a date.

Lisette and Noah were doing a quickstep, but Rose and Peter were just shuffling from side to side, their arms wound tightly around each other. Edwin was standing by the dance floor just watching and smoking a cigarette. She had half expected him to find another partner the minute she'd gone, and it was nice that he hadn't.

She was putting on some fresh lipstick when she heard the almighty crash of a bomb. It sounded as if it had hurtled down through the building, smashing everything in its path. The shock made her drop her lipstick, and then the screaming began.

Opening the door, the sight that met her eyes was so terrible that she screamed too. The bomb had come down from above the stage, and she thought 'Snakehips' and the other band members were dead. They were on the floor, their white dress shirts already red with blood.

The lights were flickering but she saw, to her horror, that a woman sitting by the dance floor had been decapitated.

Then the lights went out completely.

In that second or two while the lights flickered she hadn't been able to see any of her party because the dance floor was so packed with people who had either fallen or were trying to get away. But as she stood there, rigid with shock in the darkness, a second bomb came roaring down.

There was enough illumination from the flash of the bomb and some candles on the tables further back in the club to see that no one on the dance floor had much chance of survival. They were too tightly packed together, creating a maelstrom of flailing bodies as chunks of plaster, brick and glass from the lights showered down on them.

Mariette instinctively stepped back rather than moving forward, towards the carnage. She'd learned enough from bombing in the East End to know the whole building could come down. She was under the gallery, where, just a short while ago, they'd been sitting at a table eating dinner. There were another two galleries above it, then the long staircase leading up to the street. She knew that in a matter of minutes men with torches would appear, and then it would be possible to see who was dead or seriously injured. But unless Noah, Lisette, Peter, Rose and Edwin had left the dance floor while she was in the powder room and returned to their table, she feared they were in that tangled mass of bodies she'd glimpsed before the lights went out.

Looking up, she could see stars twinkling through the hole in the roof made by the bomb. Then she saw bobbing lights, from high up, and heard shouted instructions, ambulance sirens too. And it was only then, when she knew help was at hand, that she began to cry.

More light shone from torches and lanterns up at street

level, and a commanding male voice called out. 'Will everyone who is unhurt please make their way up the staircase to the street,' he yelled. 'There are people there waiting to take your names. Do not try to find your friends and family now, you will just make it harder for the rescue team to help those who are injured.'

Mariette couldn't bring herself to move. Her head said she must, but her eyes were on the tangled heap of people on the dance floor. The light was too poor to identify anyone, but she strained her eyes for a glimpse of Rose's pink dress or Peter's blue uniform. That she couldn't see either gave her a little hope, but she knew Lisette's black dress and Noah's evening clothes would only blend in with all the others there.

How many people were dead?

A hand on her arm startled her. It was a rescue worker in a tin hat, carrying a torch. 'Come with me, miss, there's people up the top who'll take care of you.'

'I was in the powder room when it happened,' she sobbed out. 'It's my twenty-first and I left them all dancing. I don't know if they are amongst those . . .' She pointed to the dance floor.

'They may not have been,' he said gently. 'Let's get you upstairs, you might find them there.'

Taking her arm firmly, he led her to the staircase and then up the stairs. She stopped at the first landing to look back down. There was more light now, and she could see that rescue workers, police and ambulance men were moving around the bodies on the dance floor, checking for life. Two women were tearing strips off the bottom of their dresses for bandages. She saw them helping a woman in a red and white dress to sit up, but then realized it was a white dress and the red was her blood.

Then she saw Rose, her pink dress unmistakable, with

one arm flung across her face, legs twisted as if she'd been tossed into the air and then dropped. 'That's one of my friends,' she sobbed out to the rescue worker. 'The one in the pink dress. Her mother and father and her boyfriend must be there too. Will you check?'

'I will after I've got you upstairs,' he said. 'Come along, miss, this is no place for you.'

There were so many people like her being shepherded up the stairs. All in a state of shock, moving slowly, the way she'd seen so many people do in the aftermath of other air raids. She could hear crying all around her, people pleading for help in finding someone. And there were injured people too, with cuts on their heads and faces, stumbling with the effort of climbing up one side of the stairs, as rescue people with stretchers went down the other side.

Finally, she reached street level and the club's foyer, where a female rescue worker in a siren suit took her name and asked about the rest of the group she was with: their names, ages, clothing and anything else which would help to identify them.

Mariette managed to give her the information. 'I saw Rose on the dance floor, so I think they are all together,' she added, breaking into fresh tears. 'And there was Edwin Atkins too. He's in an RAF uniform, about five foot ten, brown hair, age twenty-six.'

'That's a great help, Miss Carrera,' the woman said. 'I can see you are shivering, so I'll get someone to give you a blanket and take you nearby for a cup of tea. You can wait for news of your friends there.'

With an army blanket around her bare shoulders, Mariette was led with some other people, all as deeply shocked as she was, out of the club, along the street and down some steps to a basement room. There were forty or so people in there already, some sitting crying, others pacing the floor. She could tell those who had come from the Café de Paris as they were all in evening dress. There were other people too, in ordinary day clothes, who had clearly come in here when the air-raid warning went off a couple of hours earlier.

A big woman in a WVS uniform was manning a tea trolley, but to Mariette none of it seemed real. She felt she should be the person behind the tea trolley handing out cups of tea because that was the role she was used to. She had never expected to be the one receiving sympathy, being asked if she was warm enough and other such solicitous questions.

She took a cup of tea, but she was shaking so much that one of the helpers took it from her and led her to a seat, putting the cup on the one next to her and then wrapping the blanket more firmly around her shoulders.

Most of the other people couldn't stop talking in loud voices about what had happened. Someone said it was as well the bombs came so early; if they'd been dropped after ten, when the club was at its busiest, it would have been much worse. She gathered that most of these survivors had been on the upper galleries. Some, like Mariette, had friends or relatives who had gone down to the dance floor and were still unaccounted for, but the vast majority hadn't lost anyone, they were just here until they got some transport home.

It made her feel sick to hear them raking over the details, describing the band members who were hit, and the woman who was decapitated.

'My husband and I were dancing five minutes before the bomb went off,' one woman kept repeating. She was wearing a mink stole, and diamonds sparkled at her throat. 'My husband said he didn't like the crush down there. To think I was cross with him!'

Mariette remembered that she'd left her evening bag and

stole on her chair. She had no money and no keys to get into the house. She was freezing, despite the blanket, and could feel the concrete floor turning her feet in flimsy evening shoes to blocks of ice.

Then, just as she was thinking she'd been forgotten, Edwin came through the door. His left arm was in a sling, his evening suit was flecked with plaster and dust, and he had a bad cut on his cheek. But he was alive.

Mariette rushed to him. 'Thank heavens you are safe. But what about the others?'

He put his good arm around her and held her close. 'All gone, I'm afraid, Mari,' he said, his voice cracking with emotion. 'I just identified them.'

Mariette had heard people in her position say that they couldn't take it in, that they thought there must be a mistake, and now she could identify with them. How on earth could people who meant so much to her be snatched away from her in such a terrible way?

Edwin took charge. 'When the all-clear sounds, I'm going to take you home, Mari. I believe Rose has a brother, we will have to contact him.'

'He's called Jean-Philippe, but I've only met him a couple of times,' she said. 'He's in the navy. But I haven't got any keys for the house or anything,' she blurted out, and began crying even harder.

'I've got the keys. The police took them from Mr Baylis's pocket,' he said. 'This is the worst possible thing you will ever go through, Mari. But I'm going to help you. Now, sit down and let's talk about you. Have you got any other relatives here? Any friends who will rally round?'

It was after three in the morning before they got back to St John's Wood. Mariette still had the blanket she'd been given wrapped around her bare shoulders, and she had cried for most of the taxi ride home. But her grief became even stronger when she walked into the house and saw everything that was so much a part of Noah and Lisette. Lisette's sewing basket was by her chair, Noah's book by his. The family photographs were on the side table by the window, and even the faint waft of Lisette's perfume still hung in the air.

If not for her birthday, they would be safe in bed now. But now Rose would never have her wedding, and the house would never have Noah and Lisette's grandchildren running up and down the stairs. Only a couple of days ago, Noah had said they would go to New Zealand when the war was over. But that could never happen now.

'I think you should call your parents straight away,' Edwin suggested. 'It will already be afternoon in New Zealand.'

'They haven't got a telephone,' she said. 'When they ring me, it's from Aunt Peggy's bakery.'

'Then you must call them there. Would you like me to do it for you?'

He poured them both a brandy while she found the number in the family address book. Then he poked the fire, which had been left banked up, and coaxed it back into flames. He made her sit down by it, and dialled the operator.

'It'll take a little time, I expect,' he said, putting his hand over the receiver so the operator couldn't hear. 'Now, drink that brandy. It's good for shock. What's your aunt's surname?'

'Reid,' she said brokenly, imagining fat, jolly Aunt Peggy waddling to the phone and shouting down it the way she always did. 'She's not a real aunt, just Mum's friend really.'

He nodded, and then spoke. 'Is that Mrs Reid? Peggy Reid?'

Mariette could hear a woman's voice asking who he was. She got up and took the receiver. 'Aunt Peggy, it's me, Mari. Something terrible has happened. Could you get Mum, Papa or Mog?'

'Mog's right here, my love, she just came in to see me,' she said. 'I'll put her on.'

Mariette heard her tell Mog that something bad had happened.

'Mari?' Mog's voice sounded weak and frightened. 'Whatever is it?'

Mari blurted it out, crying as she did so. 'They've all gone, Noah, Lisette, Rose and her boyfriend, Peter. They took me to the club for my birthday. The bombs came right through the roof. I was in the powder room. They are all dead.'

She heard Mog make a sound – an exclamation of rage rather than a sharp intake of breath – but, as always, when trouble struck, Mog rallied. 'Now, where are you? And who is with you?' she asked, her voice high with distress, but controlling it. 'I'll have to go home and tell Belle, so you must tell me as much as you can.'

'I'm in Uncle Noah's house. And Edwin, Peter's friend, is here with me. He's been very kind.' Just speaking to Mog made her feel a little calmer. 'I'm not hurt at all. Not a scratch. Edwin identified their bodies. It's the middle of the night here, there's no more bombing now. But it's so awful, I can't believe they've gone.'

'Let me speak to the young man. Edwin, did you say his name was? You must go to bed with a hot-water bottle. It is a truly terrible thing,' Mog said, 'and you've had the worst kind of shock. Tomorrow you must contact Jean-Philippe. He'll know what has to be done. If I could fly, I'd come straight there to hold you, but I can't, and neither can your mum or dad. So you've got to stay strong, my darling. Now, let me talk to Edwin.'

'What did she say to you?' Mariette asked Edwin, after he'd put the phone down.

'Just what my grandmother would've said in the same circumstances. That I wasn't to take advantage of you, see that you were warm enough. And then she remembered I'd lost my best friend, and she offered her sympathy and said perhaps I needed my mother too, and some brandy.' He half smiled. 'She sounds quite a character. She said she would go straight home to tell your mother, but your father was out on a job and won't be back till late. They will ring back in the morning, meaning tomorrow evening here, at six.'

'I hadn't thought about your loss at all,' she admitted as he sat down beside her. 'I'm so sorry.'

'I understand. It's different for me – most of us in the squadron have lost so many friends, we're kind of used to it now. It's still awful, but we learn to soldier on. This is strange and different because it was so unexpected. All of us pilots think we'll die in our planes, not in a nightclub.'

'I didn't even ask you about your injuries,' she said. 'Is your arm broken?'

'I don't think so, though they did say I was to go to the hospital to get it checked. I was knocked off my feet and landed on it awkwardly. I think it's only sprained. One of the Civil Defence men said there were thirty-four deaths, and about eighty injured. If you hadn't gone off to the powder room, it would have been another two dead.'

The brandy after all the champagne and wine earlier was making her feel woozy. She got up and wobbled, grabbing the sofa to steady herself.

'Steady on! Sit down while I fill a hot-water bottle for you, then I'll help you up to bed,' he said.

'You'd better sleep in Rose's room,' she said as she sat down again with a thump.

A little later, clutching the hot-water bottle, Mariette let Edwin help her up the stairs. She pointed to the door of Rose's room and lurched towards her own.

'I think you might need help getting your dress undone,' he said.

She looked round at him, thinking for a moment he was intent on taking advantage. But all she saw in his face was concern.

'I can see it's got tiny hooks and eyes, you can't reach those,' he said. 'It would be a shame to tear such a beautiful dress.'

He was right, she couldn't have done it alone; Lisette had fastened it for her when she put it on. She turned her back to him and felt his fingers fumbling a little.

'There, all done,' he said, putting his hand on her shoulder. 'If you feel scared in the night, just call out. I'll hear you.'

She held her dress up over her breasts, turned to him and kissed his cheek. 'Thank you for everything, Edwin. I don't know what I would've done without you.'

He pulled her to him with his good arm. 'This certainly wasn't the way I imagined the evening turning out. I couldn't believe my luck when I saw you. But I've got my orders from your granny. I will look after you.'

17

Mariette fell asleep as soon as she got into bed, but she was awake again within an hour and spent the rest of the night crying into her pillow. Never before had she wanted her parents and Mog so much. She was afraid, sickened by what had happened, and she didn't know how she was going to deal with anything.

By seven she couldn't stand lying there any more with such terrible images running through her brain. When she got downstairs to make herself a cup of tea, she found Edwin sitting in the kitchen as red-eyed and troubled as she was.

'I don't know what I have to do,' she admitted, sitting down at the kitchen table opposite him. 'Will the police come here? What do they do with their bodies until the funeral?'

'I don't know either,' he said. 'I've never had to deal with anything like this. But I think the undertaker explains everything. But that isn't for you to worry about, Mari. Jean-Philippe is the one to do it. Your gran, or aunt, said you had to contact him. I could do that for you, if you like?'

'He's in the navy, so I doubt he'll be there,' she said. 'But Alice, his wife, will know how to contact him, I expect. I would be grateful if you could break the news to her, I'll probably make a real hash of it.'

She said she would get the number from Noah's study. When she came back with it, the kettle was boiling and she made them both tea. 'The thing is,' she blurted out, 'Jean-Philippe isn't very easy to talk to. Even Rose used to say it was like trying to talk to a brick wall.'

Edwin nodded. 'Peter said something to that effect too. He said Jean-Philippe and Rose were like chalk and cheese. But then he is only her half-brother, so I suppose that makes a difference.'

Mariette had often wondered who Jean-Philippe's father was. She thought, if he had died, then Lisette would have talked about it, and Lisette didn't strike her as the kind to get divorced. It was just another cloudy area in the shared past of her parents and Noah and Lisette, and one that hardly mattered now that her godfather and his wife, whom she'd come to love so much, had gone.

But Jean-Philippe was still very much alive, and she was apprehensive about having to communicate with him because she had come to suspect there was bad feeling between him and Noah. Lisette had stood in the middle, keeping them apart.

Looking back, this much had been evident at their first meeting. Jean-Philippe was polite but cold towards her, and it appeared to be a duty visit rather than any real desire to see his mother and meet the daughter of her old friend. The photograph of him in the drawing room flattered him, and made him look far more like Lisette than he really was. In the flesh he was strange-looking; his jet-black hair grew too low over his forehead, and his equally dark eyes were very small. His head could almost be described as triangular, with a very sharp chin.

He hadn't stayed that day for more than twenty minutes. At the time, Mariette didn't think anything of it, but recently, after another equally brief visit, she had asked Lisette why he didn't come more often and stay for longer. Lisette had looked embarrassed and said something about him being very busy.

Over the two years Mariette had lived with Lisette and Noah she had only met Alice, Jean-Philippe's wife, twice.

Lisette said once that her daughter-in-law suffered from her nerves, and that was why they never entertained. Mariette thought privately that she'd have a problem with her nerves too if she was married to such a cold man.

She wondered how such a warm, loving and giving woman like Lisette could have produced a son so different from her. Was his father a brute, and was that why Lisette had left him?

Edwin waited until nine o'clock in the morning to call Jean-Philippe. He said it wasn't fair to wake someone up any earlier on a Sunday and then give them such terrible news.

Mariette sat beside him on the sofa as he made the call. When a male voice answered, he hesitated for a moment or two because he hadn't expected Jean-Philippe to be there.

There was no easy or painless way to tell someone their family had all been killed, but Mariette thought Edwin did a very good job. He relayed the facts gently and tactfully. He stumbled over the words several times, and kept apologizing. But he gave an accurate account of what had happened, including Mariette's shock and concern for him, and added his own deep sympathy for Jean-Philippe's loss.

When he put the phone down, he looked shaken. 'He was so curt,' he exclaimed, looking at Mariette in bewilderment. 'It was almost as if he resented me telling him. He said he'd heard on this morning's news about the Café de Paris but asked what possessed us all to go to a West End nightclub. You heard me say it was your twenty-first? Well, he gave a kind of disparaging snort at that. He even asked why you and I survived. Didn't even ask if we were injured!'

Mariette put her hand on his arm comfortingly. 'He is a cold fish,' she admitted. 'But I expect it was the shock that made him talk like that. Once he's had time for it to sink in, he'll probably ring back and be more human.'

'He'll have to be; it falls on him to arrange the funeral and settle all his parents' affairs. I wish I could stay and help you, Mariette, but I have to get back to Biggin Hill and also report Peter's death. I did ask the police to inform his parents last night, but I'll have to speak to them too.'

'You've done more than enough for me. I can't imagine how I'd have coped last night if you hadn't been there.'

'I'll ring you as often as I can, Mari,' he said, and he put his good arm around her and drew her closer, kissing her fore-head. 'I hate to leave you here with no one to look after you. Is there a friend who could come and stay?'

'Somehow I don't think Jean-Philippe would approve of any of the friends I've made in the East End, if he found them here,' she said ruefully. 'But I will contact all the friends I made through Rose. That will keep me busy today, so don't worry about me, Edwin. But how are you intending to fly or drive with that poorly arm?'

He managed a weak smile. 'I'm not. My car's back at the air-field. I'll get a lift from the station. I'll see the MO and he'll give me sick leave or ground duties. Telling the chaps about Peter will be tough, though, he was very popular with everyone.'

She saw that his eyes were damp, and reached out to stroke his face in silent sympathy. 'Should I contact Rose's office, or leave that to her brother?'

'It might be advisable to wait until he gets back to you. The way he was with me suggests he's the kind to take umbrage at anything he feels is high-handed.'

'I'm not expecting much comfort from him,' she admit-ted. 'I might be mistaken, but I think he's got a huge chip on his shoulder.'

Edwin pulled a pen and notepad out of his pocket. 'This is the number at the airfield,' he said, writing it down. 'You can leave a message for me there, if you need help in any way.

Even if it's just that you want to talk. Don't be afraid to contact me, Mari. If this hadn't happened, I would've been beating a path to your door to see you again. I really like you, it's not just because I feel bad about all this.'

'I like you too,' she admitted. 'But you must go now, Edwin, or you'll be in trouble.'

He leaned forward and kissed her on the lips. Just a light touch, but enough for her to know he meant what he said.

After Edwin left, Mariette went into Rose's bedroom to make the bed and to find her address book. But the sight of her clothes strewn about, face powder spilt on the dressing table, the book *The Grapes of Wrath* left by her bedside, after they'd discussed it recently, brought on a huge swell of utter loss.

There had been so many, many nights when they'd sat in this room chatting and laughing. In here, Rose had taught her to jitterbug to swing music, to drink alcohol, told her about film stars Mariette had never heard of before, and they'd talked about love too. She had admired Rose's sophistication, deplored her naivety about sex, yet hoped that one day she herself would be as poised as her friend was.

She felt bad now that she'd sometimes thought Rose was a snob, bossy and mean-spirited, because the good in her far outweighed the bad, and she had become as dear to Mariette as a sister. Rose had been so generous with her time, sharing her friends, never once making Mariette feel she was a poor relation or a burden. Only now that she was gone did Mariette realize it was Rose who had given her the confidence to be what she wanted to be. Rose would never have wanted to dole out clothes to bombed-out people, or listen to their problems, but she never scoffed at Mariette for doing it – in fact, she admired her for it.

To lose Noah and Lisette, who had been so good to her,

was terrible; they had loved and nurtured her, kept her, paid for college and so much else. But she had expected to have Rose in her life for ever, to be a bridesmaid at her wedding, godmother to her children, to share everything, friends until death parted them in old age.

She lay down on Rose's bed and cried. Not tears of shock like last night, but tears for a loss she felt she could never come to terms with. Never before had she felt so alone. She would never again hear Rose singing 'Puttin' on the Ritz'. Never hear her peals of laughter, or see her wrinkle up her nose when she told Mariette of some hideous sight in the East End. Never smile at the way she used to raise one eyebrow when she didn't really believe something she was being told, or how she always checked her stocking seams were straight before she walked out of the door. All such little, inconsequential things, but they made up what Rose was – a warm, vibrant person with so much lust for life.

Mariette was still crying an hour later when the front door bell rang. She got up, ran to the bathroom to dab a face flannel on her swollen eyes and went to answer it.

It was Jean-Philippe.

'I am so sorry,' she gasped out. 'I still can't believe it. It must have been such a huge shock to you?'

'Yes,' he said, walking in and placing his trilby hat on the hall table. 'If Mother had told me she was planning to go to such a place I would have advised her against it. The West End is not the place to go when bombs are dropping. Buckingham Palace was hit too last night.'

He was in civilian clothes, wearing a dark well-cut suit under a navy-blue overcoat. She waited for him to say how awful it must have been for her, to ask for some details about the tragedy. But he said nothing further, just walked into the drawing room and poured himself a Scotch.

Mariette followed him. 'Edwin left a note for you explaining who you have to get in touch with about their bodies,' she said, feeling very awkward with him. 'I have Rose's work number too. I could notify them for you, if you like.'

'I will see to that and everything else,' he said curtly, gulping down the Scotch.

'How much leave do you have?' she asked tentatively. 'Though, under the circumstances, I'm sure they will extend it.'

'I was due back on Tuesday,' he said. 'But I have arranged another week.'

'Can I get you something to eat?' she asked. She knew he lived in Hampstead, which was no distance at all, but she felt she had to offer something.

'No, I have eaten already, and I don't have much time now. So if you will run along, I'll sort out the papers and the other things I need.'

She was shocked at being dismissed as if she was a servant.

'Is there anything I can help you with?' she asked.

'No, but in the next day or two I would expect you to find alternative accommodation. After the funeral, I will be securing the house until such time as I move into it.'

For a moment, she thought she had misheard. 'You want me to leave?'

'That's what I said. Is there something wrong with your hearing?'

'No, of course not. I just can't believe you'd say such a thing,' she retorted. 'Uncle Noah and Aunt Lisette would be horrified.'

'They were not your aunt and uncle,' he said crisply. 'You are merely the daughter of someone my mother nursed in France. You are an adult now, and you've sponged off them long enough.'

That floored her.

'Why are you being so nasty to me?' she asked with indignation. 'You know I couldn't go home once war broke out. And if your parents hadn't wanted me here, they would've said so.'

'That's as maybe, but they are gone now. So run along, I have things to do.'

'Just a minute.' She took a step closer to him. 'I don't understand your hostility towards me. I loved your parents and Rose as if they were my own family. Whatever you plan to do with this house and everything in it is up to you, I understand that. But if you think you are going to throw me out of here before their funeral, and not allow me to try to comfort the people who will come to it, or prepare the food for the wake here afterwards, then you are mistaken. Try to do it and I will inform the editors of the newspapers Uncle Noah wrote for. He was known as a compassionate man, and people would be horrified to read that his stepson shared none of his beliefs.'

'Oh yes, he was compassionate towards whores alright. Your mother was one of them!'

Mariette reeled back in shock.

'You didn't know then?' he sneered at her. 'He wrote his book about women sold into prostitution because he helped rescue your mother from that life.'

'I don't believe you,' she said weakly, although she had a nasty feeling there might be a grain of truth in it.

'Belle was brought up in a Seven Dials brothel, she witnessed a murder there and that's why she was taken, to shut her up and to sell her on into prostitution in France,' he snapped out. Then he paused, his face breaking into a smug grin. 'Later,' he went on, 'the murderer was caught and hanged for it, and your precious mother was the chief witness. So don't tell me you're going to speak to any editors. You wouldn't want that little lot coming out, would you?'

Mariette fled upstairs at that, afraid of a man who could be so vicious.

It was over an hour later that Jean-Philippe called Mariette to come downstairs. He had packed a box with some papers, and she could see some velvet jewellery boxes in there too.

She had spent the last hour pacing her bedroom in floods of angry tears. But she knew she might put herself in real danger if she told him just what she thought of him.

'I'm going now; I'll call you about the funeral,' he said. 'I realize I was a little hasty, so you may stay for two days after the wake. But if, when I return, I find anything missing, I will call the police.'

She was tempted to tell him where to go, but she bit the words back and just nodded.

Once he'd gone, she put the chain on the door – she wouldn't put it past him to sneak back and check what she was doing – then she leaned back against the door and tried to think what she must do.

But considering her future was impossible when she'd been told something so shocking about her mother. It was five o'clock now, which meant her parents would be ringing in an hour. She couldn't ask her mother about something like this on the telephone. But she did need to know if it was true.

How could she find out?

Noah's study seemed the most logical place to look.

She began by looking at the books he'd written, and found one called *White Slaves*. But after a quick flip through the pages, there didn't appear to be any real names in the case studies of victims, just details of how they were taken and lots of statistics about how many girls were reported missing and had never been found. There was also a section on foreign girls who had been brought to England, supposedly as servants in private homes, but had been sold into brothels and ruined.

Leaving that one out to read properly later, she checked his other books, but they were either fiction or about the last war. She went through a filing cabinet that held correspondence from the last five years on a range of subjects, but there was nothing about prostitution.

Noah kept things very neat and tidy, reference books arranged in alphabetical order by subject, fiction by author. There was no clutter; a few box files on a shelf were all labelled, and a glance into them proved they were full of bills, research material, recent magazine articles and reviews of his books.

She had just about given up when the telephone rang, and she raced to answer it.

'Mum?' she asked breathlessly.

'Oh my darling! I can't even begin to tell you how we all feel at the news. And how are you coping with it?'

Just the sweetly familiar sound of her mother's voice brought more tears to her eyes. 'I've been better,' she said. 'Jean-Philippe was just here, he'll do everything that has to be done.'

'Yes, I'm sure he will, he was always such a good little boy.'

Mariette gritted her teeth. She couldn't tell her mother what had been said, not even that she was to get out of the house, because she knew it would make her family frantic.

'Now tell me exactly what happened,' Belle said. 'Mog was so upset, she probably didn't get it right.'

Mariette explained everything again. 'Don't you worry about me,' she finished up. 'I've got friends who will look after me. I'll write after the funeral, just now I need to sit quietly and think things through.'

'I was so fond of Lisette and Noah,' Belle said, and it was clear she was crying. 'They helped me through some very bad times. And Rose was such a beautiful, placid little girl. It's so hard to take in that they all went together like that.'

'Look, Mum, I'm finding it really hard to talk. I'm going to sit down and write you a letter. Tell Dad and Mog that I'm alright, just terribly sad. And this call will cost a fortune, so you must go now.'

'We all love you, darling,' and this time Belle couldn't control her sobs. 'I wish I was there to hold you.'

'And I love you all too. I'll write straight away.'

Mariette felt she'd just been put through the mangle and everything had been squashed out of her. She sank down on to the sofa and cried again.

The noise of the telephone ringing roused her again. She braced herself, expecting it to be Jean-Philippe with more orders, but it was Johnny.

'Thank God you are there,' he burst out, as soon as he heard her voice. 'I don't often pray, but I did when I was told just now about the bombing at the Café de Paris. I couldn't get hold of the casualty list and, as I knew you were going there early, I was afraid I'd lost you. But my prayers were answered. What a relief!'

She couldn't bring herself to tell him Lisette, Noah, Rose and Peter were all dead. She knew he would leave his shift and come here. If Jean-Philippe found out, that would give him more ammunition to use against her. So she said that she would be at Greville's office tomorrow and asked if he could get a few hours off to meet her after work.

'It was all such a shock,' she said. 'I'm going to have a bath and go to bed now.'

'You sound like all the stuffing's been knocked out of you,' he said. 'I can get off tomorrow, I'll meet you at five thirty.'

The siren went off about half past seven that evening. Mariette was tempted to go to bed and take her chances, but she knew that was reckless, so she picked up her pyjamas and her dressing gown, filled up a hot-water bottle as she passed through the kitchen and went down to the cellar.

Lisette had added some embellishments to the cellar recently – a standard lamp, a rug on the floor – and had tacked a large colourful patchwork quilt to the wall. She said she had begun it when she was expecting Rose and while Noah was away a great deal, during the first war. But when they moved into this house, it didn't fit in with the decor in the bedrooms.

It was another reminder of Lisette's talents. She had been a serene, gentle woman who enjoyed gliding quietly about her home, caring more for other people's comfort than her own. She never raised her voice, meals were prepared without fuss, and Mariette hardly ever observed her cleaning, doing the laundry or anything else to keep the house clean, polished and tidy. Yet it always was pristine, nothing had changed since Mr and Mrs Andrews left to go and help their farming relatives. She did it all. Even down here, she had to make it homely and pleasant for her family. There were jigsaws, board games and books on the shelves, even some artificial flowers in a vase.

Mariette put the hot-water bottle in one of the beds, and turned on the electric fire, then sat down in one of the easy chairs. She could hear the soft thud of bombs dropping in the far distance, and she wondered if they were dropping on the East End again or whether some other area of London was getting it tonight.

Where would she live when she had to leave here? Where could she afford, with only two days' paid work a week?

The answer to that was obvious, of course: she'd have to get another job. But doing what? The munitions factory? Clippie on a bus?

As she sat there, she noticed in the far corner there were three stout cardboard boxes, stacked on top of one another. Noah had said to leave them there as they weren't in the way. Lisette had teased him about the contents, she said she suspected they were the first articles he wrote when he became a journalist, and he was a sentimental fool not throwing them out. Noah had just laughed, which implied she was right.

Mariette thought that she might find something about her mother in there. It could be that Jean-Philippe had looked through them, back in the days when he lived here, and that was how he'd got his information.

The first box was just as Lisette had thought. Newspaper cuttings. Noah had stuck each one on to thin card and written the date and the newspaper in which it appeared. The oldest one she could see was dated 1905, when he had been just twenty. It was about a wedding in Camden Town; he described the bride's dress, which was cream taffeta with a lace overlay, while the bridesmaids, younger sisters of the bride, were in pink.

As she looked further, she found most of the early dates were either weddings or funerals, with the occasional article about a fund-raising lunch or dinner, where he'd noted who had held it, how much was raised for the charity, and any notable people present.

He was organized even then, and the cuttings were filed in date order. She flicked through them, only stopping to read ones that had a heading that stood out. Seeing one that said 'Tarantula Terror', dated January 1910, in *The Herald*, she read about a porter in Covent Garden who was spotted with a tarantula on his shoulder. Once advised of this, the porter became rigid with terror and it took a young boy with a glass and a sheet of card to remove it and place it in a box for safety. Later, the spider was taken to London Zoo. Beside the cutting Noah had written 'My first proper story'.

From that date on, judging by the sheer numbers of cuttings, Noah was obviously getting more work, and being sent to write up more interesting events. But then, in August of 1910, there was a big article in *The Herald* about young girls who had gone missing from around the Seven Dials area. This one was the first that carried his byline.

It was a passionate article – Noah was obviously deeply concerned about the plight of these young girls – and it sounded as if he had researched the article thoroughly. All the disappearances had been reported to the police, but none of the girls had been found. He stressed that all of them were pretty, but they were good girls from loving homes, with no reason to run away. All had disappeared while out on an errand or on their way to see a friend, and he believed they could have been taken to work as prostitutes, possibly in France or Belgium. Then, at the bottom, he had listed each of the girls. And one was Belle Cooper.

Mariette was stunned.

Shutting that box up, she moved on to the second one. Again, it was full of cuttings, but there was nothing of interest to her. But she did notice that Noah's star was clearly rising in the world of journalism as many of his stories appeared on the front page of the newspaper, and all carried his name.

The last box was more of the same. But, just as she was getting close to the bottom of the box, she found what she was looking for. A report on a murder trial at the Old Bailey in 1913. It wasn't written by Noah, and it wasn't mounted on card like everything else. It was short and to the point.

Mr Frank James Waldegrave, also known as Kent, was convicted of the murder of one Millie Simmons, at Jake's Court, Seven Dials, in January 1910, and sentenced to be hanged. The principal witness, Belle Cooper, gave evidence that she had witnessed the murder when she was fifteen and was subsequently abducted by Waldegrave and an accomplice, and taken to Paris to be sold into prostitution.

Stunned and horrified, Mariette just sat there holding the newspaper cutting in her hands. She wondered how her mother could be so gentle, caring and so normal after going through something as bad as that.

She needed to know the whole story: how Noah, Lisette and her papa all fitted into it; and how Mog coped when Belle went missing. Yet, as horrific as it was, it did explain why her parents and Mog had always been so understanding of other people's frailties.

Yet if Jean-Philippe had hoped he would crush her with this family history, he was out of luck. If anything, it just made her love and admire her mother still more.

18

'I'll find somewhere for you to stay,' Johnny said, taking Mariette's hands across the café table and squeezing them. 'I'd also like to go round and give Jean-Philippe a good hiding. He's not a man, he's a snake.'

The café was close to the office in Baker Street, and she'd just finished telling Johnny the whole story about what had happened at the Café de Paris and how horrible Jean-Philippe had been.

Mariette managed a weak smile. 'That won't help things, he'd have you locked up. And then what would I do?'

'I wish I could do more,' Johnny said. 'I can't believe you went to work today. You must have steel in your spine.'

'What was I going to do all day, if I stayed home? It doesn't feel like home any more. Jean-Philippe didn't need to order me to leave – I don't want to stay there alone, and neither could I afford too. But Lisette will be spinning in her grave at the way her son is behaving. Well, she would if she was in one.'

'What did my uncle say today?'

'He was kind, very shocked, of course. Well, you don't expect one of your staff to come in and tell you four of the six people she went out with, to celebrate her birthday, are now dead. He said that I should demand to know the contents of Noah's will. But I can't do that.'

'But if you find the name of Noah's solicitor, you could tell him what's happened,' Johnny suggested. 'I expect Jean-Philippe is entitled to everything now his mother and sister are gone. But you never know, Noah might have left you something too – after all, you are his god-daughter. That snake might just tell the solicitor that you've disappeared or something. I wouldn't put it past him.'

'I wouldn't want to ask such a thing. That puts me on the same level as Jean-Philippe.'

'You don't have to ask if you've been left anything, you could just say that you want to give him a forwarding address, just in case he needs to contact you. But, like I said, I'll find somewhere for you to stay. I know loads of people who might have room for a lodger, and they don't live in slums either.'

'You are very sweet. Last night, I felt I was being crushed by the weight of it all. But when I woke this morning, I felt a bit better knowing I was going to see you this evening.'

He didn't respond for a moment, just looked down at her hands in his on the table.

When he spoke, it was haltingly, as if struggling to find the right words. 'When I thought I might have lost you, I wished I'd told you I loved you. I never dared say it before because I was scared you'd back away from me. Then, when you answered the phone yesterday, I was so happy you were alive that I thought I must tell you.

'I was watching you come out of the office this evening, and you looked like you were on your way to be executed. But as soon as you saw me, you switched on a smile. But you know what I thought?'

'No, tell me.'

'That you'd asked to meet me to tell me it was over.'

In view of everything she'd just told him, Mariette was shocked that he should be thinking of himself, and the thought crossed her mind that he was going to use her tragedy for his own ends.

'Why on earth would you think that?' she asked.

'It's easy, sweetheart. You're special, beautiful, clever, got everything going for you. Why would you want to tie yourself up with a fireman, when you could have a rich man who could give you a nice house and all the stuff you're used to? And why didn't you tell me yesterday on the phone that all your folks had been killed?'

'Because I knew you'd drop everything and come over,' she said. 'I was afraid Jean-Philippe might come back. If he found you there, it would've turned ugly.'

'I'd have kicked his teeth in. But I dare say that's just what you were afraid of.'

There was the implication in that remark that she was ashamed of him. She resented the fact that he would bring it up now, when she already had enough on her plate. It had been her intention to tell him what Jean-Philippe had said about her mother. But under the circumstances, maybe that wasn't such a good idea.

They went to a pub and had a couple of drinks, but Mariette felt too sad, dejected and worried to talk. She couldn't help but compare how Edwin had been with her the previous day to the way Johnny was behaving now. Edwin had been really comforting, and he'd only met her for the first time a couple of hours before the disaster. Yet Johnny, who had known her for months, seemed unable to grasp how bad all this was for her.

'I want to go home,' she said, when he offered her a third drink. It was only eight o'clock but she'd had enough for one day. 'I'm sorry, Johnny, but I feel too miserable to even try to chat.'

'That's OK, I'll come with you,' he said.

'No, Johnny,' she said. 'I meant alone.'

'You always said you wished we had a chance to be alone somewhere comfortable,' he said reproachfully.

'There's a time and a place for everything,' she said sharply.

'But this is not the time. And my uncle's house, so soon after his death, is not the place. Have some respect, Johnny!'

'I only wanted to take care of you. There's no pleasing some people,' he retorted.

Johnny's sulky expression played on Mariette's mind as she walked home. She really did feel he had hoped to take advantage of her when she was vulnerable, and that hurt. But maybe she was overreacting and thinking the worst of him because she had no one else to lash out at?

But when she arrived home, she was very glad that she hadn't weakened and allowed Johnny to come back with her, because Jean-Philippe was there. He had a large notepad and pen in his hands and appeared to be making an inventory of valuable items.

'The funeral is arranged for St Mark's on Friday, at two,' he said, breaking off from his list to speak to her. 'Arrange refreshments for twenty people afterwards.'

She wanted to suggest he use the world 'please', but she was more concerned by the number.

'Only twenty?' she queried. Just off the top of her head she could think of at least fifteen couples who were close friends of Noah and Lisette's, without including Noah's fellow journalists and authors, or Rose's friends and work colleagues.

'I am not providing a bun fight for all and sundry,' he said loftily. 'I have left a list in the kitchen of those I have invited back here. A few sandwiches will be quite sufficient, I believe one is allowed to have extra rations for a funeral, but I see no sense in squandering food on people at such a time.'

Mariette thought such meanness wasn't even worthy of a reply. 'But you have contacted all of the people they cared about?'

'I placed an obituary in *The Times*.'

262

She knew that meant he hadn't, and he didn't intend to telephone or write a personal letter to anyone. She was stunned by such callous behaviour.

'Don't you think your family would expect you to make personal calls to the people they cared about?' she asked.

His face darkened. 'Who are you to pass comment on what I decide?' he sneered. 'I've got more important things to do with my time than telephoning Rose's vacuous friends, or the nodding acquaintances of my stepfather's.'

Mariette thought it better to show her disapproval by walking away from him than by saying anything further. They were after all his family, not hers. And if he hadn't the good manners or the compassion to think about what they would have liked, it wasn't her fault.

Jean-Philippe left the house just after ten without saying anything more to her. He took with him the silver candlesticks and a large silver dish from the dining room, a carriage clock from the drawing room and a set of four small watercolours in gilt frames from Noah and Lisette's bedroom. She had to assume he was afraid she would steal them and, coming on top of everything else, she dissolved into tears.

The following morning, she went into work to find Mr Greville looking at *The Times*.

'Have you seen this obituary, about your uncle?' he asked, pointing to a column on the third page written by Walter Franklin, the editor. 'I know you said your uncle was a writer, but I hadn't realized he was so well known.'

She had long since realized that Greville wasn't quite as hard-hearted as he liked to make out. He'd been very kind the day after the bombing, and asked if she was alright for money. It helped to feel he cared about her, and she smiled at him gratefully as she picked up the newspaper.

Her eyes prickled with tears of pride as she read it.

Jean-Philippe might think a few lines that announced the deaths of his mother, stepfather and sister, plus the date and time of the funeral, was a sufficient obituary. But this was a real one, written by a man who knew Noah well and admired him.

The whole of Fleet Street is mourning the death of writer and journalist Noah Baylis, who lost his life on 8 March, along with his wife, daughter and family friend at the Café de Paris while celebrating his god-daughter's twenty-first birthday.

Often called 'The Voice of the Great War', the reports Baylis wrote during that conflict will stand for all time as some of the best, most informative insights into the terrible destruction and true cost of war.

He was honest, portraying not only the heroism he saw, but also the shocking waste of human life. His passionately descriptive passages allowed us to see what he had seen, to enter into that hell that haunted so many of our men for so long afterwards.

He went on to praise Noah's books and his many hard-hitting pieces of investigative journalism on the subjects of slum-property landlords, indifference to the plight of those left disabled after the war, and the extreme poverty which many people faced during the Depression years. He concluded:

Baylis had a big heart, and he used his talent as a writer to make others aware of the inequality in this country. His death is a huge loss to journalism and to all those who revered him.

Mariette didn't think she'd ever met Mr Franklin, but she hoped he would be at the funeral so she could shake his hand and thank him.

'I hope Jean-Philippe reads it and feels ashamed,' she said, wiping her eyes. She then told Greville what had happened the previous evening. 'All he cares about is grabbing everything valuable. Imagine what Aunt Lisette would have thought of his behaviour!'

'The sooner you get away from there the better,' Greville said, putting his hand on her shoulder. 'You can come and work at the factory, you know. And it would be easy enough to find a place to live down there. But, from what I hear, you'll probably want to be nearer our Johnny.'

On seeing her surprised look, he gave her one of his infrequent smiles. 'I guessed ages ago. He wouldn't be my choice for you. But it isn't up to me, is it?'

She wondered what he meant by Johnny not being his choice for her. That seemed an odd thing for anyone to say about their nephew. Did he know something about Johnny that she didn't?

Mariette cut out the obituary so she could send it to her parents. It was so very sad that this was all she could offer to comfort them on losing their dear friends.

On the Friday morning, Mariette sat up in bed and looked at her suitcase lying open on the floor. It was all packed, ready to go, just a few last-minute things to add. She would go to the funeral, come back here and say all the right things to the people Jean-Philippe thought worthy of an invitation to the house, and then she'd leave.

Joan, a friend she worked with at the old factory, had offered her a bed until she could find something permanent. It was in Bow, a tiny little house with an outside lavatory, no bathroom and gas lighting. Joan was lonely as her two children had been evacuated down to Devon and her husband was serving in North Africa. While Mariette was very grateful to Joan, and relieved that after today she would never need to see Jean-Philippe again, her heart ached at leaving a place that held so many wonderful memories.

Only six days ago she had been bursting with happiness. Her twenty-first birthday meant she was officially an adult, and she'd felt like one then, strong, capable, ready for anything that might lie ahead. But she hadn't known then that her world was going to fall apart and she would lose three people who meant everything to her. There was a hole inside her where they'd once been. Maybe, if she could go home to New Zealand, she could fill that hole with her own family. But she couldn't go home. And there was no one here, not even Johnny, who could take away the deep sorrow she felt.

She got out of bed and went to run a bath. After today, she'd have to make do with the public baths, and she knew she was going to hate that. Once she was dressed, there was bread to be picked up at the bakery – Mr Giggs, who owned it, had been fond of Lisette and he'd promised three white loaves to make the sandwiches.

It was fortunate that Lisette had been such a hoarder: there were four tins of salmon in the cupboard, two of spam, and more than enough ingredients for a large fruit cake. Mariette had made the cake yesterday, along with some sausage rolls and some jam tarts. It was a small revenge on Jean-Philippe to make sure he saw the guests eating up everything he'd probably planned to take home. She'd also packed tea, sugar and some other things in the bottom of her suitcase to help Joan out.

By half past twelve, everything was ready. The dining-room table looked pretty, with Lisette's favourite white lace-edged tablecloth, a vase of daffodils from the garden, and the food arranged on the best plates, sandwiches covered with damp tea towels to keep them fresh. Tea cups and saucers were on a trolley, and the alcohol and glasses were arranged on a table in the drawing room.

It was a lovely spring day. Crocuses had opened up in the sunshine, and there were masses of daffodils. Looking out at the garden, she was reminded that they never did get the chickens Mariette had suggested when they were on holiday in Arundel, but they had grown some vegetables last year. She wondered what would become of the beautiful garden Lisette had loved so much and on which she had lavished so much care. Mariette couldn't imagine Jean-Philippe continuing to take care of it.

St Mark's was packed, and many people had to stand. Mariette glanced at Jean-Philippe, who was standing next to her singing the first hymn, and wondered if he was suffering pangs of guilt now that it was obvious to everyone how well loved his family had been. Alice, his wife, hadn't come with him. When Mariette asked where she was, he said she was unwell. That sounded like a lie, and Mariette wondered if their marriage had broken up. That might account for him wanting to move into the old family home in such a hurry.

Mariette found the service extremely painful. She had attended services here many times with Noah, Lisette and Rose, and, although they weren't the kind of family who went every single week, they knew the vicar quite well, and she had expected him to say something personal, at least about Noah. But he didn't, and she wondered if Jean-Philippe had told him not to. At the point when the whole congregation had to follow the men carrying the three coffins out into the graveyard for the interment, she heard a couple of whispers that suggested many others were surprised by the bleak impersonal nature of the service too.

When Johnny had called Jean-Philippe a snake, it had

sounded like a very general insult. But after the coffins were in the ground, and the vicar had said the last words, Mariette noted the cautious way people approached him, most avoiding him altogether, so perhaps they too saw him as a snake that could possible spit venom at them.

Mariette kept her distance from Jean-Philippe, but she was touched that so many people came up to her to offer their condolences. Some she had met before at the house, some were neighbours, and many more were complete strangers, yet they all seemed to know who she was.

The biggest surprise was that Mr and Mrs Hayes, Peter's parents, had come. She had wondered who the aristocratic-looking couple were, sitting right behind her and Jean-Philippe in the church, but when they introduced themselves to her, she wondered why she hadn't guessed their identity. They fitted perfectly with what Rose had said about them. Mr Hayes was a big man in his sixties, with thick white hair and piercing blue eyes. His wife was slender, with high cheekbones, and the little hair showing under her wide-brimmed black hat was still blonde. Mariette thought they would make a handsome couple under happier circumstances. But today, in black mourning clothes and with faces etched with grief at losing their son, they looked old.

Mrs Hayes's eyes were damp, and earlier tears had left track marks through her face powder. 'We felt we had to come,' she said, her lower lip trembling. 'We knew from Edwin how terrible this has been for you, and we were so fond of Rose. We hoped she would become our daughter-in-law.'

'I wish I could have met you in happier times,' Mariette said, taking the woman's two hands in hers. 'I am so very sorry you lost your Peter, and I find it even more touching that you still came today, despite how you must be feeling.'

'The hardest thing is the way we've been made to feel

unwelcome by him,' Mr Hayes said, nodding towards Jean-Philippe. 'It was bad enough that we had to learn the date and time of the funeral from the newspaper, instead of a telephone call, but we put that down to his grief. But when we told him, just now, who we were, he barely acknowledged us. Not one word of consolation at losing our son.'

Mariette was shocked, she had thought Jean-Philippe's unpleasantness was only directed at her. 'I am so sorry,' she said. 'I can only suppose he is wrapped up in his own loss. I would've telephoned you myself, I certainly wanted to, but Jean-Philippe took Rose's address book and said he would see to contacting everyone.'

'He doesn't appear to have spoken to any of Rose's friends,' Mrs Hayes said with some indignation. 'We spoke to some of them we knew when we arrived at the church, and none of them had been contacted. Except that man . . .' She pointed to a small, rotund middle-aged man with a goatee beard who was talking to Jean-Philippe. 'I believe he is the man Rose worked for.'

'Sir Ralph Hastings,' Mariette said. She'd met him just once, when he had given Rose a lift home for the weekend.

'Rose would never have thought a man with a title was more important than her friends and future in-laws,' Mrs Hayes said pointedly.

'No, she wouldn't,' Mariette agreed. 'And neither would Noah or Lisette. I have to admit, Jean-Philippe has been very unpleasant to me. I have to leave the house after the wake.'

'Oh, my dear!' Mrs Hayes exclaimed. 'You mean, he is making you leave?'

Mariette nodded. 'If you should see Edwin, will you tell him? I will drop him a line at Biggin Hill, when I'm settled.'

'We'll be seeing him on Monday, when we bury Peter,' Mr Hayes said. 'He's been a tower of strength to us this last week, as have many of Peter's pilot friends. Gerald's parents came to see us too, such nice people. They asked after you, Mariette. They had high hopes for you two.'

A sudden sharp memory came back to Mariette of being in Peter's car, Rose beside him, with her and Gerald sitting in the back, all singing at the tops of their voices. Some of the best times she'd had in London had been with them, and her eyes filled with tears at the memory.

'He was a lovely, lovely man, and I miss him,' she said sadly.

Later, back at the house, Mariette busied herself pouring tea, offering people cake and sandwiches. She didn't know any of these people Jean-Philippe had invited, other than Sir Ralph Hastings, and even that had been only one brief meeting. She noted that there was only one real common denominator amongst the people Jean-Philippe had invited back here, and that was wealth and position. Not one of them was a close friend of the family; they were lawyers, bankers and the like. Presumably just people he'd found through Noah's correspondence and thought might be useful to him. That made her despise him even more, and she was tempted to fetch her case and get out now, leaving him to clear up.

A small man with gold-rimmed spectacles approached her. 'You must be Mariette?' he said.

'Yes, I am,' she said, wondering if she should know him. 'I'm sorry, but have we met before?' she asked.

'No, my dear, but I knew your mother many years ago. I'm Henry Fortesque, a retired lawyer. Noah and I were close friends when we were young, but we drifted apart, as people do. I met Belle when she was staying in his apartment prior to leaving for New Zealand, and I liked her very much. When she asked Noah to be your godfather, he was very touched.

The last time I spoke to him on the telephone, about a year ago, he said you were staying with him.'

Just to find someone who knew her mother and cared about Noah was like being given a comforting hug. 'Then you'll know Belle loves New Zealand, and I have two younger brothers, Alexis and Noel,' she said with a smile.

'I have kept abreast of her happy ending,' he said with a smile. 'I helped Noah a little in tracking down your father in France. By all accounts, he is a very charismatic man along with being a true war hero. There are few things more satisfying in life than seeing two people who deserve happiness finding it together. You have your mother's beauty and, I suspect, all of your father's charm.'

Mariette laughed softly. 'You aren't short in the charm department either,' she said. 'Gosh, it is so nice to meet someone here today who has a link with my family back home. I thought of Noah, Lisette and Rose as a second family, and to lose them all is very hard.'

He put his hand on her elbow, and drew her out of the drawing room and into the kitchen. 'Forgive me for manhandling you, my dear,' he said. 'But I had noticed a certain frostiness between you and Lisette's son. As so few of Noah and Lisette's real friends have come back here today, I formed my own opinion as to why. I suspect he only invited me because he thought I might be useful.'

'I am really mortified about how he's been behaving towards people,' she whispered. 'But he's been even worse to me. This has been my home for two years, but Noah and Lisette were barely cold before he ordered me to leave here. I'm going the minute this wake is over.'

The small man's eyebrows shot up in horror. 'My dear, that is appalling,' he agreed. 'I know Noah had come to think of you as another daughter, he told me this himself. He hoped that, when the war ended, he and Lisette could travel back with you to New Zealand to see Belle and Etienne. But we can't really talk now, walls have ears and all that. If I give you my card, will you come and see me? I'm only in Hampstead.'

There was such kindness in his tawny-coloured eyes. 'I'd like that, Mr Fortesque. It would be wonderful to be able to speak to someone who knew and cared about Noah and his family.'

'Call me Henry, please,' he said. 'Now, where are you intending to move to?'

'Bow, where a friend said she could put me up till I find something else. It might not be much but it's more welcoming than here.'

He took out a card from a silver holder and handed it to her. 'Could you make it to my house on Sunday, for lunch? My wife misses not having any of our children close by, she'd be pleased to feed you up.'

'That would be lovely,' she said. 'Thank you so much, Henry, you've made me feel a lot better.'

'About one o'clock,' he said. 'We usually eat before two.'

The guests ate everything, down to the last sandwich and sausage roll, and then began to leave.

Mariette went up to her bedroom, packed the last of her things, and took one last fond look at the room which Lisette had said was inspired by Belle's hat shop. She hoped that Jean-Philippe would never have a moment's happiness in this house, or anywhere else.

As she got to the bottom of the stairs, with her coat on and suitcase in hand, Jean-Philippe came out of the drawing room.

'There's clearing up to be done,' he said curtly.

'Yes, by you,' she said sharply. 'I'm off now, and I hope I never have the misfortune to see you again. I also hope you never have a moment's happiness in this house.'

'You little guttersnipe,' he said, and took a threatening step towards her.

'You lay one hand on me, and you won't know what's hit you,' she warned him. 'If your mother wasn't already dead, she would have died of shame at how you've behaved. Toadying around rich, influential people that she barely knew, but ignoring all those she cared about. All I can say is that your father must have been an evil man, because you sure as hell didn't learn it from your mother.'

She wrenched the front door open and left without looking back.

But she couldn't hold back the tears that had been barely contained all day, they spilled over and ran down her face. 'I'll think of something to hurt you, Jean-bloody-Philippe,' she muttered. 'Just you wait.'

Joan had clearly made a huge effort to make her shabby little home in Soame Street welcoming for Mariette. There was just one room downstairs, and a tiny scullery, but she'd cleaned, dusted and scrubbed the stone floor in readiness.

'I know it ain't what you're used to, love,' Joan said as she hugged her. 'But I'm really glad to have you 'ere. And I 'ope we can 'ave some laughs together to 'elp you put aside all yer sadness.'

Joan was twenty-eight, small and wiry. And although she was plain, with mousey hair, her personality made up for her lack of looks. Her smile could light up a room, she had energy and fire, and she made people laugh with ribald jokes and irreverent comments about everything, from religion to Winston Churchill.

"E's a fat little bastard an' a toff, but next time 'e comes down this way I'm gonna offer 'im a fuck,' she had said about Churchill the first time Mariette met her. 'See, a man like 'im probably ain't never 'ad a good 'un. 'Is missis looks to me like she's too posh fer such things.'

Her philosophy on life was a simple one: you had to search for the funny side of everything, no matter how serious the problem might seem. Mariette was intending to embrace that philosophy herself.

'So 'ow was the funeral?' Joan asked.

'About as comforting as Christmas in a workhouse,' Mariette replied. 'I'd like to get a red-hot poker and stick it up Jean-Philippe's backside. But I've brought gifts from him! Of course, he doesn't know he's given them to us, but that will make them all the better.'

She opened her suitcase and brought out a full bottle of gin, wrapped up in a cardigan. She had noted the way his guests were knocking back spirits and thought Jean-Philippe would think they'd polished off the full bottle too. Then she dug out the tea, sugar, a tin of salmon, some fish paste and a large chunk of fruit cake.

Joan's pale-brown eyes widened. 'Bloody 'ell, Mari, you've done us proud. Don't think I've ever 'ad me 'ands on a full bottle of gin. Salmon an' all! Flippin' marvellous.'

'And I nicked this for you,' Mari said, taking a lipstick from her pocket. 'It was one of Rose's, I didn't think Jean-Philippe would want to wear it.'

'From what you've said about that little maggot, I wouldn't put it past him to dress up in women's clothes,' Joan laughed. She went over to the mirror above the mantelpiece and put on the coral-coloured lipstick. 'You should've nicked more stuff, Mari, it would've made you feel better.'

'To tell the truth, I was scared he might look in my case,'

she admitted. 'I didn't want to give him any ammunition against me. And besides, I'm going to plot some revenge.'

Joan lit the fire, and they pulled the two easy chairs up to it. Clutching a glass of gin each, mixed with some orange squash, Mari launched into telling Joan about the day's events.

'So maybe this bloke 'Enry might 'elp you get a job?' Joan said.

'I'm not even going to hope for that. It's enough that he knew my mum and liked Uncle Noah. Now, tell me about Ian and Sandra? You said on Wednesday you'd had a letter from them.'

Ian and Sandra were Joan's two children who had been evacuated. Like almost all the children in London, they had been sent away in September of 1939. When no bombs fell during the Phoney War, many children and mothers with babies started drifting back to London. But Joan had resisted the desire to bring hers back because they were very happy in the seaside town of Lyme Regis, and she felt it was wrong to uproot them. It transpired she'd been very wise. When the first air raids came, the children who'd returned were sent away again, and many people Mariette had met were very unhappy about their billets.

'Ian's teacher says 'e's clever enough to pass the eleven plus and go to grammar school,' Joan said proudly. 'And Sandra come top in the class for spelling. I think I'm gonna go down and see them next weekend. Mrs Harding always lets me share Sandra's bed, she ain't the sort to put on any airs and graces. She's a good 'un.'

'You are too,' Mariette reminded her. 'So many mothers are jealous of the women who are taking care of their kids, but you've been so grateful and generous with Mrs Harding, no back-biting or trying to undermine her. I expect that's part of the reason Ian and Sandra are happy there.'

'It's flippin' 'ard, though,' Joan said thoughtfully. 'Each time I sees them they've grown another inch. And they speak quite posh now, they even 'ave napkins when they eat!'

Mariette laughed. 'Ooh, I wouldn't allow that,' she teased. 'They might expect you to provide some when they come home.'

Joan frowned. 'I get scared that I embarrass them, the way I talk an' that. I've missed so much of them growing up. 'Ow are they gonna be when they get back to this shit'ole?'

'They love you as you are,' Mariette said firmly. 'I came from a house in New Zealand with an outside lavatory and no electricity. I've got used to luxury in St John's Wood, but I'd go home to my folks tomorrow, if I could, and never moan about not having electricity. No one is ever like your own mum.'

It occurred to Mariette, that night, as she tried to sleep in Ian's lumpy little bed, that she really had learned how precious her family were.

There would be no telephone calls now, and it would be a few weeks before her parents got this new address to write to her. She certainly couldn't afford to telephone the bakery in Russell, even if it had been possible to do that from a public call box.

But she must try to see things in the optimistic way Joan did.

There had been no air raid tonight, or for the last three days. And there was Henry to go to see on Sunday.

Joan had told her a job would turn up, and perhaps she should believe that too.

She felt she ought to be glad she was living close to Johnny too. But he had unnerved her at their last meeting, and she wasn't sure she felt the same about him any more.

19

Mariette had to ask for directions three times to Willow Road before she finally found it. She had expected it to be right by Hampstead tube station, but it was a good ten-minute walk away.

But she didn't mind the walk; it was sunny, the Hampstead air was a great deal fresher than in Bow, there were very few bomb sites, and it was nice to see gardens bright with daffodils and lots of trees. There had been an air raid last night, and she and Joan had gone to the shelter. An old man with them was constantly scratching himself, and by the time the all-clear went, around two in the morning, she found herself scratching too, convinced she'd caught whatever was troubling him.

On examining herself this morning in daylight, she couldn't see anything on her skin, so it probably was 'all in the mind', as Joan had claimed. She thought she must grow to be more like Joan, laugh at such things, stop being so fussy about nasty smells and dirt, and try to think of the strangers she met in shelters as potential friends, not treat them with suspicion.

Number eleven Willow Road was a pretty, double-fronted house with a high, neatly trimmed privet hedge which grew in an arch over the tall wrought-iron gate. Henry must have seen her from the window as he opened the front door even before she rang the bell.

'You found me then,' he said with a wide smile. 'I thought afterwards I should have given you directions.'

He took her through to a large kitchen at the back of the

house, overlooking a well-kept garden, and introduced her to his wife, Doreen.

'I'm so glad you felt able to come today,' she said as she shook Mariette's hand. 'You have been through so much, and Henry tells me Noah's stepson added to it by being very unpleasant.'

Mariette had expected Henry's wife to be elegant and possibly chilly, but she couldn't have been more wrong. She looked very motherly, around fifty or so, plump, with her greying hair fixed up into an untidy bun. She wore a hand-knitted jumper and a tweed skirt, and the apron over the top had been washed so often that it was hard to discern a pattern.

'He was even more unpleasant as I was leaving. But I think I left him with some food for thought, along with all the washing-up to do.' Mariette grinned, liking Doreen on sight. 'But I did feel distraught as I walked away from the house. I had so many wonderful times with Noah, Lisette and Rose, I loved them so much, and I don't understand why Jean-Philippe was so nasty to me.'

'Noah had problems with him from the age of about twelve. The boy was insolent, he purposely damaged things of Noah's and did everything he could to create a wedge between Noah and Lisette,' Henry said. 'Noah asked me for advice because our son, Douglas, is the same age. It was my opinion that Noah had tried too hard with the lad when he and Lisette were first married. He meant well, of course, but he overindulged him, never correcting him, and the boy came to believe he could do whatever he liked.'

'I only met him once,' Doreen said, returning to some vegetables she was preparing. 'Lisette and Noah brought both him and Rose here for tea. He was objectionable, even then. I felt he was jealous of his little sister and resented his mother being so wrapped up in Noah. The whole time he was here he went out of his way to upset everyone.'

'I thought boarding school would sort him out,' Henry said. 'But he just acquired even loftier ideas of his own importance there.'

Doreen turned to her husband. 'I'm sure Mariette wants to forget Jean-Philippe today. So why don't you take her into the sitting room and pour her a glass of sherry before lunch?'

The sitting room had French windows leading on to the back garden. It was an attractive room with large armchairs and a sofa in a green and pink floral design. There was a huge glass-fronted cabinet along one wall, full of china figurines.

Henry poured them both a glass of sherry. 'Here's to the future,' he said, chinking her glass with his. 'I dare say you are feeling a little daunted about it, this damned war seems to be going on and on, and you must feel very alone now. But war often brings opportunities that don't come in peacetime, especially for women, I have heard a whisper that Ernest Bevin is about to launch plans to mobilize women, letting them take jobs that up till now have always been done by men.'

'Really?' Mariette said. 'Well, that sounds good to me. I need another job, now that I have to pay rent.'

She explained briefly about her job at Greville's, and about being a volunteer in the East End, and said that she was now living in Bow.

'A trained secretary shouldn't feel she needs to work in a munitions factory or shin up telegraph poles. I know Noah wouldn't have wanted that for you. Tell me, Mariette, did your father teach you French?'

'*Bein sûr, mon père me ferait passer –*'

Henry cut her off. 'OK, you can speak it. Sadly, I don't,' he laughed.

'I was saying that Dad would have me speaking French

to him all day sometimes. And Lisette and I had evenings when we spoke nothing else. She corrected my accent too – Dad's was more from Marseille, and she felt I should speak Parisian. But why did you ask?'

'I sometimes hear of colleagues who need a bilingual secretary,' he said, smiling at her. 'I will mull that over and see what strings I can pull.'

During lunch, both Henry and Doreen asked her many questions about New Zealand. It seemed their son, Douglas, who was an engineer, had a yen to emigrate there when the war was over.

'It is a good place for a new start,' she said. 'There's so much space, beautiful scenery and a similar climate to England, especially in the South Island. I think Douglas will have a good life there. Why don't you go with him? You'd love it.'

'It has crossed our minds,' Henry admitted. 'But it's hard to uproot yourself at our age. But then, as I often say to Doreen, if Douglas leaves England, there's not a lot left for us here.'

'You'd soon make lots of friends there,' Mariette said. 'So many people are from England, or their parents were. I should imagine that a solicitor would get as much work there as here too.' She went on to tell them about how beautiful the Bay of Islands was, about the sailing and the fishing, and how much she missed it.

'You can handle a boat then?' Henry said.

Mariette grinned. 'My dad thinks I'm better than most men. He began taking me out in boats when I was as young as three or four, and I was a strong swimmer from about the age of six. I think it must be in my blood. Dad's never happier than when he is in a boat, and I'm the same.'

'I wish I had had the good fortune to meet Etienne,' Henry

said. 'Noah idolized him. He once said, "He's the kind of man we would all like to be – fearless, strong and formidable to anyone that dares cross him – but he has such a tender side to him too. I put all my trust in him and never came to regret it.'"

'What a lovely thing to say.' Mariette's eyes prickled with emotion. 'But Dad thought the world of Noah too. Since arriving in England, I've had the feeling they went through something dramatic together, but I never got a chance to try to winkle it out of Noah.'

'I dare say that your father will tell you one day,' Henry said. 'We parents have to wait until we see our children are mature enough to deal with events in our past. Maybe, when the war's over and you go home, that will be the time.'

Mariette knew then by the way Henry looked at her that he knew exactly what had brought Noah and Etienne together. She wondered if he knew about her mother's past too. But he was as stalwart as her father and Noah, and she knew he wouldn't reveal another person's secrets.

Mariette left Henry and Doreen about five, somewhat reluctantly, as their home was bright and comfortable, the lunch had been wonderful and they'd made her feel cared for. For a few hours she'd been able to shelve her worries. But the moment she had to leave, and Doreen gave her a goodbye hug, she was reminded that Lisette had always done the same, and she felt a surge of grief again.

She knew she couldn't hope to ever replace what she'd had with Noah and Lisette. She had to grow up and take responsibility for herself. Henry had the telephone number at Greville's, as well as Joan's address, and Mariette had a strong feeling he would help her get another full-time job.

The week following Mariette's visit to Henry was a

miserable one, with the worst air raid to date on Wednesday night. She and Joan had been at the old factory all day and were walking home when the siren went off. They hadn't had any supper, and the shelter they were forced to dart into was a really bad one. There were just rough planks to sit on, a damp dirt floor, and the people already in there resented a couple of strangers in their midst.

It was a terrifying raid. Each time a bomb dropped, showers of dirt came down on them and the whole place shook. Mariette really thought they were going to die that night, if not from a bomb blast, from hunger, thirst or sleep deprivation. When the all-clear came at first light, both she and Joan could barely walk, they were so stiff. Later, they were to hear that there had been several hundred bombers that night, leaving 750 people dead; many had died in a shelter that received a direct hit. But their most enduring memory of the night was of two women going on and on about jam and marmalade being added to the list of rationed items. Anyone would think jam was vital to the nation's well-being, the way they moaned about it.

'I wanted to tell them to shut their cakeholes,' Joan said as they hobbled home, not even knowing whether the house would still be standing. 'If I'd 'ad a pot of jam on me I would've stuck it up 'er arse.'

Johnny had turned up as they were having a very welcome cup of tea. When Joan mentioned that she was intending to go to see her children at the weekend, his eyes lit up at the prospect of Mariette being alone in the house.

Perhaps it was because Mariette was so tired that she snapped at him, 'Don't you get the idea that means you can sleep with me,' she said.

'Believe it or not, I just thought it would be lovely to be able to sit somewhere warm and snug with you,' he retorted indignantly. 'But the chances are there'll be another bad air raid, and I'll be putting fires out.'

He left a few minutes later, and Mariette slumped down on a chair and held her head in her hands.

'Why did I say that?' she asked Joan.

'Because it was exactly what 'e was thinking,' Joan grinned. 'Oh, 'e covered it up well, putting fires out was a great way to remind you 'e's a blinkin' 'ero. 'But 'e'll be back, don't you worry about that.'

But Johnny didn't come back. Joan left for Lyme Regis on Friday lunchtime and Mariette went home around six, through the rain, to a cheerless house. She lit the fire, made sure the windows were blacked out and switched on the wireless for company.

There was no air raid, possibly because visibility was bad. But it transpired, the next day, that the German bombers had made for Plymouth instead and wreaked untold damage on the city, just as they had on Bristol at the start of the week.

As Mariette sat staring into the fire that evening, she thought about a woman she'd spoken to earlier in the day. She was around twenty-eight, her fiancé had been killed in North Africa, and she'd been living in lodgings a few streets away from the factory but had been recently bombed out. Like Mariette, she was now staying with a friend.

'I know everyone around here says, "We can take it." But I don't think I can any more,' she said. 'My mother died four years ago, my dad went in the last war without ever seeing me. When I met my Sidney, I thought we could build a good, happy life together, but he's gone now too. I look around at all the destruction, the hardships, and I know it's only going to get worse. I ask myself what is the point of carrying on? What for? I lost my mother and the man I love, I've got just the clothes I stand up in, nothing else. I haven't got the will to try to build a new life.'

Mariette had hugged the woman and given her a pep talk along the lines of 'you never know what's round the corner'. But the truth was, Mariette felt just as that woman did. Joan could focus on surviving the war because of her husband and children. But Mariette's family were thousands of miles away, she had no one close left here. Even Johnny, who, a few weeks ago, she'd thought might even be 'the One', didn't look as if he wanted to be her friend any more.

Henry was as good as his word. On 2nd April, Mariette received a brief letter from him asking her to contact Mr Perry at Prinknall and Forbes, in Chancery Lane. Henry wrote:

> *He could use a secretary who can also speak and write fluent French. While most of his clients are English he has a few French ones, and he anticipates more coming to him in the next year because of the situation in France. I think this might be the perfect position for you.*

After being interviewed, Mariette was not so sure it was a position she wanted. Firstly, it would mean she would have to leave Mr Greville. He might be a bit oily but she'd grown used to his ways, and had even come to like him. Secondly, she didn't like the bumptious Mr Perry, who spoke down to her, one little bit. He was fat, with a red shiny face and foul breath, and she couldn't possibly imagine even sitting near him let alone changing her initial opinion of him.

But she took the job because she needed it, and it was easier to get home to Bow from Holborn than from Baker Street.

Mr Greville was unexpectedly pleasant when she gave in her notice. 'I half expected it,' he said. 'I knew two days' work a week wouldn't be enough for you now. But tell me about the new job? I do hope you haven't gone for work in a munitions factory just because the pay is good.'

She told him that it was in a solicitor's office, and that she would be doing some French translation work.

'I'm pleased for you,' he said. 'To be honest, I have been thinking of giving up this office anyway. I could easily do everything from the factory. I wish you well, Miss Carrera. You've been a very good secretary, and I shall miss you.'

But Mariette regretted taking the new position almost from her first day. The other clerks, typists and secretaries were a chilly and snobbish bunch of women who clearly were never going to welcome anyone new to their little clique. She heard a couple of whispers about her speaking French, and the fact that she was from New Zealand, it seemed both those things were strange enough for them to decide to ignore her.

It was during her second week that her ability to act as an interpreter was tested for the first time. Mr Perry called her into his office to translate for a new French client who only spoke a smattering of English.

Mrs Dupont was Jewish. Her doctor husband had insisted she must flee Paris with their two children just a few days before the city fell to the Germans. He was fearful of the rumours he'd heard about Jews being rounded up and sent to work camps and thought they would be safer in England with relatives.

Since arriving in England, Mrs Dupont hadn't heard a word from her husband. One of her relatives had given her Mr Perry's name, hoping he could help her find out what had happened to her husband.

Mariette had no problem translating the woman's story, or Mr Perry's reply that he would do his best for her. She took down all the details of Dr Dupont, exactly as her employer asked, but she couldn't help but wonder why one of Mrs

Dupont's relatives here in London, who presumably spoke good English, hadn't accompanied her to speak on her behalf. If they had, they might have sensed from Perry's rather curt responses that he wasn't very sympathetic towards her plight.

If Mr Perry had let Mariette leave his office at the same time as he said goodbye to Mrs Dupont and showed her out, she might have been able to speak to the distressed woman and suggest she contact the Red Cross too. Unfortunately, Mr Perry kept her back to dictate an urgent letter to another client, and so the opportunity was lost.

'Do you think the Gestapo have arrested Dr Dupont?' Mariette asked him once the dictation was completed.

'I think it's highly unlikely,' he said airily. 'The chances are he sent his wife off to England for his own ends. You know what the French are like.'

Mariette's mouth opened to remind him that her father was French, and that he would only send his wife away if her life was in danger, but she stopped herself. She needed this job. And besides, she could get some advice from one of the Jewish people she often met in the shelter, and then pass that on to Mrs Dupont.

As spring slipped into summer Mariette often felt that, if it wasn't for Joan and the other friends she'd made in the East End, she would leave London and find somewhere to live away from the danger of bombs. The latest kind of bomb was a mine dropped by parachute. Some of these were as large as pillar boxes; they drifted down on the wind, exploding on impact with devastating results. Just two could obliterate a whole street.

On 20th April there was the worst air raid since December. Johnny reported that a record 1,500 fires were started by incendiaries that night, even before a rain of over a thousand high-explosive bombs and parachute mines swept the capital. Eight London hospitals were hit, part of Selfridges caught fire, and a 500lb bomb crashed through the northern transept of St Paul's Cathedral. Three days later, the bombers were back in force, concentrating on the East End, as if they hadn't inflicted enough punishment there already.

In early May, Mariette and Joan saw a newsreel at the cinema which showed the Australian, New Zealand, British and Polish troops retreating from Thermopylae, in Greece. Mariette knew her brother Alexis was there. It was reported that 7,000 men had been taken prisoner, and she was terrified he might be amongst them.

On 10th May, the bombers were back in force, using the full moon to guide them to their targets. They knocked out every main-line station and destroyed over 5,000 homes, leaving great swathes of London without gas, electricity and water. On the morning of the 11th, Joan and Mariette staggered wearily out of the shelter to find a pall of brown smoke blotting out the sun. So many streets were impassable that, for many people, it was impossible to get to work. Mariette struggled through, only to find the office locked up. A huge fire blazed in City Road. It was a gin distillery, and the alcohol made it difficult to put the flames out. In south London the Palmolive soap factory was on fire; as firemen fought to put it out, the water turned to hot froth.

Later that day, she and Joan heard that Scotland Yard, St James's Palace, the Law Courts and many other famous buildings had been damaged – even the Tower of London had been hit by a hundred incendiaries.

Johnny popped in fleetingly, a couple of days later, to tell Mariette that the Fire Service was to be nationalized, something he'd hoped would happen for a very long time. At present each local council brigade had different ranks, equipment and words of command, which made it difficult to put out a fire when men from two different brigades were firefighting side by side.

Mariette wanted to be enthusiastic about his news, but she and Joan were more concerned by the frightening figure of one million people who had been made homeless, with only 129 small, ill-equipped rest centres to give them some kind of shelter. All the windows in Joan's house had been blown out and, like so many others, they were without power, gas or water. They nailed boards over the windows, got water from a standpipe in the street, and considered themselves fortunate they still had a bed to sleep on.

When Mariette heard that 50,000 soldiers had been rescued from the beaches in Greece, in what the press called a second Dunkirk, she offered up frantic prayers that Alexis was amongst them. Those prayers were answered when a letter eventually arrived from home, in June, and she learned he was safe. But Austin Roberts, a boy she'd been at school with, and the first boy to kiss her, had been killed. She might have dealt with far greater loss recently, yet the thought of Austin dying so far away from home really upset her.

It made her blurt out to Joan that she'd had enough of London, and the war. 'I can't stand it any more. I can't bear the sight of people picking through the ruins of their houses, the smell of fire, breathing in brick dust, and knowing that one of these nights it will be our turn to cop it. I'm going to move out of London before I go mad with it all.'

As she might have expected, Joan made a joke of it. 'Then join the bleedin' Land Army,' she teased. 'You'll look swell in that uniform with them big, baggy jodhpur things! Imagine all those randy old farmers trying to have their way with you in hay lofts? You'll love milking cows, mucking out stables and planting cabbages.'

'I wouldn't mind any of that – except the randy old farmers,' Mariette shot back. 'I hate seeing all the bomb sites, hearing nothing but sad news, and struggling to make a decent meal out of nothing.'

'Come on now, you know you'd miss queuing for rations that 'ave all gone by the time you get to the 'ead of the queue! And you're forgetting how much you love all the nights in the shelter next to a farting drunk.'

'You've got me there, I would miss all that,' Mariette giggled.

'Just to cheer you up even more, they've just rationed clothes an' all. So even if we 'ad any money for new 'uns, we wouldn't 'ave the blinkin' coupons,' Joan reminded her.

Mariette laughed. 'You know, Joan, you are the only thing I'd miss in London. Well, maybe Johnny too. But I think he's gone off me, he hardly ever comes round these days. And when he does, all he can talk about is fires.'

'Why don't you let 'im get 'is leg over?' Joan, as always, didn't mince her words. 'That'll take 'is mind off fires, and you'll both be 'appier. And don't make out you're saving yourself till you get 'itched. I knows you've done it before.'

'I don't want to do it with him,' Mariette admitted sheepishly. 'All this time I've been using the excuse that there's been no opportunity, but that is just an excuse. I don't feel that way about him.' She told Joan then about Morgan, and how she was always burning up to do it with him. 'That's how you should feel about a man, isn't it?'

Joan grinned. 'Yeah, ducks, that is 'ow you should feel.'

'But he turned out to be nasty. He tried to force himself on me, in a park, just before he joined up. He couldn't read and write very well, and the last I heard he was leaving hospital in Folkestone after getting wounded at Dunkirk.'

To her surprise, Joan laughed. 'Christ Almighty, you can pick 'em!' she said. 'What was a posh girl like you doing with a gypo who can't read or write? But I reckon 'e only tried to force you that night cos 'e felt like 'e was going to lose you.'

Mariette laughed then. 'That was the quickest route to it.'

'Yeah, maybe, but blokes think with their cocks, luv. Something you said or did made 'im feel uneasy. It could've been cos 'e knew you was shocked that 'e couldn't read well, or the gypsy thing. Maybe 'e even thought 'e might be killed in the war. So 'e wanted to put 'is stamp on you, like a dog does when it piddles on a lamppost.'

Mariette giggled at that explanation but, as crude as it was, there was a kind of sense to it.

'Well, I'm never going to know the answer to that. All he left me with is a picture in my head of his handsome face, and the memory of how good sex can be,' she said. 'But getting back to Johnny, what should I do about him?'

Joan looked thoughtful. 'Well, if you don't feel that way about Johnny now, then you ain't never goin' to. So you ought to pack it in with the poor bloke. It ain't fair to keep stringing 'im along.'

'I don't know how to. He was such a good friend when the Blitz was at its worst, and I don't want to hurt his feelings.'

'You know what they say, that "you can't make an omelette without breaking eggs"? Well, it's the same with this. But you'll 'urt Johnny more if you carry on 'olding 'im at arm's length. Besides, from what I've seen of Johnny the fireman, 'e looks after number one. I can't 'elp thinkin' the main reason 'e's still 'anging on to you ain't cos 'e loves you madly but cos of who you are.'

'I'm not anyone,' Mariette said with some indignation.

'Come off it! Compared with everyone else around 'ere you're a toff! You're a secretary, you speak French and you've got class. And when the war's over, you'll be going 'ome. Johnny's got the idea your folks are rich.'

Mariette scoffed at Joan's cynicism. But once she was alone and gave some thought to remarks Johnny had made in the past – how often he talked about rich people and the opportunities to be made in wartime – she began to think Joan could be right.

After the devastating air raid on 10th May, there was a lull. After months of almost continual nightly raids, no one could really believe it wouldn't start again tonight or tomorrow. But gradually, as the streets were cleared of rubble and broken windows were replaced, people allowed themselves to think that the Blitz really was over and that Hitler was too busy attacking Russia to be bothered with them any more.

The weather was good, so when Mariette and Joan weren't helping out at the rest centre in the old factory in the evenings, they often went to a pub, the pictures or a dance hall. If Johnny wasn't on duty, he often went with them, and Mariette put aside both her idea of moving out of London and of telling Johnny that he should find another girlfriend. It wasn't that she'd had a change of heart about him, just that she felt she should wait until he had proved himself, one way or another.

One weekend, Mariette went down to Lyme Regis with Joan to see her children. She was enchanted by the beauty of Dorset and the sleepy little seaside town.

Ian and Sandra were delightful children. Their lengthy stay with Mr and Mrs Harding had given them advantages that, with the best will in the world, Joan could never have given them. Ian was going to attend the grammar school from September, and nine-year-old Sandra seemed equally bright.

Both children had Joan's wiry physique, and her joyful nature. It was obvious the Hardings loved them as if they were their own, yet they welcomed Joan and Mariette too as part of their extended family. Joan called them 'posh folk', but Mariette recognized them as being just ordinary country people, with the kind of values she had been brought up with. The children's cockney accents had been softened with a Dorset burr, they had excellent manners, and their skin glowed and their hair shone from all the good food and the peaceful environment.

'As much as I miss 'em,' Joan said soon after they arrived at the Hardings' comfortable and attractive home, 'I'd rather they was 'ere and 'appy.'

The children led Mariette and their mother up to the cliff top for a picnic which Mrs Harding had prepared. To the two adults, the hard-boiled eggs, slices of a delicious chicken pie and home-made bread were a feast. The Hardings had over twenty chickens, and Ian regaled them ghoulishly with how he'd watched Mr Harding wring the neck of the one that was now in the pie.

It was beautiful on the cliff top, with the warm sun on their skin, the sea as blue as the sky above, the clean fresh air and the long grass waving in the gentle breeze. Both the children lay on their backs with their heads in Joan's lap. Mariette watched the way Joan tenderly stroked their heads, her face soft with love for them, and fervently hoped that Rodney, her husband, would come home safely and the little family would be reunited.

'Can we come and live here for ever when the war's over and Dad comes home?' Ian asked, almost as if he'd picked up on Mariette's thoughts. 'Mr Harding said they could do with a good mechanic down here, and Dad is a good one, isn't he?'

'Yes, 'e is, love, and I'd like that,' Joan replied, and her face took on a dreamy expression. 'Imagine when they've taken the barbed wire and the mines off the beaches? I could get you buckets and spades and go paddling with you. Maybe your dad could take up fishing too. And we'd live in a nice little cottage with chickens in the garden.'

'That sounds like my childhood back home,' Mariette said, and a wave of homesickness washed over her. 'I wish I had a magic wand and could end this horrible war. And then all of us could have what we want.'

By Sunday evening, when Mariette and Joan travelled back to London on the train, they were both sunburned, with fuller stomachs than they'd had for a long time. But the two friends were very quiet.

Mariette knew Joan was dreaming of that little cottage, and perhaps thinking how she could make that dream a reality. Mariette was silently sharing her friend's pain at having to leave her children, and wondering when it was that she had changed from being entirely self-centred to caring so much.

After ten weeks of peace, on 27th July, the air-raid siren went off just as Mariette and Joan were about to go to bed. They looked at one another in astonishment.

Joan waved a clenched fist skywards. 'You bastards,' she yelled. 'We thought you 'ad better things to do than plague us again!'

'Maybe it's a false alarm,' Mariette said, but she tipped the cocoa she'd just been making into a Thermos flask and put it into the basket they always kept ready for air raids.

Joan ran upstairs and scooped up a couple of blankets. 'At least it's warm tonight,' she said as she came down. 'Of course, the downside to that is there'll be fleas in the shelter and stinky armpits.'

Within five minutes, they were in the shelter sitting side by side on the hard bench. There were no strangers tonight, only locals. They were mostly women, but there were a few men who were past conscription age.

'Sounds like miles away,' Edna, who lived a few doors down from them, remarked when they heard the first distant thud of bombs. 'I wish I'd stayed in me own bed.'

Edna's remark was a common one. Many people had given up going to the shelters after the first few weeks of the Blitz. They were convinced that, if it was their time to die, it would happen whether they were in a shelter or not. But a great many other people were so frightened by the raids that they had taken up almost permanent residence in the tube. Bethnal Green station was a very popular one because it was so deep underground and because it could hold thousands of people.

Mariette had gone into the tube a few times at the start of the Blitz, but she'd hated it. People used the tunnels as lavatories in the absence of proper sanitary arrangements, and they stank. She'd seen fights break out when someone stood on someone else's bedding. There were drunks, constant noise, babies crying, and it was said that pickpockets abounded there. She knew that wooden bunks and proper lavatories had been installed since then, and there were also canteens where you could get a drink and a snack. But she and Joan were happier either in this shelter at the end of their street, or in the one at Greville's old factory.

However tired Joan claimed to be, she always perked up in a crowd, and tonight was no exception. She was soon in full flight, telling the neighbours about their visit to Lyme Regis, so Mariette put a cushion behind her head, wrapped a blanket around her shoulders, leaned back against the wall and closed her eyes.

As so often happened, Johnny came into her mind. She was still plagued by the continuing problem of how to make it plain to him, without being hurtful, that he wasn't the one for her.

It was a puzzle to her why she kept meeting men with major flaws. First there was Sam who, apart from his looks, had turned out to have nothing else to offer. Morgan had had the looks and the sex appeal, but there was no excuse for trying to force her into letting him have his way with her. Gerald had been lovely, dependable, good-mannered, and he'd have made a wonderful husband, but he didn't make her light up. Johnny might be great company, and he had a great sense of humour, but aside from having little sex appeal, she couldn't stop think-ing that he had an ulterior motive for hanging on to her.

She had met women who had vicious brutes of husbands, yet they still loved and fancied them. She'd met other women who had married for security and were often bored stiff with their reliable husbands. If it wasn't for her own parents, and Lisette and Noah, she might have been tempted to think you had to go for one or the other – great sex or a great provider – and that it was impossible to find both in one man.

There was, of course, Edwin too. He didn't appear to have any flaws. He was good-looking, well mannered, intelligent, kind and good company. But then, she'd only spent one evening with him and, in view of the dramatic events of that night, she could hardly form a reliable opinion of him.

Perhaps she should have telephoned him at the base? But she hadn't, because of where she was living. And she didn't want to look as if she was chasing him either. But maybe she could write him a letter. Keep it light, ask how he was, and tell him about her new job. That wouldn't look like chasing him, would it?

She glanced around the shelter. The light was too dim to see most of the people clearly, but she noticed the brightness of Clara's red hair; Aggie, still wearing her yellow pinafore, was knitting frantically. The old couple opposite her, Ernie and May Forrest, were sitting so close together they looked welded to one another. They were holding hands, and each time a bomb dropped in the distance, Ernie used his spare hand to draw May's head close to his shoulder. Mariette knew from a past conversation she'd had with them that they had married when May was eighteen, when Ernie returned from the Great War. They had eight living children, and two had been taken with diphtheria. Only recently they'd received a telegram to say one of their sons had been taken prisoner in North Africa. But there they were, love for one another shining out of them. Mariette knew she wanted a love like that too, one that would last for ever.

The shrill whine of planes was coming closer now, the thud of dropping bombs much louder. As always, no one commented on it. They had long since learned to be stoic and outwardly calm; it was a matter of pride. Joan opened up the Thermos and poured cocoa for her and Mariette, but their eyes met in a silent signal of resignation at what might be a long night ahead.

People had become very knowledgeable about bombing in the past months – some could even pinpoint where the bombs were dropping, just by the sound.

A bomber passed low overhead. The crump, crump sound of the bombs hitting a target was clearly very close by. Dirt from the shelter roof showered down on them all.

'That'll be my house,' Clara said, and laughed nervously.

Usually, when a bomb hit close by, the next was further away. But before anyone could relax, there was an almighty thump right above them and the lights went out. Lumps of masonry and timber beams crashed down on to them.

'God save us!' someone yelled out.

That was the last thing Mariette heard.

20

Mariette came to, choking. Her mouth was full of dirt. She coughed and spat it out, but just that small movement brought on a fierce pain in her head. It was too dark to see anything, but she became aware that she was on the floor and something heavy had fallen on her legs; they hurt, and she couldn't move them.

For a brief moment, she thought it was a nightmare – she'd had them before, like this – but the pain in her head and the choking dust were all too real. The shelter had received a direct hit.

Her hands were free, so she lifted them to her head and felt the stickiness of blood. She then moved them down to whatever it was that lay across her legs, and found it was a wooden beam. As she'd been sitting on the bench before, something must have struck her head a glancing blow, knocking her from the bench, before the beam fell on to her legs.

'Joan!' she called out. 'Can you hear me?'

There were muffled moans coming from somewhere, but too far away to be Joan. She reached out with her right hand, sweeping in the darkness beside her, and her fingers met the familiar feel of Joan's cable-stitch cardigan. She too was on the floor. But, as Mariette felt with her fingers, finding her friend's head, shoulders and torso, she realized the same beam which pinned her to the floor was lying across Joan's stomach.

They always packed a torch in the emergency basket, which had been by her feet earlier when Joan poured the cocoa. She managed to sit up halfway, to extend her reach, and found the basket trapped beneath the beam.

'Can anyone hear me?' she called out. 'I'm trying to reach a torch, and people will be here soon to get us out.'

'Is that you, Mari?'

She recognized Aggie's voice, but it sounded very weak and distant.

'Yes, it's me, Aggie. How bad are you hurt?'

'I don't know. I hurt, and I can't move at all.'

'Help will be here soon,' Mari said as she concentrated on trying to get into the trapped basket, pulling at the wickerwork on the side. 'Anyone else want to tell me how they are?'

'My head and shoulder hurt,' a faint voice spoke out. 'It's Brenda.'

'Anyone else?'

There was no response, and Mariette knew that meant they were either dead or unconscious. She fervently hoped it was the latter. There had been eighteen people in here including old Tom, the air-raid warden – he had counted them before closing the door – and her blood ran cold at the thought of them all buried under the rubble.

Finally, she managed to make a hole in the side of the basket. She put her hand in, felt around gingerly for the small torch, found it and drew it out carefully. She knew only too well from rescues she'd observed that one hasty move could bring down more rubble.

She switched on the torch. It was a pathetically small beam of light, just enough to see through the swirling dust that she, Joan and the three people sitting on the other side of Joan, right up to the shelter door, had all been knocked down by the same timber beam. Those nearest the door appeared to have taken the full brunt of it.

Examining Joan as best she could, she found her friend

was still alive, but unconscious. The way she was twisted under the beam didn't look good. There was a great deal of blood on the ground beside her, but Mariette couldn't see where it was coming from.

The beam ended just after Mariette and, ironically, the basket had prevented it falling with its full force on to her legs. They hurt badly and they were bleeding; her shoes were gone, but she could move her toes, which was a very good sign. To her left, and beyond the end of the timber beam, there was just a huge heap of rubble. Mrs Heady, her husband and her daughter had all been sitting there and were presumably buried.

Between Mariette and the other side of the shelter was a huge lump of concrete, beyond which were Brenda and Aggie, also Clara, Ernie and May, and Edna, plus a few other people whose names she didn't know. She couldn't see any of them.

Mariette had often heard Civil Defence rescuers shouting to people buried under bombed buildings to keep still and try not to panic. It was easy enough to keep still, but very hard not to panic. She shone the torch upwards and saw a huge hole in the ceiling. This was where the lump of concrete which now lay in the centre of the shelter had come from, but the beam of the torch wasn't strong enough to see what was above the hole. There may be more loose concrete or beams which could come crashing down too.

'Brenda! Aggie!' she called out. 'Can you see the torch-light?' She jiggled it a bit to make it more obvious.

'Just a few pinpricks,' Brenda called back. 'Not enough to see anyone over here.'

'I'm going to try to get help,' Mariette called back. 'Keep still and don't panic. Try talking to the others near you, they may just have been knocked unconscious.'

'I'm scared, Mari,' Aggie called back, but her voice was little more than a whisper.

'Me too,' Mariette said. 'But we've all seen the rescue people get folk out of worse places than this, so don't despair.'

It was true what she said. But, as bombs were still dropping nearby, they couldn't expect the Civil Defence people to come until the all-clear had sounded. And even then, they might not come straight here unless someone had reported that this shelter had been hit. She had to get out and tell them people were trapped in here.

After reassuring Brenda and Aggie again, she surveyed the beam. Even if she could manage to lift the end of it and get her legs free, that would put further weight on to Joan. She needed to jack it up with something.

Scrabbling around with her hands, she found first one brick and then another. If she turned a brick on to its side, it was thicker than a leg. If she could just push one in beside her own legs, where they were trapped, then lift the beam enough to turn the brick on its side, she could get her legs out and then add a second brick for extra support.

Sliding the brick down beside her legs was easy enough, but in a sitting position it was well nigh impossible to lift the heavy beam enough to turn the brick. As she strained to do it, blood ran from her head wound into her eyes and the pain in her legs intensified.

She gritted her teeth, told herself she could do this, and tried again. Her arms weren't long enough to get a good grip on the beam from above, so she had to put her hands under it and push up. After several tries, she managed to lift it slightly. Holding it with just her right hand, she attempted to turn the brick with her left. Nothing had ever been so hard, she felt as if the muscles in her arm were being torn out, but she finally managed it.

Leaning back for a rest, she panted out to Brenda and Aggie what she'd done. 'Just got to get my legs out now,' she added.

The effort of pointing her feet downwards hurt like crazy, and she had no room to shuffle backwards to make it easier to get her legs free. But she had to do it, however much it hurt.

Her legs, when she finally got them out, were a mess; from the knee down to her ankle they looked like a bloody joint of meat in Smithfield Market, and the pain was incredible, making her feel sick. But somehow she managed to get to her feet. There were more bricks on the ground, and she managed to ease the beam off her unconscious friend and slide bricks beneath it to take the weight from her pelvis. Joan moaned just as she'd finished.

Mariette bent down to her, and smoothed her face with her hand. 'I'm going for help, Joan. Just hang on,' she said.

'Ian . . . Sandra,' Joan muttered weakly.

'You'll see them soon,' Mariette said, fighting back tears. Even by the dim light of the torch she could see her friend was in a very bad way.

It sounded as if the bombers were moving away now, and she had to get help fast. With just a quick word to Brenda and Aggie to tell them Joan was conscious and to keep speaking to her, she crept forward towards the door, shining the torch on the floor to check where she was putting her feet for fear of dislodging any more rubble.

Tom, the air-raid warden, lying next to the door was definitely dead. His head was half caved in where the beam had struck him. The older couple next to him both looked dead too, but she couldn't see their hands to feel for a pulse.

She had known even before she got to the door that the concrete stairs beyond might be blocked – and there was a fair chance she wouldn't be able to open the door anyway –

but, surprisingly, it did open just a little, enough for her to squeeze through.

Flashing her torch up the stairs, she saw they were blocked by huge chunks of rubble, and the metal handrail at the side was twisted like a big snake. But she could feel fresh air on her face, and she could see there was a gap in the middle of the rubble. She had to hope that it was like a chimney and continued all the way to the top.

She shouted for help at first, at the top of her lungs, because she knew that climbing up the rubble could bring it all down on top of her – or, even worse, she might find that the hole she could see was blocked further up – but every minute she delayed meant there was less chance for her friends. She had to try to climb out.

Climbing was something she'd always been good at. It was often said that she was like a mountain goat, but she had never before had to climb with two badly damaged legs and a head wound, or up through a hole barely wide enough for her to squeeze through. She took the belt off her dress, tied the little torch with it, then secured it around her head, tying the belt tightly under her chin. Where it touched her wound it hurt really badly, but she had to bear it; there was no alternative, if she was to have light and both her hands free.

Slowly and very carefully she began to climb, testing the rubble with her hands first to make sure it was stable. Once she was inside the narrow tube-like hole, she had no room for manoeuvre and had to wriggle like a snake, arms above her head, digging her fingers and elbows in to support herself, while she used her toes to find a foothold to lever herself up another few inches.

It was terrifying because each time she got to a large jutting-out piece of rubble, she feared she'd become stuck in there. As this debris of chunks of concrete and bricks had obviously fallen from the house next to the shelter, it was likely to become even more unstable as she got higher.

From time to time she heard an ominous rumble, and stones shifted and fell beneath her feet. Smaller pieces rained down on her, cutting her arms, hands and shoulders or catching on her lacerated legs, but she refused to think that she could fall, or be buried alive, and she crept on like a snake, ever upwards.

Then, from up above her, she saw an orange glow. She knew it had to be a fire nearby, and she was viewing it through a gap in the rubble. It was the street, there would be people there.

She'd nearly made it.

Patrick Feanny was with the first group of Civil Defence workers to reach Fairfield Road in Bow, after reports of extensive bombing in some of the neighbouring streets. There were a number of small fires from incendiaries still burning. But as the all-clear hadn't yet sounded there was no sign yet of the usual air-raid wardens, young lads and other public-spirited people out with their stirrup pumps dealing with them.

Standing in Fairfield Road, looking down what had been Soame Street, a narrow road lined with tiny terraced houses, he surveyed the scene of total destruction before him. All the houses had been destroyed, some thirty in all. There was just one wall left standing at the start of the terrace, and he could see a picture still hanging on it.

Thirty houses meant upwards of another 170 people made homeless, and his heart went out to them. Feanny had served in the last war and, at nineteen, had survived the battle of the Somme. He had enlisted for this one too, not because he wanted to fight, but because he felt it was his duty. He was turned down for active service, so he joined the

Civil Defence instead. When he joined, he thought it would be a soft option, but it had proved to be anything but that.

He couldn't count how many people he'd pulled out of bombed buildings, many of them seriously injured but even more dead. Maybe people had finally realized Hitler meant business and, as the shelters were now much improved, most had the sense to use them. But in a street like Soame Street there was always someone too stubborn, or convinced of their own immortality, to go to the shelter, and, as he looked at what remained of it, he wondered where the body or bodies would be tonight.

A shout for help from the end of the road made him climb over the rubble in the road to go to investigate. Usually it was when the all-clear went that someone would alert the rescuers that they hadn't seen Mr or Mrs So-And-So in the shelter tonight.

As he got to the end of Soame Street he saw the girl, doubled over as if in pain. By the light of one of the fires he could see she was covered in blood.

'The shelter,' she shouted, pointing to the corner where the steps led down to it. 'There were eighteen of us in there. But I know at least three are still alive.'

The all-clear sounded then, and she dropped to the ground in a faint.

Feanny blew his whistle to call the rest of his team, and ordered one of his men to call for ambulances. As he waited for help he went to the girl, to help her.

Her legs were a mess, her feet bare. She had a small torch tied around her head, which was bleeding quite badly. She was covered in brick dust, and her dress was torn and filthy.

She came round as he removed the torch from her head, and offered her some water from a bottle he carried. She drank a little, then struggled to get up. 'We've got to get them out,' she said. 'I managed to climb up through the rubble on the steps, but you'll need to clear that first.'

He shone his torch over where the steps were and wondered how on earth she'd managed to get through it. 'OK,' he said. 'Help's on its way, but tell me your name.'

'Mariette Carrera,' she said. 'I live in Soame Street with Joan Waitly, she's one of those still alive. You must get her out, she's got two children.'

'I will, but first you must tell me what it's like down there. The more we know about the conditions, the more chance we have of getting them out safely.'

She tried to get to her feet, but he could see she was in great pain. He lifted her up in his arms, took her over to a low wall that was still left standing, and sat her on it.

'A wooden beam pinned us all down on the right-hand side as you go in. Tom, the air-raid warden, is by the door. He's dead, and I think the couple next to him are too. Then there's Joan, my friend. I was on the other side of her. I managed to jack the beam up with some bricks so I could get out, and to take the weight off her. Then there's a huge lump of concrete in the middle, hiding the people on the other side. And another at the end of the beam, beyond where I was sitting. Aggie and Brenda are on the left-hand side and they both spoke to me. But it sounded like they were in a bad way. The door to the shelter will only open a crack. I managed to wriggle through it, then I climbed up through the rubble on the steps.'

'You've done well to describe that so clearly,' Feanny said. 'As soon as an ambulance gets here, I'll get them to take you to the hospital.'

'I'm not going until you get Joan out,' she said, shaking her head.

Instinctively he knew there was no point in arguing with

her. He signalled to one of the men to bring a blanket for her and then went off to start the rescue work.

Mariette had no idea what time it had been when she got out of the shelter, but it was likely to have been around three in the morning. Yet, whatever time it was, it seemed like hours before the first rays of light appeared in the sky. Twice she'd been brought a cup of tea, and she'd given the names of everyone she knew in the shelter. Several ambulance men had tried to persuade her to let them take her to hospital, but she'd stubbornly refused.

'I'll come when they get Joan out,' she said.

As the sky grew light, she saw that Soame Street was gone. Nothing remained but heaps of rubble with odd pans, items of clothing and bits of curtain strewn about here and there. She'd seen similar sights dozens of times before, and had felt deeply for the people who had lost everything. But this time they were all people she knew; she'd been in their little homes, knew about their children, their husbands and parents. Tears ran down her battered face at the cruelty of war. What had any of these people done to deserve this?

The sound of voices wafted through the swirling brick dust and plaster, and she knew it was her neighbours returning from other shelters and the tube stations. Shrieks of outrage filled the air as they saw what had happened, the shrieks turning to wails of despondency as they realized everything they owned was gone.

Some of these people came over to her, wanting to share their despair with her, but, although she tried to console them, reminding them that they were at least alive, she had her eyes firmly fixed on the rescue workers at the shelter.

While she understood they had to remove the rubble with caution, they seemed to be moving it at a snail's pace.

'Mari!'

She turned her head to see Johnny coming towards her. He'd obviously just finished a shift as he was still in his uniform, and his face was streaked with dirt. She tried to get up, but her legs buckled under her and she was forced to sit down again.

'Oh, sweetheart!' he exclaimed once he was close enough to see her injuries. 'I heard at the fire station that Soame Street copped it. Surely you didn't stay in the house?'

She explained about the shelter, and how she'd got out. 'I'm not going anywhere until I know how Joan is,' she finished up.

Johnny was well used to the diverse ways people reacted to bombing. The traumatized ones who ran wild-eyed and terrified, the shell-shocked ones who just sat and stared, and others who appeared to take it all in their stride, only to break down later. He knew that there was little anyone could do for them, other than dressing wounds, offering tea and a warm blanket, and kindness; they would eventually find their own way of dealing with it.

But he knew Mari, and this war had already taken more from her than most people had to face. She needed medical help immediately; if her head and leg wounds were not cleaned and dressed quickly, they would become infected.

'Let me take you to the hospital, before those wounds become infected,' he said. 'I promise to come straight back here and help. And let you know the moment there is any news.'

'No, I'm staying,' she said stubbornly. 'I'll go in the ambulance with Joan, when they get her out. She needs to know she's got me at her side.'

He knew then there was no point in arguing with her. That strong will of hers had always been the problem between them. Perhaps his uncle had been right in saying he'd be happier with a girl from the same background as him, someone

307

who wanted a man to look after her, who wasn't determined to do everything her own way.

'OK,' he said, tucking the blanket more firmly around her. 'I'll go and help the rescue team. But will you let one of the ambulance men standing by at least clean those wounds and put a temporary dressing on them? You won't be any use to anyone, if they become infected.'

'Alright,' she agreed. 'But you take care in there, won't you?'

After sending one of the ambulance crew to see to Mariette, Johnny joined the rescue team and introduced himself.

They were almost down to the shelter door now, but they had been constantly hampered by further loose masonry falling on to the stairs.

'God only knows how that girl managed to get out,' Feanny said to him. 'We could see the hole she'd got through, but it was barely big enough for a cat. Amazing what determination can do.'

Johnny told him she was his girl, and smiled grimly. 'Well, I say she's "my girl" loosely, she's a law unto herself. All I know is, she won't go to hospital until we get her mate out. So the quicker we do that, the better.'

Finally, the door was open and Feanny led his men and Johnny in. But his initial impression was not a hopeful one. The air-raid warden and the elderly couple beyond him were all dead. He shone his torch further, to see the woman he knew to be Joan. But before he could get her out, or the three dead, the beam trapping them would need to be lifted.

Shining his torch upwards, he saw that further beams were resting precariously on lumps of concrete, and behind these were the other trapped people. One false move and the whole lot could cave in. This was not a purpose-built shelter that had been thoroughly inspected, it was merely a large cellar running beneath three typical East End shoddily built houses. Before the war, it had been used by a second-hand furniture dealer as a warehouse. One of the houses above had already come down, and the other two could follow at any time.

He called out to tell anyone who was still conscious that he and his team were in there now and would reach them soon.

A faint response came from two women who identified themselves as Brenda and Aggie.

Crouching over, Feanny made his way carefully along beside the beam and reached over to Joan to feel for a pulse. She had one, but it was very faint, and if she was to be saved he would need to get her out fast. He could see the bricks Mariette had told him she'd used to jack up the beam and get out, and he marvelled that she'd found the strength to do it.

Feanny looked back at his men, signalling where they were to take up their positions. 'On the count of three, lift the beam and move it backwards out of the door,' he said. 'Once it's out, you, Johnny, get your girl's mate out and up to the ambulance. There isn't room enough here to use a stretcher. Ready! One, two, three, *lift*!'

A small amount of rubble moved as the beam was lifted, but the men carried on undeterred. As soon as they had lifted it clear of Joan, Johnny darted forward, picked Joan up in his arms and carried her out.

Mariette rushed towards him as he emerged up the steps. An ambulance man had got as far as cleaning her face, but she'd pushed him aside when she saw Johnny.

'Is she still alive?' she asked.

'Yes, but only just,' Johnny said as he carried her to the ambulance. 'Now go with her, Mari, and no more excuses.'

21

'I'm sorry, Miss Carrera, but there is no question of you leaving here today.'

Mariette looked up at the stern face of Sister Charles, who had been called by the nurse because she was being difficult.

She hadn't meant to be, but the moment she stepped into the London hospital in Whitechapel, the smell and the injuries all around her made her feel sick. Then, when she was ordered to take off her clothes and get into bed in a cubicle, she became frightened too, so she asked the nurse to patch her up quickly and let her go.

Sister Charles was well over forty, tall and slender with the regal air of a woman who expected to be obeyed. She pulled back the sheet covering Mariette's legs and winced at the sight of them.

'I take exception to the term "patch up",' she said crisply. 'I would never allow one of my patients to leave here knowing he or she hadn't received the right care to allow their wounds to heal well.

'Both your head and leg wounds need thorough cleaning and stitching, and I understand there is barely an inch of your body without a laceration. You also need bed rest to recover from the ordeal you've been through.'

'I only wanted to leave quickly because I need to help my friends,' Mariette explained.

'Well, you can't help any of them in the state you are in. From what the ambulance driver told staff here on your admittance, I understand that you were the one responsible for alerting the rescue workers to your friends' plight in the shelter. I can see by your injuries what you put yourself through to get them that help, and that was very courageous. But I am in charge here, and you are going to do what I tell you.'

Strangely enough, that firm order made Mariette feel easier. She didn't actually know why she had insisted she wanted to leave. It wasn't as if she had a home any longer, and Johnny would turn up before long with news of the other people in the shelter.

So she managed a weak smile. 'You sound like my aunt back home. She's very fond of telling me I must obey her. But can you just find out how Joan Waitly is? She's the friend I came in with, and she was in a bad way.'

Joan hadn't regained consciousness in the ambulance, and Mariette didn't have to ask if her condition was serious – that much was obvious. The nurse who travelled with them in the ambulance said she was afraid she had internal injuries.

Sister nodded. 'I will send someone to make inquiries. But now I'm going to get all those bits of dirt out of your wounds myself.'

A couple of hours later, Mariette had been washed, stitched up and given pain relief. She was in a bed on a ward full of women who had been injured in the night's bombing. She felt so much more comfortable that she even managed to convince herself no news of Joan was good, not bad. She fell asleep and only woke at evening visiting time, when Johnny arrived.

He had washed, shaved and changed into ordinary clothes, but she could see by his drawn face and red-rimmed eyes that he hadn't had any rest.

'Brenda and Aggie are here in the hospital now,' he told

her. 'It looks as if Brenda might have a spinal injury, but Aggie has only cuts and bruises.'

'And everyone else?'

'All gone, I'm afraid,' he said wearily. 'If it's any consolation, the doctor who came into the shelter to see them thought they were all killed instantly. They say there will be an inquiry as to why that cellar was approved as a shelter. But that's just shutting the stable door after the horse has bolted.'

'And Joan? Do you know how she is?'

Johnny took her two hands in his. 'I think you must brace yourself for bad news,' he said sadly. 'The force with which the beam hit her damaged a lot of organs. There was extensive internal bleeding, and although they've done an operation to try to save her, they aren't very hopeful.'

'Oh no!' Mariette began to cry. 'Her poor children and her husband!'

'I know,' Johnny said. 'It's terrible, but then it is terrible for the families of those killed. You know that better than anyone.'

'There's no sense to any of it,' she sobbed out angrily. 'That family had everything to live for, they deserved a better life together after the war. Why wasn't I taken too? That's twice now I've survived, when people I loved were killed.'

'My gran, who was religious, would have said that God has special plans for you,' Johnny said gently. 'I've seen lots of my mates die fighting fires, and I've thought the same and asked why I was so lucky.'

'I don't feel lucky at all.' She turned her face into the pillow and cried hard.

'I never do either, when I lose someone I care about,' he said, and he reached over to stroke her hair back from her face. 'But I am so very pleased you were spared. I couldn't bear it, if I lost you.'

The emotion in his voice was unbearable. She couldn't let him go on thinking of her that way and imagining his feelings were returned.

'Don't say that, Johnny,' she said. 'I can't be what you want me to be. I love you as a person, but I'm not "in" love with you, if that makes any sense.'

She stole a peep at his face and saw he looked stricken. She knew it was a terrible time to tell him such a thing, but if she didn't speak out now he'd be wanting to take care of her, finding her a place to live, and before she knew it she'd be in too deep to ever get out.

'I'm sorry, Johnny,' she said. 'You are the best friend a girl could have. You are kind, warm, funny and strong, everything a girl wants from a man. But I know you want much more of me than I can ever give you.'

For a moment or two, he was silent.

She prepared herself for his pleading, expecting that he might insist she was only saying such things because she was upset.

But when he did speak, his tone was very curt. 'Well, I have to say, your timing stinks. But they do say the truth comes out with drink or trauma. I'll be off now. No point in spinning it out any longer.'

He turned on his heel and just walked away.

And Mariette cried even harder.

Sister Charles, who had attended to her that morning, came into the ward just before ten, when the nurses were doing their last rounds before turning down the lights for the night.

Mariette had been crying ever since Johnny left, and she knew immediately she saw the sister that this was going to be bad news.

'She's died, hasn't she?' Mariette said.

'I'm afraid so,' the sister said, her voice soft with sympathy. 'I'm told she regained consciousness fleetingly after her operation, and asked the ward sister to give you a message. She asked that you be there when her children are told of her death because you'd know how to be with them.'

Further tears welled up in Mariette's eyes. She knew that message had been repeated word for word as Joan had said it. She could almost hear her cockney accent and her desperation that Ian and Sandra should never be in any doubt that her last thoughts were of them.

'I am so sorry,' Sister Charles said, and took one of Mariette's hands in hers. 'Have her children been evacuated?'

Mariette nodded. 'I went with her to meet them recently. Ian's eleven and Sandra is nine. Joan's husband is in North Africa.'

'The hospital will inform the army, and they'll get a message to him.'

'The children are in Lyme Regis. Joan wanted to move there, when the war's over,' Mariette said brokenly. 'She used to daydream of a little cottage by the sea all the time. They are such lovely, happy children and I so much wanted for her dream to come true.'

'I can see why she wanted you to be with them,' the sister said. 'You have a big heart, and no one could have done more than you did today to try to get help for Joan. When you feel a bit better, write down all the things you loved about Joan, and when Ian and Sandra are a bit older you can give it to them. It helps children who lose their mother when they are young to know how other people felt about her.

'I have to go now, I'm on duty again at six tomorrow morning. But you'll be in my thoughts and prayers, Mariette. God bless you.'

'You are as wise and kind as my Aunt Mog, back in New

Zealand.' Mariette sniffed back her tears and tried to smile. 'That's twice today you've said something just as she would say it.'

The sister leaned forward, her starched apron crackling, and kissed Mariette on the forehead. 'I'd be very proud to have a niece like you. Now try to sleep, my dear. You've had a day of terrible shocks and sadness.'

The lights in the ward went out, except for the one on the desk in the middle where a nurse sat writing up her notes. Her back was to Mariette, but it was comforting to see her there, in her starched cap, uniform and white apron, the guardian of all the badly injured women on the ward.

Thinking about what nursing meant brought back a memory of her mother and Mog discussing it as a career for her. Mariette had certainly wanted to go to Auckland, but she'd turned up her nose at the thought of bedpans, blood and vomit. Back then, she never thought beyond her own needs.

Would she make a good nurse now? Somehow, she doubted it. She might feel for other people now, but she was still squeamish about wounds. Even looking at her own legs today had made her feel sick.

At eighteen, she would have thought it was the end of the world to be scarred. But now she wasn't unduly concerned. She had had six stitches in her forehead, there was a bald patch on her head where they'd cut away her hair to put ten stitches in there, and there were a further eighteen on her right calf and sixteen on the other. But as long as she could walk and wasn't in any pain, it didn't matter.

When she got home, she would compare scars with her father. As a little girl, she'd always been fascinated by his – although he always told her a different ridiculous story about each one. Yet he never would tell her how he got the one on his cheek. But she would make him tell her the truth about it when she got home.

If only she could go home. She had nothing to keep her here now – well, apart from seeing Ian and Sandra. She had her job, of course, and they would always want help in the rest centre at the old factory. In fact, she would have to go there for herself now and see if someone could help her find somewhere to live and give her some clothes. All the times she'd helped other women sort through the dresses, cardigans and shoes, she'd never imagined she would one day be doing that for herself. To think the diamond bracelet Noah and Lisette had given her for her twenty-first was buried in the rubble of Joan's house! And all those other little things she had once owned that defined who she was.

Everything gone. Photographs, letters from her parents and Mog, little things Rose had given her. Clothes could be replaced – though they would never be as nice as her old ones – but she was, in fact, destitute. Even her savings account book, ration book and passport were lost.

22

The following morning, thanks to the ward sister's intervention, Mariette had a visit from Miss Coates, the hospital almoner. She was a briskly efficient woman with a plummy upper-class voice, and her manner suggested she was more used to dealing with duchesses from Mayfair than ordinary people.

Mariette was wrong, though. Miss Coates was not only very used to offering advice to people who had been bombed out but she was also very sympathetic.

Mariette's immediate concern was that Mr and Mrs Harding, who cared for Joan's children, should be notified of her death, but she explained to Miss Coates about the message left by Joan that the children weren't to be told until Mariette was present.

'I don't know their telephone number or their address,' Mariette explained. 'I could, of course, find the house if I went there. But I can't go yet, and the Hardings need to know.'

'Their address and telephone number will be on record,' Miss Coates said. 'And I am willing to break the news to the Hardings myself and explain what Joan wanted. I am quite sure they will want to respect her wishes and wait until you are on your feet again. Now, would you like to tell me everything else about your circumstances so I can see what problems I can help you with?'

Miss Coates stayed with Mariette for about an hour. She offered to telephone Mr Perry and explain where she was, and gave her advice on getting a new identity card and ration book. She also told her she was entitled to some money from an emergency fund to tide her over. She asked about friends who could put her up as a temporary measure, but the only people Mariette could think of who might be willing to help were Henry and Doreen Fortesque. Miss Coates said she would find their telephone number and ask them, and she'd come back later that afternoon with any news from both the Fortesques and the Hardings.

She was as good as her word, and returned at four o'clock.

'First things first. I traced the Hardings and spoke to Mrs Harding. She was, as you can imagine, terribly upset, but she agreed readily that she will abide by Joan's wishes. She said you struck her as a level-headed and kindly person. She also said that the children liked you and would feel comforted that you were there with their mother when she died. You will be very welcome to stay with her and her husband and the children for a few days. But she hopes this will be very soon as the children are used to getting a letter each week from their mother, and when one doesn't come they will start to worry.'

'I'll go as soon as I get out of here,' Mariette assured her. 'But what about their father? Will he even be able to get home in time for Joan's funeral? And where will we bury her?'

Mariette knew that many people who had lost loved ones in an air raid became very upset about the use of mass graves, seeing it as a pauper's funeral. But Joan had always taken the view that she'd rather be buried with people she knew; she even used to joke about it. 'Just bung in a few bottles of beer and we'll have a party,' she had said more than once.

Mariette told Miss Coates this, and the woman smiled. 'I think a local undertaker would see putting all the victims from Soame Street in one grave as both sensible and appropriate,' she said. 'They lived side by side, died together, and it is rather fitting for them to be buried together. But that will be sorted out by the undertaker, Miss Carrera, you don't need to worry yourself about it. Likewise, whether or not Mr Waitly can get home in time isn't your worry.'

'I suppose so,' Mariette agreed.

'Now, let's get back to what is yours to worry about. A place to live. I telephoned Mr and Mrs Fortesque, and they were horrified to hear what had happened. Without my even asking, they volunteered to put you up. So we are left with your lack of clothes.'

'I can't go anywhere in this.' Mariette indicated her white cotton hospital nightdress. 'I haven't even got any shoes.'

'I have a little supply of clothes,' Miss Coates said. 'People often donate things here. I'll sort them tonight. What size are you?'

Mariette was fairly certain they were dead people's clothes. But, as Mog would have said, 'Beggars can't be choosers.'

'Thirty-four bust, size four shoes . . . and thank you,' she replied.

'I'll try to find something pretty to go with your hair.' Miss Coates smiled. 'How are your injuries now?'

'Sore.' Mariette winced. 'And I'm going to be left with nasty scars. But I'm lucky to be alive, aren't I? Thank you for everything. I really appreciate it.'

Four days after Joan's death, Mariette was on the train bound for Lyme Regis. She knew she looked terrible, but perhaps it was better for Ian and Sandra to see her like this. It might help them understand that she hadn't got off scot-free.

The dress Miss Coates had found for her was hideous, a brown and white spotted dress which looked like a school uniform. It was too long, but she hadn't attempted to shorten it as it did at least partially cover her injured legs. They looked terrible, black and blue with bruising and criss-crossed cuts and scratches.

The straw hat with a turned-up brim was quite nice, and it covered her bald patch; the brown sandals with wedge heels were passable. A dressing hid the big scar on her forehead, but bruising had come up all over her since the bombing, and any bits of skin which weren't cut or scratched had turned purple.

She had to be back in London on Monday 4th August to have her stitches removed, and it was likely that Joan and the other people from Soame Street would have their funeral the following day. But that would all be arranged while she was away.

Henry and Doreen had been very kind. They'd used some of their precious petrol ration to come and collect her from hospital, and had made her feel so welcome at their house. She had only spent one night there so far, but in many ways it was like being back with Noah and Lisette. There was the same order and cleanliness, with light, bright rooms and a real bathroom. Not that she could sit in a bath until her stitches came out, but it would be wonderful when she could.

They insisted that she could stay as long as she liked, and meant it. But that old feeling she'd had about wanting to get out of London had come back stronger than before. It wasn't just the fear of another air raid, or even running into Johnny, more a feeling that she needed to try to make a new life for herself.

She felt ashamed she'd told Johnny the way she had – although, in her own defence, she couldn't think of a kinder way to tell him – but if she'd said nothing, she would only have been sucked in deeper. She had nowhere to stay, and no money or clothes. Surely it was more honourable to leave than to hang on to him just so he would take care of her?

Mrs Harding's lips trembled when she opened the door to Mariette, and she lunged forward to embrace her, quivering with emotion. 'The children are playing in the garden. I've felt such a terrible fraud, knowing and not telling them. Sandra has asked me why I was crying several times,' she said, her words falling over themselves.

Mariette hugged her back. 'I still can't quite believe Joan's gone. We were such good friends, and I thought we'd stay that way for ever. It must have been so hard for you and your husband to say nothing, but we had to do what Joan asked, didn't we?'

'Bert thought it was the right thing to do. So we've struggled on, trying to make sure they didn't realize something was up.'

'Have you heard from their father yet?'

'We had a call from an officer to say he was on his way back this weekend in a cargo plane. He'll go to the funeral first, before coming here, poor man. They go away thinking it might be them who die, I doubt they ever think it might be the other way round.'

'Will Ian and Sandra be able to stay on with you?' Mariette asked. 'I don't know what happens in cases like this.'

'Of course they can stay with us – for ever, if they want that,' Mrs Harding said, wiping her eyes on her apron. 'We've loved them right from the start. To tell the truth, we were always afraid Joan would take them away, she missed them so much –' She put her hand over her mouth. 'Oh my days, that sounds terrible.'

'It didn't sound terrible at all,' Mariette assured her. 'Joan knew how you felt about them, and it made her happy. But let's get it over with, shall we? I can't do chatter and small talk with them not knowing what I've really come for.'

Mariette knew, if she lived to be a hundred, she'd never forget that moment when she walked through the back door and saw the two children playing tennis with two old racquets and the washing line as the net.

It was a hot, still day. Sandra was dressed in a pink cotton sundress with elastic ruching around the bodice, Ian in just a pair of shorts. They were both very suntanned, the picture of health and vitality, so very different to the whey-faced children still living in London.

Sandra saw her first, shrieked with delight and dropped her racquet to come running over. 'Where's Mummy?' she shouted.

Ian clearly sensed something. He began to run over, but stopped halfway, looking at Mariette suspiciously. 'Hasn't she come with you? What's happened to your legs?'

'Come here and sit down,' Mariette said gently. Taking their hands, she led them over to a blanket laid out on the ground under a tree. Mrs Harding was standing in the kitchen doorway, holding her knuckles to her mouth.

'Something bad has happened, hasn't it?' Ian said as they sat down. 'You wouldn't come alone without Mum, unless . . .'

'Yes, Ian,' she said gravely. 'I'm afraid the very worst thing had happened. There was an air raid. Your mummy and I went to the shelter together, but a bomb hit it.'

The children just looked at her, almost as if they didn't believe her.

'Mummy was killed, and lots of other people,' Mariette went on, but her voice was wobbling and she knew she wouldn't be able to hold back her tears for long. 'I was sitting right next to her, but she got the worst of it.'

'Did the bomb fall on your legs?' Sandra asked, looking at the bandages around both her legs.

'Not the bomb, a beam in the shelter ceiling, but it didn't hit me as hard as it did your mummy. They took her to hospital, and tried to make her better, but they couldn't. She asked me to come and tell you what had happened, and to tell you she loved you.'

'And she's not coming to see us then?' Sandra asked, her lips quivering.

'She can't if she's dead, silly,' Ian said. But then he began to cry.

Sandra had looked bewildered until that moment, but seeing her elder brother cry must have made it clearer. Mariette put an arm around each of them, drew them close to her and cried with them.

'Your daddy is on his way home,' she said. 'I wish I hadn't had to tell you something so dreadful, but Mummy wanted me to be the one to explain because we were such good friends. And because I know how proud she was of you.'

Mrs Harding came over then with glasses of water for them. 'I'm so sorry,' she said to the children, her voice cracking and tears rolling down her face. 'Your mummy was a lovely, good woman, and it isn't fair she should go so young.'

Sandra got up and put her arms around Mrs Harding's middle. 'Can we stay here with you?' she asked.

'Or do we have to go back to London?' Ian asked, a look of panic in his eyes.

'No, Ian,' Mrs Harding said quickly. 'You will stay here with us.'

'For ever?' Sandra asked, looking up hopefully.

'Until the war is over, at least,' Mariette said. She knew Joan had been brought up in an orphanage, so there was no one on her side to come forward to claim the children. As far as she knew, Rodney had no close relatives either, and he'd have to go back to the army too.

'Well, that's good then,' Ian said.

Mariette knew exactly what he meant – that having to return to London without his mother would be too awful – he just hadn't yet learned to be careful how he phrased things.

Mariette remembered her mother saying that children were very resilient, and she found that to be true of Ian and Sandra in the three days she spent with them. They cried a great deal at first, then they asked about the house and the neighbours. But once that was done, it was almost as if they were closing a door in their minds on their life before coming to Lyme Regis.

By the second day, they were merely subdued, occasionally asking Mariette a question about their mother, or how it had been in the shelter. Ian asked if she had been in pain, and at least she was able to say no, which seemed to satisfy him. She found Sandra looking at a family photograph of her parents, Ian and herself. It had been taken in a studio, before Rodney left for North Africa, because he was in uniform.

'That dress is too small for me now,' Sandra said. 'Mummy made it, it was pink with smocking.'

'Have you still got it?' Mariette asked.

'Yes, it's in the drawer with all the things that are too small now,' she replied.

'Well, you must keep it, and that photo. When you are a big girl, you'll like to look at it. One day you might have a little girl of your own, and you can show the dress to her, maybe she'll even wear it. You see, things made by someone who loves you are very special. They make you remember good things, and make you happy.'

'We can't be happy without Mummy, though, can we?' she asked.

Sandra's tawny-coloured eyes were very like Joan's, bringing Mariette up with a start.

'Oh yes, you can,' she said. 'Your mummy was the happiest person I ever knew. She would hate it if you and Ian were sad.'

On the third day, Ian asked if she was their auntie.

'Not a real auntie – I'd have to be your dad or mum's sister to be that. But I'm your auntie in my heart. I'll always care about you and keep in touch. Will you write to me, Ian?'

He frowned, as if considering whether he could promise that. 'Yes, I will,' he said. 'But will you visit us too?'

'Of course I will,' she agreed. 'I'll be going back to New Zealand, when the war is over. But by then you'll be such a big boy, you won't mind.'

'I think I will. Mum said in one of her letters that you were a special friend, so that makes you special to me too.'

Mariette felt a surge of emotion and hugged him tightly. 'And you and Sandra will always be special to me.'

'How was it?' Doreen asked as Mariette returned from the funeral, just after seven in the evening, on Tuesday. It had been raining all day, and Doreen took the black coat and hat a neighbour had lent Mariette and hung them up to dry on the hall stand.

'Terribly sad,' Mariette said, her voice flat and her expression strained. 'The vicar said some lovely things about the people who died, but seeing all those coffins together was too much for everyone. Rodney – that's Joan's husband – was in a bad way. When we went over to the pub afterwards, he got very drunk with Brenda's husband. Brenda won't ever walk again, and when her husband overheard someone say it would've been better if she'd died too, he got very nasty.'

'People mean well, but they can be so tactless sometimes,' Doreen sighed. 'I've heard some terrible things said at funerals. When my mother died, her neighbour asked straight out if she could have her clothes. I would've given them to her anyway, but to ask like that was like being a vulture.'

They went into the kitchen, and Doreen made a cup of tea. 'Did Rodney say when he was going down to see the children?'

'Tomorrow. That is, if he's sober enough to get the train.' Mariette grimaced. 'Poor man, I tried to talk to him about Joan and the children. But I don't think he was taking anything in.'

'These things take time,' Doreen said. 'He's confused and hurting. I just hope he doesn't upset his children.'

'That's what I'm worried about,' Mariette said. 'I told him they were very happy with the Hardings, but he was nasty and said I knew nothing about his kids.'

That had been the most upsetting thing about the funeral. She had hoped that Rodney would want to talk to her about Joan and his children. She had intended to assure him she would keep in touch with them while he was away and be like an aunt to them. He was a big, opinionated, thuggish man, and one look at him was enough to know she wouldn't like him. Yet she had tried, reminding herself that he was grieving and that, under normal circumstances, he was probably a very nice man. But it was as if he resented her surviving when his wife had died, and he was suspicious of her interest in his children.

'The vast majority of men know nothing about their children,' Doreen said with a disapproving sniff. 'They go to work before the kids are up, return after they've gone to bed. Many of them spend the evening in the pub. Maybe Rodney was different, who knows? But even Henry had very little to do with ours, when they were small. What about your father, Mari?'

'He was always around,' she said with a smile. 'He changed nappies, walked us in a pram, shared the load with Mum. I was often out with him all day from the age of four or five. I thought all fathers were like him, and it was quite a shock when I found out they weren't.'

'Then Belle was a lucky lady,' Doreen said. 'And you make sure you find a husband like that too.'

'I'll try,' she said with a weak smile. 'I must write to my parents tonight. Tell them I got bombed out and where I am now. Tomorrow it's back to work. I'm not looking forward to that, the other women there are so snooty.'

Doreen patted her on the shoulder. 'Maybe they'll be different now that you've been hurt and lost your home.'

'Somehow, I doubt that.' Mariette laughed mirthlessly.

Mariette was right. The other women showed neither interest nor sympathy. They just looked disdainfully at her brown spotted dress, as if she'd crawled out from under a stone.

Mr Perry didn't even bother to ask where she was living now, or offer any sympathy.

She looked around the cramped, musty chambers with stacks of bulging files and walls lined with legal books. She thought it all looked like something out of a Charles Dickens novel.

She decided she would stay just a few weeks more, to save up some money, and then she would leave the job and London.

23

Sidmouth, Devon, 1942

Mariette watched the rain lashing down on the tea-shop window and wished she'd ridden her bicycle straight home instead of taking shelter in the tea shop. She'd thought it was only an April shower, over in a few minutes, but now it looked as if it had set in for the rest of the day.

She had moved to Sidmouth at the end of January, almost three months ago, as a result of Mr and Mrs Harding inviting her to spend Christmas with them and Joan's children.

The long journey to Lyme Regis had been something of an ordeal. The train was crowded, cold and slow, stopping at every station. With all the windows blacked out, and the names on the stations removed, it was a gamble whether anyone could get off at the right stop. Mariette had been amused by people only waking up as the stationmaster yelled out the station name, and then having a frantic rush to collect their luggage and parcels and get off.

But there was the spirit of Christmas on the train, and all the passengers made a real effort to be chatty and jolly. Two RAF men returning to their base on the coast had kept her entertained all the way down with funny stories. As laughter had been in rather short supply since Joan's death, Mariette welcomed being taken out of herself. She happened to mention to these two men that she wanted to move away from London, and they told her that Sybil Merchant, the landlady of the Plume of Feathers in Sidmouth, was looking for help in her busy pub.

Sidmouth was in Devon, but it was just along the coast from Lyme Regis. So, while Mariette was with the Hardings and the children, on an impulse she caught the train to Sidmouth and went to the pub, to check it out. She found Sybil every bit as warm and pleasant as the two RAF men had said. When she was offered the job, she agreed then and there to take it. She had to return to London, to work out her notice with Mr Perry and to say goodbye to Doreen and Henry, but she was back in Sidmouth by the end of January. She fervently hoped that a new year and a new home would herald a change in fortunes for both her and England. On top of her own personal tragedies, world news during November and December had been especially grim.

There had been the sinking of the *Ark Royal*, the ongoing siege of Leningrad, the Japanese attack on Pearl Harbor, the sinking of the battleships *Repulse* and the *Prince of Wales* by the Japanese, and the invasion of Malaya and the fall of Hong Kong. Then there were all the terrible stories of atrocities towards the Jews in Germany and Poland, men, women and children just gunned down in the streets, or forced into ghettos where they were starving. There were even whispers of purpose-built concentration camps where Jews were being sent and possibly killed. While no one seemed to know if the last was actually true, there was certainly enough evidence of the savage ill-treatment of Jews to make it seem more than possible.

Happily, there had been something of a lull in the bombing of London, perhaps because the Germans were putting all their energies into conquering Russia. It pleased everyone to read in the press that the German generals had seriously underestimated the severity of the Russian winter as they marched on Moscow. It was reported gleefully that German soldiers were lighting fires under their tanks in order to start the engines, their machine guns were seizing up with the cold, and they didn't even have clothing that was warm enough for the sub-zero temperatures.

The Americans declaring war against Japan also gave everyone some hope that the war could be won. Winston Churchill made an impassioned speech in December, saying that Britain, the USA and the Soviet Union would teach 'the gangs and cliques of wicked men' a lesson that would not be forgotten in a thousand years. Everyone hoped he was right.

But, for Mariette, all the horrors and sadness of the previous year, and the uncertainty about the future, seemed easier to bear when she got to Sidmouth.

Lyme Regis was quainter than Sidmouth – it was really just a small village with only a few little shops – but Sidmouth was a proper town with a school, a library, lots of shops, pubs, restaurants, cafés and much more. Its residents weren't hollow-eyed and gaunt from air raids, they smiled at strangers, they stopped for a chat, and they weren't fearful.

The gracious Regency houses on the esplanade had been built as private holiday homes for rich and influential people. In 1819, Edward, Duke of Kent, came to stay with his wife and baby daughter, Victoria, who was later to become Queen. The house they stayed in had changed its name to the Royal Glen Hotel, and it was now in use as an RAF convalescent home. In fact, practically all the grand houses on the seafront had been requisitioned by the RAF since the outbreak of war, but that hadn't spoiled their charm or beauty.

Mariette loved the winding streets of small houses behind the seafront, and she enjoyed the peace and quiet after the noise and tumult of London. She admired the carefully maintained parks and people's neat front gardens which, although devoid of flowers in January and February, promised an abundance for April and May. With seagulls whirling overhead, the sound of waves slapping on the beach and the exhilarating tang of seaweed in the air, she found her old optimism returning.

There were also long walks along the spectacular cliffs to enjoy. Sadly, there was no harbour, but there were all manner of small boats moored at the mouth of the River Sid, and she promised herself that she would befriend anyone who had one for the chance to sail and fish again.

She fell in love with the Plume of Feathers on sight because it had bow windows which, back in New Zealand, she'd always imagined an old English pub having. On a cold night the bar was very welcoming, with a big fire blazing in a huge old fireplace and the thick curtains tightly closed. Most nights, someone would bang out 'The White Cliffs of Dover' or other nostalgic songs on the piano, and everyone would sing along.

Sybil Merchant looked and sounded more like a farmer's wife than a landlady. She was short, plump and rosy-cheeked with an exuberant sunny nature. Ted, her husband, was tall and thin with a dour personality. Sybil joked that they were Jack Sprat and his wife. On first meeting with them, Mariette thought, as most people did, that they were totally ill matched.

But Mariette was soon to realize, as everyone eventually did, that the couple complemented each other. He was the still waters to his wife's babbling brook; he was the steady organizer, while her warm personality kept their customers happy.

Ted had been gassed in the last war, and he had problems with his breathing sometimes, which was why he came across as dour. But however different they were in character, they clearly loved each other dearly.

The instinct that had made her impulsively accept the job had proved to be a sound one. From the first evening she arrived, cold, tired and hungry, to be greeted with warm smiles and concern for her, she knew she'd made the right move. Her bedroom, although tiny, was comfortable and attractive. She knew, that first night, she could be happy here.

Her role was to help out with whatever was needed, whether that was cleaning, serving behind the bar, lighting fires, or cooking breakfast for any paying guests. Time off was flexible, if she wanted to visit the Hardings, take a walk along the cliffs, go to the cinema or a dance, she only had to say. Likewise if, after a busy Saturday lunchtime, the bar needed a good clean before opening again in the evening, Mariette would do it and leave Sybil to have a rest.

As February slipped into March, her birthday and the anniversary of Noah, Lisette and Rose's deaths passed. She saw bulbs coming up in the gardens and lambs being born in the fields around the town. That seemed a sign to her that the horrors of the previous year were really over. A new era was dawning, which would be happier.

She found too that she was actually happier here than she'd been with Noah and Lisette. She had loved them, of course – and Rose too – but she'd often felt that she was acting a part that they would approve of. Living with Doreen and Henry had been much the same – always needing to be polite, helpful, sunny-natured, never opposing anything they said.

She could be totally herself with Sybil and Ted, and the ordinary people who drank in the bar, and that was liberating. Along with the regular customers, there were many RAF men and WAAFs. She would flirt a little with the men, and chat with the girls. She didn't feel that she was slightly inferior to them, as she sometimes felt with Rose's friends, nor was she accused of being 'posh', as she often was with people in the East End.

Ted got Mariette a second-hand bicycle so she could get

about easily. On a sunny afternoon, when there was nothing to do at the pub, she would cycle out into the surrounding countryside and along the coast to explore. Ian and Sandra had become substitutes for her own brothers, Mr and Mrs Harding for her parents, and she visited them every week. She often felt ashamed that she'd hardly ever played board games with her brothers, or helped them with their homework. In fact, looking back, she realized she'd taken very little interest in them. Yet now she was thrilled to get a letter from them, and when Alexis recently sent her a snapshot of him and Noel together in Cairo, she had wanted to show it to the whole world.

Back when she was about sixteen, Mog had got really angry with her because she showed no interest in her family and avoided being with them.

'I almost hope that something bad happens to you one day so that you'll wake up and see how lucky you are to be surrounded by people who love and care for you, my girl,' she raged at Mariette. 'When you're old, few people will remember how clever, beautiful or talented you were. All they'll remember is how you made them feel about themselves. Right now, you make everyone you come into contact with feel uncomfortable, dull and inferior. Just think on that, Miss Smarty Pants! Is that how you want to be remembered?'

Mariette knew, of course, that Mog would never really have wished a tragedy on her to make her appreciate all she had. But she was right in saying that suffering certainly did aid the process. If Mog could see her now, helping Sandra make clothes for her dolls, or taking Sybil her breakfast in bed, unasked, or even glimpse her on her knees scrubbing the bar floor while happily singing along to the wireless, Mog would be incandescent with delight.

Yet the funny thing was, however much Mariette longed to go home to see Mog and her parents, she actually wondered if she could bear to say goodbye to Ian and Sandra. She certainly wasn't ever going to forget them, or their mother, or indeed any of the people whom she'd grown fond of while here in England.

She had been intending to ride up to Lyme Regis later today to see the children, but the heavy rain had cancelled that plan. But she had a newspaper, so once she'd read that, she would brave the rain and ride back to the pub.

The little bell tinkled on the door, but Mariette was too engrossed in reading about a ridiculous new government order – that there could be no more wasteful embroidery or lace on ladies' underwear – to look up.

'Mari!'

Her head jerked up at hearing her name. Standing there in front of her was Edwin Atkins, the airman she'd been with on the night of the Café de Paris bombing. He was with another airman, and both had soaking wet uniforms.

She jumped to her feet in astonishment. 'Good heavens!' she exclaimed. 'I can't believe it! Edwin!'

She had often thought about him in the weeks that followed the deaths of Noah, Lisette, Rose and Peter. She had been cut adrift from life as she'd known it, and Jean-Philippe's nastiness had added to the feeling of isolation. She had Joan, of course, but she was so different in every way to the family she'd lost. Maybe if she'd written that letter, as she had planned to do, telling him where she was and what she was doing . . . But she hadn't, and that was partly because she was afraid he might bring back memories of Rose, Noah and Lisette, and partly because of her friendship with Johnny.

In the light of the way she'd eventually turned Johnny down, it seemed quite absurd that she should have considered his feelings. But back then, recovering from the biggest shock of her life, and with everything seemingly topsy-turvy,

Johnny was a constant presence. He was there, as he had been right through the Blitz, as a steady source of comfort, a light in a dark place.

Then, after Joan had been killed and Johnny had left, while she was living in Hampstead, she just felt too low in herself to think of ringing or writing to anyone other than her family.

But now Edwin was standing in front of her in a little Devon tea shop, and it felt like the most fantastic and outlandish stroke of good fortune.

'I was celebrating this young lady's twenty-first birthday at the Café de Paris, when it was bombed,' Edwin explained to his companion, a short fresh-faced man he introduced as Tim Warberry. 'How wonderful to see you, Mari! And in such an out-of-the-way spot! What on earth are you doing here?'

Mariette said that she was working in a pub in the town. Edwin still looked astounded, but both men sat down at her table and Tim ordered tea and cake for them all.

'I tried to ring you after the funeral,' Edwin said, once the waitress had taken the order. 'But Rose's brother said you'd left. He was very short with me. Did you upset him in some way?'

'No, but he upset me badly by telling me to leave immediately. He did let me stay for the funeral, in the end, and I left that same evening,' Mariette said, then went on to tell him a little more about how Jean-Philippe had only contacted people he thought were important, not the family's closest friends. 'I wanted to phone you. But, quite honestly, that unspeakable man crushed me so much that I would only have blubbed to you, and you didn't need that.'

He put his hand over hers on the table. 'You should have rung, blubbing or not, you need friends when people are nasty to you. I would've tried to help.'

'I didn't feel I knew you well enough to impose,' she said. 'But never mind all that, I'm fine now.'

'So how did you end up here?'

She explained briefly about living with Joan, and how her friend was later killed in an air raid. 'Her children had been evacuated to Lyme Regis, and I'd been here to meet them and Mr and Mrs Harding, who they were billeted with. Before Joan died, she asked if I would be the one to break the news of her death to them.'

'My God, Mari! What an awful task!' Edwin exclaimed.

'Painful, certainly. But it was better for the children to hear exactly what happened from the person who was with their mum and loved her, rather than to just get a message passed on via someone who had no interest in their welfare. Anyway, I've formed quite a bond with the children and the Hardings, so they invited me down for Christmas. A couple of airmen on the train told me about the job in the pub. So I hot-footed it out of London, and here I am.'

'That is quite a story,' Edwin said, his expression full of concern. 'But how marvellous that I've found you again! I've thought of you so often, wondered how you were, where you were. I certainly didn't expect to find you in a seaside tea shop!'

He turned to Tim, his companion, briefly apologizing for neglecting him, and explained how he had met Mariette for the first time that night at the Café de Paris, and that her relatives had all been killed, along with Peter, whom Tim had known. 'It was a sheer fluke that Mariette went off to the powder room and I moved away from the dance floor – if not for that, we would've been killed too.'

A shiver of pleasure ran down Mariette's spine; she could hear Edwin's delight in finding her again in his voice. She'd forgotten how handsome he was, with his kind brown eyes and beautiful deep voice. But it was more than just how he looked: he was a link with Rose, Noah and Lisette, a reminder of all the jolly times she'd had with them, how comfortable and easy life had been then. She might feel she was happier here in Sidmouth now, but she would never forget Uncle Noah's kindness and generosity, or how much his family had changed her for the better.

'Are you stationed down here now?' she asked.

'No, we're stationed in Bristol, flying Lancasters and getting our revenge on Hitler.'

'I read that Bath and Exeter, Norwich and York were bombed in retaliation for all the damage you did to German cities,' she said. 'Just make sure you give them twice as much as they've given us. But what are you doing here in Sidmouth?'

'As you probably know, there are a lot of RAF men down here doing various jobs. We just have to be present at a meeting of bigwigs tomorrow. We're here till Monday, so I hope you'll have some spare time for me?'

Mariette had been asked out lots of times since she arrived in Sidmouth, but she'd always declined. Part of the reason was because of what had happened with Johnny. She felt guilty about stringing him along, and never wanted to be in that position again. The other reason was that she was aware men saw barmaids as 'easy', and she didn't want that reputation in Sidmouth. So, for now, she was happier to go to a dance or the pictures with some of the new friends she'd made in the bar. That way, she could have some fun without the pressure that came with being someone's girlfriend.

But she was prepared to make an exception for Edwin.

'That would be really nice,' she smiled. 'I've got to go now as I promised I'd open up the bar tonight. But pop in, it will be lovely to see you. '

As she rode her bike back to the pub, she was bubbling with excitement. She had liked Edwin right from the off, on that terrible night. She had no doubt that, if Rose and Peter hadn't been killed, they would all have gone out in a four-some again. But what really stuck in her mind was how kind he'd been to her after the bombing; a man who could show such strength and compassion towards someone he hardly knew had to be a very good man.

At half past seven that same evening, Edwin walked into the pub with his friend Tim and two other airmen. Mariette did her best to hide her delight that he'd chosen this pub, rather than one of the many others in the town. The bar was already quite busy and the men went over to an empty table, but Edwin came up to buy the first round of drinks.

He made a thumbing gesture towards his friends. 'I twisted their arms to come here,' he grinned. 'Good job there're some girls in here, or I might have become very unpopular.'

'It is supposed to be the best pub in town,' she said as she began to pull the pints. 'Not that I'd really know as I haven't been in any others.'

'So where do all the men who worship you take you?' he asked, his eyes twinkling.

'You mean the ones who buy me a port and lemon and tell me they are going to take me to the moon and back?' she laughed. 'You just can't depend on men these days. They promise that, but I never get beyond the pub door.'

'Not even one with a boat to take you sailing?'

She was touched that he remembered she loved sailing. 'No, and I'm not sure that civilians are even allowed to take a boat out to sea. My best hope is with fishermen but, as you probably know, they consider it bad luck to have a woman aboard. And anyway, most are working on the minesweepers.'

'Sorry I haven't got a boat to offer you. But how about a cliff-top walk tomorrow afternoon?'

'I'd like that, Edwin,' she said.

He paid her for the four pints. 'I wish I could stand up here all evening and talk to you, but the chaps will get shirty with me. So is it OK if I come for you about two then?'

The pub was more packed than usual so, even if Edwin had stayed at the bar, she wouldn't have been able to talk to him. But he did keep looking round and grinning at her, and she knew he wanted her company more than that of his friends.

Before going to bed, Mariette agonized over what to wear on the walk the next day. Her mother and Mog had sent her a lovely dress and jacket for Christmas. The dress was a sleeveless turquoise print with a full skirt, the short jacket was plain turquoise with the collar and cuffs matching the print of the dress. But it was more suitable for a dance, or going out to dinner, than for a cliff-top walk.

She had replaced some of the clothes she'd lost in the bombing. But they were all second-hand as she only had enough coupons to buy new underwear. None of the clothes were as nice or as fashionable as her old clothes had been. She felt dowdy in the gored tweed skirt and cream crêpe de Chine blouse that Sybil thought was lovely. The black crêpe dress was one she liked, but she wore it most nights in the bar. And if she had to wear the brown polka-dot dress once more, she'd scream.

So the only dress left was the one she'd recently run up on Sybil's sewing machine. It was just a cotton print, pastel flowers on a white background, sleeveless, with a scoop neck and a full skirt. Sybil had given her a wide blue leather belt to wear with it, and although it was a bit early in the year for something so summery, she supposed if she wore a cardigan she'd be warm enough.

She looked down at her scarred legs and winced. She'd been wearing slacks when she met Edwin this afternoon, and this evening her legs would have been hidden from view behind the bar. What was he going to think of them?

'Too bad, if he doesn't like them,' she said to herself in the mirror. 'Your papa always said people should be proud of war wounds.'

Edwin came into the pub the following day on the dot of two o'clock. Usually, Friday was a busy day as many elderly married couples came into town on the bus. While their wives shopped, the men came in here for a pint. But as it was mild and sunny today, the men were probably sitting on benches on the seafront.

Mariette had already told Sybil all about Edwin. She'd arranged to go off early as the pub was open until three thirty.

When Sybil saw Edwin, she winked in approval at Mariette. 'Don't come rushing back for opening time, I can manage,' she said.

'That's a very pretty dress,' Edwin said as they walked down towards the esplanade. 'Is it new?'

'Yes, I made it. I lost everything when I got bombed out, but I managed to buy the material for this here in Sidmouth. I think I told you before that I used to dish out second-hand clothes to people who were bombed out. I never expected that I would be in the same position myself one day.'

'I wish you had telephoned me before. You must have felt so terribly alone after losing your uncle, aunt and Rose,' he said. 'I would have taken you to meet my family, they would have all rallied round, found you things to wear and stuff.'

'With Jean-Philippe being convinced I'd been sponging off his family, I wasn't going to go cap in hand to anyone,' she said. 'But thank you, anyway.'

'Peter's parents told me he was callous towards them at the funeral. They were shocked, they'd expected Rose's brother to be as warm and caring as she was, but they put his attitude down to grief. Had they known he was so nasty to you, I think they would have insisted you go home with them.'

'He was really vile,' she admitted. 'I did plan to think up something nasty, just to get back at him, but Joan dying put that out of my head. So now I try not to dwell on him, and just remember all the good times with Noah, Lisette and Rose. I couldn't even bring myself to tell my parents just how nasty he was — they would have found it too upsetting as they'd known him since he was a small boy — so I just hope he gets washed overboard from his ship, and dies a slow and cold death.'

Edwin chuckled. 'He isn't on a ship, he's got desk duties in the Admiralty. I checked up on him. But perhaps we can hope a bomb singles him out on his way home one night.'

Mariette laughed. She had, for a short time, been twisted up inside with anger towards the man and had wanted revenge. But she realized now that she no longer cared. She was happy, and he wasn't — or he would never have been so nasty — so it was time to forget him.

It was easy to set unpleasant things aside in Edwin's company; he was so easy to be with. Conversation flowed effortlessly between them as they related things that had happened to them in the last year, chatting about friends, family and the war as it had affected them. He noticed her scarred legs and was very sympathetic, not repulsed.

'They'll fade,' he said. 'I bet in a year or two you'll have a job to see them. And with a pretty face like yours, who is going to be staring at your legs?'

He had lost even more people close to him than she had.

341

'It's a terrible thing to admit to, but I hardly react any more when one of the chaps doesn't make it back to base. None of us do,' he said. 'We go off to the pub and raise a few glasses to them, tell a few stories, then that's it, back to normal. I sometimes wonder if, when this war is over, we'll all become basket cases when the reality of who we've lost hits us.'

'I can't even imagine the war ending,' Mariette admitted. 'We all talk about it, sing "The White Cliffs of Dover" and "When The Lights Go On Again", but sometimes I think it's never going to happen, and I'll never get back to New Zealand.'

'Would you stay here, if you fell in love with an Englishman?' he asked.

That question seemed a loaded one, but she managed not to giggle or blush. 'Maybe, if we could live somewhere pretty like this.' She waved her hand towards the cliffs up ahead of them. 'But I think I'd try twisting his arm to emigrate to New Zealand.'

'I don't think you'd have to twist very hard,' he said, and half smiled. 'It's going to take years to rebuild our cities. So many homes will be needed to replace those lost in the bombing, and rationing will probably go on for years. There are already thousands of widows and orphans, and almost everyone will have lost someone.'

'From what I've learned about the English while I've been here, they can handle all that and more,' Mariette responded. 'But let's get a move on, or we'll never get to Beer.'

At seven that evening, they caught the bus at Beer to get back to Sidmouth.

'It's been such a lovely day,' Mariette said as she slumped down on to the back seat.

'What a surprise that it turned out so warm,' Edwin said. 'Freckles have come out on your nose! Looks like summer's finally here.'

Mariette just smiled. It was Edwin who had made the day so special, not the warm sun, and she didn't want the day to end. He laughed easily, could talk on almost any subject, and he didn't try to impress her or talk down to her. He was caring too.

He had told her about the pregnant girlfriend of one of his friends who had been killed. 'She's in a bit of a state, she feels she can't go home, but she can't manage on her own either,' he said, as if her plight had been playing on his mind. 'I've been trying to persuade her to write to Bill's parents and tell them – after all, the baby will be their grandchild.'

'I think it's wonderful of you to try to help,' she said, unable to think of any other man she knew who would do that. 'I agree she should try his parents, but not before she's told her own. I know my parents would be very angry if I went to someone before them. She'll have to grow herself a spine too. If she loved your friend, she should be proud to carry his baby and hold her head up high. Skulking around, feeling ashamed, only gives the gossips more to talk about.'

Edwin grinned at her. 'Well, that's direct! Or should I say fierce?'

Mariette blushed. 'I do think some girls are frightfully feeble,' she admitted. 'But then, I've had to learn how to look after myself.'

The walk from Sidmouth to Beer had been further than she realized. Once there, they'd eaten fish and chips sitting on a bench looking out to sea. Fish and chips had never tasted so good. But they had elected to catch the bus back – it was just too far to walk.

While they were sitting on a wall, waiting for the bus,

Edwin asked her if she ever wished she hadn't come to England.

She considered that for a moment. 'Now and again – mostly when I feel very alone, and I think of everyone I've lost – but I think coming to England has done me a power of good. I'm not as selfish as I used to be, and I'm more tolerant and understanding. At least, I think so. Only someone who knew me before could confirm it.'

'Is there anything more you'd like to do before you go home?'

'Yes, I'd like to do something worthwhile.'

'Such as?' He lifted one eyebrow quizzically.

She shrugged. 'I don't know really. Something that I can look back at with pride, when I'm an old lady.'

He didn't laugh at her, but he didn't make any suggestions either, so she was rather surprised that Edwin brought the subject up again, once they were settled on the bus.

'You could go in for nursing,' he began. 'You'd be good at that.'

She shook her head. 'No, I wouldn't, I'd be useless. I retch if I see anyone being sick, and I feel faint at the sight of blood.'

'I don't believe that. Your mother drove an ambulance in the last war.'

'How do you know that?'

'Peter mentioned it once. He was actually telling me about Noah, about him being a war correspondent and stuff, and that brought him on to the subject of your father. Peter said Noah kind of hero-worshipped him. Getting the Croix de Guerre and all. And then he said your mother had been out there in France too. So it's brave stock you come from.'

Mariette giggled. 'I'm certainly not brave enough to deal with war wounds,' she said. 'Sticking a plaster on a grazed knee is as far as I want to go. It's funny you should say that about Noah kind of hero-worshipping my father, though. I sensed that too. In fact, I suspect there is a great story behind how the two men met, and I'm fairly certain my mother and Lisette were right in the middle of it. Maybe, if I could do one really good thing to make my folks proud of me, then they'll tell me about it.'

'If you were my daughter, I'd be as proud as Punch at how strong and brave you've been,' Edwin said.

'All I've done is deal with the stuff that happened to me. I don't call that brave, it's just survival.'

'That's not how I see it,' he said, and he put his arm around her shoulders and drew her closer to him. 'A really brave thing to do would be to let me kiss you on the Sidmouth bus.'

Mariette giggled. There were no more than six people on the bus, and as she and Edwin were sitting at the back they couldn't be seen anyway. 'I'm feeling extraordinarily brave today,' she said and turned her face to his.

His kiss was perfect. Not too hesitant but not too bold either. His tongue flickered between her parted lips just enough to send a wake-up message to all her nerve endings. And the way he held her, as if she was something precious, made her feel marvellous.

'Umm,' she said, when they finally drew apart. 'I didn't feel scared.'

'You might, if you knew what was going on in my mind,' he said, and nuzzled his cheek against hers. 'Can I just tell you something?'

'Go on.'

'Well, that night at the Café de Paris, I was truly bowled over by you. If that bomb hadn't dropped, I would've made a complete nuisance of myself howling under your window nightly.'

'I would've thrown a bucket of water over you,' Mariette laughed. 'But that is a lovely thing to say, and I was pretty much bowled over by you too. Shame we can't turn the clock back, and meet up for my twenty-first in a different place.'

'The tragedy of that night doesn't have to prevent us starting again, does it?'

'No, it doesn't,' she agreed. 'And I'm certain, if Rose and Peter are looking down, they'll be cheering right now.'

He kissed her again then and, this time, Mariette's whole body seemed to melt into his.

She never wanted the kiss to end.

They were staggering like drunks when they got off the bus, with flushed faces and lips swollen from kissing. They felt they were floating in a kind of bubble that prevented the outside world touching them.

'What now?' Edwin said. 'I've got to go back to Bristol on Monday morning, you are working during the day, and I've got meetings and things. I can't even say when I can meet you again after this weekend.'

'We'll go back to the pub now, and I'm sure Sybil will take pity on us and let me have some time off over the weekend. As for the future, we'll just have to see how it goes.'

He slid his arms around her and hugged her tightly. 'I'm glad one of us is grounded. But I suppose I'm afraid that I'll lose you again.'

'Fate brought us together again, so let's believe it's meant to be,' she said.

'Look at his face,' Sybil whispered to Mariette later that evening.

They were busy serving as the bar was crowded. Edwin was sitting on a stool up at the end of the bar, staring into space. Mariette's stomach did a little flip because he was so handsome. She could see his dark lashes like small fans on his cheeks, and his plump lips that had so recently been kissing her.

'He's not drunk, he's only had two pints,' Sybil said went on. 'He's daydreaming about you.'

'Don't be daft,' Mariette laughed. 'He's probably thinking about flying, or fast cars.'

'No, there's only one thing that makes a man sit silently at a bar like that, and that's a woman. I watched him earlier, the way he was looking at you, all yearning and hopeful. Trust me, I've had years of practice studying men. I could write a book on my findings.'

'Well, it would be nice if he was thinking about me,' Mariette admitted. 'I really like him. But it won't be easy to see him when he's based in Bristol.'

'It's not easy for any sweethearts in wartime,' Sybil said thoughtfully. 'I met Ted when he was home on leave in the last one. We fell for one another right away, but then he got gassed. He wrote from hospital in France and told me to forget him as he'd be no use to me. As if you can forget!'

'But you made it together,' Mariette said.

Sybil smiled. 'Yes, but we had some sticky moments at first. He felt like only half a man because of his breathing, so he couldn't do any manual work. But love finds a way through anything.'

'I hope so,' Mariette said, looking at Edwin at the end of the bar. 'I really hope so.'

24

1943

Sybil popped her head round the living-room door, behind the bar, where Mariette was doing some ironing on the table. 'There's a chap wanting to speak to you privately. His name is Ollenshaw. And, by the look of him, he's from the Secret Service.'

Mariette giggled. Sybil was always guessing what people did for a living and she liked to pick ridiculous jobs. 'So is there a special look for the Secret Service?'

'Yes, you must be unable to smile, and speak in a really upper-crust, stilted way,' Sybil said. 'Shall I ask if he has the secret password? Tell him to sod off, or bring him back through here? I promise I won't listen at the keyhole, if you choose that option.'

'The last option, though I can't imagine what he wants with me,' Mariette replied. 'But wheel him through, anyway. Is he worth putting lipstick on for?'

Sybil grimaced. 'Definitely not!'

When Sybil brought the man in and introduced him, Mariette had a job to keep a straight face. He was small and very dapper in a pinstriped suit, with his bowler hat in his hand, and he was so straight-backed that he looked as if he'd left the coat hanger in his jacket.

'I'll be in the bar, should you need me,' Sybil said as a parting shot, making a silly face behind the man's back.

Mariette folded up the blanket she'd been ironing on, and

offered him a cup of tea. 'No, thank you,' he said, sitting down at the table. 'I'll come straight to the point, Miss Carrera,' he said. 'I understand you speak fluent French. Is that correct?'

'Well, yes,' Mariette replied guardedly. She noticed he had disconcertingly small dark eyes, like a pig's.

'Would you be prepared to use that ability for the war effort?'

'You mean interpreting? Yes, of course, as long as it would fit in with my job here.'

'There would be more to it than interpreting,' he said, looking at her very intently.

She knew Sybil had only been joking about him being with the Secret Service. But, astonishingly, it sounded very much as if he really was. As intriguing as that might be, she didn't like the way she was being scrutinized, or the fact that he'd just turned up here out of the blue.

'Before we go any further, I would like to know who informed you that I speak French and why that would be of any interest to anyone?'

Ollenshaw shrugged and made an attempt at a smile. But his lips only moved slightly, showing just a tiny glimpse of teeth. 'My department has ears at many doors, Miss Carrera. In your case, a casual remark made about you reached us. So we checked you out.'

'You mean you've been poking into my life without me being aware of it?' she exclaimed indignantly.

'In wartime we need to utilize people with certain abilities,' he said curtly. 'But obviously, in the interests of national security, we have to do thorough background checks. Our initial interest in you was because you are bilingual, but then we discovered you have sailing experience too.'

'Sailing! Why would you be interested in that?'

'Often, the only way to get one of our people out of France is in a small boat.'

Mariette had believed him up until that point. But surely no government officer would just talk about getting people out of France at the first meeting? Had she been set up by one of the pub customers? Playing along with it seemed like the best idea.

'When you say small, what are you talking about? A dinghy, or a rowing boat?' she asked.

Ollenshaw nodded.

Mariette burst into laughter. 'Across the English Channel? You're pulling my leg!'

'Of course, we wouldn't expect anyone to sail right across the Channel in a small craft, only to another bigger one nearby.'

Mariette looked scornfully at this little man, who didn't look as if he could even handle a pedal boat. 'Someone's put you up to this. Is it a joke?' she asked.

'Miss Carrera, do I look like a man who plays pranks on people?'

He certainly didn't. And she couldn't think of anyone she knew who might be capable of finding someone like Ollenshaw to play a joke on her. 'Then you'd better tell me something to convince me you are on the level.'

He sighed deeply, as if he'd been talking to a simpleton. 'Let me explain why I am approaching you, Miss Carrera. It is because my superiors feel you are the sort of young woman we desperately need for special missions,' he said. 'You first came to our attention some time ago, when you were working as a secretary for a Mr Greville, in London. You were present at a dinner with a senior British Army officer, and interpreted for another guest, a retired French Army officer. Am I right about that?'

Mariette knew then that this man must be what he said he was as she hadn't told anyone down here about meeting the French Army officer. 'Yes, you are right about that. I often accompanied Mr Greville to meetings with people who could give him orders for uniforms.'

'Well, you created a very good impression. A note was made about you. Since then, we have been keeping an eye on you.'

'I don't like the sound of that,' she exclaimed. 'It's creepy.'

He shrugged. 'Maybe, but it is a sign of the times. However, everything reported back to us about you is good. We know how you conducted yourself during the Blitz, the help you gave to others despite great personal loss. We also know about your family background. Your father won the Croix de Guerre in the last war and your mother served her country driving ambulances in France. The daughter of two such people is hardly likely to be lily-livered. This was confirmed to us when we learned about your actions in climbing out of a bombed shelter, with no regard for your own safety, in order to get help for those trapped inside. All in all, we have a picture of a courageous, resourceful and compassionate young woman.'

Mariette blushed with embarrassment, and some indignation at the thought that someone had been watching her every move. Yet it was also nice to be portrayed in such a good light. 'I just did what needed doing, there were no heroics,' she said. 'But although I have sailed since I was a child, back in New Zealand, and I can handle many kinds of boats, I've seen just how rough the sea can get here. I can't claim to have that sort of experience. I'd probably be useless to you.'

Ollenshaw made a dismissive gesture with his hands. 'I only came here today to get an indication as to whether you were receptive to the idea. Obviously, there would have to be a more formal interview. And then, should you pass that, on to training.'

'Training! I'm not giving my job up here.'

He shook his head. 'No one is asking you to do that. What we're talking about are special missions, a couple of days here and there. You would not be totally alone on any of them. And you would come back here and carry on, as if you'd just been away to visit a relative.'

Mariette was too busy thinking about what he'd said to make any comment.

'I should at this point, however, impress upon you that it is imperative that you tell no one about this conversation. Not even your loved ones, friends or your employers.'

Mariette gulped. It sounded so serious and scary but she had claimed she wanted to do something useful, and perhaps this was it. 'Fair enough. OK, yes, I am interested. Well, enough to know a little more.'

'Then someone will be in touch with you shortly,' he said. Picking his hat up off the table, he swept out through the bar, leaving Mariette open-mouthed in astonishment.

She could hardly believe she'd just had that conversation. Surely the Secret Service – or whoever it was that came up with rescue plans – wouldn't pick on someone like her, who wasn't even English? She went into the bar, where Sybil was polishing glasses.

Sybil looked round at Mariette. 'Well? I've been biting my nails down to the quick in curiosity!'

'I'm afraid I can't tell you,' Mariette said, making a helpless grimace.

'See, I told you he was Secret Service, I know a spymaster when I see one,' Sybil laughed.

'You don't know how close you are,' Mariette sighed. 'But please, don't ask me any more, because I really can't tell you – however much I want to.'

Sybil's eyes widened with surprise, but she put her finger

to her nose. 'Keep Mum, she's not so dumb,' she said, using the words on a poster everywhere about town.

In the days that followed the visit from Ollenshaw, Mariette veered from blind panic to thinking she must have imagined the whole meeting with him. She so much wanted to confide in someone, to get their view on it. How dangerous would this work be? She could handle a boat, she wasn't scared of that, but she was afraid of being shot. And surely, if she was helping people get out of France, that was exactly what might happen?

It was early June, and the weather good. She was sure that all over England there were people who would love to be living somewhere quiet and pretty like Sidmouth, if only as an antidote to a war that seemed no closer to ending. Rationing, high taxes and the shortages of almost everything were biting into people's way of life; while food consumption had gone down, alcohol and tobacco consumption were up.

It was bad enough to hear horror stories from all over Europe, North Africa and the Far East, but Mariette had been appalled to hear, in March, of the 173 people who were crushed to death in Bethnal Green tube station when a woman tripped and fell on the steep stairs. Those hurrying down behind her fell too, building up a wall of death. She worried about her brothers in Italy, and how her parents and Mog were coping. And, of course, she worried about Edwin too. Now she had something more to worry about – whether agreeing to undertake these special missions was really foolhardy.

Yet, whether it was foolhardy or not, it was exciting. Not just because it was thrilling to think that someone had been impressed by her. Or because she had always wanted to do something useful and brave, so she could return home knowing she'd done her bit.

But also because of Edwin.

If she'd been approached a couple of years ago, when she had first met him, she would have turned it down flat because she wanted to be with him so much, she would never have risked not being available on the rare times he got leave. Since they had run into each other that day in the tea shop, they'd only met up about a dozen times.

It was the same for all wives and girlfriends with men in the forces. But Mariette was luckier than most because Edwin was based in England, which meant she did get telephone calls and he was given leave on a regular basis – even if it was only for twenty-four hours.

If he managed to get down here to Sidmouth, on a Saturday night, they would go to the local dance, then sit on the esplanade in the moonlight, kissing and talking for hours. She had met him in Bristol twice, but neither time had been a resounding success as the guesthouse had been grim, and it had rained the whole time, so they'd had to shelter in tea shops and pubs. But then his squadron was moved over to a base in East Anglia, and that made it far harder to see him.

The move brought new danger for him. He had lost dozens of his airmen friends during the Battle of Britain, when he was stationed at Biggin Hill, in Kent. When he was posted to Bristol, he lost more. But now he was taking part in the huge bombing raids on Germany, and although he made light of it, acting like it was nothing, night after night many Allied planes were shot down.

She tried very hard not to dwell on the possibility of him being one of the casualties, and never mentioned her anxiety either in letters or on the telephone, but at night, the minute she turned the light out, fear for him clutched at her insides. She'd lost Gerald, which was something she'd never anticipated, and she really didn't think she could cope with losing Edwin too.

She loved him so much, and she wanted to see him more often, so she suggested they meet up in London, the halfway point between them. But he always said he was afraid she might get caught up in an air raid, and he'd rather know she was safe in Sidmouth.

Then, a few weeks ago, right out of the blue, Sybil asked her whether she would marry Edwin, if he asked her. She said yes, without a second thought, even said she'd leave Sidmouth and all the friends she'd made here and move to East Anglia to be closer to him. Then Sybil asked her why Edwin hadn't introduced her to his parents.

Maybe it was because her own parents were on the other side of the world that she hadn't even considered it odd that he hadn't taken her to meet his. But once it was brought to her notice, she found herself looking a lot more closely at their relationship.

First of all, she realized that while she'd been weaving happy little daydreams of them going back to New Zealand together when the war ended, he'd never actually said anything about sharing a future with her.

He'd said he loved her countless times. They were the best of friends, they laughed at the same things, and there never seemed enough time for all the things they had to say to one another. But he hadn't said he wanted to marry her, and they hadn't become lovers.

While Mariette would have been cautious about making love, for fear of getting pregnant and then Edwin being killed, she thought the main reason they hadn't become lovers was due to lack of opportunity.

Sybil wouldn't condone them sharing a room when he stayed at the pub – she didn't even leave them alone for long in the sitting room. But Mariette had always thought that the reason Edwin hadn't tried to have his way with her in his car or in a field, or even suggested they went to a hotel, was out of respect for her, and a belief that sex outside of marriage was wrong. She liked that about him, it made her feel safe and cared for.

All this time, while being crazy about the man and assuming he felt exactly the same, she had thought that marriage and children would follow in the fullness of time. But she was now forced to take a step back and consider that might not be so.

Ever since Sybil had brought up the subject, Mariette couldn't get it out of her mind. So she was glad of Ollenshaw's proposal, as it would act as a distraction. She told herself that the next time Edwin had leave, she would suggest he take her to meet his parents, and then see how he reacted to that request.

It was a week later that Mariette got a telephone call asking her to present herself at an address on Sidmouth's esplanade, that very afternoon. She was surprised that the secret meeting wasn't in London, but very glad that she would soon know more about what was expected of her.

It was a very hot day, and when Mariette emerged from the requisitioned hotel on the seafront, two hours after entering the building, she looked longingly at the sea and wished she could go for a swim. But that wasn't possible, with mines on the beach and all the barbed wire erected to keep people off. The next best thing was to sit on a bench and look at the sea, while she attempted to sort out the events of the afternoon.

The first hour had been spent in French conversation with a very severe-looking woman with iron-grey hair who was introduced as Miss Salmon. Mariette had to assume she was French, but the woman didn't give anything of herself away during their talk. She had fired questions at Mariette, on everything from first aid to growing vegetables, to films at the cinema and other often very strange topics, expecting her to respond appropriately and to ask questions back, just as if they were having an everyday conversation.

Mariette stumbled a bit, at first. But as she got into the swing of it and gained confidence, she found it was only the odd French word here and there that she couldn't remember. But just as she would do in English, she simply shook her head and admitted in French that she couldn't think of the word.

The second hour was with a man called Fothergill, who was middle-aged, stout and had piercing dark eyes that bored right into her. He began by asking her questions about growing up in New Zealand, then moved on to ask about her life in England and specifically about her wartime experiences.

When he had finished his questions, he said he felt she was ideal, then called Miss Salmon in to join them. She was all smiles – until then, Mariette hadn't believed her capable of such a thing.

'Your French is first class,' she said. 'I like it that you speak with a Marseille accent, we can build on that in the cover story we will be giving you. When we send you in, you will be playing a part, and you need to believe in that character totally or you might slip up. However helpful or kindly anyone seems, you must never, ever weaken and admit who you really are or what you are doing in France, as they might well be an informer. We will give you the name of the person who is your contact, but don't give them any personal information either. If anyone in this chain gets caught, the less they know about their colleagues the better.'

Mariette wondered if she meant the Germans would use torture to find out what she was up to, and her blood ran cold at the thought. 'You do appreciate that I don't know France at all,' she admitted, looking from one to the other and half hoping they would dismiss her as useless. 'I've never been there.'

'You don't need to have visited France,' Fothergill replied. 'You will be in and out very quickly, and we will give you an appropriate cover story.'

As if she wasn't feeling scared enough already, Fothergill dropped a final bombshell. 'You will need training in self-defence. Given the kind of situation you may find yourself in, a gun is impractical. A knife is far better, easier to conceal and silent too. On Monday afternoon, at two thirty, come here and you will be taken for a training session nearby. Now, do you have any questions?'

Mariette could feel her heart thumping as she sat on the bench on the seafront, thinking about what she'd been told. The sea was really blue today, reflecting the sky above, and as calm as a millpond. All around her people were enjoying being at the seaside. She could smell candyfloss and fish and chips, and hear tinny music coming from somewhere nearby; yet she'd just been told she would be trained to use a knife. How did she make the leap from barmaid to possible killer in just a couple of hours?

It was easy to forget here, in Sidmouth, that there was a savage war raging across half the world. If it hadn't been for the barbed wire on the beach, and the high proportion of men and women in uniform, it could be said that the war hadn't touched Sidmouth at all. As far as Mariette knew, not one bomb had been dropped here. How odd, then, that in the hotel behind her they interviewed people for jobs that would be unthinkable in peacetime.

When Mr Fothergill had asked her if she had any questions, Mariette hadn't been able to think of a single one. But they were coming to her now, thick and fast. Would she be shot if she was caught by the Germans, or would she be sent to prison? Who would inform her parents, if the worst happened and she was killed or seriously injured in France? How often would these short trips to France occur? And how was she supposed to explain to Sybil that she needed time off, without telling her what she wanted it for?

Not being able to tell anyone felt worse than the prospect of learning to kill with a knife, or being captured by the Gestapo. How was she supposed to make a decision about whether to agree to these secret missions or not, without talking it over with someone who cared about her?

'Stick it in as if your life depended on it, because it will,' the self-defence instructor, who Mariette knew only as PJ, yelled at her.

She had met PJ at the hotel on the esplanade at two thirty, as arranged, and he'd led the way on his bicycle to a farm about a mile out of Sidmouth.

The weather was hot and sultry, as if a storm was coming, and she had worked up a sweat keeping up with PJ on her bike. He was well over fifty, short, bald, wiry and with a fearsome scar down the side of his neck. She guessed he had got this in the Great War, but all he told her about himself was that he was a trainer. She spent the first hour with him in a large barn, running and jumping over obstacles, and climbing a rope. He seemed satisfied with her agility, but said she should practise running for an hour each day to give herself more stamina.

Then, just when she thought she was about to expire with the heat and exhaustion, he began the lessons in self-defence, showing her how to throw someone who had grabbed her.

At first, she was hopeless – she couldn't see how a girl of

eight stone could possibly defend herself against a man taller and stronger than herself and several stone heavier – but, after many attempts, she finally got the hang of it and managed to throw him to the floor.

He lay there for a minute, grinning up at her. 'Well done. But what you'll have to keep in your mind is that what I've taught you is only good for someone who intends to rob or molest you in some way. It will give him a shock, and the chances are he'll run for it. But in France you will be up against a soldier, who will have no compunction about killing you. Throwing him will give you a few vital seconds in which to draw your knife, and use it. By that, I mean kill him.'

He laughed at her horrified expression, and jumped up from the ground. 'You can't leave him alive to identify you, or to raise the alarm. It is you, or him. Kill or be killed. Keep that in your mind at all times. Your knife will be your best friend, the one thing that can save your life. You must learn to trust it, rather than fear it.'

PJ had sacks of straw, covered in a thick tarpaulin and shaped into the size of a human body, for her to practise on. It made her feel sick when he showed her how to get behind her victim, put her left arm around his neck to hold him, then cut his throat with her right hand. And he made her slash her knife across the straw man's neck several more times, until he was satisfied she knew how much force was necessary to sever a windpipe.

'In reality, it's a very messy business,' he said with the authority of someone who had actually cut many a throat. 'But very effective, quick and silent. However, you are much more likely to find yourself coming face to face with the enemy, so keep the knife hidden from view to make him feel you are no threat. As an attractive woman, you may be lucky enough to be able to sweet talk your way out of suspicion and avoid capture. But if you sense that won't work, you must get close enough to knee him in the balls to incapacitate him, then stab him through the heart. Or, as it is often easier to do, stab him in the side, pushing the knife upwards. Don't forget to pull the knife out again. He'll die faster, and you may need the knife again.'

Mariette wondered how PJ slept at night after teaching people such things. He made her attack the straw man so many times that the tarpaulin covers were falling apart by the time he told her that was enough for one day.

'We'll have another session in two days' time,' he informed her. 'You are showing promise, but you've got a long way to go yet. Don't forget to do some running. I'd recommend running up the cliff path; the fitter and faster you are, the safer you'll be in France.'

July faded into August. These were long, hot days in which Mariette got up early to run up the cliff path. It was very hard at first, but soon she was finding these early morning runs invigorating. Rather than tiring her, she found she had more energy. She continued her training with PJ twice a week. And if Sybil wondered what she was doing in the afternoons and early mornings that brought her home so hot and sweaty, she didn't ask.

But Edwin did notice a change in her when he came down for a weekend in the middle of August.

'You look different,' he said, the moment he saw her. He was looking at her hard, as if trying to work out what had changed.

Mariette knew she'd built up muscle during her training; her biceps were hard, her stomach as flat and firm as a board. She hadn't thought he'd notice it, though.

'I've just got a suntan,' she said. 'That always makes people look different.'

'No, it's more than that, you've lost weight, but you've got a glow about you. Have you been playing tennis?'

Mariette wanted to laugh at that because she knew he had the idea that it was rather unladylike to take part in any sport other than tennis.

'No, I've been running,' she said. 'I miss swimming and sailing, and as I was getting a bit flabby I thought I'd run instead to keep fit.'

'You aren't planning to run from me, are you?' he joked.

'Not even if a pack of wolves were after me,' she said, winding her arms around his neck and kissing him.

That night, after the bar closed, they walked along the esplanade in the dark. The sound of the waves breaking on the pebble beach was soothing after the racket in the bar earlier.

'That's the sound I grew up with,' Mariette said. 'I'd lie in bed on stormy nights, listening to the waves crashing on the beach, but by morning it would be just a faint lapping sound.'

'Are you homesick?' he asked.

'In as much as I'd give anything to see my family and go swimming and sailing, but then I couldn't see you.'

'Does that mean I'm important to you?'

'You know you are,' she said, and playfully punched him in the side. 'And, speaking of important things, isn't it time I met your parents?'

'I-I-I d-d-didn't think you'd want to do that,' he stammered out.

'Well, of course I do,' she said. 'Why would you think otherwise?'

It was too dark to see his expression, but she sensed by his hesitation that he was searching for an appropriate answer.

'They are a bit stuffy,' he said eventually. 'Old-school, dyed-in-the-wool conservative types.'

'So! You are saying they won't approve of me? Why wouldn't they? There's nothing outlandish about me, I eat with a knife and fork, I say please and thank you.'

'There's nothing wrong with you,' he insisted, just a bit too quickly. 'Look, forget about them, I don't care what they think. I love you, I want to marry you, and I'll happily go home with you to New Zealand, if that's what you want, when the war is over.'

While it was good to have him declaring his love for her and his hopes for their future together, she didn't like the idea that his family would be looking down their noses at her.

'Well, say something!' he exclaimed. 'I just said I wanted to marry you.'

'I love that you said that. But I couldn't marry anyone without knowing all about them, so I'll have to meet your folks before agreeing,' she said. 'But let's not get into this now. We should wait till the war ends, and see how we feel then.'

What she really meant was, if they were both still alive. But that was a terrible thing to say.

Sybil and Ted went up to bed soon after they closed the bar and, for once, left Mariette and Edwin in the living room.

'All alone at last,' Edwin said, drawing her into his arms on the sofa. 'Or does that make you nervous?'

'No, why should it?' Mariette asked.

'I thought maybe you were afraid I'd push you into something you didn't want to do.'

For a second or two, she didn't understand what he was getting at. But then she realized that he meant lovemaking.

'That's the silliest thing I ever heard,' she said indignantly. 'Of course I'm not afraid. In fact, I'd love to make love with you – as long as it was with precautions, so I didn't find myself pregnant.'

He looked shocked. 'You are amazingly forthright,' he said. 'Is that a New Zealand trait? I don't think an English girl would say such a thing.'

Coming on top of the suggestion that his parents wouldn't approve of her, she resented the implication that girls from the colonies were uncouth. She also didn't like the fact that he felt he had to discuss whether or not to make love.

Surely the right way to go about it was to just kiss and cuddle, and let passion take over?

'I can't see the point of being coy. I find the English upper-class way of hiding behind euphemisms rather pathetic,' she said waspishly. 'But it's late, and I'm tired, so I'm going to bed.'

With that, she got up and flounced out of the room.

Once in bed, and hearing Edwin tiptoeing along the passage from the bathroom to his room, she felt a little ashamed that she'd sniped at him. It wasn't his fault if his parents were snobs, and neither was he to know she'd been hoping for some fireworks when Sybil and Ted had cleared off to bed.

She thought of creeping along the passage to his room, to make it up to him. But why should she? She wasn't the one who'd been tactless.

Knowing Sybil would be cross, if she heard her going into Edwin's room, she decided to stay put. He had to be on the early train tomorrow morning anyway, so it was best to just leave well alone.

25

PJ picked himself up from the barn floor, where Mariette had thrown him. 'A fitting end to our last session,' he said with a wide grin.

'The training's over?' she asked.

'It certainly is. You are as ready now as you'll ever be,' he replied. 'You've got the skill, stamina, speed and agility I aimed at. I feel very confident that you will be able to defend yourself, should the need arise. You've been a good pupil.'

Mariette beamed. PJ wasn't usually one for compliments.

'So when will my training be put to the test?' she asked.

'I can't say.' PJ shook his head. 'It could be tomorrow, or two months hence. They'll come for you when they need you.'

Mariette looked at him in consternation. 'But I have to give Sybil and Ted some kind of notice. I can't just go and leave them in the lurch.' As much as she wanted to do her first mission, she was also terrified at the prospect. 'I must say, it's a bit thick expecting me to stand by, ready to drop everything at a moment's notice!'

PJ smiled at her indignation and put his hand on her shoulder, in a gesture of understanding. 'I agree. But you see, Mari, there are so many difficulties and obstacles that have to be overcome. We need a night with no moon to cross the Channel. The sea can't be too rough, and the person being passed down the escape chain also has to be in the right place. Setbacks are very common, and sometimes our people in France have no choice but to bring forward or cancel a rescue. But if I were you, I'd go home and prepare Sybil and Ted.'

'Tonight?'

'Yes, no time like the present. Ted's an old soldier – if you tell him it's a clandestine operation, he'll understand that you can't give him or his wife any details. But you will need to hatch a cover story with them about where you are, when you are called away. Visiting a sick relative is usually a good one. That way, you can use the same relative again later.'

'I don't have any relatives in England, but I'm sure I can think of something,' Mariette replied. She felt a little sad that she wouldn't see PJ any more. At the start he'd seemed very harsh, but she understood now why he'd had to push her so hard. 'I suppose there's nothing left to say but goodbye, and thank you for training me.'

He gave her one of his intimidating, penetrating stares. But she knew now that was just one of his arsenal of ploys to unnerve the people he trained. 'You will do well, Mariette, you are tough and resourceful, and it's been my pleasure to train you. May God go with you. And when the war is over, maybe we can meet up and have a drink together.'

On Sunday morning, three days after PJ had said goodbye to Mariette, she finally told Ted and Sybil about it. She had waited until then because, with the pub closed all day, it was the one time in the week when there would be no interruptions or distractions.

'I may have to go away for a few days any time now,' she blurted out. 'I'm afraid I can't explain it better than that, it's some covert work for the government. I hope you won't be cross about it, I know how much it's going to inconvenience you, but I can't help it.'

There was complete silence. They just looked at her with

blank expressions, as if she was speaking a foreign language.

'Please say something,' she pleaded. She knew Ted was never one to shoot his mouth off, but Sybil always had an opinion about everything. 'I'd rather you were angry or said you felt let down than saying nothing.'

'We're too taken aback to know what to say,' Ted admitted. 'We never saw this coming.'

'I thought there was something fishy about that man coming here, and then you suddenly taking up running,' Sybil burst out. 'And going off in the afternoons and never saying where you were going. Was that to do with this?'

'Yes,' Mariette sighed. 'But please don't ask me anything about it because I can't tell you. All I can tell you is that I'm likely to be called away suddenly, and I won't be able to say where, or what for. But if it's any consolation, I'd give anything to be able to confide in you.'

'You can tell us, we won't let it go beyond these four walls,' Sybil urged her, her face lighting up at the prospect.

'Enough, Sybil!' Ted glared at his wife. 'Mari can't tell us, she'd be in trouble if she did. All we should be saying is that she'll always have a job and a home with us, and to stay safe wherever she is sent.'

'Thank you, Ted.' Mariette's eyes welled up. Ted rarely strung more than half a dozen words together, and she was touched that he'd managed to find the very words she wanted to hear. 'They did say I'd only be away a couple of days at a time, and it wouldn't be a regular thing. To be honest, I'm scared. I almost wish they'd decide I'm no good to them and cancel the plan.'

'What does Edwin say about it?' Ted asked.

'He doesn't know, and he mustn't know. So if he rings and I'm not here, just make out I've gone to the pictures or something. I don't want him worrying about me.'

Things had been a little cool since their last meeting, when he'd said he wanted to marry her but didn't seem keen for her to meet his family.

'Is everything alright between you two?' Sybil asked.

'Yes, fine,' Mariette said, getting to her feet. She knew if she stayed in the pub all day, Sybil would keep on at her like a dog with a bone. 'I'm going to visit Ian and Sandra. I'll see you later.'

Each time she saw Ian and Sandra, she always thought how proud Joan would be of her children. They were well behaved, enthusiastic, articulate, interested in so many different things, and very appreciative of everything people did for them. Maybe much of the credit for how they'd turned out was down to Mr and Mrs Harding, but they had Joan's sense of humour and her generosity of spirit.

Sandra had joined Ian at the grammar school in September, and she was excited by the new subjects she was learning, such as Domestic Science and Biology.

'At the moment we're only learning how to make pastry and stuff like that,' she said, her face aglow. 'But soon we'll be making whole meals. And in Biology we'll be dissecting frogs before long. Imagine doing that?'

Mariette had a job not to laugh. She couldn't imagine anything worse than dissecting a frog, but it was great that Sandra enjoyed school. Mariette had always hated it.

Ian was learning to play the guitar. The Hardings had bought one for him, the previous Christmas, and he'd tried to teach himself from a manual. By Easter, Mrs Harding was feeling sorry for him because he wasn't getting anywhere with the manual and he wanted to play so badly. So she'd found someone in Beer to give him lessons, and now he was doing very well.

'Auntie Mari,' he asked, 'could I work as a guitarist? I mean, when I leave school. Do people get paid for playing musical instruments?'

'They do, if they are really good at it,' she told him. 'So stick at it, and maybe you will be able to make a career of it. But even if you aren't that good, it doesn't matter. You can just play for your own enjoyment.'

She went with them for a walk later. Although it was sunny, autumn had arrived with a vengeance at the start of October, with cold winds and a sprinkling of frost in the mornings, and it was dark by five o'clock. Looking out to sea, which today was like a millpond, she remembered what PJ had said about waiting for a moonless night. It sounded like the plot of a film, a romantic and daring dash into France to rescue someone, but she knew the truth of the matter was that it would be a long and cold journey fraught with danger. The coast of France was bound to be well guarded by the Germans, both on land and at sea, and there was the danger of mines too.

But, looking on the bright side, which she knew she must, whoever planned this must know it was viable. After all, there would be no point in sending people into France to rescue someone, if everyone involved was likely to be killed.

Yet, despite the danger, Mariette was very excited. To be out on a boat in heavy seas was the kind of challenge she welcomed. As for what she had to face in France, she would worry about that when she got there.

A call came on Monday morning telling her to report to Miss Salmon that afternoon, at three thirty, at the same hotel on the esplanade where she'd had her initial interview.

'PJ informs me you are ready,' Miss Salmon said, when Mariette had been ushered in to see her.

The woman was as sour-faced as she had been at their first meeting; Mariette wondered if she drank vinegar to keep herself that way. In a dark brown wool dress, without even a lace collar or a brooch to lessen the severity, it was clear she cared little for appearances and was probably wincing at the brightness of Mariette's apple-green jacket and strawberry-blonde hair.

'We have a mission planned for Wednesday. You must be at Lyme Regis harbour at five p.m. Wear suitable, warm dark clothes for the boat. But you must also have smart street clothes and a cocktail dress with you.'

Mariette looked askance at the older woman. Surely she wasn't expected to be socializing?

'Come, come,' Miss Salmon tutted. 'You will have more than one part to play on this mission. Now, let me tell you the cover story.'

Sybil lunged forward as Mariette went to leave through the pub's side door on Wednesday, just after one o'clock. She caught hold of Mariette and hugged her tightly.

'You come back safe,' she said, her voice cracking with emotion. 'Ted and I have come to think of you as family, and we'll be on tenterhooks until you return.'

Mariette disengaged herself from Sybil's arms, touched by her affection. 'That's a sweet thing to say, but try not to worry about me, I'll be fine. Now, if Edwin should telephone, just say I'm out. Don't tell him I'm with the kids – which is what I've said to everyone else – as he knows the Hardings are on the phone, and he might ring there. But I must go now, or I'll miss the train.'

'Were you hoping to disguise yourself as a man?' Sybil asked teasingly, referring to Mariette's wool trousers and the fact that she was wearing a naval pea jacket which had been left behind in the bar last winter. 'Because if you were, you failed. Even with your hair tied back, you still look totally feminine.'

Mariette grinned. 'I doubt I will with this on,' she said, pulling a black knitted hat from her pocket. 'But I'm not walking through Sidmouth wearing it. I'm saving it for when it's dark.'

She wondered what Sybil would say if she knew just what kind of place Mariette was heading for in France. She had lowered the neckline of the black dress she wore so often behind the bar, and had sewn dozens of sequins on the bodice. Sybil would have guessed the part she was expected to play right away, if she'd seen her in the altered dress.

And she'd have been even more worried.

As the train chugged along the coast, Mariette thought about Sybil's emotional reaction to her leaving. She had grown very fond of her employers too, and it seemed so odd now that her younger self, back in New Zealand, had never formed any attachment to anyone other than family members. And she hadn't even been very caring towards them!

Would age have made her kinder and more caring, even if she'd stayed in New Zealand? Or was the change in her character only down to getting a wider view of life in England and experiencing tragedy?

Her stomach was full of butterflies. When she'd slipped the razor-sharp flick knife that PJ had given her into the bag with her clothes for the trip, she'd felt physically sick, convinced she could never use it. But PJ had assured her that the training she'd had would automatically kick in if she was in danger. She hoped he was right. She wondered too how her parents would react, if they knew what she was about to embark upon. They'd be scared for her, of course, but somehow she felt they'd be really proud that she was brave enough to risk her life for someone else.

But she didn't feel brave; for two pins she'd jump off the train at the next station and run back to the safety of the pub. Yet whoever it was she was going to collect in France, she guessed that at this very moment he was probably every bit as scared as she was, cowering in some hiding place, terrified he'd be caught and shot. She couldn't let him go through further torment by not turning up as planned – to do so might be the same as signing his death warrant, along with others in the chain.

Mariette arrived in Lyme Regis too early to go straight down to the harbour, so she went into a busy tea shop to wait. From her tiny table in a corner she could observe every-one, and despite her nervousness it was very entertaining.

At the pub most of the customers were men, and the women who did come in were very ordinary – mostly wives or girlfriends of regulars, or young women in the forces or doing war work in or around Sidmouth. She rarely came up against what Sybil called 'lah-de-dahs', middle-class ladies with fox furs around their necks and loud, braying voices. That kind of woman was more likely to be found in the cocktail bar of one of the grander hotels, sipping gin and tonic.

But the Copper Kettle in Lyme Regis was clearly another gathering place for such women, and while some of them might be here on holiday, looking for fossils – which Mari-ette had discovered was one of the attractions of Lyme – she thought, from the snatches of overheard conversation, that most of these women lived close by.

'She asked to see my identity card!' one woman, with a Roman nose and a long speckled feather sticking out of her hat, exclaimed loudly. 'As if she didn't know who I was! Such impudence. That girl was in service to my sister before the war, but now she's been taken on as a receptionist at the Bellevue she thinks she's royalty.'

One by one the friends of the feathered-hat woman chipped in with little anecdotes of ungrateful servants, and Mariette smiled to herself. The tide had turned for such women. They couldn't get servants any more because no one wanted to be in domestic servitude when they could earn far more in factories, and have no restrictions placed on their private life. Without their maids and housekeepers, these women were in exactly the same boat as the ordinary working classes, as likely to be bombed out as anyone else, and existing on exactly the same rations. Many of the women, who lived in big old houses, were struggling to hold their homes together as all the tradespeople who once handled routine maintenance work had been called up.

Mariette didn't have much sympathy for them. She felt their female servants would probably have stayed with them, if they'd been treated well and valued. She also despised the way such women lorded it over those they considered beneath them. She hoped the war would bring an end to class snobbery, but somehow she doubted it would.

Just after five, Mariette made her way down to the harbour. It was pitch dark now, and chilly, but luckily there was very little wind. She trained her torch on to the ground, slipping and sliding on the cobbles. Her instructions were to stand by the lifeboat holding a white handkerchief in her hand. The skipper of the boat would approach her.

She put her woolly hat on, pulling it right down over her ears. It wasn't just about warmth; with her hair covered, she would be taken for a man and would not raise any suspicions.

'Elise?'

373

The gruff voice coming from behind her startled her, and for a split second she forgot she was to be called Elise Baudin.

She spun round to see a short, squat man with a bushy dark beard, but it was too dark to make out further details about him.

'*Bonsoir, je suis Elise. Armand?*'

He nodded. 'It's OK, you can speak English. Now follow me.'

Leading the way across the stony beach, he didn't speak again until they came to a rowing boat which had been pulled halfway out of the water. He took her bag from her, threw it in, and told her to hop in too. He pushed the boat out into the water, then jumped in and took the oars.

He rowed fast and so smoothly there was scarcely a sound, reminding Mariette of the way her father rowed; the man was entirely at one with the oars, as if they were extensions of his own arms. Just that similarity was enough to calm some of her fears.

Armand reached a moored fishing boat, caught hold of a ladder on the side to keep the rowing boat steady, then told Mariette she was to go first. As she climbed up the ladder, another man appeared on deck and held out his hand to help her.

Within a few minutes, the fishing boat was chugging out of the harbour. Mariette had been ordered to put on waterproofs by the second man, who said his name was Henri. By the light of a tilley lamp below decks, Mariette saw that both men were at least fifty, possibly even older. They were both English and, like her, they had been given French names for this mission. They didn't seem inclined to talk, but Henri told her the fishing boat was fast, and it needed to be, as they had to meet up with a French fishing boat off the Brittany coast before dawn.

Henri must have realized she was puzzled, and he explained. 'We can't go right in as the Germans would blast us out of the water, so we meet up with a French boat and pass you on. As it's such a dark night tonight, we hope we won't be spotted by anyone.'

The boat was a little larger than her father's boat back in New Zealand, and the engine was a lot more powerful. It sped through the waves and, to Mariette, it was wonderful to be back on the sea at last.

It was soon clear to her that neither man wanted her in the wheelhouse – perhaps they were worried about it being unlucky to take a woman aboard a fishing boat – so Mariette went into the tiny cabin and sat down. It was just like every other fishing boat she'd been in; it smelled bad, not just of fish, but of stale cooking, cigarettes and sweaty feet. There was a narrow bunk fitted in towards the bow, while seating was on the boxes either side, where equipment was stored, with a narrow table bolted to the floor between them. The tiny galley fitted in between the bunk and the seating.

Everything was very dirty, but Mariette was well aware that most fishermen, especially ones who go out in their boats night after night, would not have the time to concern themselves with such things. She could remember her mother tutting over the state of the cabin in her father's boat. She always said it was a waste of energy cleaning it up, it would be just as mucky again the next time she looked. But after a few moments of sitting there looking at unwashed crockery, Mariette put the kettle on to wash up.

Despite the speed they were chugging along at, the boat remained surprisingly stable, and she was able to wash the crockery and make coffee for Armand and Henri without being thrown around.

When she took the coffee to the wheelhouse, both men looked surprised and pleased.

'We're making good time,' Armand said as he took his mug and waved away the tin of condensed milk she'd brought with it. 'If I were you, I'd try to get some sleep now, we'll have to call on you to keep watch for ships as we get closer to France.'

'I'll try,' she said, knowing full well she was far too pent up to sleep.

'Tomorrow will be a long day for you,' Henri said, and his smile was warm and even sympathetic. 'With luck on our side, we'll be meeting up with the French boat again, with you in it, around ten in the evening. Then we'll be back to England at first light.'

'Have you done many of these trips?' she asked.

'Don't ask, Elise. Better not to know.'

Lying on the bunk a little later, trying to sleep, Mariette wondered what Henri had actually meant. Had the previous person doing her role been captured or shot? Or did he just mean that it was best not to ask questions about anything?

Armand woke her at four in the morning and gave her some binoculars to scan the horizon for ships, while he had a sleep and Henri took the wheel. Mariette saw the occasional light on a ship a great distance away, but nothing worryingly close.

The sky was just beginning to lighten when she spotted a fishing boat coming towards them. 'Is it the one we're supposed to be meeting?' she asked Henri.

He nodded. 'Go and wake Armand and get your bag, we need to do the changeover fast.'

The other boat came alongside, and Mariette jumped across to it. Her bag was thrown after her.

'Good luck!' Armand called out, and without a second's delay sped away, back towards England.

The two Frenchmen on the other boat had quite a haul of fish aboard. They were younger than Armand and Henri, tough-looking men with weathered skin and thick beards. They did not introduce themselves, just ordered her down into the cabin in rapid French. They told her to stay there, out of sight, until they called her.

Mariette lay on the bunk, thinking with trepidation about what lay ahead. She knew that their destination was Portivy, a tiny fishing village on the Atlantic side of a long, narrow isthmus. The Atlantic side of this land was known as the Côte Sauvage, which, she guessed, would mean it had high winds and rough sea. The inner, protected side that formed the Bay of Quiberon would be far less hostile, but any attempt at making an unseen escape from there would mean sailing right round the isthmus. At the top of the isthmus, only about a mile from Portivy, stood Fort de Penthièvre, built back in the eighteenth century to protect France from the English. It was now a German garrison, and Miss Salmon had been unable to find out just how many soldiers were stationed there.

When they arrived at Portivy, Mariette was to go to La Plume Rouge café on the harbour to see Celeste Gaillard, who ran it. Celeste ran a brothel alongside her café, and as new girls came and went frequently Mariette's sudden appearance would not be thought odd. The cover story for anyone who might question her was that her mother, back in Marseille, was an old friend of Celeste's. But then, if everything went to plan, she would be leaving the small fishing village that same evening, hopefully without arousing anyone's interest in her.

Miss Salmon had said Celeste was a member of a very

active Resistance group in Brittany who were responsible for hiding many people until they could be got out of France. Some of these were other Resistance members, but they also included Allied airmen who had been shot down and some Jewish people escaping before they could be sent to German work camps.

While Miss Salmon had been anxious to point out that there were dozens of people who played their part in rescues, all of whom risked their own lives, she had said Celeste was especially courageous as she faced spite and condemnation from many local French people who had no idea of the secret work she was doing and believed her to be collaborating with the Germans who frequented her café and brothel.

Mariette hoped that some of Celeste's courage and dogged determination to thwart the Germans would rub off on her. But she was all too aware that she was entering France illegally, with false papers that she couldn't be sure would stand up to scrutiny, going to a brothel of all places. She just had to hope that those who had recruited her knew what they were doing.

Soon after Mariette had caught her first glimpse of Fort Penthièvre, which was a huge and forbidding grey stone building with the German flag fluttering above it, one of the two sailors came into the cabin and introduced himself as Luc. He was a big man, possibly thirty-five or so, with wild dirty straw-coloured hair and a moustache to match.

'You must stay in here,' he said, lifting the lid of a storage box which was used as a seat. 'It has air holes, and I will release you as soon as it's safe. But it may be some time. Often, German soldiers come straight to the boat to buy fish, and we have to pretend to be glad of their business. When they are gone, we can get you to Celeste.'

Mariette climbed in with some trepidation as she could

see it wasn't long enough to lie out straight, and it smelled awful. Luc put her bag in the storage box for a pillow, and she smiled weakly up at him.

'There are worse things,' he said and he smiled back, suddenly looking far less fierce.

She heard the sounds of people in the harbour even before she felt the slight bump as the boat touched the quayside. The boat lurched as one of the men jumped off to secure her, and then there was thumping and bumping as they carried the boxes of fish off the boat.

She could hear the two fishermen talking to other people, but not clearly enough to follow what they were talking about. She thought some of it was haggling over the price of the fish, but every now and then there were bursts of loud laughter. Trapped, cold, hungry and very uncomfortable, Mariette found herself imagining they were telling German soldiers where to find her. She expected the lid of the box to open and to be hauled out at any moment.

The sound of voices moved away from the boat, until all she could hear was the calling of the seagulls. It was very tempting to raise the lid of the box just enough to see what was happening. But she didn't dare do it, for fear a German soldier had remained on the deck or was standing close enough on the quayside to see into the boat.

After what seemed like hours, Luc came back. 'Quickly,' he said. 'Change your clothes, leave what you are wearing now in the box, and then we must get you off the boat.'

He left her, and Mariette quickly stripped off her trousers, thick jumper and heavy shoes, then put on a brown wool dress, stockings, high heels and a camel coat with a red fox collar that Sybil had given her. Mog had made and sent her the dress, and Edwin had always said she looked sexy in it as it was pencil slim with a crossover neckline that enhanced her breasts. With her bright red lipstick, and her hair brushed and worn loose under an emerald-green beret, she was ready. She slipped the flick knife into her coat pocket and picked up her bag containing her black cocktail dress and washing things.

Luc smiled in surprise at the transformation. 'A friend will be along in his van to collect some fish, very soon,' he said. 'He will pull up very tight to the gangplank. I will go to the back of his van with the fish. You must peep out of the port-hole, and when I put my pipe in my mouth that means it is safe for you to come out. Run to get in the front of the van, then lie down on the floor and cover yourself with a blanket. In a few moments, my friend will drive off and take you to the back door of La Plume Rouge. Celeste will give you the instructions for later tonight.'

Mariette couldn't speak as her mouth was too dry with fear, so she just nodded.

'Most of the soldiers who were out here earlier have gone now, but we don't want anyone to see you come off the boat. There are some in Portivy who would sell their own soul to the Germans.'

Miss Salmon hadn't told her any of this. Mariette had imagined Celeste's place was so close to the quayside that she would just run there from the fishing boat. All Miss Salmon had said was the next part: Mariette was not to divulge any-thing to any of Celeste's girls and must stick to the pre-arranged story that she'd had a fight with her mother, back in Marseille, and had taken the train to Paris. When that didn't work out too well, she'd come here. Mariette needed to act as if a brothel was normal to her, perhaps even give the impression she'd worked in one in Marseille.

A large old blue van, belching smoke and backfiring, pulled up by the gangplank. Mariette went over to the port-hole to peep out. Portivy was tiny, just a dozen or so houses clustered around the harbour, with maybe a couple more streets behind them. She could see La Plume Rouge on a corner; it was an unprepossessing place with steamed-up windows and peeling red paint. The little port looked forlorn under the pewter sky, but she guessed it would be pretty in summer with flowers spilling over the walls, and a blue sea rather than the cold grey expanse it was now.

There weren't many people about, just a couple of fishermen mending their nets on the quay, three women standing in a huddle gossiping, and another couple walking with baskets over their arms to the bakery. What did worry Mariette were the German soldiers. She could see six, standing in pairs, and although they seemed more intent on their conversations with one another than guarding the town, their jackboots and rifles sent shivers of fear down her spine. She'd seen pictures of them often enough, in newspapers and on Pathé News at the cinema, but in the flesh they looked bigger, tougher and very scary.

'Ready?' Luc asked, taking his pipe out of the pocket of his striped apron in a reminder that it was the signal. Then he went out on the deck, picked up a couple of boxes of fish and walked down the gangplank.

The van driver was old, with a cloud of white hair, gold-rimmed spectacles and a bright red muffler tied around his neck. He shouted a jubilant greeting at Luc as he got out of his van, then he walked round on the passenger side and opened the door wide as he passed along to the back doors.

Both Luc and the old man put on a great show of delight at seeing one another, laughing and thumping each other on the back, then appeared to be having a more serious conversation about the fish in the boxes. But Mariette could see that both men were actually scanning everyone in the harbour, and particularly the German soldiers.

Luc took his pipe out of his apron pocket and started gesticulating to the old man with it. Mariette's heart was thumping so loudly, she felt sure the soldiers would hear it out on the harbour, but she tucked her bag under her arm, kept her eyes on Luc and braced herself for flight when his signal came.

He lifted his hand with the pipe in it several times, only to lower it again. She didn't dare take her eyes off him to see what was going on all around the harbour.

Then the pipe went into his mouth.

Mariette took off like a rocket down the gangplank, squeezed her way alongside the van and curled herself into the well of the passenger seat. There was a blanket on the seat, which she pulled down over her.

She could hear the old man saying a cheery goodbye to Luc, then he slammed the back doors of the van shut, came along the side and shut the door next to where she was hiding. Starting up the engine, he yelled something about lobsters out of the window, and she heard Luc laugh, then away they went.

'Stay where you are, my dear,' the old man said quietly in French as the van rumbled over cobbles. 'It's not far.'

It was about five minutes later that he stopped. 'You can sit up on the seat now. You can say I gave you a lift from the station at Quiberon.'

Mariette shook off the blanket and got up on the seat. They were in a narrow lane with high walls on either side. She thought it must be the back of the houses which faced the quay. She straightened her beret and smiled at the old man. 'Do I look like someone just up from Marseille?'

'You look like a film star,' he said gallantly. 'You certainly don't look like someone who spent the night on a fishing boat.'

He drove on a few more yards and then stopped outside a tall wrought-iron gate set in a wall. 'Through there,' he said, and pointed. 'Anyone asks, Gilpin brought you here.'

'Gilpin?' she repeated.

'Everyone calls me that,' he said, and reached out to pat her arm. 'Be wary of the girls in there, and good luck.'

26

'Could I see Celeste, please?' Mariette asked in French of the girl who opened the back door to her knock. She was no more than fourteen, small, thin and her dress and apron were too big for her. 'Tell her it's Elise.'

'Wait there while I see,' the girl replied, and shut the door in Mariette's face. She was left standing in a little walled yard. There were dozens of plant pots, but the plants in them were all dead or lying dormant for the winter.

The door was opened again by a plump red-headed woman of around fifty. 'Elise!' she exclaimed loudly, as if for someone else's benefit. 'I was only thinking about you and your mama just now, and here you are.'

She then wrapped her arms around Mariette. 'When we go in, make up some story for me about falling out with your mama,' she whispered against her neck. 'The girls are always eavesdropping, so don't come out with any true stuff until we can be entirely alone.'

Celeste took Mariette into a large living room, with the kitchen in front of the windows overlooking the backyard. Along with a table and chairs, and two shabby sofas, there was a chiffonier that was almost disappearing under a vast amount of china, ornaments and a hundred and one different items, from bits of jewellery to letters and medicine bottles.

It was a shambles, but the range made it very warm and it had a cosy atmosphere. It was just as well it was warm as there were three girls sitting around, dressed in nothing more than petticoats.

'So what brings you to see your old aunt?' Celeste asked Elise, not even bothering to introduce her to the other girls.

Mariette told the kind of story which could have been a true reflection of her when she was living at home in New Zealand: that she'd run to her aunt because her mother didn't approve of her boyfriend and complained that she was too proud to be a servant or a waitress.

Mariette really warmed to the story. 'She screams at me that I've got to bring some money in. And I would, if they'd take me on in a dress shop or an office. But I'm not cut out for cleaning, working in a factory or dishing out food, so I came here.'

She was very aware the other girls were looking astonished. Whether this was because they would rather do any kind of work than sell themselves to men – or perhaps because, for the first time, they were hearing someone owning up to what they believed in – she didn't know which it was.

'Oh, Elise.' Celeste shook her head sadly. 'You surely aren't saying you want to work here?'

Mariette pulled a disgusted face. 'Not the mucky stuff, Aunt Celeste, but I could be at front of house, a bit of style and glamour, like you used to do.'

She saw that Celeste struggled not to laugh, and in that instant Mariette knew they were going to get on.

An older woman in a floral apron came through a door to one side of the room, and Mariette had a glimpse of the café beyond. It was a dreary-looking place with oilcloths on the tables and rickety chairs. The woman said something about vegetables, and Celeste looked back at Mariette.

'I have to sort this out, so we'll talk later,' she said. 'You'd better have some breakfast, and afterwards you can help with some cleaning. I don't carry passengers here, not even my niece.'

By mid-afternoon Mariette had learned a great deal about what it was like to live under German occupation, with German soldiers creating fear and menace. The girls at Celeste's had no choice but to entertain them. If they refused, they were likely to find themselves on the next transport to a labour camp. One, a sullen-looking girl with curly black hair, said that they'd all been accused of being collaborators, and most of the local people were as cruel and spiteful as the Germans. One of the other girls rolled her eyes at this, as if it wasn't strictly true, and Mariette wondered what the truth was.

But she did discover how a brothel was run, and some of the opinions she'd held about such places were quite wrong. For a start, she'd always thought girls were forced into prostitution – as she'd believed her mother was – but she found out that all of Celeste's six girls had come to it of their own accord, and they quite enjoyed it. She'd always imagined too that only horrible, dirty old men used prostitutes, but Celeste said this wasn't so.

'We have many bachelors, and men who have an invalid wife, or they are simply married to a woman who refuses to sleep with them,' she said airily, as if they were discussing the merits of a finishing school. 'Young men come to get experience before marriage. And, of course, there are the men working far away from home, including soldiers, who need a woman. I like to think my girls give them more than just release, even a bit of affection and fun too.'

Celeste had come to this part of France in 1920, when she was twenty-six, after being a nurse in field hospitals during the Great War.

'France was left devastated by the war,' she said simply. 'A quarter of our men were killed, and so many more were unable to work because of the wounds they received. There were so many weary and bitter people who had lost everything – their loved ones, their homes and their livelihoods – and most had no idea how to build a new life. I came here to try to rebuild mine.'

She paused for a moment and smiled, as if she was remembering something good. 'I liked the quiet here, the wildness of the coast, and so I stay and opened a café. It was little more than a shed, around the back here, but it was somewhere for people to gather and talk, and maybe, because of my nursing experience, they found me sympathetic. Anyhow, it became a success and soon I was able to rent this bigger property. I had intended to make the house a hotel – indeed, I did rent out rooms at first – but one of those first guests was in fact a prostitute, and that was how it began.'

Mariette found that her previously held beliefs on prostitution were becoming blurry. She liked Celeste, and, from what she'd seen so far, none of the girls who worked at La Plume Rouge was unhappy. Celeste said that most of the German soldiers treated the girls well, and they paid more than the local men. The girls were looked after, they ate well, had regular check-ups with the doctor, and they had the company of the other girls.

But however fascinating it was to be privy to the details of how a brothel worked – something that would be unthinkable back home – Mariette was mindful that she had a real purpose in being here. She wanted to know who she would be helping to escape, and where they were hiding now.

Celeste had kept up the story of being her aunt superbly, not only making little jokes to Mariette, as if they really had a shared past, but also rebuking her for upsetting her mother and being too full of herself to take a job she thought beneath her. At lunch, when all six girls were present, she said she must insist Elise return home, and she would get someone to take her to the station for the evening train to Paris.

Mariette managed to force a few tears and protest that Celeste didn't know how mean her mother could be. But Celeste stuck to her guns, and said a daughter's place was with her mother, especially in wartime. 'We'll go for a little walk later and talk some more,' she ended up, finally letting Mariette know she was ready to discuss their real business.

It was late afternoon when they finally went out, going down the little lane Gilpin had driven up that morning.

Celeste paused at a gate much like the one at La Plume Rouge. 'The airman is in the basement there,' she whispered. 'I'm not risking taking you in to meet him. I'll explain the plan as we walk on.'

The lane came out behind the last house along the harbour, and from there a path led through grass and sand to a few further scattered houses. The beach was around five or six feet below this path, and it was mainly rocks, but there were strips of shingle with shells here and there, leading down to the open sea, and now and again patches of sand.

'Tonight there will be a rowing boat left down there,' Celeste whispered, pointing to a particularly large rock. 'The tide will be going out, and the boat will be on a strip of sand. You will push the boat straight on, following a clear path between the rocks out to the open sea. You see that buoy?' She pointed to a large red and white buoy secured some five or six hundred yards out to sea. 'That is what you will be rowing to. You won't be able to see it, of course, once it's dark, but you'll hear its bell. When you reach it, tie the boat to it, then wait for the fishing boat to come and get you.'

'And the airman I'm helping?' Mariette asked. 'Do I bring him here?'

'No, someone else will do that. Mostly the airmen go on the regular escape route through Spain, but this one has an injured arm and leg, and he can't make that long trip.'

'Is the beach mined?' Mariette asked.

'No. Thankfully, the Germans seem to think the rocks alone are enough protection against a landing. The harbour is not mined either, because they need to come in and out all the time in their boats, but they have vigilant lookouts at the fort, and searchlights too. But you will be just out of range here, and hidden by the harbour wall. There are foot patrols all along the coast, but on a cold night the guards tend to huddle in shelters. They know all the fishing boats and won't stop them unless they suspect something is going on. Hopefully, they will have no reason to be suspicious. Our biggest fear is that they get wind of something and send out a fast launch to intercept the fishing boat. But that hasn't happened yet. Now, do you think you can handle rowing out to that buoy in a heavy sea?'

'Yes, I can,' Mariette said with confidence. 'But I'll need warmer clothes than these.' She was shivering now, and her shoes would be a liability on a beach in the dark.

'I have your clothes back at the café.' Celeste smiled, and then reached out and touched Mariette's cheek affectionately. 'I would be so proud, if you were really my niece. You are a very brave girl.'

'I haven't done anything yet,' Mariette said.

'That is to come, and it can be very dangerous. The reason I asked you to bring an evening dress was because I thought it might have been necessary for you to be one of my "girls" for the evening. A seemingly drunk woman can get away with quite a lot. But with this man's injuries we had to take a different approach and, I must admit, I am glad you don't have to put yourself on display at the café.'

'So I meet him here?'

'Yes, if all goes to plan he will be in the rowing boat waiting, ready for you to jump in and take him away. We just have to pray the sentry for this section is his usual lazy self. If he comes into La Plume, as he often does, I'll give him a large brandy to make him disinclined to go any further.'

'What do I do, if someone does come?'

'You have trained for that, I believe,' Celeste replied.

Mariette gulped. It was one thing to learn the theory of stabbing someone, quite another to actually do it, in the dark, down here on a beach where just one step on the pebbles would sound as loud as a gunshot. 'Let's just hope it doesn't come to that.'

Celeste took her arm. 'Come on now, we'll walk back. You must make a mental note of the way. Things can look very different in the dark, and you'll be on your own.'

Later, Mariette found Celeste's words to be true. Nothing looked familiar in the thin beam of her torch.

She had said goodbye to the girls and Celeste over an hour ago, playing on her reluctance to go home right until the end. Gilpin had called in, supposedly to drive her to the station, but he had only taken her twenty yards down the back lane, to a shed where the warm clothes she'd been wearing when she left England were waiting to be changed into. Gilpin drove off, and she had to stay in the shed until she heard the church clock strike seven.

Waiting gave her time to think of all that could go wrong, and when the church clock finally struck she was very jittery. Several people had walked by; each time she heard heavy male footsteps, she was convinced it was a German soldier who had been tipped off about the plans.

Once she finally set off, it was hard not to keep looking round to see if she was being followed. She had a moment of indecision at a point where the lane forked – she didn't remember seeing that fork before, and thought she'd come too far – but she could hear the sea, so she followed the sound and, all at once, found herself back at the beach.

The wind was much stronger now. The waves were slapping against the beach, and she could make out white horses, even in the dark. Her mouth was dry and her stomach was churning as she flattened herself against the garden wall of the last house while she checked to see if anyone else was here. But there was no one, just the sound of the wind and the sea, and she quickly ran down towards the big rock Celeste had pointed out earlier, eager to find the airman and the rowing boat.

'It's just me, Elise,' she whispered in English. She knew if the airman was there in the dark, he would be anxious at the sound of footsteps. 'I can't see you yet. Where are you?'

'I'm beside the boat,' he whispered back, and it sounded as if he was only a few yards away. 'I was afraid you wouldn't come.'

All at once she saw him lying down beside the boat. His face looked long and pale in the little light there was. 'Stay there while I push the boat closer to the water,' she whispered. 'I know you are hurt, but will you be able to climb in?'

'I have to,' he said, and got to his feet very gingerly.

Mariette glanced at him and saw he was wavering from the effort. She reached out and took his arm, helping him down the beach towards the water.

Returning to haul the boat down, she found it was very heavy and hard to move. The airman took a few wobbly steps to help but she reproved him. 'No, stay there, you might make your injuries worse. I can do it.'

Putting all her strength behind it, at last the boat began to move. As soon as the bows met the sea, it became easier. Holding it tightly by the mooring rope, she signalled to the airman to get in.

It was so dark, she could barely see his face, but she sensed he was in great pain and was finding it very hard to swing his leg over the side of the boat to haul himself in. Her heart went out to him but there was nothing she could do to help. Once he was in, and sitting in the bows, she pushed the boat out further, then leapt in.

As she picked up the oars to push the boat further from the beach, she thought she heard something, and her stomach flipped with fear. But she couldn't see anyone, so she began to row out towards the buoy.

Since leaving New Zealand she had only rowed a boat on London's Serpentine, and a couple of times on the river at Arundel, and never since the war began. It felt very strange to be in a boat out on the sea again, battling against a current and a fresh wind.

It was further to the buoy than she'd expected, and she pricked up her ears, waiting for a shout that meant they had been spotted. But finally, they were at the buoy and she secured the rowing boat to it.

'I don't know your name,' she whispered to the airman. She could no longer see the shore, so she doubted anyone would spot them either, but sound carried a long way.

'Alan White,' he whispered back. 'You don't know how good it is to hear an English voice.'

'For me too,' she agreed. 'But we'd better be quiet now,' she said. 'We can talk on the boat.'

It seemed for ever before Mariette saw a pinprick of green light, which was the signal that Luc was close by. They had seen lights on other boats, in the distance. Some appeared to be heading towards Quiberon Bay, perhaps making for St Pierre on the other side of the isthmus, while others appeared to be heading towards or away from the Bay of Biscay. She had no way of knowing whether they were French or German boats.

Finally, the boat came close enough to see, aiming straight at them, only sweeping round when it was almost upon them.

'Will you be able to manage the ladder?' Mariette asked.

'I'll have to,' Alan replied. 'I don't fancy spending all night in this rowing boat.'

Mariette held the ladder steady for him, and Luc leaned down to help him too, but they were both aware of how hard he found the climb. When he got on to the boat, he collapsed from the effort.

Luc and Mariette hoisted him up, supporting him between them, and took him into the cabin where they laid him on the bunk.

'There's a bottle of brandy over there.' Luc pointed to a box by the stove. 'Give him a tot, he's like a block of ice.'

The relief as the fishing boat steamed away to meet up with the English boat was enormous, but Mariette knew they were by no means safe yet. They still had to pass the fort where, if any suspicions had been raised, they could be intercepted. Once they were past that danger, they could be bombed by aircraft, hit a mine in the water, be torpedoed, or be fired on by a German ship. But she wasn't going to think about that.

Alan was clearly relieved too. He lay there, grinning like a Cheshire Cat. 'I really didn't think I would get out of France,' he admitted. 'I thought I would die from gangrene in that cellar. Or if they got me to the beach, I expected a couple of storm troopers to appear and shoot me.'

'I had visions of being captured and facing a firing squad,'

Mariette admitted. 'But don't let's talk about that. Tell me where you are from?'

'A place called Saffron Walden, in Essex,' he said. 'Mother is going to be very joyful to hear I'm alive and well. I expect she was told I was missing, presumed dead, after I was shot down. I don't know whether they pass on the news that you are alive when they are planning to get you out.'

He reminded Mariette a little of Gerald. It was not so much his looks – he was taller, with broader shoulders, and he had good teeth, which Gerald hadn't had – the similarity was in their ages, in the way they spoke and their confidence, signs she recognized as coming from a loving middle-class home and a first-class education. But he also had that puppy-dog look Gerald used to get, as if he was afraid of displeasing her.

'You are awfully young and pretty to be doing such a job,' he said, looking appraisingly at her. 'And where are you from? I can detect an accent.'

'New Zealand,' she said crisply. 'But how I look is immaterial, in this job or any other.'

'Oops!' He put his hand over his mouth. 'Sorry if I offended you.'

'You haven't offended me. It's just a bit trying to be judged by your age and looks. No one does that with men. But never mind that. How are your wounds? Can I do anything to make them more comfortable? Are you feeling alright?'

'I am, now we're away from France,' he said with a boyish lopsided grin. 'I can even believe that in a day or two I'll be drinking a pint of beer at my local, taking my girl, Valerie, out and listening to my mother wittering on about the length of the queue at the butcher's.'

Mariette hoped that would be the case. After all he had been through, it would be terribly bad luck to be captured now, or for the boat to hit a mine.

But they were lucky. It was a very choppy crossing, and Alan was seasick, but no German boats challenged them, the bombers that came over flew past, and they made the rendezvous with the English boat on time. It was eleven in the morning when they sailed into Lyme Regis, and Alan was taken away to a military hospital.

He tried to thank Mariette, but his eyes filled with tears and his voice quavered.

'Don't, Alan,' she said. 'I was just one link in a chain of people who helped you. Getting you back here was the result we were all working towards. Now just get well again. Go home and see your mum and Valerie, and keep out of trouble.'

27

Sidmouth, February 1944

Mariette looked out of the back window of the pub at the thick layer of snow covering roofs, walls and gardens, and a shiver of fear ran down her spine. Snow would make the planned rescue even more dangerous.

It wasn't a question of the cold for, however miserable icy weather made everyone feel, it often worked in their favour. German soldiers were inclined to take shelter when it was very cold rather than patrol as they were supposed to. Snow, however, meant better visibility in the dark, and footprints were a clear signal of paths used and how many people were involved.

Tonight would be her ninth trip to France and, so far, they'd all been successful. Not all the escapees had been wounded airmen: two were French Resistance men, who were being hunted by the Gestapo, and there had been some young Jewish women who Celeste had been hiding.

There was now no doubt in anyone's mind that the war would eventually be won. The Americans were piling in, and the RAF planes were inflicting grievous damage on German cities. The Russians had finally managed to triumphantly end the siege of Leningrad, and even Rommel in North Africa looked beatable at last. There was the question of the Japanese, of course – some said they were almost beaten, but others said they would fight on to the last man.

People might have different opinions on many aspects of the war, but the one thing that unified everyone was their weariness of the rationing, the blackout and all the shortages of everyday goods. Oddly, they moaned more about these things than about the terrible tragedies played out daily, with husbands, sons and brothers killed in action and civilians dying in air strikes. Thousands were homeless, many more were living with severe bomb damage to their homes, and children were growing up without their fathers. And yet, such things were not mentioned as often as the scandals of wives and girlfriends being led astray by fun-loving GIs.

Just a few days ago, there had been a heated discussion in the pub about unfaithful wives, black marketeers, looters and other wartime examples of wrongdoing. Sybil's view was that people were losing their moral compass, and all the things they had once thought so important – like honesty, loyalty, pride, good manners and sticking with a marriage even when it became a bit rocky – were being abandoned.

Mariette didn't agree. In her opinion, people still had the same values, but the challenges and deprivations of wartime had just altered their outlook. She knew from her own experience that, right up until she began the training for her secret missions, she would have married Edwin in the blink of an eye, if he'd asked her, and been more than happy to settle down and make a home for them both.

She had been hurt by his reluctance to introduce her to his parents, but it was her training and the danger of the missions which had given her a new perspective. She had learned a great deal about herself, and what she wanted out of her future life. Now she wasn't so sure Edwin was the right man for her.

She still felt the same physical attraction to him, and she longed to spend a whole night in his arms. But Edwin continued to be the perfect gentleman. He never suggested taking her to a hotel, as almost every other red-blooded man would do if he had nowhere else to go with his girl, and whereas she'd once admired his self-control, she was now inclined to think there was something cold-blooded about a man who didn't allow his heart to rule his head.

But, on the other hand, it could be that he was terrified he'd be killed and leave her unmarried and pregnant. However, she knew they were drifting apart. They had once had so much to say to one another, there was never enough time for it all. Now there was little to say.

He talked about his airmen friends, what they'd said and done, and she talked about the regulars who came into the pub. But it was dull, and there was no spontaneity or excitement.

Sybil said perhaps he didn't feel able to talk about his experiences on the bombing raids, and that Mariette ought to understand that – after all, she couldn't talk about her missions to France. But it wasn't that. She felt Edwin had withdrawn from her a little because he'd had second thoughts about her. She knew from things he'd said about his family when they first met that they were rather grand, and recently he'd said they were stuffy. Added to that, when she thought about the slightly critical remarks he made sometimes about the way she spoke, dressed and approached people, it all seemed to suggest to her that he knew his parents wouldn't approve of her working behind a bar, or of her being from New Zealand.

A great many English people seemed to have the idea that New Zealanders and Australians were uneducated oafs, and perhaps his parents subscribed to this view too.

While it was hurtful to think anyone would make judgements about her without ever meeting her, maybe Edwin was right to think she might not be the kind of wife his own mother had been. Mariette had seen 'county' women, there were plenty of them around in Devon and Dorset, and she couldn't see herself fitting in with that sour-faced, bridge-playing, riding-to-hounds set who sent their sons off to boarding schools. Her own daydreams of marriage and home-making were always set in Russell. She wanted to be the kind of wife and mother Belle was – very affectionate, fun-loving and unpredictable. Belle didn't need a week's notice to organize a party or picnic, an hour was long enough for her. She was joyful about everything, from bottling fruit to collecting the hens' eggs in the morning, or making herself a new hat that would raise eyebrows at church on Sunday.

During one of Mariette's trips to France she had taken a long walk along the coast of Quiberon and saw why the Atlantic side of the isthmus was called the Côte Sauvage. Strong winds scraped the harsh, flat landscape and the few feeble trees were bent over in the wind. It reminded her of certain places back in New Zealand, and she knew that, although it was inhospitable now in midwinter, in summer it would be lovely, with yellow gorse filling the air with its perfumed flowers, long waving grasses, and clumps of pink thrift and other wild flowers softening the stony ground.

She even found herself looking at houses that had been shuttered up since the German occupation and imagined owning one, opening it up, whitewashing the outside and planting geraniums in tubs by the door. She knew if she told Edwin that she'd like to live somewhere like that, with a boat moored on the beach, brown-skinned children running wild, spending the days fishing and gathering wood for the fire, he would think her crazy.

It was, of course, only the vague similarity to New Zealand that made her nostalgic; she didn't want to live in France, only in the Bay of Islands. She could see the clapboard houses of Russell before her, feel the sun on her skin, hear the voices of all those people she'd grown up amongst. She imagined Russell parties, with everyone from aged grandparents to newborn babies – and every age in between – gathered together for a celebration. She'd watched her parents at these parties, laughing and dancing together, still as much in love as they had been when they married. Yet they had their own separate identities, her father with his building skills, his fishing and sailing, and her mother drawing and painting and making pretty hats.

It was ironic that she had to go to the other side of the world to discover that her own parents lived the life she wanted. But Edwin would never adapt to Russell.

He was too polished and sophisticated, too fixed in his outlook. He was, even if he claimed otherwise, a city man. He might like sailing, swimming and fishing, but only on a holiday, not all year round. She couldn't see him tolerating the lack of electricity for long, or the bad roads. And what would he do for work in New Zealand? Maybe he could pick up where he'd left off in accountancy, move on to law, or become a pilot for one of the new airlines he seemed to think would start up after the war? But that would mean they'd have to live in Christchurch, Wellington or Auckland.

But, over and above all the niggling anxieties she had, she knew Edwin would be horrified when he found out she wasn't a virgin. At the start of their relationship she had always imagined a night of passion with him would be all that was necessary to wipe out the past – the way it had been with Morgan – but Edwin would want assurances that it was her first time. He was just made that way.

Then there were her parents, and Mog. It would soon become obvious to anyone that all three of them had enjoyed a colourful past. Some men might like that, but she didn't think Edwin would. He was far too conventional. She couldn't bear the thought of spending her life with someone from whom she had to hide things, for fear of his disapproval.

Since getting to know Celeste better, Mariette had confided in her about what Jean-Philippe had said about her mother. Celeste had smiled knowingly and said that, when Mariette got home, she was to ask Belle about her experiences.

'Don't ever make the mistake of thinking that all women who are, or have been, whores are bad women,' she said. 'My experience is the exact opposite. I've seen great kindness and self-sacrifice, generosity of spirit, and courage too. Any woman who could produce a daughter like you would have to be a good woman through and through. So listen to her story, when the time is right for her to tell it to you, and be proud of her.'

Mariette knew that she had seen enough of life in the raw since the war began to accept anything her parents might have done in the past. But Edwin certainly wouldn't be able to. He'd try to, of course – he was, after all, a tolerant and good man – but as Mog had been very fond of saying, 'You can't make the blind see, or the deaf hear. However much you want to.'

Turning away from the window, Mariette pulled on a pair of flannel pyjama trousers, tucked the legs into her socks, then put thick wool trousers over the top. On her top half she wore a wool vest, a flannel shirt and two jumpers. She had to make sure she kept warm while at sea, otherwise it was utter misery.

Today, just like every time she went on one of these missions, she hoped it would be the last. The fear never left her.

She'd had one close shave, when German soldiers came running down the beach just as she was rowing away. That time, she'd had the Jewish women in the boat with her, and the Germans opened fire. Fortunately, the boat was just out of range and the bullets hit the water harmlessly. But the terror hadn't stopped there. They'd fully expected the soldiers to call for assistance and a fast boat to be launched from the harbour to cut them off. For whatever reason, that didn't happen – Luc was of the opinion that the soldiers were supposed to have been somewhere else, and raising an alarm would mean questions would be asked – but although she was thankful for their luck that night, Mariette knew it was unlikely to be repeated.

Edwin seemed to think the Allies would invade France in early summer. She fervently hoped he was right. From Celeste and the French fishermen she'd heard how much their people were suffering under occupation. The farmers had seen their livestock and crops taken, and sometimes farmhouses were ransacked and then burned to the ground. Children went hungry, and old people were dying because they had too little food and not enough wood for the fire to keep warm.

It was Luc who told her Celeste used the profits she made from her café and brothel to help local people. 'Some people call her a collaborator because she entertains the Germans, but every sou she takes from them is distributed around our people, and she takes such a big risk supporting the Resistance. There are folk in town capable of informing on anyone just for a loaf of bread or a few eggs, so it's only a matter of time before one of them points the finger at her.'

Mariette knew now that all those terrible rumours of camps where Jews were gassed were true and not anti-Nazi propaganda. She also knew that all those working for the Resistance were shot or sent to labour camps when they were caught. A labour camp might sound better than being shot, but by all accounts it was worse because it was a slow, painful death from starvation and disease. This made Celeste's dogged determination to outwit the Gestapo even more admirable.

'If you don't want to miss the train, you'd better hurry,' Sybil shouted up the stairs, bringing Mariette abruptly out of her reverie.

She moved away from the window and put the last few things in her bag. She didn't want to go, but she had to, people were depending on her. Sybil never tried to pry into what she did any more. She certainly knew it was dangerous, though, because each time Mariette left, the goodbye hug was longer, and the relief on her face when she returned was greater.

In the bottom of her wardrobe Mariette had left a tin containing letters for her parents, Mog, her brothers, Edwin, Sybil and Ted, and Ian and Sandra, just in case she didn't make it back. She had explained in the letters what she had been doing all these months, and said she hoped they would forgive her for choosing to do something so dangerous. She had written in one of them:

I felt glad that speaking fluent French and being able to handle a boat enabled me to help a few people. Mum and Papa always said I was defiant as a child, and I've been proud to defy the Germans by slinking in and out of France right under their noses.

Each one of the letters was tailored individually to tell her loved ones how much they meant to her and why. It struck her, as she put the letters into the tin, that they were all she had to leave anyone. Her clothes and other belongings would fit into a small suitcase. And if she did die in France, no one would even know where her body lay.

It was seven the following morning before the English boat met up with the French one for the handover. The sky was leaden and it felt as if more snow was due. Luc and Guy, the regular crew members, greeted her. Guy was his usual sombre self, only nodding to her, but Luc seemed preoccupied. They had become quite good friends over the past months but this time he barely greeted her.

Once she'd put on her waterproofs in the cabin, she went up to the wheelhouse with a cup of coffee for the men and some cheese and onion flan she'd brought from home.

'You made this?' Luc asked after he'd tasted it. 'It's very good.'

'Thank you,' she said. 'Now, tell me what's wrong?'

He gave a deep sigh. 'It's children you'll be bringing out tonight. Four Jewish children, and I believe it's far too risky.'

Mariette understood his fears. Children could cry and give the game away, they couldn't be left to use their own initiative if things went wrong, they couldn't run as fast, or help to push a boat out. In every way they were a liability. But, to Mariette, children were the future, and they were innocents who deserved saving. She'd been told about the trainloads of Jews sent out of Paris, crammed into cattle trucks with very little air or even water. She couldn't bear the thought of anyone being submitted to that, let alone children.

'Poor little mites,' she said, imagining how scared they must be and what their fate would be, if they were caught. 'But I'm sure we can manage it.'

'I never agreed to take children,' Luc said stubbornly. 'The risk is too great. I have children of my own to take care of; if

404

I get caught, it will be the firing squad for me. And what will become of them?'

Mariette could understand his dilemma, but she knew the people who organized the escapes must have a very good reason for getting these four children out of the country. 'Then we have to make sure we aren't caught,' she said, rather more firmly than she felt.

Mariette hadn't been able to go to Celeste's place for the last three missions because a niece turning up with such regularity, and only staying a few hours, would begin to look suspicious. But at least it meant she didn't have to dress up for the part, and could stay in her warm clothes.

There was only a light sprinkling of snow on the harbour. She was whisked away from there, as usual, by Gilpin in his fish van, and dropped by a shed in a back alley where she had to hide until Celeste could come to her with further instructions. Gilpin seemed nervous too, and he hardly said a word.

Mariette waited three hours in the freezing shed before Celeste finally arrived, wrapped up in a man's tweed overcoat, with a red woolly hat dusted with snow pulled right down over her ears.

'I am so sorry,' she said on finding Mariette shivering in a corner with a sack around her shoulders. 'But it was impossible to get away earlier. Things get harder every day now, I have to be so careful who I trust. But I've brought you some hot soup to warm you.'

Mariette drank the hot soup gratefully, even though it had no real flavour.

'I used to pride myself on my cooking once,' Celeste said. 'Now it's so hard to get even the basic ingredients, I just have to use whatever I can find.'

'It's the same back in England,' Mariette told her. 'People

make jam from turnips, the dried egg is disgusting, and the other day we got some dried potato powder called Pomme. You're supposed to mix it with hot water to make mashed potato, but it's vile.'

'I wish I could spend longer with you today, or at least take you somewhere warm, but I can't,' Celeste said, with sorrow in her eyes. 'I think someone back at the café is informing on me; I've seen a man watching the place. After this one, we must stop for a while, it's getting too risky.'

'Luc said it's children tonight,' Mariette said.

'Yes. All I can tell you about them is that they are the children of two of our people. The youngest is four, the eldest fourteen, and we must get them to safety.'

Mariette guessed by the deeply troubled expression on the older woman's face that she feared if these children were caught, they would be used as hostages to get to their parents and other people in the escape chain.

'Is it the usual plan?' she asked.

'Yes. The children are already in hiding close to the beach. The rowing boat will be in the same old place, and you must leave by half past five because of the tide. The soldier on guard duty along that stretch of shore normally reaches there at quarter to six. But as he always comes into the café for a cognac when it is very cold, I will get him to linger a little longer in the warmth.'

Mariette wasn't going to ask if Celeste was sure she could do that. She trusted her.

'You leave here when the church bell strikes five,' Celeste said. 'The oldest boy, Bernard, knows to be ready too. As you approach the beach, give your usual signal so he knows it's you.'

Mariette nodded. She had invented her signal herself; she rattled a few small pebbles in a tin because using a whistle, or calling out, was too risky.

'This may be our last meeting,' Celeste said, reaching out to hug Mariette. 'I feel better times will be coming soon. I hope I'm right. But if we don't ever meet again, I thank you now for all you have done for us. Your courage is admirable, and I wish you every happiness in the future.'

Celeste left swiftly, leaving Mariette feeling a little emotional. She had come to like and admire the older woman so much, and she couldn't really believe she might never see her again.

Huddled in the shed, she heard the church clock strike one, then two, three and four. It seemed far longer than an hour between each one because she was so cold. After four, it was getting dark. She got to her feet and ran on the spot for some time, to get her circulation going.

Finally it was five, and she opened the shed door cautiously, listening carefully. When she was sure there was no one about, she hurried on down to the beach.

As usual, a night with no moon had been picked, but she could just see the shape of the big rock where the boat would be tucked away out of sight. Even over the sound of waves she could hear the tinkle of the bell in the buoy, signalling the direction in which she had to row. She picked up a handful of small pebbles, put them in her tin and rattled it.

At a faint sound she turned and saw the four children slinking like shadows through the garden gate of the house closest to the beach. Celeste had said the house belonged to wealthy Parisians who, before the war, always spent the whole summer here. It was all locked up now, the shutters closed and the doors padlocked, but Mariette guessed Celeste had the use of a cellar or outhouse.

She went over to the children and touched each of their cheeks in silent greeting. The oldest boy, who she'd been told was named Bernard, was taller than her. Both he and the

407

other boy, who appeared to be around six or seven, wore dark balaclavas on their heads. The two small girls wore dark coats and bonnets.

'Come,' she whispered in French, holding out her hands to the girls. 'I'll put you in the boat first and come back for your brothers.'

Telling the boys to go back into the garden and hide behind the wall, Mariette hurried the girls down the beach. At this point in a rescue she always feared the boat wouldn't be there, or that a soldier would suddenly appear. But the boat was there, secured in place, as always, some hours earlier. She lifted the children in and told them to lie down out of sight while she got the boys.

She had almost reached the two boys, back up the beach, when to her horror she heard footsteps coming along the coastal path from the little town. Just the heaviness of the footfall told her it was a soldier in heavy boots, and her blood ran cold. If the girls in the boat called out, or their brothers tried to reach them, all would be lost.

When she reached the garden gate, Bernard's anxious expression was evidence he understood the danger. She silently indicated that the two boys were to hide under the wall, and put her finger to her lips to remind them they had to stay silent.

While they crouched down beside the garden wall, Mariette stayed by the gate. She hoped that, as the guard had come early, his intention was to do his patrol as quickly as possible and get back into a warm place. But to her dismay he stopped walking just a few feet from her hiding place, gazing down the beach as if looking for something.

Although there was some snow on the ground, it was less than an inch thick, and she was sure it was far too dark to see all the footprints. But could one of the girls have cried out, or spoken, and he'd heard? This seemed unlikely as the noise of the waves slapping against the rocks was enough to drown out anything but a loud scream. Was the soldier just watching to see if the few snowflakes fluttering down were going to settle?

She waited and waited. But the guard wasn't moving.

It suddenly occurred to her that he had been sent to guard that area, and he wasn't going to move on. She felt sick because posting a sentry here meant the Germans must have a suspicion that people were being smuggled out from this beach.

Mariette was stuck in an impossible position. She couldn't get to the two little girls, and before long they were likely to get so cold and panicked they would climb out of the boat. And there was no way she could get the boys to the boat either.

The soldier would shoot the children, if he saw them. She knew that with utter certainty. She couldn't let that happen.

PJ's words came into her head. 'You will find you will be able to use your knife, as I have shown you, if your life or someone else's depends on it.'

She put her hand in her pocket and closed it around her knife. There was no alternative but to kill the guard. She couldn't let four children die just because she was afraid.

But she was afraid. If she had been dressed in women's clothes she could have boldly walked out of the gate, acted surprised to see the guard there, and then said something flirtatious to get closer to him. But dressed as she was, he would be suspicious of her immediately. That meant she had to take him by surprise.

Taking her courage in both hands, she first signalled to Bernard that he was to stay where he was. She then crept down behind the garden wall, away from the guard, and stopped at a point where a thick bush grew up over it.

Picking up some stones first, she climbed on to the wall.

Then, hidden from sight by the bush, she threw one of the stones. It made a sharp crack. Peeping through the bush, she saw the soldier's head turn in the direction of the sound, but he didn't move.

She threw another stone, this time throwing it further on to the beach, where it made a rattling sound. This time, the soldier did move. He began walking towards the place where she was hidden, peering into the darkness of the beach as if he thought someone might be lurking there.

The path was no wider than three feet. There was a short drop on the other side, which anyone would be wary of in the dark as it was impossible to see how far the drop was, or even if it ended on rocks or just sand and grass.

Mariette climbed silently down from the wall on to the same path the soldier was on, still remaining hidden by the overhanging bush. She was only four feet from him now, so close she could smell tobacco on his greatcoat.

She weighed him up. He was only slightly taller than her, but he was heavy and slow moving. His rifle was still slung over his shoulder and he had both hands in his pockets. As long as she could spring at him as quickly as she'd done in training, she could cut his throat before he even got his hands out of his pockets.

In order to make herself do it, she pictured the two frightened little girls waiting in the boat and the boys on the other side of the garden wall, afraid that at any moment they would be caught and then killed. She had to do this right for them. Failure would mean they would all die, and Luc, Guy and Celeste would almost certainly face a firing squad.

She crept closer to the soldier's back. She hoped the sound of waves breaking on the beach would drown out any sound she made.

Taking a deep breath, and rising on to her toes, she leapt

at his back. Her left hand grabbed his chin and yanked his head back to expose his neck. He made a roar of surprise, and his helmet thudded against her shoulder. With the knife firmly in her right hand, she slashed it hard across his throat.

He struggled, made a gurgling sound and she felt blood spray out, warm against her cold hand and face. She could smell his blood too, like iron in the icy air. He was sagging back against her, and she pushed him forward so he fell on to his knees, then she ran for the boys.

'*Vite, vite,*' she called.

They moved like lightning down the beach, with only the briefest of sideways glances at the soldier lying on the path.

Mariette had always moved slowly and cautiously on the beach before, to keep noise to a minimum, but she didn't care now. Her only thought was to get the children into the rowing boat and out to sea.

As Bernard tossed the younger boy into the boat, the two little girls jumped up looking alarmed.

'Stay down,' Mariette ordered as she pulled on the rope, which was attached to a metal stake secured in the sand.

Bernard strained to help her push the rowing boat into the water. The delay in getting down here meant that the tide had receded some distance, and it was hard going. But finally, the bows reached the water.

'Jump in,' Mariette ordered Bernard. 'I'll just push it out a bit further, and then I'll be in too.'

The boy did as he was told. As Mariette felt the boat begin to float, she threw herself on to the side of it to roll in. She heard a sharp bang, but before her brain had even registered that it was gunfire, a searing stab of white-hot pain hit her right knee.

'He wasn't dead!' Bernard exclaimed. He grabbed her, hauling her right into the boat.

A second shot rang out, and a wail of shock and pain came from the smaller boy. To Mariette's horror, she saw that he had been hit in the shoulder.

She grabbed the oars, pushed off from the large rock, and the tide began to draw the boat out to sea.

Another shot ran out. She saw the flash from the rifle, low down on the ground and wild, which seemed to suggest the soldier was shooting with his dying breath.

'Bernard, take this and hold it tight against the little boy's wound,' she ordered him, pulling off a scarf from around her neck. 'What's his name?'

'Isaac,' Bernard said. 'He's the brother of Sabine, the little girl. Celine is six, and she's my sister.'

'OK, Isaac,' Mariette said as she rowed briskly, trying very hard not to scream at the pain in her knee. 'You've been shot, and so have I, but we'll be patched up when the boat comes for us. But we have to be quiet until the boat comes. Can you be really brave and not cry until we are safe?'

'I'll try,' he whispered. 'But it really hurts.'

'Mine does too,' she admitted. 'But we're going to be brave soldiers.'

The buoy was ellusive. Mariette could hear the bell tinkling, but she couldn't see it as the waves were so high. They were all drenched now, and little Sabine was whimpering, big dark eyes full of fear as she clung to Bernard. Celine was holding the scarf to Isaac's wound and doing her best to comfort him. It struck Mariette that these four children must have already been through several kinds of hell to remain so controlled in what was a terrifying ordeal. It was dark, freezing cold, they were soaking wet, waves threatened to turn the boat over, and they were with a woman they didn't know.

She wished she could be so controlled. But she was in pain, and she was afraid that the gunfire might bring other soldiers running, and then the dead man would be discovered. It was too dark to see anything on the shore, but that didn't mean there was no one there. What if Luc had already been prevented from sailing because the Germans had suspicions about him? How long could she stay out on the open sea, with four children, just hoping help was going to come?

Between her own pain, and her fears for the children, she felt this was the very worst kind of nightmare. She had a mental picture of Celeste trying to charm Nazi officers who had come to search La Plume Rouge. Would they arrest Celeste and take her away?

What was she going to do, if that was the case? She couldn't keep the children out here all night, and by morning they'd be dead from the cold. If she couldn't even find the buoy, how would she manage to row the boat further along the coast, and get them safely on to land there? And even if she did manage that, the shed she'd spent the day in was as devoid of comfort as the rowing boat.

On top of all that, there was also her wound and Isaac's. She knew little about medical matters but she knew her knee was shattered. And at the rate blood was running out of it, she would pass out soon. Isaac was just a child, and without prompt treatment he might get an infection that could kill him.

What was she going to do?

She was feeling faint, but she gritted her teeth and made herself think of what her father had gone through in the Great War. He had fought on with severe injuries, and so must she.

All at once she could see his face in front of her. He was saying something, and she had to strain her ears to hear. 'True courage is when you can hold on to what is right,' she heard him say, 'whatever the cost to yourself, even if it seems all hope is gone.'

She knew that was what he'd said to her before she left New Zealand, but it felt as if he was here, whispering it in her ear.

'*Elise!*'

She roused herself at the name she hardly recognized.

Bernard was prodding her arm. 'I think the buoy is right here, I saw it a second ago. You got us here.'

The little boat was tossed up by a big wave and, as it came down again, Mariette saw the buoy. With all the skill she'd perfected in her youth, back in Russell, she managed to throw a loop of rope over the top of the buoy and pull the boat closer.

'You are so clever,' Bernard said admiringly.

'I've had a lot of practice,' she said, and managed a weak grin even though her knee felt as if it was going to explode.

'Isaac is getting very sick,' Celine said anxiously. 'And Sabine and I are so cold.'

'It won't be long now,' Mariette said. 'Let's play who can be the first to spot the fishing boat?'

It seemed like they waited for ever, the little boat pitching up and down, sprayed by icy water, the cold wind searing their faces. Five pairs of eyes peered into the darkness, and Mariette silently prayed that rescue would come.

Then, just as little Sabine began to cry, Bernard saw the small green light from the fishing boat. 'That's got to be it,' he cried out gleefully. 'If it was a German ship, they'd have a big searchlight.'

Later, as Mariette lay in the bunk wrapped in a blanket with Luc cleaning and dressing her knee, she learned that it was only seven o'clock when he picked her and the children up. It seemed impossible that the ordeal from leaving her hiding place to find the children, to cutting the soldier's throat, getting the children in the boat, rowing out in a heavy sea with a knee which was smashed to pieces, then waiting for Luc to come had all happened in just two hours.

Just the part when they were in the rowing boat on the open sea, waiting for Luc, had seemed hours.

'Short of being blasted out of the water by a torpedo, or fired on by a German plane, the nightmare is over,' she said with a snigger. She didn't think she could ever adequately explain to him how wonderful it was to see his boat steaming towards them.

'Not quite,' Luc reminded her sternly. 'You've got to get aboard the English boat yet, and this knee is going to take some sorting out.'

'We're all alive, that's what matters,' she said. Her knee hurt like hell, but it had been heaven to get out of her soaked clothes, which smelled of blood. 'How is Isaac's shoulder?'

Guy was at the wheel, and Bernard and Luc had fixed up a makeshift bed for the children on the cabin floor with some cushions and blankets. After Isaac's wound had been cleaned and dressed, he'd been only too glad to get into bed with Celine and Sabine.

'It is only a flesh wound,' Luc said, smiling down at the sleeping children. 'Look how deeply he's sleeping, it can't hurt too bad.'

Mariette smiled at the children too. Sabine and Celine were such pretty little girls, with dark curly hair, soft spaniel eyes and wide mouths. Isaac had light brown hair with a cowlick in the front that made it stand up, and a sprinkling of freckles on his nose. Now that he was relaxed in sleep, he looked as if the only sorrow in his life was losing at marbles.

'And you, Bernard? How are you doing?' she asked the older boy, who was sitting at the little table wrapped in a blanket.

He looked round at her and tried to smile. 'I'm alright, thanks to you.' He was a tall boy, very thin, with dark eyes that looked too big for his face, and his thick curly black hair was badly in need of a cut. Mariette suspected he was brooding on her killing the soldier. It was shocking enough for her to discover she was capable of killing but even more shocking for a child to witness it.

'It's time you got some sleep,' she said.

Luc said he had to go back into the wheelhouse with Guy.

As soon as he'd gone out of the door, Bernard looked back at Mariette. 'Have you killed many people?' he asked.

'No, tonight was the first. And I didn't do it very well, or he wouldn't have fired at Isaac and me.'

'I couldn't believe you did that,' he said in a small voice. 'I mean, you sort of leapt at him like a wild cat, and when you pulled his head back I saw how you killed him.'

'It was him, or us,' she said. 'I hope that makes it right for you.'

'I know people have to be killed in war. And after what the Nazis are doing to my people, I should be glad to see another one die. But a knife seems far more personal than a gun,' he said, his voice wobbling.

Mariette wished she could get up to give him a hug. He was too young to be seeing such things, but she guessed he'd already seen more horror than most people saw in a lifetime.

'Try not to dwell on it, Bernard,' she said. 'I shocked myself that I was capable of it. But I'm glad I was, or none of us would be here now. And your parents would have been very proud of the way you handled yourself tonight too. Climb into this bunk with me now. You are exhausted, and there's room for two of us.'

He wriggled in on the inside of the bunk, and fell asleep almost as soon as his head touched the pillow. Mariette wished she could sleep as peacefully, to wash away the pain in her knee, the smell of blood which seemed to be lingering on her, and the sadness that she'd only been able to save four Jewish children when there were tens of thousands who would perish before the war was over.

28

Russell, New Zealand

'I can't believe something so terrible could happen to her.' Belle sobbed against Etienne's chest. 'We should never have sent her to England.'

'She'll be fine now she's in hospital,' Etienne assured her, hoping this was the case. He was still reeling from being called to Peggy's bakery at daybreak to take the telephone call from Sybil.

To learn that their daughter had been shot on some kind of secret mission in France, when they believed she'd been safely working behind a bar in a sleepy seaside town in England, was a terrible shock. Etienne had always believed he could deal calmly with anything life threw at him, but he was wrong. It wasn't possible to stay calm when one of your children was hurt or in danger.

'Why would she volunteer to do something so dangerous?' Belle sobbed. 'Doesn't she understand we've got enough worry, with the boys over there, without her adding to it?'

'I think we should be proud she chose to do something to help in this war,' he said. 'Did you stop to think how Mog would feel if you were killed, when you signed up to drive ambulances in the last war?'

'That was different,' Belle sniffed.

Etienne grinned. Belle had been just as impulsive and daring as Mari when she was younger, but for some reason she had always seen Mari's spirit as a bad thing. Boys were allowed to be daring, but girls should be quiet and obedient.

'It wasn't different at all,' he reproved her. 'You drove ambulances because you wanted to do something to help in the war. And, although we don't know what Mari was actually doing in France, I'm sure it was something similar. So dry those pretty eyes, and just be happy she's lived to tell the tale.'

Belle grimaced. 'You always did take her part when she acted impulsively.'

'Just as you took Alexis and Noel's part when I took them to task for being too timid! That's the whole point of having two parents, they balance each other out.'

He smiled at Belle, who was pouting. If she'd had her way, she would have wrapped the boys in cotton wool. But her pout was so sexy, he felt a strong urge to kiss her.

'It was nice that Sybil sounded so fond of Mari. She said she was a credit to us,' Belle said reflectively. 'I just wish so much we could go to her. Letters and phone calls aren't enough, not when she's in hospital.'

'If there was a way to get to England, I'd try,' Etienne said. 'But we know it isn't possible, and Sybil said we can phone the pub any time for updates.'

Peggy came bustling into the shop then, her big face flushed with both the heat from the ovens in the bakery and from distress, because when she answered the person-to-person call from England she thought it had to mean one of their children was dead. To see Belle and Etienne's white faces, and the way they were clinging together, only confirmed this for her.

'Is one of them –' she broke off, unable to say that terrible word.

'No, they are all alive and well, Peggy, just Mari with a

busted-up knee,' Etienne said, understanding what their friend had thought. 'The lady who called was Sybil, the owner of the pub where Mari works and lives. We're only upset because it seems Mari has been doing secret work in France, and this could have been a lot worse than a bullet through her knee.'

'You mean she's been spying?' Peggy asked.

Etienne laughed. 'No, I don't think so, we assume she was working for the Resistance. But her injury has put paid to that! It seems it will be a long job getting her walking again. But the hospital in Southampton is a good one, so she'll get the best of care.'

'Thank heavens for that. But you'd better take Belle home now, and give her some special care,' Peggy said, noting that Belle was shaking. 'If you need to use the phone again, you know you can come any time.'

Etienne put his arm around Belle to support her as they walked the short distance home. He was worried because she was so shaken and pale. He could see Mog up ahead, waiting for them on the veranda, and even from a distance he could sense her agitation.

The war and worry for their children had taken its toll on all of them. He might still be lean and healthy at sixty-four, but when he looked in the mirror it was a shock to see how lined his face had become and that his hair was white, not blond any more.

Mog had just had her seventy-second birthday, and her hair was snow white too. She had arthritis in her knees and walked with a stick. But although she joked that she was growing senile because she forgot things and repeated stories, Etienne knew that she was far off that.

As for Belle, at forty-nine she was still a beautiful woman, even with grey hair and glasses. She had kept her figure, the brilliant blue of her eyes and the sweetness of her smile, and there was hardly ever a morning when Etienne didn't wake up and look at her and think how lucky he was.

They'd been through a great deal, both before their marriage and after, but the love between them had grown even stronger with the birth of the children, in spite of the hardships of the Depression and now this war. Mog, Belle and Etienne all felt empty and rudderless without the children; the house was too quiet, too tidy and too big. He missed them coming out in the boat with him, the chatter at mealtimes, and even having to break up the squabbles between them.

Mog still did all the dressmaking and alterations work in Russell, but Belle rarely made hats any more. Instead, she grew vegetables and fruit in their garden and on a piece of land they had acquired near their house, and she sold the surplus produce.

With all the younger men in Russell having gone off to the war, Etienne had more than enough building or repair work to keep him busy, and the three of them were better off financially than they had ever been. But that was no compensation for missing the children, or for the ever-present fear of getting that telegram telling them one, or both, of the boys was dead or missing in North Africa.

Ironically, they had never really worried about Mari being killed; perhaps that was purely because she'd cheated death twice in bombings in which her companions had died. They did worry about the boys, though, because their regiments were right in the thick of the action, but so far neither of them had received so much as a scratch. He just hoped their luck would hold out.

Three boys from Russell had been killed, boys who had gone to school with his children, played on the beach with them and come to the house for parties. At each memorial service he and Belle had felt deeply for the bereaved parents, and it drove home the message that today the service might be for Tom, Roger or Andrew, but next week or next month it could be for Alexis or Noel.

'What was up? Is she sick, in trouble?' Mog called out as they got closer.

They waited until they were sitting down on the veranda bench before Belle explained to Mog all that they knew. But it wasn't enough for any of them. Even Sybil had said that, when the man called to tell her Mari was in hospital, he'd been reluctant to say anything more than the fact that she was hurt. She'd had to drag the information out of him that it was a bullet wound in her knee.

'Her knee is very badly damaged,' Belle said. 'Sybil doesn't know how it happened – why, or even where – but she said she was planning to go to see Mari in hospital tomorrow and she'll ring us again then. But doctors can do wonders now, Mog, it's not like it was in the last war.'

Etienne could see by the haunted look in Belle's eyes that she was remembering the time when she was told how her first husband, Jimmy, had lost an arm and a leg at Ypres.

'Trust Mari to stick her neck out and volunteer for something dangerous,' Mog said.

Etienne smiled. He could see that Mog felt proud of Mari's courage.

'There hasn't even been a hint in her letters that she was doing anything like this,' Belle said indignantly. 'How could she write home and tell us about the pub and Edwin, and leave this out?'

'You can talk! As I recall, you put very little in your letters about the conditions when you were in France,' Mog retorted.

'They were too bad to write about,' Etienne said. 'But if Mari was working for the Secret Service, she wouldn't be able to divulge anything.'

'What if she can't walk any more?' Belle said fearfully.

'Will you stop it!' Etienne said. 'There's no point indulging in this "what if" speculation. We must wait till Sybil rings us again with more news. Maybe Edwin will ring us too – that is, if he's been told. Poor chap, I expect he's as shocked as we are to find out what she's been up to.'

Belle excused herself and went indoors and up into the bedroom to cry. She knew everything Etienne had said made perfect sense. But he didn't understand that discovering her daughter had been involved in something dangerous was far worse than facing danger herself.

She wanted Mari back just the way she was when she left here, five years ago. She may have been disobedient, devious and selfish, but at least she was safe.

Belle knew her daughter had changed dramatically in those five years. When she first arrived in England and wrote home, Belle's instinct told her Mari was playing along at being a caring, sensible girl, and many a sleepless night was spent wondering how long it would be before her daughter disgraced herself.

It was after Noah, Lisette and Rose had died in the bomb blast that real maturity shone through in Mari's letters. There was no self-pity, only grief that she'd lost a family she'd come to love. She never said that Jean-Philippe had made her leave the house, but Belle and Etienne sensed he'd been mean to her, and Belle knew only too well what a come-down moving from St John's Wood to the East End would be. Yet Mari didn't moan about her reduced circumstances. In fact, she wrote about her friend Joan in glowing terms, grateful for a roof over her head.

Yet it was when Joan died in the air raid, and Mari was left with nothing – no home, not even a change of clothes – that the real transformation in her character happened. Her pain at losing her friend Joan was all too clear. She said in one impassioned letter that it wasn't right that a woman with two children should be taken. Then she moved to Sidmouth, and, although she never said that it was because Joan's children were there, Belle knew it was. And she was deeply touched by her daughter's compassion towards them. Five years ago, Mari wouldn't have thought beyond her own needs. She might have got a rich man to take care of her, and it certainly wouldn't have occurred to her to try to help two motherless children who she barely knew.

Belle buried her face in the pillow and cried.

She felt guilty that, whenever she felt anxious about Mari, she always imagined her doing the sort of shameful things she'd done herself when she was in a tight spot. What sort of mother was she that she hadn't worried about bombs or stray bullets, and had only anticipated an unwanted pregnancy, dishonesty or guile?

Why hadn't she been able to trust Mari to do the right and honourable thing?

She heard Etienne come into the room, but he said nothing. He just sat on the bed beside her and scooped her into his arms. He let her cry against his shoulder for some time before speaking.

'You know, we've had more than our share of good fortune,' he said eventually. 'We found each other again, we've got three beautiful, bright and healthy children, and we live in paradise. If all we have to grieve about is one of our brood in hospital with a bullet wound, then I think our luck is holding out.'

'You always manage to look on the bright side,' she sniffed. 'But I feel responsible for this because I thought it was a good idea to send her to England.'

'It *was* a good idea. If she'd stayed in New Zealand, she would have got into some kind of trouble,' he said. 'As it turns out, England seems to have been the making of her. All I hope is that Edwin doesn't keep her there for ever.'

'That's just it,' Belle sighed. 'She doesn't tell us her plans, or what she thinks about. She's never even said outright that she loves Edwin, or that they're planning a future together. I'd feel so much happier if I could sit down with her for an hour or so and find out everything.'

'Do children ever tell their parents everything?' Etienne chuckled. 'I certainly never told my father anything because he was always drunk. I doubt you told Annie anything either.'

'No. But I had Mog, and I did talk to her.'

Etienne moved and propped himself up on his elbow, looking down at her. 'I bet you didn't tell her you'd met me again in France and been unfaithful to Jimmy?' he said, arching one eyebrow.

'No! How could I tell her that? She loved Jimmy.'

'I'm just reminding you that there are many reasons for not telling the whole truth,' he said pointedly. 'Maybe Mari doesn't think Edwin is "the One". Or maybe she knows he doesn't care as much as she does. Or he could have some hideous disfigurement.'

Belle managed a faint smile. 'Now you are being silly!'

Etienne smoothed her hair back from her face. 'Come out on the boat with me today. We'll take a picnic, and I'll make love to you on a deserted beach.'

'Why is it that you believe making love is the cure for everything, from a headache to fallen arches?' she asked.

'Because, *ma chérie*, you have been exceptionally healthy

since I began making love to you. That is all the proof I need.'

Belle giggled. Etienne still had the power to make her feel eighteen again.

It was just two days after the phone call about Mari's injury that Mog returned from the shop with a letter in her hand. Belle and Etienne were still in the kitchen, lingering over breakfast.

They had gone out in the boat on the previous day, and had spent a lovely afternoon together. They hadn't returned until after dark, and Belle had been reminded that it was a long while since they'd been spontaneous, and done something just for fun.

'There was this letter for you, from England,' Mog said, handing it to Etienne. 'It looks very official. Could it be about Mari?'

Etienne opened the envelope with a knife. As he read the contents, he frowned.

'Bad news?' Belle asked anxiously.

'No,' he said, 'just surprising news. It's from a solicitor. It seems Noah left my old place in Marseille to us.'

Belle was so surprised, she could only stare for a moment. 'Really?' she exclaimed, after a moment or two, knowing she must respond. 'That is amazing! And how like Noah to do something lovely for us.'

Etienne had bought the land long before she met him. He had repaired the tumbledown cottage, planted lemon trees and kept chickens. During the Great War, when she met up with him in France, he had told her about it. He had even suggested she should run away from Jimmy, her husband, and hole up there until the war was over. But then Jimmy lost his leg and arm, and she couldn't leave him like that.

She had thought Etienne had been killed in the war, and so, when Jimmy died too, she and Mog emigrated to New Zealand. It was Noah who discovered that Etienne was still alive. He tracked him down to the farm, and urged him to follow Belle out to New Zealand. Noah bought the little farm from him; he said he and Lisette would love to have a summer home in the South of France.

'Why has the solicitor taken so long to contact us?' Belle asked.

'It appears they've had some difficulty finding out where we are.'

'Why?' Belle asked. 'Surely Jean-Philippe knows exactly where we are?'

Etienne grinned. 'I suspect Jean-Philippe didn't want to say. The solicitor says, "Mr Foss challenged his stepfather's will, claiming that the French house had been promised to him." He then goes on to say the court ruled that Mr Baylis's wishes must be upheld.'

'And so they should be,' Belle said, with some indignation. 'I'm quite certain Jean-Philippe was well taken care of anyway. But, you know, Lisette did say in a letter some years ago that Jean-Philippe could be difficult with Noah. She didn't elaborate. But she must have felt bad about it, considering that it was Noah who saved her and her son from the clutches of French gangsters and gave them a new life.'

Etienne nodded in agreement. 'I only met Jean-Philippe once,' he said. 'And I recall him being a very sullen little boy. Noah was embarrassed by him not answering my questions. But I had assumed he would improve as he got older. Seems he didn't.'

'It's an ill wind and all that,' Belle said with a smile.

'A place in the South of France isn't worth much to anyone right now, it could even be a liability,' Etienne said

427

doubtfully. 'The chances are it has been damaged, requisitioned or even burned down. I recall Noah sent us a picture of his family taken there, and it looked marvellous, because he'd done the place up. But that must have been fifteen years or so ago.'

'I'll try to find that picture,' Belle said. 'They went there every summer. Lisette loved it as much as Noah. She told me in one letter that people around there still talked about you.'

Etienne smiled. 'Well, by the time the war's over and we have enough money to go there to take a look, I'd say most of those people will have passed on. We'll have to sell the place anyway. It's too far away.'

'Noah must have realized that we wouldn't go back to Europe,' Belle said. 'So why did he leave it to us?'

'He was a sentimental man, he knew how much it had once meant to me, and I guess he felt it was right to give it back to me. But I really hope he also wanted to annoy Jean-Philippe,' Etienne said with a wicked grin. 'I never told you, because Noah asked me not to, but at the time I was talking on the phone to Noah about sending Mari over there, he admitted to me the lad was a nasty piece of work. He said he was resentful, mean-spirited and very jealous of Rose. He often tried to hurt her. Noah said Lisette was bewildered by it, and they both felt very relieved when he got married and moved away.'

'Why didn't you tell me this before?' Belle asked with some indignation. 'Surely you should have said something when Mari left Noah's house so quickly after the tragedy? Didn't you think that Jean-Philippe must have been nasty to her?'

'Yes, I did. But I could hardly leap over there and flatten him, could I? We were both so upset at losing Noah, Lisette and Rose. And it wouldn't have helped you to know what Noah had told me.'

'What else have the solicitors said?' she asked.

'I have to confirm I am Etienne Carrera, get someone to witness the document, and then they will send me the deeds. Maybe I'll also ask if I can see a copy of the will, just to make sure that Jean-Philippe hasn't blocked anyone else's inheritance.'

'What might the house be worth, darling?' she asked.

Etienne shrugged. 'I haven't the faintest idea. It's in Vichy France, and I don't know if that makes it more likely to be intact, or less. I don't even know if Noah had someone taking care of it. But the land will have value, once the war is over, and people start going to the South of France again.'

'Maybe once Mari's leg is better, she will be able to go to look at it for you?' Belle said.

'Yes, maybe she will,' Etienne replied.

But he couldn't look Belle in the eye as a sixth sense told him the repair to Mari's leg wasn't going to be a quick one.

29

Southampton

Etienne's instinct was right. Mariette's knee had been badly smashed by the bullet, and she had her first operation on it the afternoon she arrived at Southampton Hospital.

The journey from France was all very hazy to her. All she remembered clearly was being on deck, ready with the four children to transfer from the French boat to the English vessel, and the pain in her knee was so bad that she couldn't stand on her right leg.

In the end, Luc jumped across with her in his arms because she passed out. Or so Armand said, on the way back to England. She had no recollection of it.

The rest of the journey, arriving in Lyme Regis and being transferred to an ambulance, was like a series of brief, disconnected snapshots to her, with faces she didn't recognize leaning over her and white-hot pain engulfing her.

She only became aware of being safe in hospital the next day, after the first operation on her knee. A man called Whitlock came to see her, sent by Miss Salmon, and Mariette asked him to contact Sybil to tell her where she was. But Whitlock was more interested in hearing the details of how the rescue went, and reminding her that she wasn't to divulge anything to anyone, than in reassuring her that Sybil would be told.

So she was left not knowing whether he would contact

Sybil, or not. And she was wondering how she was expected to explain her injury to people, especially here in hospital. She was fairly certain a gunshot wound bore no resemblance to a wound acquired falling over or being hit by a car. Was she supposed to say she couldn't answer that question, if the doctor asked who shot her?

As it was, the doctor who came to see her after she came round from the anaesthetic just said that he'd removed the bullet from her knee. Then he explained that she'd need a further operation in a day or two as the bullet had splintered other surrounding bone. He didn't ask any questions about how she got the injury. All he did say was that she would be in hospital for some time.

Apart from the constant pain in her knee, it felt good to be in bed in a warm room, with no further responsibility. She was alone in a small side ward. If she craned her neck, she could just see the big ward through a glass panel in the wall. She was glad she wasn't in there. Women patients always made a point of trying to find out what was wrong with everyone else, and she needed rest and time to make up a story before she was ready to talk to anyone.

Yet whenever she closed her eyes, she saw again how she had killed the soldier. She heard the gurgling noise he made, and felt the spurt of warm blood on her hand from his throat.

She wondered if she would ever be able to forget it. Was she going to see that scene for the rest of her life? She could rationalize it, tell herself that the lives of four innocent children were more valuable than the life of one soldier. She just hoped that other good people in Portivy didn't lose their lives because of what she had done. Especially Celeste, Luc and Gilpin. Would she ever get to hear any news of them?

Sister Fairclough, a thin horsey-looking woman, came to

see her at nine that night to tell her Sybil had rung the ward to ask how Mariette was, and to say she'd be coming to visit the next day. 'She said a Mr Whitlock contacted her,' the sister said. 'That was the gentleman who came this morning, wasn't it? Is he a relative?'

'No, I sort of worked for him,' Mariette said, hoping that would stop any further questions. 'I asked him to ring Sybil. I lodge in her home, and I knew she'd be worried about me.'

'I'd be worried too, if my lodger had a bullet in her knee,' the sister said tartly.

'I'm not allowed to talk about it,' Mariette replied. 'I'm sorry.'

Sister sniffed, put a thermometer in Mariette's mouth and pushed up the sleeve of her hospital nightdress to take her blood pressure.

It seemed as if she'd taken the hint.

The next morning, after a long night that Mari had spent mostly awake with the pain in her knee, a young nurse came in with a bedpan and a bowl of water for washing. She was a plain girl with dark hair and glasses, but she understood immediately that Mariette was embarrassed at having to use the bedpan. She somehow managed to get it beneath her, then disappear as she used it and come back at the right moment to discreetly remove it.

'I'll leave you to wash yourself while I nip off and find you a toothbrush and toothpaste,' she said cheerfully. 'I'll find you a clean gown too.'

Mariette managed to wash herself quite well – considering each time she moved her leg, it hurt like crazy – but she was very glad when the nurse came back and helped her into a clean gown and combed her hair for her.

'You've got such pretty hair,' the nurse said. 'But it looks like you've got blood in it. How did you manage that?'

Knowing it was the soldier's blood made Mariette feel sick. She lay back on the pillow without replying.

'I'll bring you some breakfast,' the nurse said, backing out with the washing bowl, clearly realizing that she'd somehow upset her patient.

Mariette lay in bed, on the verge of dropping off, when she suddenly heard a man's voice outside her door.

'I was told I've got to take someone down to X-ray,' she heard him say, and Mariette was instantly wide awake. His voice was so familiar.

She shook herself, remembering that many Londoners sounded the same.

It couldn't possibly be Morgan.

But when the little nurse with glasses came into her room, carrying a breakfast tray, she had to ask.

'A man came just now to pick up another patient for X-ray,' she said. 'His voice sounded like someone I used to know. What's his name?'

'I don't know,' the nurse said. 'I haven't been here long, and most people just call him "Porter". Some call him "Scar", though,' she said, then clamped her hand over her face in a sudden gesture of embarrassment at what she'd said. 'I'm sorry, that was horrid of me, especially as he's a nice man, very gentle and kind to the patients. And very rude, if he should be your friend.'

'He isn't,' Mariette said, remembering Morgan's handsome face. 'If he had been, you'd have described him very differently.'

At eleven o'clock that morning, she heard the porter's voice again. And this time he had come for Mariette, to take her to X-ray.

As he pushed the trolley into her room, he stopped short and stared open-mouthed at her.

433

If he hadn't reacted to her, she might never have realized it was Morgan.

Because he had changed so dramatically.

His black hair was streaked with grey, presumably a result of the shock of the burn that disfigured his right cheek and neck. It slightly puckered his eye and one side of his lips, but it looked as if he'd had extensive plastic surgery because the scar tissue was pale and shiny, almost like snakeskin. It was only by looking at the left side of his face that she could recognize the face of the man she'd fallen in love with on the way to England. That cheek was as golden and smooth as she remembered.

'Morgan!' she gasped. 'I thought I heard your voice this morning. But I convinced myself it was just someone who sounded like you.'

'Mariette! Of all the people in the world!'

'That you hoped you'd never run into again,' she added pointedly.

He hung his head. 'I'm sure you can see why I didn't want you to come and see me in Folkestone. I looked like a monster.'

'Did you really think I was that shallow?' she retorted. But even as she spoke, she knew that, in fact, she had been back then. And he must have looked a million times worse than he did now.

'You were just an impressionable young girl then, and I'd also treated you very badly the last time I saw you,' he said. 'I was amazed you even wrote to me afterwards.'

As he turned the good side of his face towards her, she was astounded to feel that old familiar tugging sensation in her belly that she remembered so well. It seemed ridiculous, considering all she'd been through since they'd last seen each other.

'You've got a very bad knee injury, I'm told. The surgeon needs an X-ray to look at how he will rebuild it,' he explained.

He manoeuvred the trolley to the side of her bed and then removed her bed covers so she could shuffle over.

'Can we talk sometime?' she asked.

He let go of the covers and lightly touched her cheek with one finger, just the way he had on the boat coming to England. 'What is there to talk about?' he asked. 'Maybe, on the ship, it did seem special. But you lived in one world, and I came from another. You didn't deserve the way I treated you; the only excuse I can offer is that I knew I was out of my league.

'I don't know why I wrote to you when I was in the Folkestone hospital. As soon as I'd posted the letter, I regretted it. Anyway, it was all a long time ago now. Let's leave it and just remember the good parts.'

30

Mariette lay on the trolley looking up at the ceiling and tried to think of some way to open up a conversation with Morgan as he wheeled her to the X-ray department. But she knew his silence was the kind that meant he had no intention of holding a conversation, no matter what she said.

Once they got to the department, where they had to wait to be called in, he moved away from her trolley. It was then that she noticed how he hung his head slightly, as if trying to hide his scars, and her heart went out to him. It was bad for any man to be disfigured, but for someone as handsome as Morgan had been, it had to be a terrible disaster.

After the X-ray, he wheeled her back to the ward, once again in silence.

But, as he helped her from the trolley back into bed, Mariette felt she must say something. 'I wish you had told me the truth about your injury and given me the chance to help you get through it.'

He just looked at her hard for a moment. 'You would have run away. Or, even worse, pretended you didn't mind when actually you couldn't bear to look at me.'

'Maybe I would. I admit that, back then, I wasn't the most compassionate of people,' she agreed. 'But you weren't the nicest of men, were you? I was really hurt by the way you behaved that night in Green Park.'

'I know, and I was really ashamed of myself.'

'A lot of water has gone under the bridge since then, so that doesn't matter any more. But considering you said in a letter that you cared about me, you should've been honest about your injuries and let me decide what to do. I was left thinking you'd found someone else.'

He turned away from her. 'I was never right for you, Mari, we both knew that. I couldn't read or write well, I had nothing to offer you. You needed a man who could take you dancing at the Ritz and all that. I went out to your uncle's place before I had to report to the army training camp. I couldn't write well enough to express why I'd behaved so badly that night we went out, but I thought I could explain it to your face. Yet as soon as I saw how you lived, I knew there was no point in even trying to make you understand and forgive me. You could never be happy with a ship's steward, or an enlisted man. You needed a toff who could keep you in style.'

Mariette felt chastened. She wanted to say that he had misjudged her, but she knew he hadn't. Back then, she really had been the person he was talking about.

'Maybe I was that shallow then,' she agreed. 'But the war has knocked that out of me. Uncle Noah, his wife and daughter died in the bombing of the Café de Paris. We were there to celebrate my twenty-first. I only survived because I was in the Ladies when the bomb dropped.'

His eyes softened. 'I'm sorry to hear that,' he said.

'I'm not asking for sympathy,' she said. 'I just need to explain why I'm not that way any more. Right after the funeral, Aunt Lisette's son made me leave their house. So I went to Whitechapel to stay with a friend – not a good place to see out the Blitz, but I was happy there. Do you remember telling me I should go to see the East End?'

Morgan nodded.

'Then you'll be glad to know that I came to understand what you meant. I never did find a man to take me dancing at the Ritz, and with this knee I doubt I'll be dancing any-where again.'

There was a perceptible change in Morgan's body language. His shoulders relaxed and when he turned back towards her, his expression was one of understanding.

'I saw on your notes that you had a bullet in your knee. How did that happen?'

'It's a long story, and I'm not really allowed to tell it,' she sighed. 'But if you want to know about me, as much as I want to know all that's happened to you, come and visit me when you aren't busy. Looks like I'm going to be here for a while.'

He hesitated.

She felt he wanted to, but he wasn't sure it was a good idea.

'Come on, Morgan!' she exclaimed. 'Nothing bad can happen just talking.'

He smiled then. 'No, of course it can't. Are you likely to have visitors this evening?'

'No, the only person who knows I'm here is my landlady. I think she's coming this afternoon.'

'Then I'll pop back when my shift ends. I must go now, there are people to move around,' he said as he began to push the trolley out through the door.

A few minutes later, Staff Nurse Jones came in to check the dressing on her leg. Mariette had only spoken to this plain, buxom nurse for a few moments on the previous day, but she'd found her to be warm and chatty. She seemed a good person to ask about Morgan.

'I met Morgan Griffiths, the porter, when he was a steward on the ship on which I came over from New Zealand,' she said companionably. 'He remembered me, but I think he was embarrassed because of his scar. Can you tell me anything about him?'

'Only that he is a kind and dedicated man,' Nurse Jones said. 'Officially he's a porter, but he's almost qualified as an SRN too. He knows as much about nursing as the most senior of us. I can't count the times he's helped us out in an emergency. Some say he should be a doctor, he reads up about everything.'

Mariette felt a glow at hearing such praise for him, and delight that he'd learned to read. 'He used to look like Errol Flynn,' she said. 'He was so handsome, you wouldn't believe.'

'When you spend a little time in his company, you find yourself thinking he's still like that,' the nurse said, and laughed lightly. 'He has such a way with people, you just don't notice his scar. Of course, it's a great deal better now than it was; he's had a few operations since then. He's never going to have film-star looks again, but I think the woman who manages to capture his heart will be very lucky.'

'Hasn't he got anyone then?'

'No, the silly man doesn't socialize. I think he spends all his spare time with his nose in a book.'

'I suppose when you've been very handsome, and suddenly you lose those looks, you are likely to want to hide yourself away,' Mariette said.

'Yes, just as you are likely to cover this leg up,' the nurse said, looking away from the bullet wound she was cleaning to the many other scars on Mariette's leg. 'Looks like this isn't the first time you've been in the wars?'

'I was in a shelter when it got a direct hit and a beam fell across my legs,' Mariette said, looking objectively at her badly scarred legs. She'd grown used to them, and rarely gave them any thought, but the new livid wound in her knee, surrounded by inflamed skin, made the old scars look much worse. She had to admit that, along with being very painful, her leg looked hideous.

'Poor you,' the nurse said.

'I was the lucky one, I managed to wriggle out of the rubble. Only two other people were saved. Not being able to wear shorts, or have bare legs, is a small price to pay for your life.'

'So how did you get a German bullet in your knee? Everyone wants to know,' the nurse asked with a conspiratorial grin.

'Running away from a German in France,' Mariette grinned back. 'Well, actually, getting into a rowing boat to get away.'

'The Resistance?' The nurse's eyebrows lifted.

'I'm not allowed to give any details, sorry,' Mariette said. 'So tell me about you? Do you come from Southampton? How long have you been nursing?'

'Well, that tells me all I need to know,' the nurse laughed. 'A reluctant heroine!'

3 1

Sybil arrived to see Mariette mid-afternoon carrying a large bouquet of hothouse roses which must have cost her a fortune. She dropped the flowers on the bed and enveloped Mariette in a tearful hug.

When she eventually let her go, her eyes were puffy. 'I spoke to your mum in New Zealand,' she said. 'I'm going to ring them again tonight to tell them how you are. Your mum sounded as if she wanted to jump on the next boat here, and your dad was standing by asking questions. Of course, I had nothing much to tell them. Only that you had a bad knee.' She paused to look at the cage holding the blankets off Mariette's knee. 'How bad is it?'

Mariette tried to smile. But it was hard, because her knee was hurting a great deal. 'I've got to have another operation, it's pretty badly smashed. Let's say I won't ever win a "Lovely Legs" competition. But I made it out of France with the kids.'

'You were rescuing children?'

Mariette put her hand over her mouth. 'I wasn't supposed to say that, so forget it. This secret stuff just isn't me, and I'm really glad I'm out of it now. My nerves would never have coped with another mission.'

'No one could be happier about that than me,' Sybil said. 'Except, perhaps, your mum. She, of course, couldn't understand what you were doing in France, or even why you were doing anything other than serving drinks in the pub. Edwin is trying to get down to see you. I had twenty questions from him on the telephone, he sounded quite cross really. I said, "You should be very proud of her," but all he could say was that you should've told him what you were doing.'

Mariette sighed deeply. 'He, of all people, should understand why I couldn't say anything.'

'I know, but it must have been a shock to hear that someone you love, and who you thought was at home, safe and sound, has been shot in France.'

'You know, Sybil, I really don't think Edwin is for me,' Mariette admitted wearily. 'He needs someone his family will approve of, some quiet, well-behaved young lady who won't ever give him a moment's anxiety.'

'Don't be ridiculous,' Sybil said. 'He adores you just the way you are.'

'He might have done, at first, but I think that's worn off, and he's too much of a gentleman to admit it. But then, I don't know that I even want a gentleman like him. I want a man like my father, strong, noble and capable, who doesn't give a fig about what anyone thinks of him.'

'You're being a bit mean about him,' Sybil reproached her. 'He's a fighter pilot, the bravest of the brave. He's a gentleman because that's the way he was brought up. If you were my daughter, I'd want you to marry him.'

Mariette picked up Sybil's hand and squeezed it between both of hers. 'You are a great stand-in mother,' she said with affection. 'But I think my real one would say there has to be passion to make a marriage work. She also wouldn't like the fact that his parents don't think I'm good enough for him.'

'You don't know that,' Sybil said with some indignation.

'I do, that's why he's never taken me home. And this little escapade won't make things any better. They'll think I'm wayward, too spirited, a bit dangerous, which, perhaps, I am. And maybe I need a man who likes that about me.'

Mariette's leg was throbbing now, and it was making her feel quite odd. But she didn't say anything, just carried on talking to Sybil, moving on after a while to tell her about meeting Morgan again. She admitted they'd had a torrid romance on the ship coming over here. As she went on to explain that he'd been badly scarred, Sybil looked very anxious.

'It sounds as if you want to start it all up again with him,' she said.

'I don't know about that,' Mariette admitted. 'I was a silly, empty-headed girl when I met him, and he was a handsome but uneducated ship's steward. The war has changed us both. But there was something about seeing him again, rather like opening a book again that you hadn't finished reading, and finding it's really good. So maybe!'

'Oh, Mariette,' Sybil scoffed. 'Life isn't like that. He's been a recluse because of his scar, and he's probably got a huge chip on his shoulder. And as for you! Well, you are clutching at straws. As soon as you are well enough to travel, I'm taking you home to nurse you there. OK, so maybe Edwin isn't "the One", but I can't believe a man who has been skulking in hospitals for years, rather than telling you what happened to him, is right for you either.'

Mariette felt very much worse after Sybil went home. She was feverish and weepy, but she put it down to her irritation that Sybil hadn't agreed with her about Edwin and had poured cold water on to her meeting up with Morgan again.

She was also hurt that Edwin hadn't sent a loving, concerned message via Sybil. She knew that she was being entirely irrational, given that she'd just been complaining about him. But she knew he would have expected her to be at his bedside the very next day, if he'd been shot down.

She also felt cross with the doctor because he hadn't come

back to her to discuss what the X-ray revealed. She had expected her knee to be painful for some time, but not as bad as it was, and no one had come near her to check if she needed stronger painkillers.

The smell of the mince and carrots for tea made her stomach heave, and she didn't even try it. The orderly who came to take her plate told her off for not eating her dinner, and Mariette snapped at her, saying it wasn't fit for a dog.

Afterwards, she was ashamed. She lay back on the pillow and cried.

She was still crying when Morgan came in. 'Hey, what's wrong?' he asked.

'I don't know really,' she replied. 'I just feel miserable, and my knee is really throbbing.'

He put his hand on her forehead, and she saw a look of concern on his face. 'How long have you been hot like this?' he asked.

'A while,' she said.

'How long is it since they took your temperature and checked your blood pressure?'

'The staff nurse did it when she changed my dressing this morning,' she said.

'Not since?'

She shook her head.

Morgan got up and went out of the room. He returned a few seconds later with Staff Nurse Jones, who was just about to go off duty. She took the chart from the foot of Mariette's bed and pursed her lips as she looked at Morgan.

'It seems she was forgotten. We have been very busy this afternoon, but that is no excuse. But never mind, I'll do it now.'

She took Mariette's pulse, checked her blood pressure and put the thermometer in her mouth. After checking her temperature, she looked concerned and said she was going to call the doctor. She asked Morgan to stay with Mariette.

'Was my temperature high? And what does that mean?' she asked him, once Staff Nurse Jones had left the room.

'I think it must have been high, and that could mean you've got a little infection. Or you could be coming down with something. Either way, they'll soon put you right.'

She wondered if he was holding her hand because that was what he did with anyone who was ill. Or was it because she was special? She really didn't feel well, and it was more than just feeling weepy because Sybil had been short with her, or the doctor hadn't come.

'Were you out in the cold, on the open sea, for a long time before you were picked up?' he asked.

'I think it was only an hour,' she said, 'but it seemed like for ever. The children were very quiet and brave. I hope they are all somewhere nice now.'

A little voice at the back of her head reminded her she wasn't supposed to talk about the rescue. But she felt too woozy to care, and closed her eyes.

'I had to kill a German to get away,' she heard herself say. Her voice sounded a very long way off. 'I cut his throat, and his blood was all over me. But I can't have done it properly because he was the one who fired at me, just as I was getting into the boat.'

She opened her eyes to find Morgan staring at her. 'I shouldn't have told you that,' she said wearily.

'Maybe you needed to,' he said, and stroked her forehead soothingly. 'I won't be telling anyone else.'

'Is it kismet that we met again?'

He chuckled. 'I think it must be. It's funny that I was so scared of you seeing my face. And yet, now you are poorly, you're looking at me just the same way you used to.'

'I'm seeing the same man,' she said. 'But he's just a little hazy now. Don't go away, will you?'

A little while later, a nurse popped her head round the door to say the doctor was delayed as there was an emergency elsewhere in the hospital.

Morgan was growing more and more concerned because, by now, Mariette was barely conscious.

'I think this is an emergency too,' he whispered to the nurse. 'She's burning up.'

He had already soaked a cloth in cold water, wrung it out and put it on her forehead. While he hoped it was just flu, or a very bad cold coming on – something which could easily be treated – a gut feeling told him an infection had got into her wound.

He'd seen it happen so often before, especially when there was a long period of time between the patient being wounded and arriving in hospital. One minute the patient was cheerful and chatty, the next running a fever. But, even worse, all too often this led to the infected limb being amputated.

People often asked Morgan if he would rather have lost a limb than be burned. He always told them he'd rather have the burn, as it wasn't the curse others saw it as.

He had been retreating to Dunkirk with his regiment when a German plane fired on the truck he was driving, and it burst into flames. Before he could get out of the truck, the flames had licked up his face, and the searing pain almost paralysed him. In that moment, he thought he was going to die.

But another soldier hauled him out of the truck and smothered his face in a wet cloth. Fortunately, his uniform had protected his body, and the burns on his hands were only superficial.

He did feel very sorry for himself, at first. The pain, the shock of being disfigured and the fear that he would be a

446

kind of outcast for the rest of his life made him feel like killing himself for a while. But when he was still at the hospital in Folkestone, he was told he could transfer to the vast Netley Military Hospital, near Southampton, to be seen by Dr Franz Dudek, a brilliant Polish plastic surgeon.

Dr Dudek might have improved his appearance with his patience and skill, but it was Mr Mercer, a surgeon at Netley, who really turned Morgan's life around purely by giving him the will to learn to read and write.

'You must master it,' he said simply. 'A handsome face may have opened doors for you before the accident, but a scarred one may slam those doors shut unless you can prove to people you are smart.'

Mr Mercer asked Mrs Lovage, a former primary school teacher and the wife of one of his friends, to teach Morgan. He left the ward three afternoons a week for his lessons with her, in a small office which was rarely used. Three months later, during which time he had undergone three separate operations on his face, he could read as well as Mrs Lovage. And she'd also schooled him in writing letters.

Because Morgan was afraid of having to leave the hospital, where he felt safe and accepted, he made himself useful on the wards, portering, feeding patients and cleaning. Sometimes, when he helped bath or feed soldiers who had lost both legs, been crushed by heavy machinery, or been shot in the head and suffered severe brain damage, he knew he was lucky it was only his face.

He was a voluntary worker at Netley for almost a year, happy to work for bed and board. At night-time he read any book about nursing that he could get his hands on.

It was Mr Mercer who persuaded him to take a porter's post at Southampton Borough Hospital, where he also operated and could speak up for Morgan. As he pointed out,

Morgan couldn't hide in a military hospital for ever, he had to learn to mix with civilians again.

As it turned out, the Borough was a much happier place for him than Netley. It wasn't run on military lines, as Netley had been, and it wasn't so vast, or impersonal. People did stare at him, and sometimes he overheard remarks too, but he found that it bothered him less and less as time went by, and the majority of staff were warm and friendly.

The management made a special case of him, allowing him to do his nursing training on the job, and giving him time off from portering to attend lectures. He found that working in a hospital wasn't that different from being on a ship – everyone had their jobs, and they all pulled together. He found lodgings close to the hospital, and he even made some friends.

In three months' time, he was due to take his final nursing exams. He didn't know if any other hospital would want a male nurse, so he might have to stay at the Borough, but that was fine by him, he was happy there.

When he was first injured, he had thought about Mariette constantly. While he was still in Folkestone he wrote a letter telling her not to come and visit him, half hoping she would disobey him. He tortured himself with thoughts of her with another man too. Later, once he'd been transferred to Netley, he was tempted to write again and beg her to visit him, if only to prove to himself that he had been right in thinking she'd run a mile from him.

But gradually she slipped into the place where he put every-thing that was 'before the accident'. He didn't want to see anyone from that time, or even think about them, because to do so would only bring home to him what he'd lost.

Books took the place of women in his life. They took him to places he'd never been, they taught him things, made him laugh and comforted him too. He told himself no woman could do that for him.

But then, suddenly, there she was in the side ward, with that strawberry-blonde hair, the wide blue eyes, and that soft mouth that he'd so often woken from dreaming about. He'd heard rumours that a heroine of the French Resistance had been brought in with a bullet lodged in her knee. He'd taken that with a pinch of salt as rumours like that circulated around the hospital almost every day, and the truth was usually something quite dull.

But then, when he saw who the supposed heroine was, he did believe Mariette was capable of it. She'd been daring – unique, even – and that vital spark she'd had was never destined for an ordinary life.

The surgeon who had removed the bullet from Mariette's knee was in London and couldn't be contacted. When her temperature soared higher, and she became delirious, Morgan begged the ward sister to call for Mr Mercer.

She agreed, but Mercer wasn't able to come immediately as he was in the middle of a delicate operation. By the time he did arrive and examined Mariette, the expression on his face, and the rank smell coming from the wound, left no doubt in Morgan's mind that Mercer knew amputation was the only course open to him. But he didn't say so, he just told the ward sister he would have to open the wound again and take a look around.

He asked Morgan to bring Mariette straight to the theatre.

Once Morgan had delivered her, he took a seat in the corridor by the theatre to wait. He intended to stay, however long it took.

But it wasn't long, just half an hour, before Mr Mercer came out of the theatre, removing his mask.

449

'I understand she is an old friend of yours?' he said.

'Yes, she is,' Morgan replied. 'It's bad news, isn't it?'

George Mercer had a great deal of respect for Morgan. He admired the way he'd dealt with his injury, never complaining, or seeking to blame others for his misfortune. He'd stuck doggedly at learning to read and then used it to educate himself. That was why he had argued Morgan's case with the hospital board, so he could train as a nurse, while continuing to act as a porter too. The idea had broken new ground, but he didn't know anyone in the Borough who didn't believe Morgan was an asset to the hospital.

It was quite obvious that this girl meant a lot to him, and George felt sorry for both her and Morgan.

'I had to remove her leg just above the knee. The infection had got too strong a hold for me to save it. It's a tragedy for someone so young and lovely, especially as I believe she was shot helping people escape from France. There are times when life just isn't fair.'

Morgan felt as if he'd been punched in the stomach. He remembered Mari in shorts on the ship, those shapely long legs attracting the eye of every passing male. He knew her interests were all physical ones – swimming, sailing and cycle rides. This wasn't just unfair, it was cruel.

'I see from the hospital notes that she is from New Zealand. Are her parents over here? Is there anyone we can contact?'

Morgan took a moment or two to compose himself, then explained that he thought the only person to notify was her landlady, who had visited Mari earlier. 'She will know how to contact her parents,' he added. 'And if it's alright with you, sir, I'll stay here to take Mari back to the ward when she's ready, and I'll remain with her.'

*

When Mariette came round and saw Morgan sitting beside her bed, she tried to smile.

He lifted her a little and held a glass of water to her lips for her to take a few sips.

'They took my leg off, didn't they?' she said as he laid her down again.

Morgan hadn't intended to tell her straight off, but he couldn't lie when she'd asked him a direct question.

'Yes, Mari, they had no choice. I'm so sorry.'

'Just before they put me under, I heard the nurse say something about the smell. So I knew that meant it would have to come off.'

Her voice was flat and emotionless. Whether this was resignation, or because she was still under the effect of the anaesthetic, he didn't know.

'They make amazing prosthetic limbs now,' he assured her. 'I saw people with them all the time at Netley. Once you get used to it, you'll be able to do everything you did before.'

Mariette closed her eyes again.

She was too sleepy to talk. And what was there to talk about anyway?

32

Sybil had to sit down when Morgan telephoned her about Mariette. He said he had put himself forward to break the awful news to her because he felt it would be better coming from someone who really knew Mariette.

It did help Sybil, because the way his voice cracked with emotion was evidence that he was very fond of Mariette and as distressed as Sybil herself.

He said he'd had a lot of experience with amputees at Netley Military Hospital, so he knew the problems, and what could be done to help them improve their life. Sybil had no doubt that in a few weeks she, Belle and Etienne would be glad to talk such things over with him, but right now she was too shocked to think beyond what this would mean for Mariette, and how she would tell her family.

Once Sybil had put the phone down, she burst into tears. It was too awful for words, and yet she knew she must ring Belle right away because it would be morning in New Zealand now. Then there was Edwin; she would have to ring the number at the airfield and try to get hold of him. It was a bit odd that he hadn't rushed down to see Mariette as soon as he knew she was hurt, but maybe he couldn't get leave. But to have to tell him now that his girlfriend had lost her leg was frightful.

But telling Belle would be much, much worse. How did you tell any mother that her beautiful and brave daughter was now crippled?

Morgan had said he believed Mariette would just accept it.

He said his experience was that those who took big risks, as she had, were usually the most stoic.

Sybil hoped he was right. She had never seen any vanity in Mariette, despite her good looks. But she did remember the girl laughingly admitting that, back in Russell, she'd thought she was the cat's pyjamas.

But however much you thought you knew someone, sometimes, in a crisis, they could do the exact opposite to what you expected. Sybil couldn't be sure how anyone would react to such news.

Belle did not take Sybil's news calmly. She broke into hysterical crying and her friend Peggy, at the bakery, had to take the phone and say they'd ring back later, when Belle had composed herself.

It was Etienne who eventually rang back; he said Belle was in pieces.

'Her first husband lost a leg and an arm in the last war,' he explained, his French accent making Sybil feel quite fluttery. 'He became a changed man because of it, and Belle is afraid that is what will happen to Mari.'

'I can understand her fear,' Sybil agreed. 'I can barely take it in because it was such a short while ago that I was with her, and she seemed fine then. But you must tell Belle that I don't think Mari is the kind to feel sorry for herself, or let it spoil her life. Of course, it's far too early to speculate on what she will or won't do. But she has an old friend, Morgan, there with her, and I think he'll help her to come to terms with it. It was he who rang me to break the bad news.'

She told Etienne that Mariette had met Morgan on the ship coming to England, but omitted the fact that they'd had a fling. She explained that, as a result of facial burns at

453

Dunkirk, Morgan had lost touch with her, and they'd only met again by chance as he worked at the Borough Hospital.

'I asked around about him before I left,' she added. 'People couldn't say enough good things about him, and it was he who alerted the ward sister that Mariette was poorly.'

'I see.' Etienne's tone was sharp, and Sybil suspected he didn't like the idea of a damaged man helping his daughter. 'What about Edwin? Has he been to see her yet?'

'Not yet, but I'm sure he will get some leave to see her soon. I'm afraid I'm not able to go back to the hospital for a couple of days. But please reassure your wife that I will, just as soon as I can. I hope you don't mind, but I gave your number to Morgan and suggested he telephoned you. As he works at the hospital and will be seeing Mari a couple of times a day, he is far better placed to explain things to you than I am.'

She ended the call by telling Etienne that Mariette was welcome to come back to Sidmouth to live with her and Ted, whenever she was able to. 'We think of her as family, not as an employee. We'll look after her, as if she was our own, until the war is over and she can go home to you.'

When Sybil hung up, Etienne leaned his forehead against the wall and sobbed. It had been bad enough to know his daughter been shot, but he had never expected her to lose her leg. He'd thought horror like that had died with the last war. He cried for some little time before wiping his face and going back into Peggy's living room.

Belle was still sobbing her heart out in her friend's arms. 'I should never have let her go to England,' she wailed. 'I was being selfish because I was fed up with worrying about her. What sort of mother does that make me?'

'That is rubbish! It was not selfishness. We wanted her to

have more chances than she had here,' he said firmly, taking Belle out of Peggy's arms and enfolding her in his own. 'Now look, just think how much worse it could be. She could be dead – next to that, a missing leg isn't so bad.

'But remember, Belle, this is our Mari. She got this injury because she was brave and strong-willed, and she was protecting children. She's not going to take to her bed, or give up on life. She'll fight her disability, you'll see.'

He told her then what Sybil had said about Morgan. He might be suspicious of the man's motives, but he knew it would comfort Belle to think she had an old friend in the hospital.

'In one of the letters she wrote home while she was on the ship, she mentioned someone called Morgan. He worked in the sickbay and looked like Errol Flynn.' Belle mopped at her eyes and tried to smile. 'Mog said she hoped he wasn't a womanizer, like the actor.'

'I doubt he looks like him any more, if his face was burned,' Etienne said. 'Fate can be so cruel sometimes, yet sometimes kindly too. Fancy Mari ending up in the same hospital where he works.'

'Do you suppose Edwin will appreciate a man from her past turning up?' Belle asked.

'It didn't sound as if Edwin was pulling out all the stops to see her,' Etienne said, frowning. 'So maybe it wasn't a serious love affair, after all. I wonder how he'll react to hearing she's lost her leg?'

'I'd say with fear,' Belle sighed. 'I was terrified, when I heard about Jimmy's injuries. Not very compassionate, I know, but that's the truth. I don't feel that way about Mari, though, only desperately sad for her.'

A lone tear ran down Etienne's cheek. 'I can't imagine our beautiful, perfect daughter with a limb missing. I've got a ball of misery inside me, and I can't imagine anything will ever take it away.'

Mariette didn't want to think about what life would be like for her with only one leg. She found that by taking any painkillers offered to her, and closing her eyes and shutting down mentally, she could sleep for most of the day and night. She was continually woken, of course, for dressing changes, for checks on her temperature and blood pressure, and for meals too. But, for the most part, the time just slipped by.

Sybil was very weepy when she came to visit Mariette, two days after the amputation.

Mariette told her not to come again as it was a long journey and too distressing. 'I don't need reminders of how I used to be,' she said. 'I'm OK alone, I'm just letting my body and mind heal until I'm strong enough to try out crutches. I know you and Ted care about me, and I love you for that. But you've got a pub to run.'

But if seeing Sybil was difficult, when Edwin arrived on the third day with a huge bouquet of flowers, it was far worse. He looked very handsome in his uniform, and she guessed that he'd made quite a few of the nurses' hearts flutter, but he was so ill at ease. He went through the motions of kissing her, holding her tight as if nothing had changed, but she noticed how stiff he was, and how his eyes kept wandering towards the cage under the bedclothes. She sensed he was afraid he would have to look at her stump. That was ridiculous as she had no intention of showing it to anyone, least of all to him.

'You can tell me how you really feel,' she said. 'It's better to talk about it honestly.'

'I love you just the same, with or without your leg,' he said, far too quickly.

'That isn't true,' she said. 'You are afraid of what it looks like, and what it would be like to be seen out with a girl on crutches. But that's alright. I'd be exactly the same, if it was you who had lost a leg.'

But that wasn't the only problem Edwin had with her. She sensed that losing her leg had just put the tin lid on the other anxieties he had.

'Why do you always have to force issues?' he said crossly. 'It seems to me it's a cultural thing with Australians and New Zealanders. I've come across a few of your airmen, and they are all the same. Have to get everything out for an airing, regardless of who they embarrass or upset.'

Mariette would agree that by and large colonials were more outspoken than the British middle-class male appeared to be. But she resented that he would try to blame her nationality for wanting to understand his feelings.

'Well, I'm going to force another bloody issue too,' she snapped. 'You have been aware for some time that your family wouldn't approve of me. But if they didn't like the sound of a colonial barmaid, what will they say to your one-legged girlfriend? You know perfectly well it's going to cause a terrible stink, but you just don't know how to tell me that without looking like a real cad.'

He looked horrified at her outburst and tried to say she was mistaken.

'Come off it, Edwin. I'm not a fool. You thought I was wonderful, at first. But when your family started asking awkward questions, you drew back from me. You've never taken me home to meet them because you knew how it would be.'

'That isn't true,' he said. 'My parents are stuffy and out of touch, and the only reason I haven't taken you to meet them is because I know you'll find them difficult.'

'That amounts to the same thing. But even more importantly, you don't show any real passion for me.'

'How can you say that?' he exclaimed, looking outraged. 'Just because I haven't tried to persuade you to go for dirty weekends away or to throw you down on the ground in the woods, it doesn't mean I don't want to. It's because I was brought up to believe a gentleman waits until he is married for that.'

'I do know the difference between a man showing respect, and a man who feels no passion at all,' she retorted. 'And if you didn't feel any passion before, you certainly won't feel any when your hand touches my stump of a leg.'

'You are so crude sometimes,' he said with distaste.

'And you, Edwin, are a bit of a pansy,' she said pointedly.

'Are you saying that I'm queer?' he asked in a shocked voice.

'No. I'm quite sure you'll rise to the occasion with someone your parents approve of. Just be a man and admit it isn't me, and then we can go our separate ways.'

His eyes narrowed, not liking the implication in her words. 'You haven't been exactly truthful,' he shot at her. 'You must have been training with the Secret Service for months, but you never even gave me a hint of what you were up to. Then you go off to France and don't say a word about that. How can I think of marrying a girl who keeps such secrets?'

'We're at war! All over England there are people keeping secrets like that from their families,' she retorted. 'You wouldn't tell me which city you were going to bomb tonight, would you? But, for your information, I didn't put myself forward for this work. They contacted me because I could speak fluent French. But how dare you feel aggrieved? I saved lives, you should be proud of me. But perhaps you think there's only room for one hero? Is that it? You don't like competition from a mere woman?'

'Don't be ridiculous. Of course I'm proud of you, but this has all been such a shock.' He tried to smile, and put his hand on her cheek in a display of affection.

Mariette wanted to believe him, but she saw the coldness in his eyes, felt the lack of tenderness in his caress.

'Go, Edwin,' she said, her voice quavering a little because she had hoped for so much more from him. 'Back to your squadron and your family. No hard feelings, we just weren't meant for one another.'

'You don't mean that. You are just overwrought with the shock of it all,' he said.

She was overwrought – no doubt she would regret most of what she'd said later – but she knew in her heart of hearts that he wanted to go, he just didn't like the idea of how bad that would make him look. He probably hoped she would say something really nasty, because then he could leave feeling completely justified, but she had no intention of making it that easy for him.

'I'm letting you off the hook because you are no more use to me than I am to you,' she said, trying hard not to cry. 'Go and find yourself a girl your folks approve of. Be happy with her.'

He took a step towards the door, but then stopped, his expression one of puzzlement. 'Did you ever love me?'

If she hadn't been in pain, and so close to tears, she might have laughed. 'I did, until I realized that you are a cold fish and dominated by your parents,' she said. 'Please go, Edwin, there is nothing to gain by stringing this out. Goodbye.'

He went then. If he'd had a tail, it would have been between his legs.

*

459

Morgan came to see her soon after Edwin had left, and found her with a red blotchy face.

'You've been crying,' he said. 'Is your leg hurting?'

'It does ache, but no worse than usual,' she said.

'So what were the tears for?'

'Disappointment, I guess,' she said ruefully. 'Edwin came to see me. I sensed he wanted out, so I showed him the way. But it would've been nice to see him put up some sort of fight.'

Morgan just put his hand over hers in sympathy. 'Better that he showed his true colours now,' he said.

'Yes, that's true, and I'm not broken-hearted, I knew he wasn't right for me. But –' she broke off, unable to say what was on her mind.

'You are afraid no one will ever want you again?'

She looked up at Morgan, and her eyes brimmed with tears. 'Yes, I suppose so.'

'That's how I felt too,' he said. 'Horrible, isn't it?'

'We're a fine pair,' she said, and attempted to laugh.

As her body healed, the need to sleep all the time soon lessened, and then the time really dragged. She found herself dwelling on how difficult life would be with only one leg, fearing she would never marry and have children, and remembering the joy she used to feel running up the path on the cliff top at Sidmouth. She wished she'd realized then that her days of running were numbered, so she might have appreciated what she had a little more.

By eight days after the amputation, she felt she might go mad with boredom. It didn't help that she kept picking at the scab which was Edwin. Should she have tried to conform and become the kind of woman his type married? Was she foolhardy agreeing to go to France on the secret missions?

Should she have just said nothing about any of it until she was on the mend?

Yet, however she looked at her relationship with Edwin, it always came back to the same thing. He hadn't loved her enough to overcome any problems that presented themselves. And while she was scrutinizing things under a microscope, she could see that just maybe she had fallen for the image of a fighter pilot from an illustrious family, not actually for Edwin himself.

Facing up to her new status was painful. She'd always imagined going back to New Zealand on the arm of a handsome and wealthy husband, looking sophisticated, beautifully dressed, and with a wealth of experience behind her that she could use to dazzle her old friends.

But she would be going back alone, poor, badly dressed, and her experiences were ones no one would want to hear. To top all that, she had a missing leg. She would never again be able to leap into a boat wearing just a swimsuit, leaving the men of Russell goggle-eyed.

'I am not going to succumb to self-pity,' she muttered to herself, whenever such thoughts came to her. 'I may never be able to leap again, but I can learn to get about under my own steam.'

To this end, she insisted on trying a wheelchair, and once she'd mastered getting about in that, she asked to try out crutches. She was urged by the physiotherapist to take it slowly, but she didn't listen. Crutches were harder to master than she'd expected, and she had a couple of tumbles.

'You will do yourself a serious injury, if you don't listen to what I tell you, Miss Carrera,' the physiotherapist said wearily. 'It takes time to adjust to your body weight being unevenly distributed now. You have to learn to balance, just the same as you did when you were a child and learned to stand and hop on just one leg. Ten minutes a day, for now, is more than enough.'

Mariette knew her stump had to be completely healed before she could even be measured for a prosthetic leg, and it would then take weeks to learn to walk with it. But patience was not one of her strong points. She wanted to go back to work in Sidmouth because she missed the banter of working behind the bar. Or, failing that, she intended to find a job here, in Southampton, so she'd be close to the hospital.

But the reality of it was that no one was going to employ a one-legged woman.

When Sybil had last visited, even she had joked that a barmaid on crutches was about as useful as a chocolate fireguard. She wanted Mariette home, but she'd pointed out that, realistically, Mari would have to accept that she could only sit in the bar and talk to the customers.

Mrs Harding brought Ian and Sandra to see her one day. Even though Mariette made out to them that she was fine about everything, was enjoying being in hospital, and had lots of people to talk to, she suspected she didn't really fool them.

Sandra hugged her, when she was leaving, and whispered, 'We like you just as much with only one leg. And so will everyone else.'

It was strange that a child could pick up on her real fear – of not being liked, or being ignored, or even being treated differently. She remembered there had been a girl at school who had a club foot, and no one really wanted to be her friend. Her family had moved to Auckland eventually, and Mariette could remember one of the bigger girls saying it was because she had no friends in Russell.

But she reminded herself that she did have a friend in

Morgan, and he came to see her every day, even if he could only spare a few minutes.

'You've got to use all this spare time productively,' he told her, when she had moaned that she was bored. 'You can't expect people to entertain you, just as when you get out of here you can't expect people to wait on you hand and foot. They'll have a lot more time for someone who makes an effort to do things for herself. Believe me, I know.'

She took note of what he said, and she did try to pass the time productively. She wrote letters home, she read a great deal, and she started a cross-stitch tapestry that another patient had brought in and then left behind when they went home. She even asked the nurses to give her little jobs to do.

But sometimes it was just too hard to be sunny-natured, optimistic and never to grumble about her lot. She would think dark thoughts about how unfair it was that people like Miss Salmon, who had talked her into training for the rescue missions, sat in safety in an office all day. The woman hadn't even come to see her in hospital to ask if she needed anything!

It wasn't so much that she wanted to see Miss Salmon, but she did want to know about the children she'd rescued that last night, and maybe get an address to write to them. She was worried too about Celeste and the other links in the chain in France; the dead soldier must have caused problems for everyone. Yet what made her really cross was that Miss Salmon and her colleagues had spoken so often about the need for humanity in this war, but now that she was hurt, and of no further use to them, the word meant nothing to them.

But at least letters to and from home were getting through faster these days. By using the special envelopes and light-weight paper, they went by plane now, and often they were delivered within ten days of writing. The day she got the letter from her mother about Uncle Noah leaving his house in Marseille to her parents was a real red-letter day. She forgot her aches and pains in her glee at imagining how angry that must have made Jean-Philippe.

Her father had written to someone he knew well in Marseille to get a report on the condition of the house, to find out if it had been requisitioned. His plan was to find someone who could act as caretaker for him until the war was over and he could sell the property.

Mariette hoped that something really unpleasant would befall Jean-Philippe before too long. His wife running off with someone else would do nicely, or his house being flattened in a bomb blast and him losing everything he owned. Maybe it wasn't very nice of her to be thinking such things. But then, he had been so evil towards her.

Finally, after almost four weeks in hospital, Mr Mercer came to see Mariette and said he was recommending that she be moved to a convalescent home in Bournemouth. He said that it specialized in fitting prosthetic limbs and helping the patient to use them well.

'Bournemouth!' she exclaimed. She was about to say she didn't know anyone there. Why couldn't she stay in Southampton, or go home to Sidmouth? But then she realized Mr Mercer was doing what he thought was best for her. 'Oh, that will be lovely,' she tagged on, and hoped she sounded as if she meant it.

'I know you'd probably like to go back to your friends in Sidmouth,' he said. 'But it's my experience that family and close friends do too much for those with missing limbs. You must become independent. Anyway, Bournemouth is very nice. And with spring around the corner, you will enjoy it there. I did hear a whisper we're going to invade France before long. Maybe one more year and the war will be over.'

She liked Mr Mercer; he had kind grey eyes and a very gentle manner. He was the sort of man anyone would want for a grandfather. Morgan had told her how good he'd been to him too, encouraging him to learn to read and getting him into nursing training. 'I do hope so.' She sighed. 'Everyone has suffered more than enough now.'

'You must use the year ahead to master your new leg and be ready for a different kind of life in peacetime. I bet your family in New Zealand are longing to see you?'

'Yes, they are. And for my two brothers to come home safely. They are in Italy with their regiment now. From what I've read in the newspapers, the Allies appear to have the Italians on the run.'

'So I believe,' he agreed, and smiled broadly. 'God knows, we need it to end.'

Mariette was taken to Stanford House, in Bournemouth, by a volunteer in a private car, and Morgan went with her.

The volunteer was a middle-aged woman in tweeds – a hearty 'county' type – and her car was a Riley, which Morgan was very excited about. 'Not just a day out of the hospital with pay, but also a ride in my favourite car!' he said.

'You have good taste, young man,' the lady owner boomed out. 'If you behave yourself, I may let you drive on the way back.'

The woman's name was Mrs Dykes-Colman, and she told them she had four boys. One, an airman, had been shot down over France and was now in a POW camp in Germany, the next was a lieutenant in the navy – she said he was somewhere around Gdańsk – the third was in the RAF, but on the engineering side, and the youngest was a Royal Marine, serving out in the Far East.

'Their father died in 1922, of lung disease after being gassed in the trenches of the Great War,' she explained. 'Such a waste, as he was a wonderful man. His boys are like him, thank heavens, and I'm praying I get them all home in one piece.' She glanced round at Mariette and Morgan, and a cloud passed over her face. 'That was a little tactless of me. I'm sorry.'

'We survived, that's lucky,' Morgan said. 'And we knew each other before the war and met up again at the Borough. So that's pretty lucky too. Can you tell us anything about Stanford House?'

'I can, indeed, as I go there most days to help out,' she said. 'They have very dedicated staff, all experts in their field. You are fortunate, Miss Carrera, that you've been sent there. They'll have you mobile before you can say Jack Robinson. Now, young man, if you want a bed for the night when you come visiting Miss Carrera, I'd be happy to put you up. I live close by, and it's always nice to have someone in the house.'

Morgan looked at Mariette and raised one eyebrow. 'Do you want me to visit you?' he asked.

'You know I do,' she said. She was actually afraid he wouldn't keep in touch, and that would really hurt. 'But only if you get time. I know you've got your nursing exams soon.'

He took her hand in his and squeezed it. 'I'll always have time for you,' he said. 'But you are going to meet lots of good people at Stanford, so you won't need me.'

A week later, Mariette thought of what Morgan had said about meeting good people at Stanford. He'd been right. The other seventeen patients, and around eight staff, were all good. But they were good as in grateful, worthy, sincere, optimistic, dedicated and enthusiastic. Lovely – but, like a diet of chocolate, it was getting rather sickly.

She wanted someone like herself who couldn't see anything good in losing a leg, who would grouse about it, curse the world, yet also see the funny side of it. No one did that here, not even those who had lost two limbs. They were constantly saying how humbled they were by all the help they were getting, how miraculous prosthetic limbs were, and how grateful they were that, in a few short weeks, they would be able to go home and take up their old life.

Only eight of the men were soldiers; all had lost a limb in some kind of explosion. They'd been brought here, rather than Netley, because it was believed they would benefit from the specialist care at Stanford.

The other ten people – six women, including Mariette, and four men – were civilians. Two were policemen, another was a farmer who'd got his arm torn off in a threshing machine, and one man had fallen while trying to cross railways tracks and been hit by a train. The women, with the exception of Mariette, had all sustained grave injuries during bombing raids, and later infections had resulted in amputation.

She didn't feel guilty that she wasn't as grateful as the rest of them, because she was not convinced they were as happy and content as they purported to be. How could they be? It was pie in the sky to think they could go back to their old life, as if nothing had happened. The two policemen wouldn't be able to go back on the beat, and the farmer would find it hard to drive his tractor with a false arm. As for the man who had been hit by the train, Mariette was convinced that he'd actually intended to kill himself, but when he survived, he was too ashamed to admit it, so he made up a different story.

The women all had husbands who were soldiers. She soon realized their motives for appearing so calm and grateful was because they had small children. These children were either with relatives, or in care, and the women knew that they had to learn to walk again if they wanted to get home to them. Any grousing might see the women returned to the care of a general hospital, where there was no expert to help them. Yet Mariette couldn't understand why they didn't indulge in a private whinge, now and again. She thought it would be good for them.

She wasn't fooling herself that she'd be able to swim and sail, as she had done before – although she intended to, if it was humanly possible. For now, she was satisfied with being nifty in a wheelchair, and being able to climb stairs on crutches while she awaited the arrival of her new leg.

And she kept a diary of how she was progressing.

A diary wasn't perhaps the right name for it, because she aired all her grievances against those who were irrepressibly cheerful, the ones who lectured her on taking courses on everything from dressmaking to electrical work, and those who were grateful for just being alive. She enjoyed ridiculing them on paper, made herself laugh as she painstakingly described them. Her diary would be as dangerous as a bomb, if anyone found it and read it, so she carried it around with her most of the time.

Luckily, she shared a room with Freda, who was neither a reader, nor a nosy parker. She was a quiet, rather frail-looking woman of twenty-eight, with watery blue eyes and hair the colour of old sacking. She was always knitting for one of her two children and, when she wasn't practising walking on her new leg, she spend a lot of time gazing at a photograph of them.

'Do you think all children are embarrassed by people with an artificial leg?' she said suddenly one afternoon.

Mariette had just returned from the preliminary fitting of her prosthetic limb. 'If they are, they need a clip around the ear,' she said. 'Why? What makes you ask?'

Freda's children, Alice and Edward, were with her elder sister in Salisbury. Freda had previously said, in passing, that

468

they'd only been to visit her here once because the weather had been so bad.

'My sister said in a letter that she thought it was wrong to embarrass them,' Freda said. 'She's suggesting that it's better for them to stay with her.'

'It is always better for children to be with their mother,' Mariette said firmly, thinking of Sandra and Ian and how they still spoke longingly of Joan. 'You are coming on a storm with that leg, you can cook, do the washing, everything a mother needs to do. I can't imagine what your sister is thinking of.'

'She loves my children, and she hasn't got any of her own,' Freda said in a small voice. 'She pointed out that they've got used to living in a much bigger house, in a nice safe place with fields at the end of the road. We were in two rooms in Southampton, down near the docks. And I haven't even got that since I was bombed out.'

'Why isn't she inviting you to live with her?' Mariette asked. 'Surely that's the answer? She'd still have the children there, and she could keep an eye on you too.'

Freda didn't respond for a little while. She was biting her lower lip, as if she thought she shouldn't be talking about her family to a comparative stranger.

'Well?' Mariette prompted.

'She wouldn't want me there. I'd show her up.'

Mariette was astounded that Freda's sister could be so callous. 'If you aren't good enough for her, then neither are your children,' she said forcefully. 'She's proved to you that she has no heart, and therefore she should have no permanent place in your children's lives. You've been very brave with your leg; now you must be braver still and stand up for yourself. And I'm going to help you!'

33

'I understand you've been motivating some of the patients to stick up for themselves,' Dr Hambling said as he examined Mariette's stump for blisters and sore places.

She'd finally got her prosthetic limb three weeks earlier. But instead of taking it slowly, as she'd been instructed to do, practising in short bursts, she immediately went at it like a mad bull. Dr Hambling knew she was surprised by how difficult it was to learn to walk with her new leg. But she had the idea that, if she just kept on and on, she would get the hang of it more quickly. The result was some sore places. But luckily, he'd managed to slow her down before she did herself any real damage.

'Who's been talking?' she asked, immediately on the defensive.

Dr Hambling first became aware that Mariette had become something of a counsellor when Freda came to him and told him that her sister wanted to take her children from her. Freda had lost her frightened mouse look, and she said Mariette had made her realize that she had to fight for her children. She'd asked for help to get a home of her own so she had a safe place to take her family.

Before long, Dr Hambling and other staff were noticing that Mariette was often having very earnest conversations with other patients, and all at once those meek and mild people were asserting themselves, asking to be put in touch with organizations that might help with their problem, or just looking and acting more positive about their future.

'Nothing goes unnoticed here,' Dr Hambling said. 'But it's excellent that you are getting other patients to talk. Often the psychological problems with an amputation are greater than the physical ones. You probably know that Freda came to me, asking for help in getting rehoused, and she would never have been brave enough to do that under her own steam. I honestly think her sister had convinced her that she was of no use to her children and that it was kinder to abandon them.'

Mariette beamed at Dr Hambling's approval. She'd half expected to be told to back off and not to stick her nose in other people's problems. She had found she was very good at getting people to open up about their anxieties, and she could see for herself how much it helped them to be able to discuss possible solutions. It also helped her to put aside her own worries and sadness.

'Will you be able to help Freda? She's desperate to get her children back.'

'It's all in hand. But let's talk about you, young lady! Will you slow down and take this leg at the pace we suggest? We do know a thing or two.'

Mariette laughed. She liked Dr Hambling, with his wild, white hair and bushy beard. He was old, he'd been operating on the wounded in the First World War, and it was the things he saw there which had made him want to work on prosthetics and help amputees to lead normal lives. Morgan had told her he was considered the best in his field.

'OK, I've learned my lesson,' she said. 'May I put it back on and show you how I'm walking now?'

The first time she saw her 'leg' she almost burst into tears. She'd seen other people's, but it hadn't prepared her for her own. That sickly pinky-beige Bakelite covering, the hefty straps and the sheer weight of the beastly thing made her think she'd rather use crutches for ever.

471

She couldn't help but remember Morgan on the ship, running his fingers from her toes, along her feet, and right up her legs. He said she had the best legs he'd ever seen. No man was ever going to want to do that to a one-legged girl. She couldn't even imagine a man holding her in his arms and kissing her. She might still have a pretty face, but an artificial leg would put anyone off.

Dr Hambling watched as Mariette strapped the leg on. He could see by her expression that it repelled her, but she had decided to come to terms with it. And love it or hate it, she needed it.

To the doctor's mind Mariette was a fascinating curiosity: defiant, impatient, bold, funny, given to wild ideas, often pig-headed and very brave. But she also had a very tender side to her, and she cared about people, especially those less able than herself. If she'd been born a man, she would have made a fine officer.

She was also undeniably beautiful.

Mr Mercer had commented on it, saying, 'She lights up any room she is in.' How right he was.

Some might say that it would be easier for a beautiful woman to adjust to a prosthetic leg than a plain woman, because people would want to help her. But Dr Hambling had found the reverse to be true: people shied away when they saw flawed beauty. But he had a feeling that, as long as Mariette was still breathing, she would never stop striving to be everything she had been before she lost her leg. And a real man would see her true worth and never think of her disability.

'Another couple of weeks and you'll be fit to go home,' he said, as she walked up and down in front of him. He wished he could tell her that her walk was identical to a normal two-legged person's, but he couldn't. She had to swing the prosthetic limb in order to take a step, and she was still at the stage where this was very obvious. With practice it would become less noticeable, but she would never walk as she once had.

'I wish that was "home" home,' Mariette said with a grin. 'But I guess there's no chance of a ship taking me to New Zealand?'

'Now surely you want to be here for the end-of-the-war celebrations?' Dr Hambling teased. 'And before that to see what happens when we invade France?'

'I suppose so.' Mariette made a dramatic sigh, and then laughed. 'It would be a bit rude to push off just as all these soldiers are flocking down to the coast. There are Yanks on every street corner. Shame I'm not up for jitterbugging, I'm told it's wild at the dance halls on Saturday nights. But how's the walking looking? Better than when you last saw me?'

'Very much better,' he said. 'You are still swinging it a little too much, but practice will sort that out. The main thing is that you aren't hesitant, and that is very good. But back to the dance halls – I don't see you falling for some wet-behind-the-ears Yank. Not even if half the girls in England are going that way. My money is on you and Morgan.'

Mariette was astounded that the doctor was aware of something between her and Morgan. Everyone else thought it was nothing but friendship. But Morgan did still make her heart flutter, and she was fairly certain she did the same to him. But although he'd made the journey to come and see her almost every week since she'd been here, he'd never admitted any feelings for her. He had never even tried to kiss her.

Dr Hambling guessed what Mariette was thinking, and sympathized with her inability to move things on with Morgan.

'Unfortunately, Morgan has the same problem as many of

the patients here that we've tried to help,' he said. 'I've seen a photograph of him as he was, and I can perfectly well understand why a man who was once so handsome would imagine he had nothing to offer a woman now he has lost those looks. He's wrong, of course, we both know that. You, Mariette, aren't a different person because of your leg. And he is no different because his face was burned. But getting patients to understand that isn't easy.'

'But it's also about how others see us too,' Mariette said. 'In the past, when I walked down a street, I'd get men turning their heads to look at me. Now, when they see my limp, their expression changes, they drop their eyes. That's how it is for Morgan too. Women used to stop in their tracks to look at him, but now they avoid looking directly at him.'

'But you don't avoid looking at him,' Dr Hambling said pointedly. 'I've seen you with him, you retain eye contact all the time. And he looks at you as you walk away, as if he is afraid he'll never see you again. I'd say you two have something good to build on.'

'There won't be any opportunity to build on anything, once I'm back in Sidmouth,' she said. 'And if the invasion does go ahead, the Borough will be run off its feet with wounded, and he'll never have the time to come visiting.'

'Then perhaps you should go back to the Borough?' The doctor smiled mischievously. 'I seem to remember you told me you had secretarial training? The Borough might very well need someone in administration.'

Mariette's eyes lit up. 'Do you think they'd take me on?' she exclaimed. 'Am I able to do a job like that now?'

'Yes, I think they'd take you on, if I have a word in the right ear. As for whether you are able to do it, well, only you can answer that. Physically you are able – you know now how long you can walk with the leg, and which things you still find difficult – but secretarial work is mainly sitting down. Far more suitable than working behind a bar. So I think you'll be fine.'

'Won't Morgan think I'm chasing him?'

Dr Hambling threw back his head and laughed. 'Oh, Mariette, no man on earth would mind someone like you chasing him! I think Morgan will be overjoyed. Chase him, and kiss him once you've caught him, and I'm sure he'll be yours for life.'

Mariette remembered how she had shamelessly pursued Morgan on the ship. 'I used to be so sure of myself, when I was younger,' she said, looking very pensive. 'I never had a moment's doubt about anything really. Now I have doubts about almost everything.'

'That's part of growing up,' Dr Hambling assured her. 'Nothing to do with your leg, the war, or anything around you. As we become adults, we learn to be cautious. But that isn't to say we can't take risks, especially when the odds are all in our favour. Off with you now, and next time Morgan visits tell him you want to stay close to him.'

Mariette smiled and began to walk towards the door. 'I shall miss you, when I leave here,' she said, turning towards the doctor before opening the door. 'But I'll let you know how it works out.'

'You haven't seen the last of me yet, my dear,' he said. 'I'll be seeing you again, before you leave. And I'll need to see you every two months after that.'

'You are coming to the Borough to work?' Morgan said incredulously. 'I thought you'd be on the first train back to Sidmouth when you left here. Why the Borough?'

Mariette took a deep breath. 'Because you are there,' she said.

It was a warm day in May, and when Morgan arrived to visit her she'd suggested they sit in the garden of Stanford House to make the most of the sunshine. She'd received a parcel from home just that morning, containing a pair of cream-coloured linen slacks and a very pretty pale green blouse with ruffles down the front. Mog had made them, of course. As always, she seemed to know exactly what Mariette needed. She had put them on immediately and, with her legs covered, she felt ready for anything.

'You must know that I can't live without you?' she went on. 'Now, just tell me you only feel sorry for me, and nothing more, and I'll bugger off to Sidmouth.'

He hung his head. 'You know it isn't that,' he said in a small voice. 'I want to be near you too, but I can't be the man you need.'

'Allow me to know what I need. And it's you,' she said firmly.

He looked up, and there was such desolation in his dark eyes. 'You don't understand –' He opened his mouth to say something, then shut it. 'I can't even tell you,' he said eventually.

'Tell me what? I know you feel the same about me,' she said. 'So you've got a scarred face and I've got a missing leg. That makes us an odd couple, but it means we'll always have something to talk about, even if it is only who gave us a funny look that day.' She moved forward, put a hand on either side of his face, then stood on tiptoe and kissed his lips.

He responded immediately. His arms went around her, and his tongue flickered into her mouth. Mariette leaned in closer, just the feel of his firm body against hers making her nipples harden.

Morgan broke away first.

'I have to tell you,' he said, and his face was contorted as if in pain. 'I can't do anything any more. It disappeared at the time I was burned.'

Mariette sensed that admitting this was the hardest thing for him to do. She hesitated in replying, in case she made him feel worse. 'OK, do you mean you don't get hard any more?'

He nodded, and turned his face away to hide his embarrassment.

She took his hand and led him over to a bench by a bed of tulips. 'Have you told a doctor this?' she asked after a few minutes of just sitting there holding his hand.

'I did once, and he said it would come back in time. But it hasn't.'

There was a tragic irony in that the man who had shown her how much pleasure she could have from sex should be telling her it didn't work for him any more.

'When we were kissing, how was that?' she asked.

'Lovely, because it was you. But it didn't trigger anything.'

'But it was just a kiss in the garden. Don't you think if we were in a comfy place, all alone, that would be a better test?'

'I suppose so,' he said.

Mariette turned to him. 'You are always pushing me to do this or that. What you've achieved since your accident is utterly inspiring, so I find it very sad that you have allowed yourself to believe this problem can't be overcome.'

'Forget it now,' he said sharply. 'I don't want to talk about it.'

Mariette got up from the bench. 'I can't make you talk about it, to me or a doctor. But you know as well as I do, a burned face couldn't destroy any man's sex drive. It's all in your head, and if it was you who put that idea in there because you didn't believe any woman would want a scarred man, then you can remove that idea too.'

'I can't,' he said. 'God knows, I've tried.'

477

'Then we'll try together,' she said stubbornly. 'If I can rise above being scared of exposing my stump to you, I see no reason why you can't rise to the challenge.'

She giggled then, covering her mouth with her hand.

Morgan laughed too, and soon both of them were hugging and laughing, more from the relief of getting an awkward subject out of the way than because it was truly funny.

'So are you glad I'm coming to the Borough?' Mariette asked a little later.

'You haven't said what you are going to be doing there,' he said with a grin. 'If it's just to check up on me, I might not be so pleased.'

'Administrative work,' she said. 'Typing up requisition lists, writing letters, that sort of stuff. But as Dr Hambling told them I was very good at listening to people's problems here and helping to find solutions, I will also be working with the almoner.'

'Good luck with that one!' Morgan raised one eyebrow. 'Miss Wainwright is a real fire-eating dragon. I don't think she actually listens to anyone with problems, she just shouts them down.'

'Maybe I'll be able to tame her,' Mariette said.

'If anyone could, it would be you,' he said. 'Have they found you some accommodation?'

She nodded. 'I've got a room in the nurses' home. Mr Mercer apparently suggested that. I've been lucky that I had him and Dr Hambling on my side.'

'How about Sybil and Ted? Are they disappointed you aren't going back to them?'

Mariette pulled a face. 'I don't think Sybil approves at all. I think she'd like to baby me and display me as her private war trophy. But I don't want that, and I want to be near you.'

'We won't see much of one another when the invasion begins,' Morgan said. 'I'm hoping there won't be as many wounded as there were at Dunkirk, but it could possibly be worse.'

34

It was a general assumption that the Allies were going to invade France during the late spring or early summer of 1944 because of the vast numbers of troops arriving all along the south coast, but especially in Portsmouth and Southampton. Mariette never went into the centre of Southampton, but she often heard the nurses talking excitedly about the sheer numbers of American soldiers there, and arranging to go to dances to meet some of them.

As spring turned to summer, there was a palpable buzz of expectation as people thought the invasion was imminent. But no one knew anything for sure – not the date it would start, or which part of France would be targeted. Around the start of June, a rumour flew around that it was going to be through the Pas-de-Calais. But that turned out to be false information, leaked so that the German generals would send the bulk of their troops there to defend it.

Yet it was obvious that the invasion was about to start when people reported 2,000 naval ships lying in the English Channel, barrage balloons flying to protect shipping from enemy fighter planes, and countless minesweepers clearing enemy mines. On 5th June, hundreds of Allied bombers roared off overhead, and the muffled sound of heavy bombing could be heard coming from the coastal towns in France.

Everyone had theories, and many claimed to be 'in the know', but it was generally thought the invasion must take place on 6th June. There would be a full moon that night and a very high tide on the beaches of Normandy, which would get the boats over the traps the Germans had set on the beaches to rip out the bottom of any landing craft.

At all the hospitals along the south coast, nurses, doctors and other staff were poised for the inevitable casualties. At the Borough as many wards as possible had been cleared in readiness, though the bulk of the wounded would go to Netley Military Hospital, which had been taken over by the Americans.

Morgan had passed his final nursing exam with distinction, and doctors at the Netley had asked for him to be sent over there to help them. They felt he had special abilities; he had been a soldier himself, severely wounded, and he was known to be extraordinarily knowledgeable about battle wounds. Although Mariette was very glad his talents were being recognized, it was ironic that he was to be whisked away from her just as she had got close to him and was seeing him every day.

But she had more than enough work to keep her busy, taking dictation from senior personnel and typing out their letters and notes. So far Miss Wainwright hadn't allowed her to talk to any of the patients who came to the almoner's office with problems or questions. All she would let Mariette do was type up reports and file them. Morgan had been right about her: she was a dragon, rude to patients, insensitive to their problems and very high-handed. But then, she was going on for sixty, and she'd been at the Borough for eighteen years so had made the job her own.

Despite Miss Wainwright, Mariette loved her new job. It wasn't difficult, and after being so bored for so long it was a pleasure to be busy and needed. She already knew a few of the nursing staff from when she'd been a patient at the hospital, and she soon made new friends too. She didn't feel like a freak either. Perhaps it was because the staff in a hospital were used to seeing all kinds of injuries and disabilities, but they didn't stare or, even worse, avoid eye contact. She was often asked how she'd lost her leg and how she felt about her prosthetic limb, and she found she preferred openness to awkward silence.

Her room in the nurses' home, which was a detached house in the hospital grounds, was tiny, so small that some of the nurses called it a cupboard. But she had so few belongings that it didn't matter. And she only slept in there, as there was a communal sitting room downstairs where all the off-duty nurses gathered in the evenings.

On the evening of 6th June, everyone dropped everything to gather around the wireless and listen to the news. They heard how there had been a pre-dawn drop of paratroopers into France who had cut telephone and power lines. At 6 a.m., tens of thousands of soldiers had gone ashore in amphibious vehicles or landing craft on four different beaches in Normandy. The navy, which had been bombarding the coastal area with heavy fire, kept it up for an hour after the landings.

There was jubilation and awe in the voice of the news-reader. Jubilation, as it seemed all the many plans to deceive the enemy into thinking the invasion would be at Calais had worked, and the German troops in Normandy had been caught napping. Awe, as the huge scale of the operation was revealed, a magnificent show of brilliant organization, sheer power and guts.

But even as the nurses were cheering and hugging each other – because this invasion would surely bring the Germans to their knees and bring an end to the war – they all knew that within twenty-four hours they would be tending the first wave of hundreds, maybe thousands of casualties. It was a sobering thought too that many of the men who had jumped so bravely from their boats and other craft, and waded ashore ready to fight, would have died on those Normandy beaches.

As far as Mariette knew, her brothers were still in Italy, although there were New Zealanders, Australians and Canadians fighting alongside the American and British soldiers in France. She could imagine how fearful her parents would be when the news of the invasion reached New Zealand. They would be remembering the horrors they had both been through in France in the last war, and they couldn't be certain that Alexis and Noel weren't in the thick of it.

Sometimes Mariette wished she was home so much that it made her cry. She longed to feel her mother's arms around her, to hear that trill of laughter that was so instantly recognizable as Belle's. But more than anything she would like to sit down with her mother and really talk, not idle gossip about what the neighbours were doing, or the latest fashions, but about the experiences Mariette had lived through in England, and about her mother's life when she was a similar age. She wanted to know the real Belle, not the mother, but the girl, and to understand all the forces that had shaped her and made her the woman she was now.

Her father too. He was a tough, strong man – sometimes a touch scary – who had taught her to sail, swim and fish, but could comfort a small child just as well as any woman. Even as a small girl she'd always sensed there was more to him than papa, fisherman and sailor. Noah had hinted at things in her father's past, and Mariette wanted to know about them.

And then there was Mog. No one had ever really explained how Mog had come to be like a mother to Belle. Mariette knew Mog came from Wales, but she'd never said what happened to her family, or even if she had ever gone back to see them. She'd always just been a grandmother figure – loving, sweet-natured – a fantastic needlewoman, and the person Mariette had confided in.

Nearly six years was too long to be away from them. She ached for family dinners around the kitchen table, evenings spent playing board games, and sitting with them all by the fire in the winter. It was funny that she'd had to go to the other side of the world to see what treasures she had back home. She felt that when she finally got back to Russell, she would never want to leave again.

But, however much she wanted her home, she wanted Morgan too. With him being moved to Netley, she'd had no time to work on him. And even when he was here, it was almost impossible to be alone. She couldn't walk far over fields and rough ground, and Morgan wasn't keen on going into pubs or cafés where people were likely to stare.

Would it always be like that? And if there were always barriers, how would she ever find out for certain if Morgan was the man she really wanted to spend the rest of her life with?

On the evening of 9th June, the first casualties of D-Day, as everyone was calling the invasion of France, arrived at the Borough. They had received emergency care at dressing stations and on the ship that brought them back to Southampton, but some were very seriously injured.

Mariette happened to be going past the emergency treatment room and saw one man with half his face blown away. She was told later by Julia, a nurse she'd become very friendly with, that there were spinal wounds, eye injuries, legs and arms blown off, and that many of these soldiers would never walk again.

The following morning, Miss Wainwright told Mariette that she was to go and get the personal details of the injured.

Each of them had to be listed and their families contacted, if they weren't able to do it themselves.

Miss Wainwright was a bully, a sixty-year-old tyrant with iron-grey hair and a sour expression who had managed to keep her job as almoner because, although unsympathetic to patients, she dealt with them in an efficient manner. Mariette wanted to laugh when she realized she'd found a chink in the woman's armour. She was squeamish! That was why she was sending Mariette to do a job she should be doing herself.

'Don't take all day about it,' the almoner barked at her. 'You'll find the forms we use for this in the stationery cupboard. And mind you get all their details.'

'What do I do if they are unconscious and can't tell me?' she asked.

'Then get the details recorded on their dog tag,' Miss Wainwright said irritably. 'As long as we know their name and regiment, that will suffice for the time being.'

As Mariette walked into the first ward, with twenty-four men lying there, some with heavily bandaged heads and chests, others with cages under their blankets or arms already amputated, she thought of her mother. Belle had once described her first day at the Brook War Hospital in London, where she had been a volunteer. She said the horror of it was almost too much to take in, with the sight of blood-stained bandages, white faces etched with the pain, the smells and the low moans of pain the men couldn't control.

Mariette saw all that now, and more, especially how young some of these soldiers were. Her heart swelled with compassion as their eyes turned to her, silently begging for her help.

She had seen so many injured civilians whilst she was in the East End, and that had been heart-rending, but these men made her think of her brothers who might, for all she

485

knew, be lying in a hospital bed somewhere, afraid, hurting and feeling very alone.

All the men on this ward were English. Mariette supposed that the Americans had gone to Netley. She did as she'd been told and got the forms filled out, but she didn't leave it at that. She asked each man how he was feeling. And if he wasn't married, she asked if there was someone special, other than his parents, that he wanted to send a message to. She told them all how proud their families would be of them, and how proud England was of her brave boys.

Some cried, held her hand and sobbed out how terrifying and confusing it had been on the beach at Normandy. One told her that after he was wounded, he ran along the beach trying to find his platoon, but he was afraid he would be accused of desertion. Another told her that his best friend had his head shot off right in front of him. He needed to talk about it, and Mariette didn't care if Miss Wainwright took her to task for taking so long, she was going to listen.

It was late in the afternoon when she returned to the almoner's office with the completed forms. Miss Wainwright looked as if she'd spent the day sucking lemons.

'And where have you been?' she said.

'Collecting all the information,' Mariette said.

'And why, pray, did it take so long?'

'Because some of them wanted to talk, and I listened,' Mariette retorted.

'You are not here to take the place of a relative or psychiatrist. You are merely here for clerical duties. And now you'll have to stay late to type the letters for those unable to do it themselves,' she said.

'I was intending to do that anyway,' Mariette said. 'And, with respect, I believe that it is everyone's duty to support and help those who have fought for our country. If listening helps, then I will do it.'

'You insolent little baggage!' Miss Wainwright exclaimed. 'This is my department, and I will have it run my way.'

Mariette was tired, her leg was aching, and it had been a long and distressing day. She had done what she thought was right, and she wasn't going to lie down and let this woman walk all over her.

'And you, Miss Wainwright, are an apology for a human being. You are more suited to being a wardress in a prison than an almoner.'

The woman got to her feet and looked like she was going to strike Mariette. 'How dare you speak to me like that!' she snarled. 'I shall speak to Matron and get you dismissed.'

'Good luck with that.' Mariette shrugged. 'Now, if you'll excuse me, I've got work to do.'

Miss Wainwright picked up her handbag and her cardigan, and swept out of the office. Mariette sat down at her desk and began typing an address on an envelope. There was a special preprinted letter to be used to inform relatives when a member of their family had been admitted here. No details were ever given at this stage; the relatives had to telephone or visit to be told. Mariette had no intention of going against the rules, but she did have the addresses of two sweethearts that the men were afraid wouldn't be informed.

Some of the injured men came from the north of England. As she typed the addresses, she wondered if anyone would be able to come to see them. She remembered how low she had felt while in hospital, and how much she would have liked to see someone from her family. If it hadn't been for Morgan, she didn't know how she would have coped.

It was after nine, and a beautiful warm evening, when she walked back to the nurses' home. She was very hungry, but she had missed the evening meal and would have to make do with a sandwich. She wasn't going to dwell on the unpleasantness with Miss Wainwright, or the repercussions it might have.

She would deal with that tomorrow.

But after several days with no reprimand for being rude to Miss Wainwright, Mariette assumed that the older woman had decided not to complain after all. She was just as frosty as before, but she ordered Mariette to go back on to the wards and check with each of the soldiers to see if they wanted any help or advice about anything.

'Of course, it's the army's responsibility really. If they were in Netley, an officer would have already been round to see to them,' she said airily. 'But you can do it, until someone else comes.'

Mariette didn't know whether Miss Wainwright was just giving her a job she didn't want to do herself, or if one of the ward sisters had suggested Mariette. But, however it came about, she was glad. It was far more satisfying to write a letter home for a soldier who couldn't hold a pen than to type out reports and requisition forms. Many of the men had questions about their future now they were seriously wounded, and although she didn't know the answers to their questions, she could get the right person to come and discuss matters with them.

But the men were mostly just glad of someone to talk to. And for men who had already had a limb amputated, it helped them a little to hear from her how long it took to get used to a prosthetic limb, and what it felt like.

On 12th June, there was news of a new kind of pilotless bomb which appeared to be launched from France. People took it for a plane at first, because it had wings. But it wasn't long before there were many more arriving, by night and day, throughout the south, and targeted on London. The bombs sounded like a motorbike, with an engine that would suddenly cut out prior to falling and exploding. They had clearly been designed to create terror, and they did.

Two old ladies who lived together were brought into the hospital after one of these bombs, which people were calling 'doodlebugs', fell into their garden and caused their bungalow to fall down around them. Apart from many cuts and bruises – and one lady had a broken arm – they weren't too badly hurt, but the shock had been enough to give them a heart attack.

'We knew what to expect in the Blitz,' the older of the two said to Mariette, her voice quavering. 'But you hear this, then it stops, and if you are underneath it you don't stand a chance. What are we going to do now without anywhere to live?'

It was tough on anyone bombed out of their house, but for the elderly it was particularly cruel to lose belongings collected over a lifetime – especially if, like these two old ladies, they had no money to replace anything. Mariette said she'd contact someone to help them, but she knew priority was being given to families, so she doubted these two old dears would get anything more than one room in a shared house.

She told Morgan her concerns about housing when he came over to the Borough to see her. They sat on a bench outside the nurses' home because it was a warm evening.

'I despair for everyone,' Mariette sighed. 'They will need thousands of houses to replace all the bombed ones. And it's going to take years to repair all those with just missing tiles and broken windows. I can't imagine life here after the war, it certainly won't be anything like it was before. Thank goodness I'll be going home.'

Morgan didn't reply.

When she turned to him, she sensed that her last remark had upset him. 'Come with me?' she said, taking his hand in hers. 'I don't want to go without you.'

'What would I do for a living?' he asked. 'From what you've told me, Russell is too small for a hospital.'

'There is the Bay of Islands hospital in Kawakawa, that's not far away,' she said. 'Wounded servicemen went there in the last war, and it's been pretty busy in this one too. It's also a TB hospital.'

'I doubt they'd want a male nurse.'

'You, Morgan, can be very negative,' she said lightly. 'Do you want to stay here without me?'

He made a gesture with his hands. She knew exactly what he meant by it, that he wanted to be with her, but he wouldn't commit himself to it, not the way he was now.

'What would your parents say about bringing home some-one like me?' he said.

'You spoke to them on the phone when I first lost my leg, so you know how grateful they were to you for helping me. They know you've been burned, that won't make a scrap of difference to them.'

'But I'm not what they would've wanted for you.'

Mariette felt herself growing angry with him. 'I'm sick of this! They aren't the kind of people who go by looks. I'm not going to ask you again, I'll just go on my own.'

She got up to leave, but Morgan caught hold of her arm and pulled her back on to his knee.

'I'm afraid,' he said.

'Afraid of what?' she asked, exasperated with him.

'We met when we were both perfect. We thought it was love, but we didn't have long enough together to be sure of it. Then we meet up again five years later, and we've both got something wrong with us. How can we be sure we aren't just making do because we know it's unlikely anyone else will want us?'

'Making do!' Mariette exploded. 'Is that what you are doing with me? Better to have an imperfect girl on your arm, than no one?' She jumped up from his lap so fast, she forgot her leg and nearly fell flat on her face.

Morgan caught hold of her and pulled her back to him. 'I wasn't talking about my feelings for you, but how you might feel about me.'

Mariette looked at him in bewilderment. 'Why do you think such things? You were the one who abandoned me. You knew I cared for you.'

Morgan dropped his eyes from hers. 'I behaved shamefully outside the Ritz. You were everything I wanted in a girl – smart, sexy, beautiful – but at the same time I felt I was going to lose you because I'd told you I could barely read or write. So I was rough with you; that's what I'd seen so many gypsy men do to women when they felt second rate. If I'd been able to write better, maybe I could've explained how it was. I tried to forget you; but I couldn't. I was one mixed-up idiot, wasn't I?'

'If it's any consolation, I wasn't that sweet and kind then,' Mariette admitted. 'I liked the way Uncle Noah lived, I wanted that kind of life for myself. I was in two minds about meeting you that day in Trafalgar Square, because I didn't think you'd fit into my plans, but I couldn't quite let you go either.'

'Did you ever think of me, after I stopped writing?'

Mariette nodded. 'A great deal. I even thought of you while I was going out with other men. None of them ever made me feel the way you did, and I haven't slept with any man since you.'

Mariette wasn't sure why she admitted that.

'And I haven't had another girl since you either,' he said. 'Over in France I never got a chance. And then the fire put paid to it all.'

Mariette held his face in her two hands and kissed him lingeringly. 'I don't see your burn any more,' she said as she broke away. 'To me you are just Morgan, and I do love you.'

Suddenly they heard that dreaded motorbike sound of a doodlebug coming closer and closer to them. Morgan picked her up in his arms and ran towards the air-raid shelter with her. As he ran, nurses came charging out of the nurses' home, some overtaking them. They had just got the door of the shelter open when they heard the doodlebug's engine cut out.

'*In!*' Morgan yelled, pushing Mariette and the other nurses inside and quickly following them.

The crash as the doodlebug landed was so loud that the ground shook. 'The nurses' home!' one of the nurses exclaimed. 'Did everyone get out?'

Morgan struck a match and found a candle by the door to light. There were seven nurses in the shelter. When he questioned them about missing girls, it seemed they had either gone into town or were on duty.

'I think we can open the door now,' Morgan said, and gingerly opened it a crack to peer out.

They were all expecting billowing brick dust, and a scene of utter devastation. But to everyone's surprise Morgan laughed.

'The nurses' home is fine. The bomb landed on the waste ground, beside the garden. There's a huge crater!'

Everyone began giggling with relief. Mariette realized she'd been holding her breath from the moment they first heard the bomb. And there it was, at the bottom of a deep hole, a wisp of smoke rising from it.

'If it had fallen on the hospital!' one of the nurses said as they all came out of the shelter to view it.

'That doesn't bear thinking about,' another one added.

'Not our night to die,' Morgan whispered in Mariette's ear. 'I'm really glad of that as I have some unfinished business.'

'What?' she asked.

'Come with me,' he said, taking her hand and leading her away from the group of nurses who were all still staring at the deep crater the flying bomb had made.

He led her round the other side of the hospital, through a gap in a fence and into a small wood.

It was getting dark now, and Mariette was always nervous about walking on uneven ground in darkness as she felt she might trip. 'Where are you taking me?' she asked.

'Here,' he said, 'where there are no prying eyes, and hopefully no more doodlebugs.'

Mariette laughed as she realized what he meant.

He pulled her into his arms and kissed her. The kiss went on and on, their bodies pressing into one another's, arms clinging tightly. Mariette wasn't sure if Morgan was aroused, but she certainly was. If he chose to throw her down on the ground now and have his way with her, she wouldn't try to stop him.

'My darling,' he whispered as he broke off. 'I do love you, more than I ever thought I was capable of. And I think my problem seems to have rectified itself.'

'That's good to hear,' she whispered back, rubbing her nose gently against his. 'So what are we going to do about it?'

'We'll plan a weekend away,' he said, 'in a hotel. We'll do the Mr and Mrs Smith thing. Or even Griffiths, if that appeals to you.'

'It does,' she said. 'Does that mean you'll come back to New Zealand with me?'

'Well, I couldn't let you go on your own, could I?' he laughed. 'But I've got to get back to Netley now, so we'll plan it all next time I see you.'

'The next time I see you . . .' Mariette murmured the words Morgan had said that evening in the woods, and wondered when on earth that would be.

She hadn't seen him for weeks. He'd sent her letters, and twice he'd managed to get her on the telephone at the nurses' home. But Netley was snowed under with casualties from France, and he couldn't get away.

'Think of the six weeks on the ship sailing to New Zealand,' he'd written in one letter. 'You will be stuck with me morning, noon and night. You'll be screaming to escape me after two weeks.'

She was really busy too as the Borough was full to capacity, not just with war casualties but with everyday things such as people having their appendix out, giving birth, and having heart attacks too. Almost every one of these patients had some problem they needed help with. Life went on despite the war.

It was now early September, and there was no doubt the Allies were winning. German generals had made an attempt on Hitler's life, but to everyone's disappointment it had failed. The Allies had taken Cherbourg, liberated Paris and freed Belgium. Over in Italy, Florence had been captured, and the Poles in Warsaw had risen up too.

Mariette felt very relieved to hear that both her brothers were still in Italy, and unhurt. A letter had come from them, saying how much they were looking forward to a family reunion once the war was over.

But although there was so much to be optimistic about, Hitler had sent a further surprise, even worse than the doodlebug. It was the V2 rocket. It couldn't be intercepted and flew faster than the speed of sound. The destruction it could cause was enormous, and the damage to public morale was terrible.

With rationing becoming more severe every month, the number of people who were homeless or living under appalling conditions growing ever larger, and the casualty lists ever longer, there wasn't much to be cheerful about. Sometimes, when Mariette heard of one of these new rockets taking out fifty people or more in a single blast, she really wondered how much more England could take.

But she had a rosy glow within from thinking about Morgan. It really did seem plausible that, next year, they might be home in Russell for Christmas.

35

'It's lovely,' Mariette lied as she surveyed the little cottage Morgan had managed to borrow from someone at Netley for the weekend. 'Very atmospheric.'

'I'm glad you didn't say romantic, or I might have slapped you for telling fibs,' Morgan said. 'I'd call it creepy, and I think this may be Jim's idea of a joke.'

The cottage was only a mile or two outside Southampton. Jim had described it to Morgan as being like something out of a fairy tale, very picturesque, in a little wood. He'd said the bus would drop them at the top of the track that led to it.

He hadn't said that the fairy tale was one about a witch, that the cottage hadn't had any repairs in years, or that the track was the best part of a mile long and very muddy from recent rain. Mariette found the long walk in such poor conditions quite difficult, and she looked tired now.

It was the first week in November, and cold and blustery. The wind was banging a gate which was hanging off its hinges, and the trees all around the cottage were creaking ominously.

'I'm sure it will be lovely inside, once we've lit a fire,' Mariette said. 'I brought some firelighters with me, just in case there weren't any here.'

'I think we're going to be very glad of all your "just in cases"!' Morgan smiled as he looked down at the big bag he was carrying for Mariette. She'd already told him it contained clean sheets, a pot of stew – which she'd bribed the cook at the nurses' home to make for her – candles, various grocery items including milk and bread, and a half-bottle of brandy which she'd won in a tombola.

'Let's go in,' Mariette said, a hint of trepidation in her voice. 'This is turning into a bit of an adventure, isn't it?'

Morgan unlocked the door and mentally kicked himself for not booking a hotel room. But Jim had said the cottage in the woods was romantic and Mariette would love it.

They both might have done, if they'd been able to come in the summer. But the way things were at Netley, with new casualties flooding in from France daily, Morgan could never get more than a few hours off.

The door needed a hard push, and as it opened they were greeted by a smell of damp. 'It just needs airing,' Mariette said. 'First job is to get the fire lit.'

It wasn't as bad inside as it looked from the outside. There was one main room with a big fireplace, a scullery leading off behind it, and a bedroom at the far end. The furniture was plain, the kind a farm worker would have had back at the turn of the century, and the carpet on the bare boards was frayed and old.

'Jim's grandmother lived here,' Morgan said. 'She left it to him. He said he spent all his school holidays here as a kid.'

'Perhaps that's why he hasn't noticed it could do with a bit of smartening up,' Mariette said as she emptied the contents of her bag on to the table and rummaged for the firelighters. 'But look how much wood there is,' she added, pointing to a stack of logs at the side of the chimney which almost reached the ceiling. 'At least we won't be cold.'

Morgan took off his coat, and began laying the fire. He looked round to see Mariette inspecting an oil lamp.

'That's lucky, it's full up,' she said with a smile. 'I'll just trim the wick and light it. We can pretend we're at home in Russell.'

Morgan had the fire going in no time as all the wood was

very dry. He smiled to see Mariette playing house; she'd not only got the oil lamp lit but had worked out how to prime the water pump in the scullery, how to turn on a cylinder of gas for the gas stove, and the kettle was now on.

He found it immensely comforting to watch her stacking up the food in the scullery, checking the pots and pans and generally making herself at home. He had been very nervous all week about how things would be when they went to bed. Somehow he'd imagined them rushing through the door and into the bedroom immediately. This was much better, it didn't feel like a challenge.

'The bed feels a bit damp,' Mariette called out from the bedroom. 'It's a feather mattress, but if we give it a shake and prop it up in front of the fire for a bit it should be fine.'

'We had a horsehair mattress when I was a kid,' Morgan said as they hauled the mattress out into the living room and shook it. 'Hard as nails and usually full of bedbugs. Mind you, the mattresses on the beds at Netley are horsehair too, only no bedbugs. But I'm always so tired when I fall into my bed, I've never really noticed how hard it is.'

'You can get used to anything,' she said. 'At my Uncle Noah's the beds were sprung and beautiful. The first night at Joan's in the East End I thought I'd never sleep again, with so many lumps and bumps in the mattress, but I did. I used to sleep OK in the shelters too.'

'Do you think you'll sleep alright with me?' he asked.

She reached out and ruffled his hair. 'Yes, as long as you don't snore. But I'm a bit scared,' she blurted out.

'Why?'

She shrugged. 'My leg, of course. I'm afraid it might put you off.'

Morgan laughed. 'If my face doesn't put you off, why should your leg affect me?'

498

She put one hand either side of his face. 'I know your face is scarred and kind of shiny, but in my head it's just the same as it used to be. Your voice is the same, and so are your eyes, even your touch is just as it used to be. But let me tell you something else. I'm so proud of you now, Morgan, because you didn't wallow and feel sorry for yourself, but became a brilliant nurse.

'When I first met you, I saw the handsome face, the charm, but there wasn't much else there. Now there's a wealth of compassion, strength, tenacity and knowledge. You are a man to love now, Morgan.'

She saw his eyes well up, and she wiped the tears away with her thumbs. 'Even if we can't set the world alight tonight, it won't matter,' she said softly. 'I'm here with you, and that's all I want.'

'You've changed so much too, and all for the better,' he said with a teary smile. 'Back then, you struck me as calculating and self-centred, but you were very young and I was knocked out because you were so pretty. You aren't pretty any more, you are beautiful, inside and out. I love that you care about the soldiers, that your first thoughts these days are for other people. Your missing leg is like a badge of honour because you lost it protecting children. I love you more than I thought it was possible to love anyone.'

They hugged each other, heads resting on each other's shoulders, hearts beating as one. No more words were necessary; being together was all that mattered.

It remained that way. They ate the stew, cuddled on the couch and even dropped off to sleep for a short while because the cottage had become so warm. It was dark by four o'clock, and the wind was howling outside. Mariette was nervous about going to the lavatory outside, so Morgan went out there first and lit a candle in a jam jar to make sure there weren't any spiders.

'I'll stay outside the door, if you think the Bogey Man will come and get you,' he joked as she went in.

'I'm not that pathetic,' she shouted back.

But as she came back into the scullery, he leapt out at her from behind the door.

She nearly jumped out of her skin. 'You beast!' she exclaimed, but she laughed with him because it reminded her of how she and her brothers used to frighten one another. It was funny that she could feel frightened and safe at the same time.

Later, they put the aired mattress back on the bed and laughed a great deal as they made it up with the clean sheets. But although they kissed many times, Morgan made no attempt to take it any further.

They drank the brandy and played cards, giggling because they were a little tipsy. Then Morgan suddenly stood up, lit a candle, took her hand and said it was time for bed.

'I had plans for us to lie in front of the fire,' he said, pulling her to him in a tight hug. 'But I think we'll both find it cosier in the bed.'

She knew he meant 'easier in the dark', but she liked him using the word 'cosy'. That felt safe, and not a bit frightening.

He disappeared, perhaps to check the doors were locked and the oil lamp extinguished. Mariette unstrapped her leg, put on her nightdress and quickly got into bed. By the light of the one lone candle the bedroom looked pretty. The faded pink roses on the wallpaper and an embroidered sampler, perhaps done by Jim's grandmother as a child, evoked a feeling of home for Mariette.

'How is the bed?' Morgan asked as he came into the room. He must have been washing as his chest was bare. Mariette saw that it was as bronzed and rippling with muscle as she remembered from the voyage to England.

'It's like a snug nest,' she said. 'So soft you could drown in it, and very warm. But how come you are so brown? I thought you didn't get a minute to yourself at Netley?'

'I joined some of the ground staff and recovering patients, cutting grass and pruning trees, when we had that hot spell in September,' he said. 'Getting the wounded out into the sun and looking at nature often does more good than drugs.'

She almost said that, in the dim light of the candle, he looked no different from how he had been when she first met him. And that lying in a warm, comfy bed, she felt no different either. But she didn't say it, just patted the bed for him to join her.

'Well, here we are at last,' he whispered to her, once he'd blown the candle out and they were lying face to face in the bed. 'So dreams can come true.'

The wind was blowing even harder, the rain rattling down on the roof, but his breath was warm and sweet on her face, and his hand on her hip felt heavy with promise.

'You've dreamed about this?' she whispered back.

'All the time, when I was in the hospital having my burns treated. Not exactly real dreams, but I made myself think about you to distract myself from the pain. It worked too. Later, after the first couple of stabs at plastic surgery, I used to have these fantasies in which you came to visit me, laid your hands on my face and all the scarring disappeared. I told the army shrink that, and he said it was a very good sign that I allowed myself to think love could conquer anything. But he asked why I hadn't contacted you, if that was how I felt.'

'So what reason did you give him?'

'That I was too cowardly. I thought you would reject me.'

He was being so honest she thought she should be too. 'I would like to think I wouldn't have done that,' she admitted.

'But I'm afraid I might have. I was so wrapped up in myself, back then. I only started to feel real sympathy for others when the Blitz began and I saw houses crushed to a pile of rubble and people digging with their bare hands to find a loved one buried in the debris. Then losing Noah, Lisette and Rose on my twenty-first birthday, that was utterly devastating. It was as if I'd had a hard coating around me till then, and with each terrible blow, some of it chipped off. I think the last piece went that night in the rowing boat with the French children and a bullet in my knee. I was so afraid I wouldn't be able to get the children to safety. I didn't even think about myself.'

'I love you,' he said softly, sliding his arm around her and drawing her close to him. 'Here in this little cottage nothing matters, not the past, the future, nothing but us.'

He was so gentle and hesitant, as if he thought she might stop him if he did anything she didn't like. But as his hands crept under her nightdress to cup her breasts, Mariette was suddenly so aroused that she wanted it fast and furious. But Morgan set the pace, his hands stroking every inch of her with gentle deliberation. He removed her nightdress as if by magic and moved down to suck at her nipples while he pushed his fingers into her, making her moan and writhe with pleasure.

She could feel his penis hard and erect against her leg, yet when she tried to take it in her hand, he pushed her away. So she gave herself up to the exquisite pleasure with abandon, let him probe, stroke and rub her until an orgasm erupted, making her scream out his name.

He pulled her on top of him then, his penis so hard and big that she thought she couldn't take it all, but she was wrong, and while still feeling the reverberations of her orgasm, she delighted in the feeling of pleasuring him too.

She sat up on him, and he lay back, cupping her breasts with his hands, moaning with delight.

As his movement beneath her became faster, he sat up, holding her so tightly to him by her buttocks, moving her in and out while kissing her with such passion that it seemed impossible it could get any better. But it did. Another orgasm hit her like a tidal wave, and at the height of it she was aware of him telling her he loved her, as he came too.

Weak autumnal sunshine woke Mariette as it hit her face, and she opened her eyes to find Morgan watching her.

'Morning, beautiful,' he said. 'I was beginning to think you would never wake up.'

She could only smile. They had made love for hours, only falling asleep when the first rays of grey morning light began to lighten the patch of sky they could see through the window.

'I want to stay here all day, it's so warm and snug,' she said.

'Well, that's fine by me,' Morgan laughed. 'But a cup of tea and some eggy bread would be good. I did see a couple of eggs, didn't I?'

'You did. Feel free to make our breakfast then,' she said. 'And while you are at it, the fire needs clearing and lighting. You could also heat some water for me to have a wash.'

'I'm relegated to the role of servant now then, am I?' he said, sitting up on the side of the bed and pulling on his trousers. 'I seem to remember last night I was a god.'

'And so you are,' she said, running one hand down his bare arm. 'But any woman subjected to such serious and prolonged lovemaking needs to lie still in a darkened room.'

He laughed and went off into the living room, where she could hear him raking out last night's fire. She must have fallen asleep again because suddenly he was back, carrying a tray with two cups of tea and a plate of golden, fried eggy bread.

'You are the breakfast god too,' she said, sitting up and pulling the covers over her bare breasts.

Morgan pulled the covers back down. 'Leave it, I like to look at them.'

'Do you now? Well, I'm a bit chilly. But speaking of covering up. You didn't use anything last night, did you?'

He looked a bit crestfallen. 'I meant to, but it went out of my head.'

'What if I get pregnant?' she asked, taking a mouthful of eggy bread and rolling her eyes with the delight of it.

'We'll get married,' he said. 'That is, of course, if you'll have me?'

Mariette waited till her mouth was empty. 'Any time,' she replied. 'But we'd better be careful in future. I want my folks to know I married you for love, not because I had to.'

'It might be better to get married here,' Morgan said, suddenly serious. 'They might not let me into New Zealand otherwise. And even if they agreed, the chances are we'd be put in separate cabins – and that means sharing, like when you came over here.'

'My parents and Mog would be sad that they weren't at the wedding,' Mariette said thoughtfully.

'We could do it in a registry office, then have a proper church ceremony in Russell,' he said. 'I think they call it a blessing, though. A bloke I knew on the ships got married in Cape Town, and he had that when he got home. His bride was in a white dress, bridesmaids and the whole thing. I expect lots of Yanks will do it, as their girls might not be allowed home with them unless they are married.'

'How long do you think it will be before the war ends?' she asked.

'I spoke to an officer in Netley the other day, and he said the war in Europe couldn't last more than six or seven months. The Allies are in Germany now, and Rommel's dead. No one believes he died of his old war wounds. They think Hitler forced him to commit suicide because he believed Rommel was in on the attempt on his life. Just the fact that Hitler is so paranoid, he'd kill off one of his most highly respected officers, suggests he knows the war is over bar the shouting.'

'But ships won't sail to New Zealand while the Japs are still fighting us, will they?'

'No, they won't,' Morgan said. 'And unless we get lucky, we'll have to wait for all the Kiwi troops to sail back first.'

'But you do want to come back with me?'

He smiled broadly. 'It's what I want more than anything else.'

36

Sidmouth, May 1945

'Mariette! The phone!' Sybil yelled up the stairs. 'It's your mum and dad.'

Mariette came down the stairs as quickly as she could, dressed only in her petticoat, her hair still damp from washing.

'Just wanted to wish you a wonderful day,' her mother said. 'Are you nervous?'

'A bit,' Mariette admitted. 'But mostly about whether there will be enough food and drink, not that I'm doing the wrong thing.'

'He sounds to me like the best of men,' her father chimed in. 'I really appreciated him ringing me to ask if he could marry you. I hope it won't be long before you can come home.'

'Everything feels a bit of an anticlimax after VE day,' Mariette said. 'That was wild, so much excitement, drunkenness and all the stuff you'd expect. But since then it's been back to normal, with horror stories every day in the press about the death camps. Morgan and I couldn't stomach some of the newsreel at the pictures, it was too shocking.'

'Everyone here is just waiting for their men to come home,' Belle said. 'We'll be counting the days till we see you and the boys. Now Mog just wants a word, and Peggy said to tell you she's going to bake a real wedding cake for when you get here.'

Mog came on the phone, and at the sound of her voice

Mariette's eyes welled up. Mog had made her a beautiful dress, ivory satin with hundreds of seed pearls on the bodice. It made her think of the wedding dress Mariette had helped her with when she was seeing Sam, only without the long train. It was just another reminder of how Mog had always been the listening ear, never judging, never shouting, just offering gentle wisdom and kindness.

'Does the dress fit properly?' Mog asked. 'I was afraid it wouldn't arrive in time.'

'It came three days ago – I thought I would have to borrow one. But it fits like a glove, and I feel like royalty in it,' Mariette said. 'One of the sisters at the hospital gave me the ivory satin slippers she wore at her wedding. No one will even know about my leg, if I walk slowly.'

'Love him like there's no tomorrow,' Mog said, her voice cracking with emotion. 'And if he doesn't do the same to you, I'll box his ears when you get here.'

They had to go then. The last Mariette heard was all three of them wishing her luck and love.

It was a beautiful warm day, without a cloud in the sky. The wedding was at St Giles and St Nicholas Church, at two o'clock. Belle had been against a registry office wedding. She said firmly, 'A step as big as marriage should have God's blessing.' It was also the church Mariette had slipped into before each of her missions to France, so she felt that the setting was a good omen.

Ted was going to give her away, young Sandra was to be her only bridesmaid, and Ian was an usher. The best man was Mr Mercer. Morgan had asked the surgeon because, without him, he'd never have been able to train as a nurse.

Sybil was a stand-in mother of the bride. She'd dug out a beautiful pink dress and jacket with a matching flowery hat that she'd only worn once before, in 1936, to a nephew's wedding. With rationing and shortages of almost everything needed for a wedding, Sandra's pale blue bridesmaid's dress was made from one of Mrs Harding's old evening dresses. The cake was a decorated cardboard one – beneath it was a modest sponge – but many of the customers had made contributions to the wedding feast. There was a very large ham, several dozen tins of salmon, and a local farmer had brought round a sack full of new potatoes.

Sybil, with Mariette's help, had made trifles and a huge batch of bread rolls. It had been so long since either of them had eaten soft white bread – the only stuff in the shops tasted like sawdust – that they ate three each, as if they hadn't eaten a thing in months.

Sybil and Ted had insisted she and Morgan get married from the pub, even though the only contact she'd had with them since going to work at the Borough was a brief weekly telephone call. Sybil said they would always think of her as an adopted daughter, and they thought it was wonderful that she was marrying Morgan.

Mariette had not left her job at the Borough Hospital, and she would be going back there after a brief honeymoon in Lyme Regis. Miss Wainwright had finally retired, though some claimed she'd jumped before she was pushed, and Mariette was now the hospital almoner.

Morgan was still at Netley and would remain there at least until the end of the year. Wounded men were still being brought back to England, and some of the seriously wounded patients were in no condition to be moved nearer to their homes. But Morgan did not work such terribly long hours now, and he had found two rooms midway between the two hospitals where he and Mariette would live. They were saving as much money as possible for going back to New Zealand.

Sybil came to the doorway of Mariette's room and stood there for a few moments, just looking at the bride sitting in front of the dressing table.

She had always thought Mariette was beautiful, but to see her in her lovely wedding dress, her skin aglow with excitement and her hair a froth of strawberry-blonde curls cascading over her shoulders, made a lump rise in her throat.

'Are you nearly ready now?' she managed to ask. 'It's half past one. I must put your veil on for you before I leave for the church.'

'I wish my parents, Mog and my brothers could be here today, Sybil,' Mariette said, taking Sybil's hand and squeezing it. 'But you and Ted have been wonderful. Not just about the wedding, but ever since I first came here. Thank you for all the kindness and the support, I don't know what I would have done without you.'

'You'd have done just fine,' Sybil said, wiping a stray tear from her eye. 'You, my girl, have more guts than anyone I know, and Ted and I are proud to know you. But let's get that veil on. The cart will be here soon, I just hope they decorated it like I asked.'

Mariette sat still while Sybil secured the veil. The idea of the cart made her want to laugh. Back home, in Russell, people walked to the church to get married, but she understood that a car was the norm in England. With the shortage of petrol, a car was difficult, but Sybil had got the idea of a cart. All Mariette could hope for was that it didn't look like the kind of tumbril they used for people going to their execution.

They went downstairs then to check the tables were all laid up in the bar for the reception. There were snowy-white tablecloths, sparkling glasses and pink flowers on each table. Janice and Molly, two of Sybil's friends, were organizing the reception and staying behind to have everything ready when they returned.

'You wait till you see the cart,' Janice called out from the kitchen. 'They've done you proud.'

Mariette and Sybil went outside, and there it was. The driver, who was wearing a rather battered top hat with a rose pinned to the side of it, grinned sheepishly.

'Just look at that!' Sybil exclaimed, clapping her hands with pleasure.

It did look very pretty, the rough wood completely swathed in white sheets, including the seat on the back, which looked suspiciously like the bench from the back of the pub. Garlands of ivy and flowers, some just common weeds like Queen Anne's lace, plucked from the hedgerows, were tacked all along the sides of the cart, with pink ribbons fluttering in the breeze. The seat itself looked like a double throne, the sheeting covered with a dark green velvet tablecloth, and the arms and back smothered in flowers.

Even the old carthorse pulling it had his mane plaited and a garland of flowers around his neck.

'I have to go now to beat you to the church,' Sybil said. Turning to Ted, who had just come out to join them, she waved a warning finger at him. 'Help Mari in and out of the cart, and don't go charging down the aisle with her. Slowly, in time to the music.'

'Yes, dear heart,' he said with a touch of sarcasm. Then, turning to Mariette, he swept her up in his arms, and deposited her on the bench. A second later, he was sitting in the cart beside her. A great many people had come out of their houses to watch, wave and shout their good wishes. As the driver flicked the horse with the reins, instructing him to walk on, Mariette waved back.

'You've won a lot of hearts in this town,' Ted said, 'including mine and the wife's. Reckon that's why the sun's shining for you too.'

Ted did exactly as he'd been ordered, walking at a slow pace down the aisle to where Morgan was waiting.

Mariette noticed that Morgan was wearing a new navy-blue suit, and it fitted him almost as if it had been made to measure. She remembered him saying he would try to get one, as his old one was threadbare, but she hadn't expected him to find the coupons that would be necessary. He turned to look at her, his lovely mouth curling into a joyous smile. The way the light slanted down on him from the high windows meant she couldn't see his scar, and he looked as handsome as when they'd first met.

'Almost there, my beautiful girl,' he whispered, as she took her place beside him.

In that moment, before God and in His house, she absolutely knew for certain this was a marriage which would be made in heaven.

It wasn't until they had been through the ceremony and been pronounced man and wife, and she was walking back down the aisle with the ring on her finger, that Mariette saw the four children.

She couldn't believe her eyes.

She stopped dead by the pew where Bernard, Isaac, Sabine and Celine were standing. The four Jewish children she'd brought out of France.

They were dressed up for the occasion, the two little girls in pretty smocked dresses, the boys in smart blazers, white shirts and grey trousers. But it was their big dark eyes that moved Mariette the most; they were no longer full of fear, but happiness. Their broad smiles said they were as pleased to see her as she was to see them.

'What a wonderful surprise!' she gasped, and quickly told Morgan who they were.

Bernard laughed, as he could see the congregation were anxious to move things along. 'Go on, you can't keep everyone waiting,' he said, in halting English. 'We will see you at the party.'

'How come they are here?' she asked Morgan, once they were on the cart and riding back to the pub, waving at everyone. Almost all the guests were trotting along behind the cart in a procession, which made people turn and gasp. 'I'm thrilled they are here, but I'm mystified too.'

'I've no idea,' he shrugged. 'But it is the best of surprises, and Sybil must have had a hand in it.'

Back at the Plume of Feathers, they all sat down at the tables and were offered sherry for a toast. Sybil said Mariette would have to wait a little while before she found out how the children were here. The tables were laid for about thirty-five guests, some of whom were Mariette and Morgan's friends from Southampton. Mr and Mrs Harding were there, as were Henry and Doreen Fortesque and several regulars from the Plume of Feathers who were particularly close to Mariette. But the four French children were seated at the biggest table, with Mariette, Morgan, Mr Mercer, Sybil, Ted and Ian and Sandra.

As best man, Mr Mercer – who had insisted Mariette call him by his Christian name, George – was to make a speech before the meal. He began by saying how he had met Morgan, and expressed his admiration for a man who, although disfigured, wished to help others who had been crippled or scarred by war. Then he said that he had first met Mariette when he had to amputate her leg.

'I was, of course, very curious to know how such a pretty

young woman came by a German bullet in her knee,' he said.

He paused for dramatic effect.

'When a rumour circulated around the hospital that she had brought four children out of France by rowing boat, under fire, I had to know more. It proved difficult because Mariette would only say she wasn't allowed to talk about it.

'By this time, Mariette had met Morgan at the hospital. It seemed she had met him previously, when he was a steward on the ship that brought her to England. I asked Morgan what he knew about this rescue of four children, but Morgan didn't know much more than I already did. However, he did say that Mariette was desperate to know how the children were.

'I tried many avenues to get this information, but failed miserably. But then, many months later, right out of the blue, I received an inquiry written on official government stationery, asking how Mariette was progressing. It had, of course, to be from the department that had sent her to France. So I wrote back, and I pointed out they were rather late in showing concern for her. I added that she would dearly love to know about the children – how and where they were.'

Mercer halted, looking around at the expectant faces on all the tables, and then he grinned broadly.

'In a nutshell, and with Sybil's help, we made pests of ourselves until we had an address. And we finally succeeded in getting the four children here with us today, something I knew would make up to Mariette for not having her own family here.'

He raised his glass.

'And now, ladies and gentlemen, will you please raise your glasses to Bernard, Isaac, Sabine and Celine!'

The four children stood up, prompted by Sybil and Ted.

Bernard looked very composed; he was old enough, at fifteen, to understand completely why Mariette was so special. Isaac and Celine looked shy; at seven, they could remember that night in France very well, especially Isaac, who had been winged by a bullet. Only five-year-old Sabine looked bewildered. But she clearly did recognize Mariette, and smiled at her.

'But for Mariette's courage, strong will and powers of endurance,' Mercer went on, 'these children would not be alive now to hug her and tell her of their new life in Brighton with relatives. Mariette gave them life. And I'm even happier to tell you all that, just a few days ago, the children learned that their parents are alive, and they will be reunited with them within a month or two.'

There was a huge round of applause, and many people were wiping their eyes.

'Now to the ultimate love story,' Mercer continued, once the clapping had subsided. 'Morgan was a handsome steward on the ship that brought the beautiful, young Mariette to England. They fell for each other, but Morgan joined the army when war broke out. When he was so badly burned at Dunkirk, he decided Mariette would not be able to deal with his disfigurement and so he decided never to contact her again.

'While Morgan was courageously making himself indispensable in the Southampton hospital where he had many skin grafts and plastic surgery, and was also training to be a nurse, Mariette was helping Blitz victims in London. She lost all the family members she was staying with in London on the night of her twenty-first birthday, in the bombing of the Café de Paris, and so she moved to the East End of London to stay with Joan, whose two children – Sandra, our bridesmaid, and Ian, our usher – are here today.'

'Mari tried to save our mum when the bomb hit the shelter

they were in,' Sandra called out. 'She climbed out to get the rescue men, but Mum died in hospital.'

'That's right,' Mercer nodded. 'And Mariette came to live and work in Sidmouth purely so she could be near Ian and Sandra, who had been evacuated here to Mr and Mrs Harding. It was while working in the Plume of Feathers that Mariette was recruited for missions to get people out of France. She was chosen because she is bilingual, but I think they must have seen far more in her than a pretty girl who speaks fluent French.'

He paused to look at Mariette, who was blushing furiously.

'Ted and Sybil could only guess where she went off to from time to time,' he went on. 'Sybil told me she lived in constant fear for Mariette's life. But tragic as it was that she was shot in the knee while saving the children, she was brought to the hospital in Southampton, to meet up with Morgan again –'

Wild clapping broke out, and Mercer had to wait until it died down before continuing.

'To cut a long story short, and so we can get on with our meal, let me tell you that the spark of love, which had lain dormant for years, finally flared up between them. And the end result is this happy-ever-after wedding. I can't think of two people more suited to one another, or more deserving of happiness. I give you Mariette and Morgan!'

At six o'clock, Mariette slipped upstairs to change into the slacks Mog had made for her, plus a new checked jacket. The Hardings had managed to get some petrol for their car and had said they would give the newly-weds a lift to the hotel in Lyme Regis, if they didn't mind having the children on their laps.

When she came back down to the bar, George Mercer was talking to Morgan.

George turned to Mariette. 'I've got something before you go,' he said. 'It's a message from Miss Salmon.'

'Really?' Mariette said. 'It was she who got in touch with you?'

'Yes, that's right. She's a cold fish, if you'll excuse the pun. At first, she said it was impossible for you to see the children, but then suddenly she did an about-turn and offered to have the children driven here today. All very odd, very Secret Service. The woman wouldn't even put anything in writing! She also told me to tell you that Celeste is fine, still running her bar, and she is safe now from accusations of collaboration as word got out about the risks she took to help people escape.'

'Thank God for that,' Mariette exclaimed. 'I was afraid she might have been arrested by the Gestapo. She deserves a medal for all she did.'

'Miss Salmon said that too, but then she appears to be far more interested in those who did the rescuing than in those who were rescued. It was quite miraculous that she got the children here today.'

'Well, I am very grateful. It really made my day,' Mariette said, and she beamed. 'To see them all looking so healthy and happy has made everything worthwhile. And how amazing to learn their parents are still alive!'

George nodded. 'Miraculous, considering they were all Jewish and working for the Resistance. From what I understand, the Gestapo normally shot such people on sight. But to return to you, Mari, it seems Miss Salmon's department does feel an obligation towards you. When I told her you intended to go back to New Zealand as soon as possible after your wedding, she said they would be pleased to give you some assistance.'

'Good God!' Mariette exclaimed, looking hopefully at Morgan. 'Did she mean financial assistance, or getting on a ship?'

'I think it might be both. She told me to tell you to get in contact with her at the address you know.'

'That would be marvellous,' Morgan said. 'I can imagine what a scramble there will be for berths on ships. Without help we might be waiting for months.'

'The Hardings are ready to go now, and I must go and say goodbye to the children,' Mariette said. She inclined her head to a burly man who was standing by the pub door. 'I think that's their driver.'

The three smaller children clustered around Mariette, all anxious to hug her. She spoke to each of them briefly in French, telling them they were to work hard at school and keep out of mischief.

Then she turned to Bernard. 'It's made me so happy to have you here today,' she said. 'I know the little ones don't really understand everything, and I'm glad of that. I hope, in time, you and I can forget it too.' She put the address of the Plume of Feathers into his hand. 'Write to me here, when you are reunited with your parents. The landlady will send it on to me. I'd like to keep in touch.'

To her surprise, Bernard embraced her. 'You were so brave,' he said, speaking quietly in French into her ear. 'We owe our lives to you. I am so sorry you lost your leg, but I am glad you have a good husband now to take care of you.'

Mariette could feel herself welling up. 'I couldn't have done it without your help, Bernard. You were very brave and strong too.' She disengaged herself from his arms and smiled at the whole group of children. 'Your driver is here to take you home. I'm so glad you came, and I hope you had a nice time.'

'I read in a magazine a while ago,' Morgan said as they were in the car, driving with the Hardings to Lyme Regis, 'that when anyone looks back at their life, there is always someone who was inspirational, or someone who changed the course of their life. Do you think that's so?' he asked.

'Well, these two changed the course of our life,' Mrs Harding said, turning her head round to look at him and the children on the back seat. 'We'd given up hope of having children of our own, and we got talked into having a couple of evacuees. We were the only people prepared to have a brother and sister; everyone else who agreed to have two children wanted the same sex.'

Mr Harding said he had been inspired by a man he was apprenticed to as a young lad.

'I was inspired by both Dr Dudek, the plastic surgeon, and Mr Mercer,' Morgan said. 'But I was really thinking about the French boy, Bernard. Will he think of Mariette as inspirational?'

Mr Harding smiled into his mirror. 'I think every single person at the wedding today will always think of both of you as inspirational. We'd be very happy if these two kids of ours learn something from you two.'

'Happy?' Morgan asked as they lay in bed. Their guesthouse was right by the Cobb in Lyme Regis, and through the open window they could hear the sound of the sea slapping against the wall.

'It was such a lovely day,' Mariette sighed. 'If only you could bottle days like this. And every now and then, in the future, take the cork out and relive it.'

'I do hope Miss Salmon does help us get a passage to New Zealand,' Morgan said thoughtfully. 'I can't see the Netley carrying on as a hospital for much longer. It's too big and badly designed, and there aren't many other hospitals that want male nurses. We can't live in two small rooms for long either. I'd like to believe the politicians when they rabbit on

518

about a National Health Scheme, jobs and homes for all. But where's the money going to come from for all that?'

'I don't know,' she said sleepily. 'The only thing I know right now is that I've never been so happy before. Or so glad I'm with you. So I guess it doesn't matter how long it takes us to get to New Zealand. Or where the politicians get the money from.'

37

August 1945

'Surely there was some other way of ending the war than dropping atomic bombs?' Mariette looked up from the newspaper she was reading with tears running down her face. 'They say that seventy thousand people were killed instantly in Hiroshima and Nagasaki, and many more will die later. They weren't killing soldiers, these were just ordinary people – men, women, children and even babies.'

The news on 15th August that Japan had surrendered, and that the war was finally over everywhere, was wonderful. There were parties, fireworks and general jubilation throughout England. But now that Mariette knew just how that victory had been won, she felt ashamed that she'd celebrated. And she was pretty certain tens of thousands of others must feel the same.

'I know, it's dreadful,' Morgan agreed. 'But, in fairness to the Yanks, I don't think they fully realized what the bomb was capable of.'

'What sort of a person creates a weapon and uses it without knowing the end result?' she said, angrily wiping her tears away. 'I don't believe they didn't know. I bet they did, and they dropped the bombs regardless.'

It was Sunday morning and, for once, Morgan had the day off to spend with Mariette. They had planned to catch the bus later to Brockenhurst and have a picnic in the New Forest.

'Stop looking at those pictures,' Morgan said, and snatched

the paper away from her. 'You've been weepy and worked up about lots of things lately. Why is that?'

'I don't know,' she said, looking up at him. 'I started crying the other day at work, when a patient told me her dog had died while she'd been in hospital. She had to console me, she said the dog was very old and it had had a good innings.'

'You couldn't be pregnant, could you?' he said. 'You are looking very rosy and fuller in the face.'

Mariette just stared at him. 'I don't know! That never occurred to me.' She jumped up and dug her diary out of her handbag. 'I had the curse just after our honeymoon,' she said. 'I put a cross on the 5th of June. There's another one on the 3rd of July . . .' She leafed through a few more pages, then looked up at Morgan. 'Nothing at the start of August, but I could just have forgotten to mark it.'

'Or it didn't happen. And what with the war ending, and all that excitement, you just didn't notice?'

'Oh my giddy aunt!' Mariette exclaimed. 'I don't know whether to cry again or laugh. Is it good or bad? What am I saying? Of course it's good. But not really at the right time, what with hoping to get a passage home.'

Morgan began to smile, and it gradually stretched over his entire face. 'As far as I'm concerned any time is the right time. But maybe we should chivvy Miss Salmon up to get us there quicker. It wouldn't be ideal, if the baby was born at sea.'

Mariette got up and put her arms around Morgan. 'Well, nursey, how long before we know for sure?'

'Take a pee sample into work tomorrow and get them to test it,' he said. 'Might be a bit too early, but worth a try. But I believe another reliable way of finding out is examining the breasts, the areola turns brown. Let me look?'

'You are making that up,' she giggled. 'You are not examining them, because you know what that will lead to.'

'Exactly, my sweet,' he grinned. 'But, as I'm your husband, I have a perfect right to examine any part of your body I feel needs it.'

She fled into the bedroom, but he caught her and pushed her down on to the bed.

'Do you submit to examination?' he asked, holding her two hands above her head with just his left hand while, with his right, he undid the buttons down the front of her blouse and pulled up her bra.

'I submit,' she giggled.

'Umm, as I suspected, brown areolae. And if I'm not very much mistaken, Mrs Griffiths's breasts are a little fuller than normal. They will need to be kissed on a daily basis from now on.'

'So I am then?' she asked, but Morgan was too busy sucking at her nipples to answer.

Mariette smiled to herself. She might not have thought of having a baby yet, but now it looked as if there was one on the way. She felt a warm glow all over her.

She couldn't be happier.

On Monday morning, the first thing Mariette did was to ring Miss Salmon. Mr Mercer had given her the woman's London number after the wedding and suggested she phone to remind her of the offer of a passage home.

Mariette hadn't done it. Her excuse had been the excitement of the wedding, and moving into their own little flat, but the truth of the matter was that she was a little intimidated by the chilly woman. But now she thought she was pregnant, and she was a match for anyone.

To her surprise, Miss Salmon was in her office and actually

seemed pleased to hear from Mariette, asking how the wedding went and if she'd enjoyed seeing the French children again.

'It was the best wedding present ever,' Mariette said. 'And I was so thrilled that they are going to be reunited with their parents too. But Mr Mercer did tell me you would be prepared to help with a passage home to New Zealand for my husband and me. We would like you to honour that promise now. I've just found out I'm pregnant, and obviously I want to be home before the baby comes.'

'Well, I don't know if I can arrange anything quickly.' Miss Salmon's voice suddenly took on its more normal chilly edge. 'As I'm sure you realize, there are many important people who are very anxious to get out to your country, and one has to prioritize.'

'Isn't someone who risked her life to save servicemen and members of the Resistance a priority? Especially someone who lost a leg saving others?' Mariette wheedled.

'Well, of course, Mariette,' she said, her tone oily. 'I'll see what I can do, but I can't promise anything.'

Mariette felt she had to drive her message home or be fobbed off and perhaps never get help. 'Thank you, Miss Salmon. The only other way we can be sure of getting a passage is to bribe someone, and we can't afford to do that – not unless we sold my story to a newspaper.'

'You can't do that!' Miss Salmon exclaimed, and it sounded like panic in her voice.

'I don't want to, of course,' Mariette replied. 'But I need to leave within the month, if I'm to be home for Christmas.'

There was silence for a second or two.

'Leave it with me,' Miss Salmon said eventually. 'I'm sure I can arrange something.'

When Mariette put the phone down, she felt victorious. She could almost imagine Miss Salmon snatching up the phone and demanding tickets for them. She wouldn't want the general public to learn about her department and how little they cared for those they had recruited to risk their lives on secret missions.

Mariette passed the next week in a state of anxiety. She wouldn't really go to a newspaper, and she wondered if Miss Salmon realized that.

But at the end of the week, she received confirmation that she was pregnant. The baby was due late April, and nothing seemed as important as that news. It was tempting to ring home and tell them, but Morgan said she should wait a little longer, so as not to tempt fate.

Then, three days after her pregnancy was confirmed, a plump brown envelope arrived by post. To their absolute delight it contained tickets on the *Ruahine*, sailing from Southampton to Auckland on 25th September.

'Blimey!' Morgan exclaimed. 'That's an old ship; she was due to be scrapped and was only saved because of the war. I think she's just been carrying troops and cargo since then.'

'I don't care how old or shabby she is – I'd paddle myself in a bathtub, if that was the only option. Oh, Morgan, we're going home!'

She flung her arms around him, her face radiant with joy. He lifted her up by the waist and danced around with her. In the last letter from home her parents had written that Alexis and Noah were still in Italy, winding things up there, but they thought the boys would be home for Christmas.

'And we should be home for Christmas too,' Mariette screeched excitedly. 'Could things get any better?'

In early December, sitting on the deck of the *Ruahine*, Morgan turned to look at Mariette. She'd fallen asleep on a steamer chair, as she did most afternoons now it was warm enough to sit out in a spot shielded from the wind.

He didn't think he'd ever seen a woman look so good pregnant. Her hair shone, her skin was radiant, and her rounded belly was adorable to him.

In a week's time they would be docking in Auckland, and from there they would get the steamer up to Russell, to arrive on 20th December, in plenty of time for Christmas. But however good it would be to meet Mariette's family, at last, and to see her little hometown, which she talked about so often, he was also a little sad the voyage was coming to an end.

Back in England work had always got in the way of them spending much time together, so it had been marvellous to wake up each day on the ship with nothing more pressing to do than go for meals, stroll around the deck and just be together. The *Ruahine* had been refitted in 1933, to carry 220 passengers in tourist class, then relegated to cargo only in 1938. But the passenger accommodation had been reactivated later to carry troops.

Fortunately, he and Mariette had been given a cabin that must have been intended for an officer. It was spacious, comfortable, on the top deck, right next to a bathroom, and it even had a double bed. From what they understood from other passengers, mainly ex-servicemen returning home, the other cabins were very poky and airless.

The cabin was a real retreat from the other passengers, and also from memories of war, the hospital, and even real life. They played cards, board games, lay on the bed reading, and there was also a great deal of lovemaking. They were two of a very small group of passengers who hadn't suffered from seasickness. The passengers who had cabins down in the bowels of the ship really suffered in rough seas. Despite telling himself before they boarded that he wouldn't tell anyone he was a nurse, so that he wouldn't be called upon in an emergency, Morgan had helped out, and so had Mariette. It had seemed wrong to lie around enjoying themselves when so many of the passengers were ill.

One of the best things about the voyage, apart from being with Mariette, was having time to reflect on both his past and his future. He'd gone from being an illiterate Jack the Lad, who bedded any girl that crossed his path on the cruise ships, to being a soldier. And then came his injury – which, at the time, made him wish he was dead.

Those first few months of pain and total dejection had been terrible, but good things had come out of it. He'd discovered that his looks weren't his only attribute, that he was intelligent, he had compassion towards the sick, and he had the ability to learn new skills.

He had felt pangs of real sorrow saying goodbye to the many friends he'd made at Netley and at the Borough. The two hospitals had been his entire world for five years – until Mariette turned up, out of the blue, he had thought he would be there for his whole life.

Mariette had stopped him thinking about his disfigurement. He could even look in the mirror now and just see himself, not the burn.

But now a whole new chapter in his life was about to begin. He had no anxieties about being a husband and father, but he did have some concerns about finding a job and adjusting to a life that wasn't centred around a hospital. Mari's father sounded tough, and he just hoped he could get on with him and her mother.

What he really wanted to do, though he didn't know yet if it was possible, was to work in a burns unit. He supposed the closest one would be in Auckland, and maybe Mariette wouldn't want to live in a city.

But he wasn't going to talk to her about that yet. It could wait until after the baby arrived. By then, she just might be thinking that Russell was actually too small and lacking in challenges for her, after all. New babies had a way of making people change their ideas about all kinds of things.

'We're nearly there now!' Mariette put her arm through Morgan's and squeezed it tightly with excitement as they stood at the steamer's rail. She had been moved to tears so many times on this last lap of the journey from Auckland to Russell, by the clear blue sea, the lush greenness of the trees along the rocky coast, and the dolphins. They had put on a display of gymnastics alongside the boat, which she was convinced was just to welcome her home.

There was no longer a regular weekly boat to Northland – people went by road now – but this one had been chartered to serve all the holidaymakers going up to the Bay of Islands for Christmas, or further into Northland where they had friends or relatives. There were also quite a few men in civilian clothes, who she thought were returning servicemen, but she didn't know any of them as they weren't from Russell.

'There it is!' she exclaimed, as they sailed into the bay and they could see houses in the distance. 'Do you think they'll all be there to meet us? My heart feels like it might explode with excitement. I don't think I've ever been quite as excited as this before, but I'm scared too.'

'What of?' he laughed, putting his arms around her and hugging her.

'That they'll be upset by the way I walk, that they won't be the way I remember. Alexis was fifteen when I left, Noel was fourteen. They'll be grown men now seven years on. I was always so mean to them, they are probably dreading me coming back.'

'Silly goose,' he said affectionately, kissing her forehead. 'Seven years and a world war will have changed how everyone acts and feels. You aren't the same girl who left, and they won't be the same boys.'

Belle, Etienne and Mog were waiting on the wharf, as excited as Mariette was, and just as fearful. For them it was worry over whether Mariette would approve of the redecoration of her bedroom, anxiety that Morgan might prove difficult, and fear that Mariette had been away for so long that she'd never fit back in. They'd suggested Alexis and Noel stay at home, for now, as they were afraid Mariette would be overwhelmed by too many people meeting her at the ship.

'No more than ten minutes now,' Etienne said, putting his arms around both Belle and Mog's waists, but not taking his eye off the ship sailing towards them. He wanted that first sighting of his daughter's beautiful hair.

Waiting like this took him back to the day he'd arrived on the old SS *Clansman*. It had been pouring with rain and he'd stood up on the deck in readiness, his heart thumping with fear that Belle might have found a new love since arriving here a year earlier.

She hadn't, and she was miraculously waiting on the wharf, just as they were doing now. Not for him, of course – she didn't know he was coming – but to collect a parcel. He remembered her startled expression when she first saw him, a look that told him she thought she was seeing things. Then, suddenly, she was running into his arms. The girl he'd held in his heart for so long still wanted him.

He bent to whisper in Belle's ear. 'Remember the day I arrived?' he asked.

She smiled up at him, older now, a little plumper, and with her hair turning grey, but still his beautiful girl.

'Yes, and nothing's changed,' she whispered back. 'You still make my heart sing.'

'What are you two whispering about?' Mog asked.

'That would be telling,' Etienne said, and looked back to the boat. 'Look! Is that her, up in the bows? Wearing something green?'

All three of them peered at the boat.

'I think it could be,' Belle said. 'Her hair is fair.'

They were aware that others had arrived to meet the boat. They could hear feet on the gravel path along the foreshore, voices raised in greeting. In the days when the *Clansman* came every week, bringing post, household goods and even the odd piano, there had been a tradition that everyone came to meet it.

That tradition had died along with the demise of the SS *Clansman*, but Belle knew that most of the people coming here now wanted to see Mariette and her new husband. They would all insist it was to welcome her home. But Belle knew word had got out that Mari had lost a leg, and Morgan was scarred by a burn, and they were curious.

Although she was irritated by people being so morbid, she thought it was better that they see her daughter and son-in-law here, to satisfy their curiosity, rather than calling round to the house on some pretext.

'Coo-ee!'

Belle turned her head to see Peggy hobbling towards her. She had a problem with her feet now, and found it hard to walk any distance.

'I couldn't get the shop shut,' Peggy said breathlessly, wiping her perspiring face on her apron. 'People kept on coming in. There are so many of them on holiday here, goodness knows where they are all staying.'

'We think that's Mari, up in the bows,' Mog said, pointing her out.

'I bet she's been standing there for the whole trip, she always did like the wind in her hair. I just hope Morgan likes the sea too,' Belle said.

'He must do, if he worked on ships,' Etienne said.

'Let's all wave now, whether it's her or not,' Mog said. 'Her eyesight will be better than ours. If she waves back, we'll know for certain.'

They waved frantically. Sure enough, the figure on the boat, and the man with her, waved back too.

In real time it took less than ten minutes for the ship to reach the wharf, be secured and for the gangplank to be put in place. But it seemed like an hour to those waiting on the wharf.

As Mariette took her first slightly hesitant step on to the gangplank, Belle broke away from Etienne and rushed forward, reaching her daughter just as she touched land.

'My darling girl,' Belle cried out, flinging her arms around her daughter. 'Welcome home! There were times when I thought I was never going to see you again.'

'Let other people get off the boat,' Etienne said behind her, drawing both his wife and daughter to one side.

'Papa!' Mariette exclaimed, and all at once she was crying, trying to hug both parents at once.

Mog turned to Morgan. Smiling, she held out both her hands to him. 'Welcome home too, Morgan. I'm Mog, and we've all been dying to meet you. They'll get around to saying that too, any minute. But I think the sooner we can get back to the house the better.'

For Mariette it was the strangest feeling to be back home again. Everything – the sights, the sounds and the smells – were all so familiar, as if she'd left only yesterday. But it had a dreamlike quality to it, as if she might wake up and find herself back in England.

Everyone had so much to say, so many questions to ask, and Mariette found it quite unnerving that her two brothers were now grown men with deep voices and wide shoulders. Yet their deep cobalt-blue eyes seemed to reflect all the danger and hardships they must have experienced.

With everyone talking at once, Belle told Etienne and Mog to take Morgan and the boys into the kitchen, and she would take Mariette and her luggage up to her old room.

'That's better,' Belle said, shutting the bedroom door behind them. 'I've got you all to myself for a few minutes.'

Mariette sat down on the new double bed, which had replaced her old single one, and looked around her. The pictures of film stars she'd pinned up were gone now, and the walls were papered in a pretty blue and white paper. All the furniture was the same, though, just given a fresh coat of white paint. There was an enlargement of a photograph of Mariette on the wall; she was standing at the helm of a yacht, wearing oilskins, because it was a heavy sea.

'Where did that come from?' Mariette asked. It was far too good a photograph to have been taken by anyone she knew.

'A photographer who was here on a fishing holiday took it. It must have been the year before you left for England. Anyway, a couple of years ago he came back here again and gave it to us. As you can imagine, your father was thrilled. He made the frame, and we put it in here when we did the room up for you.'

'It's all lovely,' Mariette said. 'So pretty and fresh. And it's so very good to be home again.'

'Mog thinks you and Morgan will want a place of your own by the time Christmas is over,' Belle said. But she laughed, as if unsure whether that was likely or not.

'I don't think so,' Mariette said. 'Come and sit here, so we can cuddle.' She patted the bed beside her. 'Or do you think I'm too old for that now?'

Belle was there in a trice, hugging Mariette tightly. 'There were times when I thought I'd never, ever do this again,' she said, her voice cracking with emotion. 'Now I just want to hold you and never let you go.'

'You'll be a grandmother before long,' Mariette said. 'I won't get a look-in with you, once there's a baby to compete with.'

'You'll always be my baby,' Belle said fondly, patting her daughter's cheek. 'That's why I've got to ask about your leg. I need to see it. Is that peculiar of me?'

Mariette laughed. 'No, I think I understand. I've been told that all new mothers check to see their baby has all its fingers and toes. I guess it's the same instinct.'

'Then you don't mind showing me?'

'No, well, as long as it's once and for all. To put your mind at rest.'

Mariette stood up and unfastened her slacks so they fell to the ground. She heard Belle's sharp intake of breath but she said nothing, just let her see the prosthetic leg and how it strapped on. She understood that the hardest thing in the world for any mother was to see their child injured.

'It doesn't hurt, Mum,' she said as she sat down and began to unstrap the leg. 'I'm used to it now, and I don't mind it any more. I want you to feel that way too. I can do most things I did before, I just can't run or jump. There!' She exposed the stump, took her mother's hand and laid it on her upper thigh. 'I'm still the same, Mum, there's just a bit missing, that's all.'

She watched as her mother's fingers hesitantly touched the stitching on the stump, and saw the tears rolling down her cheeks.

'Don't cry, Mum,' she said. 'I really am OK about it.'

'When you were a baby, I kissed your tummy, your bottom and those plump little thighs,' Belle whispered. 'I played "This Little Piggy" with your toes. It never crossed my mind that anything could ever spoil your perfect body. But thank you for letting me see. It's not awful like I expected.'

'We've got so much to talk about,' Mariette said as she strapped the leg back on and pulled up her trousers. 'I don't mean about this, but things we never discussed before. You, Papa and Mog, how you all came together, your adventures both before and during the last war. I want to know it all.'

Belle chuckled. 'And I shall be quizzing you about your adventures too.'

Mariette stood up and took her mother's hand. 'But not today, we've got a lifetime for all that. Let's go down now and see the boys. I bet they've got lots to tell too.'

Later that evening, after a celebratory dinner of roast lamb, something neither Mariette nor Morgan had eaten for years, Belle suggested they should all move outside as it was such a lovely warm evening.

On the way back to New Zealand, Mariette had run through her head all the conversations she would have with her family. Especially her two brothers, because she was very well aware that they hadn't really communicated at all before she left for England.

Yet, despite all that planning, once they were all sitting around the table together, the conversation was as trivial as if they'd only been apart for a week. Mariette and Morgan spoke about the voyage home, and Alexis and Noel told them about a few incidents when they'd been kicking their heels in Auckland for a week, unable to come home until they'd been officially demobbed.

As they all got up to move outside, Alexis caught hold of

Mariette and held her for several minutes without saying a word. When he finally released her, he touched her cheek tenderly.

'It's great to be home with you again, sis, and to know that Noel and I are going to be uncles. Tonight isn't the time to discuss the war and what it has done to all of us. It's just a time to be glad we are all home, safe again. To welcome Morgan to our family, and to look ahead to Christmas.'

Noel patted her shoulder, as if to say that he was in total agreement with his elder brother.

'Wait till you see what the old man's been up to while we've all been away,' he said, grinning like a Cheshire Cat.

'Less of the "old",' Etienne reproved him. 'I had to find things to do, with all my children gone, and my wife off growing fruit and vegetables.'

Etienne took Mariette's hand and led her outside. When she saw the transformation, she gasped.

When she was growing up, there had just been scrubby uneven grass running downhill from the back doorstep to the chicken run. In winter it was like a swamp, and in the summer the grass had huge bald patches because of all the ball games played there.

But now it was a raised terrace of rather splendid crazy paving, with the walls surrounding it designed to be planted up with flowers. It looked beautiful, with a riot of bright red, orange and yellow flowers cascading over the walls. A couple of steps led down to the rest of the garden, where there was a real lawn, lush and green, with pretty flower beds. Mariette could see neat rows of vegetables growing behind a trellis.

'It's beautiful,' Mariette exclaimed, and all at once she burst into tears. Somehow, the transformation in the garden brought home to her the realization that she and her brothers were grown-ups now. That her parents and Mog had been forced to make a life just for themselves while the children were away. They were all home together again now, but she, Alexis and Noel would all have to find their own path soon, which might even take them away from Russell.

Morgan sat down and pulled Mariette on to his lap, letting her cry on his shoulder.

'She's understandably emotional,' he said, looking around at her family, who all looked confused by her tears. 'She's kept an image of this house, of Russell and all of you, in her heart for seven years. But that image is out of date now. There's so much to say to all of you, so many stories about each of you that she wants to hear. But she's forgetting there is no rush, that we've got endless time ahead of us to catch up.'

Etienne put his hand on Morgan's shoulder. 'Well said, Morgan. And can I just say how glad I am to find that my daughter has married the man I would have picked for her myself?

'I can imagine what was going through your head on the long voyage, not really knowing what lay at the end of it. I made that trip into the unknown myself once. But I know you and Mari are going to be as happy as Belle and I have been, and a new life begins for you now as a member of this family.'

He sat down then, next to Morgan, and took Mariette's hand in his. She had begun to cry even harder because of what her father had said.

'Tomorrow, we'll go out on the boat,' he promised. 'And you'll find nothing has really changed here.'

Belle came closer and bent down to kiss both Morgan and Mariette's cheeks. 'What a future we have now! All of us older and wiser, but with a baby joining us soon. Babies have a habit of making everything real, they show you what is important and what isn't.'

'Just before you were born, Mari, your mother got in a terrible state about everything,' Mog said. 'She wailed that she knew nothing about babies, and that you might die of neglect at her hands. I laughed at her because I'd seen that, whatever life threw at her, she could deal with it. And besides, she had me and your father too. You are just like Belle, capable of dealing with anything, and you've got the whole lot of us too. An army of help.'

Mariette sat up and sniffed back her tears.

'I guess coming home has reminded me of what a self-centred person I was when I left. But I just need to tell you that going away taught me how precious all of you are,' she said, looking around at each of them. 'I've got millions of questions for all of you, and there's so much I want to share with you too. But I guess my lovely Morgan is right, there's plenty of time for all that.'

'There are thousands of tomorrows,' Belle said, reaching out to tweak her daughter's cheek. 'All of them empty and waiting to be filled with laughter, love and happiness. Time for us to talk over all the things we didn't have the time or inclination for in the past. Tonight is just a celebration of all of us being here, together again, at last.'

Acknowledgements

I owe Olive Bedford in the North Island of New Zealand so much. Not only has she been the most stalwart of fans for over twenty years, but for this book she did a tremendous amount of research for me about New Zealand.

I only met her in the flesh for the first time in 2011 – until then we merely wrote letters to each other – but on her eightieth birthday, when she'd just lost her husband, I visited her while in New Zealand. Since then she has moved home, learned to use a computer, travelled to England alone, keeps abreast of world news, knits for my granddaughter, and is my dear friend and confidante. She calls herself my honorary mother, but I would be very proud to have her as my real one, as she is just the bravest, brightest, kindest woman I've ever met. I love you, Olive!

Also a huge thank you to the little museum in Russell in the Bay of Islands, where I spent so much time pouring over old photographs and scraps of information to learn what life was like there back in the 1930s and 1940s. If I've got any facts wrong, please forgive me. Thanks also to the fabulous Imperial War Museum, in London, which is just the very best place to learn about both world wars and how they affected ordinary people.